I0669260

Terrible Children

By

Chris Travis

W & B Publishers
USA

Chapter 1

Spruce and Shadow

Earth Mother mourns, for the world gone mad.
Scars of strife, mar her flesh.
Prodigal people, the fruit of her loins,
Rape, ravage, and tear her asunder.
Black blood of her bosom, stains the hands of man.

Nycolos Arcadia had a theory; a theory born of childlike wonder and impossibility. He believed his parents controlled the weather. It always seemed to storm when his parents argued. Sometimes rain would come down light and hazy, like walking through fog that brushed your cheek and lead you astray. Sometimes rain came down in a sun shower; those were neat. The worst storms occurred when they fought late and loud; thunder clapped almost in time with their screams, and the rain fell in thick sheets, pelting windows and doors. The wind came to life, ripping at storm shutters and doors alike, occasionally finding enough purchase to rip something off the little yellow farm house.

Lately he thought he would never see the sun again. As it was, it had been raining for the last two weeks. The little brown boy sat on a cushioned bench he moved from the piano to the sliding glass doors of the living room. The room behind him was earthy. A wooden coffee table was an old door from a ship, thick, heavy and stained black with age and water. Across from the love-seat sat a wooden bookshelf of dark walnut where they kept their books. An old rocker on a circle rug occupied the corner, two grooves worn in the fabric from years of rocking. Nycolos leaned against the sliding doors, his rounded brown nose pressed against the windowpane, fogging the glass with each breath. Large curls fell around his ears and neck like a curly crown of brown curls. The undisputed King of Hide and Seek, at least that's what his parents called him.

That night was particularly bad, the clouds roiled through the heavens, lightning illuminated the small yellow house nestled at the foot of one forested hill. The night wind whined and whistled through the cracks in the old farmhouse. The wood house settled and creaked, providing an eerie accompaniment to the raging storm without. A less distracted youngster would've been frightened stiff. Nycolos Arcadia however, couldn't have been farther from the dark living room. The boy's face a mask of heartache and pain. Raindrops and tears raced for his chin, running juxtaposed over the same tracks, wet tears crested his cheeks, topped with silhouettes of raindrops on the other side of the windowpane.

Outside in the darkness, beyond the big sugar maple and the tire swing, was the forest and his best hiding place ever. The uncontested King of Hide and Seek, he was never found unless he wanted to be. The screaming from upstairs died down; the boy still heard the creaking floorboards of his parents moving, so at least they had not killed each other—yet. He knew the forest back there like his bedroom floor. His favorite rock outcrops and secret gardens nearly infinite even though his parents made him stick close to the house. His father had given him a book on being a naturalist last year for Christmas. He read it, but never really used it. It didn't seem right to kill bugs and animals just to put them in a jar in his room on a shelf. His father hadn't said much, just asked about it while they were hiking and saw some tadpoles in a vernal pool deep in the forest.

"Did you bring any jars, maybe collect a couple?" His father asked.

"Nah, I think they'd rather stay out here." Was all Nyc had said.

And that had been that. His father had tousled his hair and they walked on in silence.

The rain raged, sounding like surging waves of an angry sea, sheets tore at the siding of the house, the North wind hurled angry liquid claws, tearing at wood, stone and mortar. The wind howled, giving voice to the angry boreal gusts, frustrated at the roof, walls and the warm dry hearth protecting the souls within. Nyc could hear his mother screaming something, and his father yelling back; a shutter banged on one of the upstairs windows. The storm sent out raindrops and hail like small-arms fire the boy thought would blow out windows, sending glass flying in all directions; it was all he could do not to throw his arms around his head and dive to the hard-wood floor.

Moving farther from the sounds of the yelling, he migrated onto the sofa, where he sat sniffling. He wiped his snotty nose with the back of one shirtsleeve; placing his chin in his palm, he resumed his sentry of the backyard. Imaginary broken windows or not, the storm was more than a little scary. Out there beyond the tire swing something moved in the darkness. True, sometimes they would get black bears moving down from the forested hills during particularly hard summers. Drought and lack of good forage brought them down only when absolutely necessary. This was not a bear, and it had not been a hard summer. Like most people he had heard stories of Bigfoot, the abominable snowman and the like, and for a few moments that's what he thought he saw. If he had to guess or put a name to it he would've said what he saw looked more like a bear-man, or man-bear.

A large bear-like creature with massive head, shoulders and chest stood next to the sugar maple. Standing upright, looking perfectly natural, like he had all the time in the world to lean against that tree and pass the time. The child stopped the absent-minded kicking of his foot against the cushions of the sofa. His breath steamed the window once he had his forehead and nose neatly pressed against the window. The bear that was not a bear, there was something odd about the haunches and back. The bear stood far too straight, knees halfway down the rear legs, front legs bent slightly where elbows would bend on a human. In fact it looked to have its arms crossed across a massive chest as it leaned against the tree. The boy squeaked a little, excitement bubbling in his stomach.

The giant bear-man moved from the trunk of the big maple; like a shadow come to life, a bear that walked like a man had come to their yard in the midst of a torrential downpour. The yelling upstairs stopped. Nycolos Arcadia couldn't hear footsteps, yelling or anything breaking. He turned and looked up the stairs, resting his cheek on the cool glass. The light in his parent's room was still on, spilling under the doorway onto the landing, fading just short of the first step, leaving the stairs in darkness. He looked outside; the were-bear was gone. The rain continued, though the horrible raging thunder and lightning had ceased. The rope swing swayed in the breeze, abandoned by the blustery North wind. He was gone in search of more trouble; momentarily docile and spent after the tantrum he had thrown at the yellow farmhouse.

The boy checked the landing outside his parents' bedroom once more; no movement, just some whispered murmurs from the other room. He stepped off the couch, treading with carefully chosen steps. He grabbed his raincoat from the peg next to the door. Placing the flat of his palm on the brick red back door in the kitchen he opened it slowly and slid into the night. His child's mind was aflutter with thoughts and feelings. His parents were obviously in a very bad way. First, just his mother was sad, then just his father, and now they were both sad. They told him over and over it had nothing to do with him, but he sure heard his name a lot when they were arguing. He was scared, not of the giant creature he was running toward in the darkness, but of what was going to happen to his family. Mud sucked at his boots, threatening to pull them from his feet and compromise his balance.

He stopped in meadow behind the house, halfway to the tree line, the meadow was full of goldenrods and flowers. He crouched to tighten the laces on his boots. It was after he finished the second boot when he saw something. Out of the corner of his eye he saw a shadow move, something darker than a shadow. He shot after it like a bat out of hell.

He hit the tree line at a dead run and had to pull up hard and get his bearings. Moving through the forest in the dark was harder than Nycolos remembered. The overcast clouds made the night darker still. Water dripped down his forehead and into his eyes, from the end of his nose, down the back of his shirt, everywhere. He knew the forest this close to the house blindfolded. It was a good thing too, for he could see nothing. The boy moved slowly, dragging his feet on the forest floor. The rain sounded loud in his ears, drumming off the waterproof lining of his hooded raincoat. The rain had soaked through all his clothes, despite the rain jacket. He shivered in the chilly night air. Summer arrived weeks ago; flowers bloomed, and babies were long since born, but the air was cool like the coming autumn. Nycolos Arcadia shuffled and danced a slow waltz, sliding his feet down the forest trail. Alone amongst the oaks and beeches, spruces and pines, Nycolos crept down the trail. The maples and birches watched his progress with mute indifference. Naked branches shook and groaned, vibrating with the roar of windy gusts. He bumped into a tree, which wasn't where it was supposed to be.

He sidestepped, and his left foot came down on a small rock that nearly sent him to the ground. That wasn't supposed to be there either. Nycolos spun in the darkness, instinctively searching with his eyes in every direction. It was useless, he might as well have been blind for all he could see. Step by step he approached the edge of the ravine that should have been about ten feet from where he stood. Lying down on his stomach he crawled forward, dragging knees through decomposing leaf litter that smelled sweet with decay and moisture. Thankfully the soil here was not mud yet. He crawled approximately three meters, so scared he was panting. With shaking outstretched hands he felt the ground, too excited to notice how much he was shaking or how cold he really was. And then he felt it, or rather didn't feel it. His hands no longer came in contact with the forest floor. He bent his elbow and felt for the ravine wall. Soft moss and wet stones lined the flanks of the ravine. Crawling backward five feet, the boy rose. He knew this ravine ran for nearly a mile in each direction. The bear-man or whatever would have to climb down and in to cross or go around, either way this was probably where he would have the best chance to see it again.

A train of lightning marched into the forest, illuminating the night and exploding barely fifty feet from where the boy stood. Nyc was looking into the ravine when the darkness was torn asunder, and he had seen the beast. It was a bear, a massive black bear, standing in the center or the ravine some thirty feet down, looking up at him with golden eyes and his enormous maw open to roar. Nycolos Arcadia was disappointed, he had really thought it was something else, and now he had to flee with an angry bear not fifty feet away, and the heavens throwing death like Zeus in a fit. All his thinking and scrutiny were irrelevant however as the concussion of the lighting strikes and the crack of thunder deafened him and shook the earth, throwing him to the leaf-covered ground. He attempted to rise, fear bubbling in his chest for the first time. This had been a really bad idea. Standing on shaking legs, deaf and blind, the little brown boy leaned against a tree and tried to remember which way the ravine was so he didn't accidentally fall in. He heard the bear roar, and the scraping and clattering of loose stone in the ravine, a sound that was coming closer. Pushing away from the tree, struggling to regain his composure Nycolos prepared to break into a run. He definitely knew which way to go and he was certain he could get into the meadow before this crazy bear made it out of the ravine.

Zeus hurled another bolt of lightning that impacted the ground in time with Nyc's first step. He managed to see the branches in front of his face in time to close his eyes so as not to lose one, but he ran full speed into branches he was certain had not been there a moment before. He stepped backwards, the crack of thunder vibrating in his chest, the earth shook and rock exploded somewhere. His foot caught on a root as he back-pedaled, and he fell. He fell into blackness, absolutely shocked; that root had not been there a moment earlier. He thought of his mother's smell and the way his father would tousle his crown of black curls. They were going to get divorced. The undisputed King of Hide and Seek heard his own voice screaming in the darkness and wondered if his parents had even noticed he was missing yet. He hoped they could find him in the ravine. A particularly violent volley of lighting ripped from the heavens. In his twisting descent Nycolos turned his body enough to see he was falling into the arms of the standing bear. The last thing he saw was the black bear standing at full height with arms outstretched and snarling to boot. He heard the heavens clap with thunderous strikes of lightning that were so tremendous and terrible the entire forest may have well exploded. Then darkness...

****

Lyndon Arcadia ducked a flower vase with ease but nearly got a clock embedded in his skull as his wife hurled objects with both hands. For her size, Rosa Arcadia was strong and fast, and when angry, she had the strength of ten men. Her dark skin shone with sweat, her bosom heaved mightily with exertion and boiling emotion. He retreated behind a chair and stumbled over the debris of a lamp that had once illuminated the nightstand. She was very angry. Brown locks tumbled to mocha shoulders which she flicked irritably and neatly pulled an orange handkerchief from the back pocket of her tight boot-cut jeans and tied the curls behind her head.

She started to jinga. She made the Brazilian capoeira look so smooth and fluid he almost caught her heel with his face. The two hundred-pound Lyndon raised his hands in a sign of surrender, bowing his head and hunching his shoulders. She would have none of it. She continued to dance, spinning through two leg sweeps that would've taken his legs out from under him if not broken his ankles altogether. Another couple of spins, a meia lua de frente also known as a half moon crescent kick, followed by a spinning roundhouse that would've broken his sternum and clavicle both.

Rosa's anger and frustration boiled to the surface like a champagne bottle shaken and left on the counter. An explosive pop and the liquid rage kept tight under the cork spilled up and over the lip of the bottle, effervescent like the liquid party beverage, but bitter like bile rising in the back of one's throat. Molehills to a man become mountains to a woman. At least that was what their most recent fight was about. All this spinning, kicking and talk of divorce had come as a result of one such mole hill that was now a mountain and he, standing on a very narrow precipice, felt he had just slipped off the edge and was falling to his certain death.

Lyndon settled onto his haunches and sat with his buttocks propped on his heels with his toes pointing backward. Rosa wasn't just angry, she wasn't just going through the forms. She was showing him exactly what she would do to him if he stepped within those ten square feet. He wasn't bad at capoeira, but not on par with his wife. They had met in Salvador, Bahia, Brazil. She, a brown goddess, one of many female capoeiristas he met in the rodas on the beach, in town, wherever. She had been different than the rest and had taken an interest in him after their second fight. Like their first, he had been headed toward quick defeat when she threw sand in his eyes with her feet as she spun, and something inside him raged.

The malicia or gamesmanship or whatever it was, cracked his veneer. He didn't understand malicia back then and his ignorance had been evident if perhaps a blessing in disguise. He had covered his face, half blind and walked straight at her. She rained fury back with heels, spinning elbows, backhands and the like. He took it all, grabbed her arms and wrapped her up in a bear hug.

He took her to the ground with his weight, flat on her back, sand spraying outward from the impact on the sand. It had taken a few seconds of heavy breathing, feeling how soft she really was beneath him before he realized the berimbau had stopped as well as the drum accompaniment. He scrambled up, literally lifted her to her feet and placed her gently in the sand, muttered an apology and limped off the beach. A few days later she found him at his hostel and offered to show him some moves since he was "mas o menos," she said he was so-so in beautifully melodic in Portuguese. Not bad coming from her. He never bested her except when she let him; once she knew of his speed and strength wrapped in his 6' 4" frame she was all sweeping ankles and pointed toes, whirling back-hands and even sharpened nails once. She did enjoy his athletic ability; he learned quickly and was good on his feet despite his large size. Maybe he never beat her, but he had given her a run for her money on a number of occasions. This was not one of those occasions.

Lyndon supposed that was what she wanted right now. She wanted him to walk into the melee of raining blows and blurred feet. Maybe she wanted him to take every kick and punch, and then put her on her back. Not likely, more probable was that she wanted to knock him out. A spinning back kick took the round top off the bedpost. A block and shift turned into a cupping motion and a vase crashed into the wall above his head. The situation was very grave indeed.

A date, it had all started with a date they made last week. The date had been for tonight, to go see one of their friends play in a local reggae band. The first spark and what should have been his first sign of warning had been when she blithely asked,

"So what are we doing tonight?"

He had known what game she was playing and had played right back.

"Dunno, what do you want to do tonight?" He should have sensed her mood and been sincere, instead he played along until she was convinced he did not intend to attend the agreed-upon engagement. Which was when the stuff hit the fan so to speak. Somewhere in the midst of the yelling and blame game he decided he was sick of it.

Tired of the fighting, tired of the yelling, tired of being tired, and he had said the four words. With one final leg sweep she spun to the ground and stopped. Chest heaving and sweat starting to bead on sculpted shoulders, she sat with her head bowed, elbows resting on raised knees.

"So you want a divorce?" The question was rhetorical at that point, but he answered anyway.

"Yes."

Lyndon Arcadia approached slowly, kneeling to wrap his arms around her curled form. Like an uncoiling snake she struck hard and fast, punching him in the abdomen, causing him to grunt. Pulling her balled fist back she grabbed his hand and pulled him to the ground, laying her head on his chest. He held her sobbing in his arms, smelling the back of her neck. So sweet, so soft, his heart ached and burst, filling his chest with the sorrow of love lost. They clung to each other and wept, as the finality of it all crashed upon them in unforgiving waves. The storm outside howled, giving voice to their pain.

****

They woke to the sound of banging coming from downstairs. Lyndon checked the clock that was on the floor in the corner. They hadn't dozed for more than ten minutes. Rubbing the sleep out of their eyes they rose together. Rosa picked up the broken and tattered lamp and set it on the table. They moved out of the room without speaking, Rosa going right, down the hall towards Nyc's room. Lyndon went left downstairs to investigate the banging. The answer was evident when he reached the foot of the stairs. The back door had blown open, the screen thrown back as well, both doors banging furiously in the wind. The red ceramic tiles of the back entrance were wet with rain. Lyndon stepped outside and pulled the screen door shut with one arm, closing the backdoor with the other. He turned, looked upstairs and saw Rosa looking frightened, her face pale.

"He's not in his room." The words hung in the momentary stillness between claps and rumbles of thunder, the rain sounded loud, pelting against windows, pinging loudly on metal somewhere. Lightning streaked outside, the light penetrating the many windows of the living room and lighting them in that instant like an old magnesium flash bulb.

Thunder exploded like a bomb, the window of the backdoor-shattered inward throwing glass on Lyndon. He turned, covering his face with a raised arm, and nimbly jumped backwards a few steps. And well he did—the backdoor followed suit, barely emitting a groan before blasting off its hinges. Lyndon was struck with the full weight of the wooden door and his skull rang with the impact. His left foot slipped on red, rain-wet tiles, sending him crashing to the floor, his posterior taking the blow, head whip lashing back and bouncing off the tiles. The door ricocheted off Lyndon's knee and elbow, flying through the air, crushing the chandelier above, raining glass down on his unconscious form, leaving only the chain whipping wildly connected to nothing. The door and main bulk of the chandelier impacted high on the far wall with a crunch and the sound of splintering wood. Rosa jumped over the banister and landed lightly next to Lyn's prone form, glass crunching under her sneakers.

He was unconscious but—most frightening—with open eyes. Glazed-over beautiful hazel eyes she had never seen so close to dead. She had seen him hit hard, she had even hit him hard, but he had never been knocked cold like this. She gingerly checked the back of his head, no blood, which was good. Removing her hand she flexed her fingers. He wasn't in as good a shape as when they first met, but punching him still hurt. Punching his stomach was like punching a wood plank where before it had been stone. She stroked his face and kissed it, softly murmuring sweet nothings between kisses. That sucker punch she had gotten in upstairs had been worth it at the time, but now she felt sorry about it.

Lyndon blinked twice and appeared to return to himself. He sat up with her help and winced. She gathered his arm in her hands and fondled it gently.

"It's not broken…," she paused briefly and ran her hands down the rest of his body and stopped over his knee for a moment, again the gentle probing and she nodded to herself.

"Go figure." Dry humor was still intact.

She didn't say a word, only stood, extended her left hand to his and pulled him up.

"We need to find him." She didn't say any more.

"Let's go then." He winced and looked at her with his open eye.

Only then did he notice the maple branch pushing through the back door and five feet beyond.

"Jiminy crickets." He muttered combing his good hand through his hair.

He followed her through the dining room limping, his knee wasn't broken or surely she would have said something. Rosa turned on the stoop gesturing with dark arms already glistening with rain from their leafy intruder. "I'll go to the tree-house, and the tea-house, there's a lantern in both, so he might've gone there."

"Alright, I'll do the meadow and ravine and we can meet in the middle." He jerked his head a little, bad arm cradled to his chest. She moved close, pulled his head down, and kissed him, then she disappeared into the night.

Lyndon turned and made his way around the house. The yellow siding seemed bright in contrast to the dark night, but he could've made his way around the house in his sleep. He rounded the southwest corner pushing past some walnut saplings, and stopped at the edge of the back patio. The blue stone reflected what little light came from their upstairs window like black onyx in the night. The huge maple with the rope swing still smoldered, embers still glowing in the darkness despite the downpour. Splintered wood creaked anew with gusts of the returning storm. One of the two leaders of the tree had been hewn off, neatly cutting the tree in half. The falling branch had found little resistance from the back door on its journey to the ground.

Lyn's heart beat loudly, bringing the thunder of pounding blood to his ears to accompany the thunder of the heavens. Anxiety wrapped around him like a blanket; a cold, wet, leaden blanket that threatened to drag him to the ground sobbing. He yelled for Nycolos once, he waited, nothing. Fear rose in his throat like a murderous apparition jumping from the night, threatening to strangle the life from him. Anxiety grew to panic, lightning struck in the meadow, frighteningly close, raising the hairs on his arms and head. Again he called for Nycolos, still nothing. Lightning forked from the heavens again and again, exploding against the earth. Shock waves and flying soil nearly forced him to the ground. Eerily, the lightening marched in a straight line towards the forest and the ravine, one bolt after another, and once above the conifer treetops fell like raindrops. Lyndon Arcadia knew where his son was.

Blood drained from Lyndon and his head spun, he found himself on his one good knee, wet mud seeping through the fibers of his pants, chilling his skin. He felt the break before he saw it. Subtle vibrations through the ground, the accompanying creak and splintering of wood giving way were all the warning he had. Without looking up he leapt with every ounce of strength he had. His right foot slipped through mud ineffectively, his left foot caught purchase on one of the flagstones. Adrenaline and fear poured through his legs as he dove. His right knee exploded in pain, and he flew through the air, landing atop the already downed branch, practically sailing through the blocked back door.

The ground shook briefly with the impact of the second half of the massive sugar maple. A large lateral branch of the once magnificent sugar maple impaled the ground where he knelt moments before. The bark and wood were burnt black from the lightening strike, and charred leaves fell like embers, red veins hissing angrily as they extinguished in the mud.

Sliding from the first limb to nearly claim his life that night Lyndon ran with abandon past the second limb, headlong into the waist deep meadow that separated the house from the forested Mount, or so the kids had named it. Generally he let the meadow grow wild though he had sown many hours worth of wildflowers in order to attract wildlife and his wife's attention. He tore through grasses, milkweeds, and cosmos. High stepping to keep his feet out of the mud nearly cost him his consciousness as pain sliced through his leg and up his spine to his shoulder and down to his sprained arm. Limping, he made his way across the meadow, quicker than he ever had.

The forest of trees and shadows met him like cloaked sentries guarding a forbidden treasure. No stranger to this forest, he glided through the stands of spruce, maple, beech and oak. Branches ripped at his clothes, and roots tore at his shoes. Strange, even limping as he was he could generally move through the woods like a shadow regardless of his size. It felt like the forest was clawing at him. Branches hung low scratching his hair; he stubbed his foot on a rock that had made its way to the middle of the trail. In the dark he knew the trail, as did his son, given they made sport of walking down the forest trail on nights of the new moon. In the darkness he could sense the emptiness, the void space despite the fact he could see nothing. He approached the ravine and stopped, he could hear Rosa screaming in the distance, she sounded panicked.

A bolt of lightning lit the forest, the ravine flanked his left, and Nycolos lay at his feet. Dirty and soiled with mud in his pockets and across the front of his shirts and jeans, the boy's rain jacket was open and dirty. He looked for all the world to have crawled through the mud. His brown skin was coated with mud, wet and black across his neck. Something large and heavy stepped nearby, breathing loudly with some unseen effort. Lyndon Arcadia, gathered the boy in his arms and hobbled as quickly as he could out of the darkness, failing to notice tree limbs no longer scratched his head, nor did roots tear at his feet. The boulder in the path must have rolled on, and Lyndon carried his son into the cool rain of a summer night.

Chapter 2

Love Hurts

Tears trail through slate gray skies.
Whipping winds and waves rise with woe,
Calamity crests o'er levy and sea wall.
Chosen children, flora and fauna,
Answer her beck and call.

Nycolos slept for several days after the incident, as did his father. Lyndon's wrist was sprained, he wore a brace on his knee and his right arm in a sling. Lyndon had suffered a concussion but that didn't explain his goose bumps, the knot in his stomach, or his nervousness whenever he walked by the spot where their favorite sugar maple almost claimed his life. They spent the night of the storm at the hospital, after arriving bedraggled, soaked through, and bloody at the emergency room doors. The first nurse to attend them nearly fainted when she saw them, and ran off screaming for a doctor. Lyndon placed the unconscious Nycolos on the nearest gurney as if he were a newborn, sat down in a plastic waiting room chair and passed out.

The following morning Rosa uncurled from the hospital bed next to her son and spoke to the doctor. He assured her everything was fine and father and son were clear to go, but he was curious about the scratches on Nyc's back.

"Mrs. Arcadia, they look like claw marks." The doctor said.

"An animal attacked him?" Rosa's heart stuck in her throat. Nycolos sighed in the bed next to her. She lay her hand atop the blue fabric of the hospital gown. His heart beat strongly beneath her trembling hand.

"There are bears and some other wildlife around the house." Her voice sounded hollow in her own ears. She was thinking that bears didn't come near the house and bears didn't attack humans unless they were provoked.

The doctor peered over his wire rimmed glasses at Rosa, blinking dark eyes in a thin face almost as white as his lab coat.

"The wounds are not that deep. He should be fine, just check his wounds for infection every day."

"Yes." She murmured, but she was remembering the middle of the night. Nycolos had been restless, and his sleep fitful, murmuring something about bears.

"Bear-man," he mumbled in the middle of the night, "the bear man is a good guy," he said.

He yelled out again near dawn, telling the bear-man to leave them alone: "We don't need any help."

****

The little family rode home in silence, Rosa drove. When Lyndon tried to slip into the driver's seat ahead of her, she would have none of it.

Halfway home she asked Lyndon, "Did you see anything out there where you found him?" She chose her words carefully, thinking about what the doctor said.

"Did I see anything?" Lyndon's eyes were unfocused, as though he was looking at someone far away. "I heard something...something big." His gaze remained somewhere distant.

"The doctor says Nyc was attacked by an animal, he has claw marks on his back." Rosa Arcadia looked at her husband, trying to gauge his reaction.

Lyndon sighed. The ambiguous response Rosa knew meant Lyndon wasn't convinced and needed to digest the information. Rosa smiled; she had grown to love his thoughtfulness, and to regret the fact that this thoughtfulness seldom included her.

The family spent the next several weeks occupying themselves with mundane summer activities around the house—once the massive maple was sawed up and hauled away, the back door replaced, and the 9-foot blackened pike that had once been a branch, was extracted from the earth. They practiced capoeira on the patio, and in the capoeira barn. They played in the meadow, catching fastballs one day and butterflies the next. There were moments, though, when they caught Nycolos staring toward the tree line in thoughtful silence. The woods were off-limits, at least for the time being.

Lyn and Rosa even cleared enough of the meadow to make a half soccer field. They suited up and played in the mornings and the evenings. Mother and son took bending shots at the comical one-armed Lyndon, who entertained them with his antics, regularly bringing them to their knees in laughter. They talked trash, made fun of each other's plays, laughed a lot, and generally made good sport of it.

The summer was benign, no more thunder or lightning, just languid days. The subject of the divorce was not mentioned though each of them knew it loomed like storm clouds on the horizon. Nyc did his best to distract them, talking about the bear, the bear-man and insisting that he was good, not evil. His persistence irked his parents – who could see the scars on his back whenever he took off his shirt. One morning, Rosa decided to do something about it.

The kitchen smelled sweet with the scent of toasting raisins and cinnamon. Steam rose from the sliced bread and butter melted in the center of each piece. Nycolos looked up from his hot cider, oatmeal, and side of raisin bread. He held the cup tight with both hands as if warming them, melted butter glistening in the corner of his mouth, but his eyes were miles away

"I should've been at the bottom of the ravine." Nyc said.

"What?" Rosa couldn't believe what she was hearing.

"He caught me. I fell off the edge in the lightning. I remember falling towards the bottom and seeing the bear-man, except he was a bear again."

"Honey," Lyndon chided gently, "first of all, that ravine is nearly forty feet deep. A bear would have to be fifteen feet or taller to catch you."

" I think he was. " Nycolos was serious.

"You probably just tripped on some tree roots and hit your head." Lyndon resorted to a more logical approach.

"Then why did I see him leaning on the maple? A bear wouldn't be out at night leaning on a maple tree watching the house!"

Assuming that he had seen what he claimed, Nycolos had a point. Neither parent would acknowledge it, but it would indeed be strange behavior for a bear to stand behind a house doing something other than pawing through garbage cans. Nyc's conviction had Rosa and Lyndon Arcadia concerned about his emotional well being. Considering the dysfunction he had been subject to that night, Rosa feared that perhaps the giant bear-man was the personification of Nyc's fears in the face of his parents' troubled relationship.

Nyc was a smart kid, and though they hadn't discussed their separation or divorce, both parents knew he would soon, or perhaps he already had, put the pieces together. If they didn't say something about it soon, Nycolos would.

"Why don't we go for a walk in the woods as soon as we finish breakfast?" Rosa's abrupt change of topic surprised Lyndon and Nycolos. Even more surprising was her suggestion that they walk in the woods. She had strictly forbidden either one of them from entering the woods. She expected their obedience to be short-lived, their restlessness was apparent after the first week. She looked back and forth between them, the fork sliding out between her rounded lips, her raised eyebrows giving them a look that said, "obviously boys".

What they didn't know was that Rosa was a little concerned about their uncharacteristic lack of defiance. What she had expected and what was in character would be for them to sneak off and break her rules together, leaving muddy boots by the door as only one of many clues for her to find. They loved night hiking, fishing, climbing massive boulders that had been dropped deep in the forest.

She confronted Lyndon about it one night after a passionate session of lovemaking. She lay on her back, feeling Lyndon's warmth slowly dissipate from her body,

"I know you two guys went on a night hike tonight. I always know when you guys break the rules, you leave too much evidence around."

Lyndon rolled over and looked lovingly into her face with a twinkle in his eye, and smirk on his face.

"We know you know, mommy; didn't you know?"

She smiled at his trickery and kissed his shoulder. Tired and satisfied they both drifted into a deep and satisfied sleep.

Rosa was called back to the present from her reverie when Nyc answered her. "All right," Nyc said, not even hesitating to think.

"Sounds good to me," Lyndon's agreement was almost as quick. The entire Arcadia family loved the forest and she saw no reason to make it off limits.

Breakfast finished, the white father, black mother, and their little mixed-race son left the kitchen. Walking single file the family moved through goldenrod, milkweed, and cosmos toward the tree line. In the already warm August morning, heat radiated up from the earth in humid waves and they began to sweat even though the family was dressed for summer. Cargo shorts all around; Lyndon and Nycolos wore white cotton t-shirts and Rosa was wearing a blue tank top that reminded Lyndon of the sky and ocean at the same time. School was starting next week and they all felt the changing season just around the corner.

The heat dissipated as they moved into the deep shadow of the forest. The trio paused, peering into the depths of the forest as if expecting something to move. Nycolos squeezed between his parents and Rosa and Lyndon parted easily, each taking one of his hands. They moved three abreast down the trail, moving quietly except for the occasional cracking twig or rustle of the underbrush. Nycolos noticed that roots and stones were not where they had been the night of the storm, but he did not mention this to either of his parents. Lyndon didn't miss Nyc's head swiveling as he scanned the ground.

Lyndon was glad to see it, it meant that Nycolos had noticed something strange too. Roots, stones, and branches that had thrown him off balance, made him lose his footing and almost lose his boots, were missing, or in different places. Using the same logic he had tried on Nyc earlier that day, Lyndon tried to convince himself that the fear and adrenaline rush of that night effected his memory and perception. Seeing Nyc's reaction to trail, Lyndon found it harder to cling to his own logic.

The cool under story was welcome after the steamy meadow. They ducked with muted footsteps into a stand of spruce trees and over pungent smelling needles, moving through dark pockets of forest where shadow so deep prevented the growth of underbrush, until they reached the ravine edge. The limestone walls were dark where water moved out of the soil along root channels, flowing down the face of the rock, staining it black. On the far side of the ravine sunlight penetrated through the trees and warmed the air, illuminating lush mats of unruly grasses that flanked a downed log. Some forty feet below the ravine floor was mostly limestone, adorned here and there with large boulders and fallen trees or shrubs.

Stillness settled over the little family standing on the edge of the ravine. Nothing stirred save a few finches and sparrows in the spruces above. No marks were evident within the ravine or on either edge that might indicate what had occurred there a few days ago. No bear, no monster, nothing but trees, sunshine, rocks and stillness. Diaphanous mats of roots were knotted cords, twisting and intertwined, penetrating rock with patient tenacity, dowsing for water and minerals. Roots erupted from the rock face in places, flowing down the ravine sides in braids colored red, orange and black. It was clear to both parents why Nycolos loved this place, and Lyndon wondered how he could've forgotten how lovely it was. He and Rosa had walked the trail almost every day when she had been pregnant with Nycolos.

Lyndon pulled them along and led Nycolos along the length of the ravine. Rosa, still holding Nyc's other hand, trailed behind. They moved along the edge, remarkably peaceful and calm with the truth before them. Lyn found an area where the ravine narrowed sufficiently for them to jump across. Though barely four feet across, Lyndon took no chances. He grabbed Nycolos and hefted him smoothly across the gap. Rosa arched an eyebrow at him but said nothing.

"Jeez Dad, I...thanks." Nycolos sounded surprised to find himself on the other side of the ravine.

The adults followed easily, barely making a noise as they leapt over. Lyndon grabbed Rosa and Nyc's hands and led them onward. He pulled his family through a stand of Norway spruce, pendulous branches thick and heavy with green needles hanging so low they had to duck in order to pass. They crossed into a sun-drenched clearing full of ferns and tall grasses that circled a fallen log. The ferns were a bright shade of green and smelled of hay, suffusing the air with a sweetness that made Rosa smile. Lyn put his hands on her hips, and looked deep into her eyes; eyes that sparkled in the sunshine, deep green like jade and more precious to Lyndon than any gemstone. Lyn beheld her perfection, her perfectly sculpted legs and bottom, and full lips so sweet her kisses could make the dead live again. At least that's what he always told her. He hugged her tight, and though it took a moment, her hands slid up his back.

Nyc's rustling footsteps and the crack of breaking twigs told them their son was resuming the exploration without them. Rosa separated from Lyn as an errant cloud skidded in front of the sun. He saw a question dart through the recesses of her lustrous green orbs; her eyes gathered in shadow seemed as deep as the forest itself. Eternity and Infinity met in the depths of her eyes, and she had love aplenty to sustain his wayward soul. The question, whatever it may have been remained unasked; she turned away and led him toward the sound of their son's footsteps.

Nycolos hadn't gone far but was hidden by a large log they had seen from the other side of the ravine. The tree was bleached white from years of rain and sun. When they reached Nyc he was staring at something in his hands. He was holding a large claw and at his feet, a piece of blue cloth hung from a root, a piece of Nycolos's blue raincoat, torn and sodden with rain and blood.

"Wow, nice bear claw." Rosa's voice was taut, like a string ready to pop.

"I knew it," Nyc exhaled loudly in the gathering silence. His words ricocheted off the walls of the ravine, bouncing from rock face to rock face, echoing 'I knew it... I knew it.... I knew it...' until his voice sank to the bottom and settled there. The unspoken fear they all shared lay bare before them, stripped of pretence by Nycolos Arcadia with three words. Despite the chaos and the trauma of that fateful night, doubt had taken root in Lyndon's mind. Lyndon, whose arms and legs were as strong and supple as green wood, hugged his son tight. There on the ravine's edge he lifted his little brown boy in one arm, gathered his wife in the other, and squeezed them close.

Lyndon considered what had brought them out to the ravine that morning, and what brought Nycolos there that terrible night, was the same thing. They were all in desperate need of answers, answers to questions Lyndon was afraid to ask -- answers that he was afraid to hear.

"No matter what Nyc, your mother and I are here and we love you, regardless of what we're going through, or headed toward, we are still a family." Nyc's eyes darted to his father's, the boy squirmed and pushed away until Lyn put him down again.

Rosa leaned close to Nyc and rested her arm on Nyc's shoulder, speaking very gently.

"That looks like a bear-claw sweetheart, a regular bear." She did not have to say what she meant – the claw was not from a were-bear, it was not from a man, who could turn into a bear, or a bear that could become a man, it was simply a bear claw. Nyc shrugged a non-committal response, leaned his head on her breast and wrapped his arms around his mother. The little family stood on the brink: the undisputed King of Hide and Seek, his mother the Jaguar Princess and his father a bear of a man. They took the long way back to the house, walking hand in hand down an unused section of the trail. The trail ran parallel to the ravine for a mile or so, the ravine floor gradually rising up to meet the surrounding earth. The deep dark forest the trail cut through transitioned from a mature forest to young forest, with thin beech and maple saplings growing tightly together. Finally they moved beyond the gorge into an old open field.

They laughed as they meandered home. Morose, ponderous thoughts were dispelled like the deep shadows of the forest, scared into hiding by the bright light of the sun. Nycolos picked a purple coneflower from the field, which Rosa put behind her ear, the bloom contrasting beautifully against her black skin. The boys chased Rosa, tackling her into the field and tickling her until she wept. They chased swallowtail butterflies, not to catch, but to run free with unpredictable, chaotic abandon.

They wandered home, navigating through an emotional gauntlet. The adults were trying to avoid confrontation, while attempting to cast aside demons within and without. Trying in vain to dispel the gathering darkness with the splendor of afternoon tomfoolery. They lounged beneath a gorgeous old burr-oak, easily 150 years old by Lyn's reckoning. The stately old-timer was the only remaining tree in that particular field, it provided them with welcome shade and gnarled grandeur. Lyndon sat leaning comfortably against the old tree, with Rosa's head in his lap, a long piece of grass between his teeth, gently stroking Rosa's face and hair. He was nearly dozing when her stomach grumbled loudly.

She laughed and opened her eyes, sitting up she hit him on the leg. "Well, I guess that's our cue." She was right and they got to their feet. Nycolos moved down from his perch somewhere high in the tree. Hanging from a branch, the boy dropped lightly to the grass.

"I think I'd like to take Nyc camping." Lyndon spoke, trying to get the words out as quickly as possible. Rosa's green eyes darkened and she stiffened, dropped his hand, and pushed him away.

"Sounds good to me," she said, her voice hollow like the sound of rain on a tin roof.

"When do you want to go? I can make some food." She smiled at Nyc, who had stopped running and stood behind his mother listening. She tousled his hair and hugged him tight, with glistening eyes and tight lips. Lyndon tried to catch up to Rosa on the way home, but she wouldn't hold his hand anymore.

****

The following day Lyndon and Nycolos were out of the house before dawn. Rosa stood on the front porch, waving goodbye. She hugged Nyc goodbye so tight she almost cracked his ribs, but kept her distance from Lyndon, giving him the silent treatment. Hawk Mountain was about an hour from their house and Lyndon had them on the trail as the sun crested the eastern ridgeline. They hiked through stands of sugar maples and beech. Nycolos found some spicebush on the way and played with the leaves, enjoying their citrus scent.

They hiked through the day, filling their lungs with clean air and the organic scents of decay and renewal. The day was perfect with crystalline blue skies, and wispy white cirrus clouds high in the sky. The sun gained strength, and by midday father and son were down to shirtsleeves, jackets packet away in their backpacks. Ferns grew thick around the moss-covered log they sat on for lunch. Nycolos stared into the sun, feeling the beams warm his face. He was waiting for the ball to drop and for his father to start the conversation he felt hanging in the air like a pregnant cloud. But nothing came. They finished their turkey sandwiches on wheat bread and got back on the trail. The rest of the day was a harmonious blend of green and brown, the trail becoming more overgrown and dense the further they moved into the forest.

Lyndon called the hike to a halt around 4'oclock and they made camp. Before long, dinner of beans and rice were bubbling away on the campfire while Lyndon heated tortillas on a large flat skillet he pulled from the depths of his pack. They ate hearty burritos, two a-piece as they were ravenous. The sun set somewhere out of sight to the west and night crawled into the woods draping them in shadow.

Lyndon and Nyc sat in the ring of firelight in the comfortable silence of family. The fire popped, and Nycolos lost himself staring into the dancing flames. Lyndon played his flute softly. A quenacho, a large bamboo flute from the Andes Mountains in South America that produced sad, melancholy notes that evoked longing in Nyc's breast.

He played softly, as much to fill the silence as to comfort them. His eyes were far away, and his mind with them. Nyc's eyes remained on the apex of the fire, the embers dancing like Will-o-the-wisps in time to the flute, orange tongues licking the air beneath the dancing balls. The flute's song turned light and airy like the dancing embers. The song stopped short as Lyndon's eyes caught movement across the fire. A female form entered the circle of light, and Lyndon was on his feet with a knife in his hand in a flash of silver steel.

"Please." The woman spoke, her tone imploring. She didn't say anything else, but moved closer. Lyndon visibly relaxed, and Nyc watched the muscles in his father's back relax. A cool breeze caressed them easing their tension and calming nerves. The wind fanned the fire, shooting sparks into the air. The woman was fair-skinned with straight auburn hair that hung to her back. Her eyes shone golden yellow in the firelight and shadows flitted across her chiseled features. Her high cheekbones were prominent and her face smooth and unblemished. Her cheeks sloped to her well-formed mouth and sculpted chin. Her nose was slightly hooked, and presently her mouth hooked down at the edges. She was an undeniably attractive woman, though something in the way she looked at them was predatory.

"I did not mean to startle you, nor do I intend to harm you." Her voice was high and sharp, and her gaze weighty.

"Hello, little one." Her gaze shifted to Nycolos. She raised her skirt and sat on the log next to Nycolos. Her clothes were in earth tones. Her skirt was brown, with red accents on the hem. And her blouse was a creamy brown flecked with brown chevrons that looked like plumage. She wore a sky blue amulet that changed color in the flickering firelight. The shape was foreign to Nycolos but he would've guessed it was a leaf or something similar. Nyc didn't say anything but waited for his father's reaction. Lyndon sat on the log between Nycolos and the strange woman, gently nudging Nyc down the log, away from the woman.

"Who are you?' Lyndon may have relaxed, but suspicion filled his voice.

"Just another camper, I saw your firelight and came down to say hello. I'm camped about a mile up the trail." She inched closer to Lyndon, lightly touching his arm with one finger. "I thought perhaps I could find some comfort beside your fire."

Lyndon considered her for a long time, eventually speaking to her quietly.

"Well, you are welcome to sit by the fire, and I am not in the habit of turning away a woman in the forest at night, but we will be turning in shortly, we have a long hike tomorrow." Nyc didn't think they were really going to bed that soon, but understood. The woman turned away from them, peering into the dark woods. She was smiling when she turned to face Lyndon again.

"It is of no consequence, I will not disturb you anymore, have a good evening." With that she stood and melted into the darkness. Lyndon sighed deeply, over and over again. Steeling himself for the conversation he wanted to have with Nycolos. Nyc felt anger flood his chest. He had never considered his father a coward before, but very nearly called him one, what with all the sighing. He wanted to scream at his father to get it over with, but he didn't have the heart. Finally, they turned in, Nyc first, he stretched out in his sleeping bag reading a book by the light of his headlamp. He was asleep by the time his father entered an hour later.

****

The next morning Lyndon and Nycolos left the campsite after a breakfast of corned-beef hash and leftover beans. Lyndon walked in front, he smelled like wood smoke, his hair was wild, and he wore wrinkled jeans and a roguish grin. Lyndon couldn't deny the spring in his step. He stepped out with long strides, his eyes sparkling when he checked to see if Nyc was keeping up every couple of minutes. Nyc thought his father was a different person in nature. He never shone so bright as when they managed to get lost, off the trail, or simply turned around.

The trail climbed gradually until it reached a meadow surrounded by tall hickory and beech trees, their tall straight trunks racing each other to the sun. Large boulders jutted up from the earth, half submerged like giant whales swimming through the black soil. They both loved camping, especially in backcountry places like Hawk Mountain. Nycolos knew there was a reason why his father had brought him out there. Lyndon wanted to tell him something last night at the campfire but he couldn't seem to do it before, or after they were interrupted. Nycolos guessed the news would come sometime that day.

A hawk cried high above and Nycolos ran ahead. He climbed a large boulder, shielded his eyes and looked upward.

"Come on, nature boy," Lyn beckoned to him, "we can't see the hawk very well from here but there's a clearing up ahead where you should be able to get a good look at her." Lyndon lifted Nycolos from the rock, lengthened his stride, and covering the remaining distance to the clearing at a gallop. He carried Nyc until they reached a clearing full of white asters. Nyc's father put him down, but the boy didn't notice the way Lyn's breath caught in his throat. Nor did he hear the sound of gnashing teeth. Nyc's mind was elsewhere though his body stood arms outstretched, head back, face bared to the sun and sky.

Nycolos Arcadia felt as if he were the hawk soaring through the heavens. He felt the warm air of thermals rising from the meadow below. Buoyant beneath his wings, the warm air lifted him higher, and higher. A sense of euphoria swelled in his breast, and he saw the world with eyes more powerful than any binoculars. He felt he could see every detail of the world below: a large lake sparkled in the distance, field mice skittered through a clearing directly below him, and all around, miles of forest rippled in the late summer breeze. The mice scurrying in the meadow drew his attention. *Later*, he thought and turned his focus instead on three individuals standing in the clearing. He saw a large human male frozen with fear, with his arm outstretched toward a small human male. The adult's face was ashen, his eyes bulged in his head and the rise and fall of his chest was rapid. Nycolos, the hawk, watched the boy, with his face turned to the sky, arms raised. The third figure in the clearing he was very familiar with. A massive grizzly bear, black like the night, towered over the two small humans.

Nycolos the raptor watched the larger human grope numbly at the child's sleeve. He could almost sense the fear welling up within the man, who pushed the boy to the ground, directly in front of the bear. For that moment, frozen in time, it looked as if the father was offering his son to the bear, like a sacrifice one might make to appease an angry god. The trio froze; Lyndon stood above the prone, seemingly unconscious boy, staring in horror at the bear.

The black beast reared up on its hind legs and roared. Lyndon screamed he was sorry and lightning struck from a cloudless sky, tearing the earth asunder some thirty meters behind group with an ear-splitting crack. Nycolos's awareness was ripped from the hawk and hurled to earth with teeth-jarring force. He entered his body so fast Nyc was sure he would die on impact.

Instead he slapped his hands to his ears and cried out in pain. The bear's roar and the thunder's clap drove all thought from his mind. In the silence that followed Nycolos Arcadia felt a strange understanding. He recognized this bear from the ravine. The animal was enraged, Nycolos could tell, though he couldn't say how -- infuriated with Lyndon Arcadia for offering his son as a sacrifice.

"Dad, it's him." Nycolos thought his father should know, but he barely managed a whisper. He didn't get a chance to find out if his father heard.

Towering over them, some 25 feet tall, the giant bear roared again, raised its arm and took a swipe at Lyndon. His father dove on top of Nyc, sheltering the boy with his body. He rose to a crouch and spun to face the attacker. Lyndon whispered instructions over his shoulder to Nyc.

"Walk backwards slowly, stay close to the ground, run back to camp, and get help if you see someone." That was all he said. He sprang to his feet and ran at the beast, ready to embrace death.

Nycolos obeyed part of the instructions. He crawled backwards, so low to the earth his belly scraped the ground. He did not run to their camp however. Instead he crouched behind the bole of a beech tree just beyond the clearing. Lyndon dodged to-and-fro once he had the bear's attention. When Lyndon sensed Nyc's departure he tried to flee towards the middle of the meadow. With dizzying speed, the bear pounced. One massive paw struck Lyndon, sending him flying into the air. He landed on his right side ten meters away. Years of capoeira helped Lyndon roll with the fall, and he was back on his feet, knife in hand, starting to jinga, the dance of the capoeirista. Nycolos couldn't even tell if his father was hurt.

The bear stopped, sniffing Lyndon. Dropping onto all fours the animal turned away and headed in the other direction. The bear's movement was a feint, in the blink of an eye the black mass of fur charged Lyndon. Lyndon cartwheeled sideways on one hand, kicking the bear in the muzzle with both feet while slashing at the bear's ankles with his other hand. Lyndon only just returned to his feet when the bear smothered him. Nyc watched in terror as his father disappeared beneath the monstrous bear. A cry that froze his blood came from beneath the bear. Nycolos could not look away, but he wept none the less. His father screamed as the bear's muzzle ripped downward, seeking flesh from bone. High in the sky, a red-tailed hawk's cry echoed Nyc's anguish.

The bear roared in outrage and stumbled backwards. Lyndon emerged from beneath the bear's body, crawling on his stomach. He dragged himself several meters before rising to his feet, holding the bloodstained knife in front of him. The monster reared on unsteady legs. Nyc saw the fur-covered belly and chest glistened with oozing punctures in at least a dozen places. Each wound stained the surrounding fur with dark blood that spilled from severed arteries and veins. Lyndon's shirt was stained red and black, and a large piece of flesh was missing from his right shoulder. He held the knife in his left hand, his right arm dangled uselessly, spilling his life-blood onto the white asters below.

The hawk's cry cut the air and Nyc though his head might burst. The sound signaled the beginning of the final round. The monster barreled into the human, attempting one more deadly embrace. Lyndon's left arm stabbed repeatedly as the as the bear's momentum carried them tumbling backwards head over heels. When they came to rest and both man and beast sprawled lifelessly to the earth.

Nycolos scrambled to his feet and stumbled to his father's body. A pink tongue lolled from the bear's open maw, its massive chest gurgled in a death rattle, and black blood seeped from its mouth onto the earth. Lyndon lay on his back; his severed arm a meter away. His jeans were torn and bloody but his legs were whole and unbroken. White aster blossoms were stained red with his blood. He looked at Nyc, and stroked his face with the hand that remained him.

"You are such a brave, beautiful boy." he whispered, eyes fixed not on Nyc but on the hawk circling above their heads. He turned his head and looked into Nyc's eyes. "I love you buddy. I love you and mommy both so much." The hawk cried again and Lyndon closed his eyes and stopped breathing.

Panic filled Nyc's ten-year old heart. He screamed at his father to get up. He begged his father to forgive him; he told him he didn't mind if he divorced them; grief finally dulled his senses and Nycolos wept. He didn't hear the bear making noises until his own sobbing ceased. Lying on one side, the monster sounded like it was drowning in its own blood. Suddenly Nycolos was filled with rage; he wanted to stab the bear, cut out the bear's eyes and teeth, stuff the beast and put it on the wall. Maybe he should eat the flesh and use the hide to make a robe or a rug. Perched atop his father's body he noticed Lyndon's blade buried to the hilt in the bear's chest.

Nycolos crept close, crawling on all fours, heart hammering wildly in his chest, as if the creature were merely sleeping and not dead. Crouching low he counted to sixty Mississippi looking for any signs of life. Seeing none he crossed the last few meters. His eyes filled with tears again and again, but he brushed them away. He would grieve later.

He concentrated on the hilt, wrapping his small, shaking brown hands around the knife, he took a deep breath and pulled hard. His fingers slipped from the bloody hilt and he backpedaled on shaking legs tripped on one of the bear's outstretched paws and fell backwards. Once he was flat on his back, even though he was aching all over, Nycolos could see the beast's massive head and golden eyes, clear and bright, looking right at him. The bear's chest was barely moving and the eyes were... alert. Scrambling back to the bear, Nycolos once again grabbed his father's knife with both hands and placed his left foot on the animal's chest. He paused a moment to focus whatever strength he had left. The blood coating Lyndon's knife was so thick it reminded Nyc of molasses. It welled up from the wound onto the blade, over the hilt and onto Nyc's hand. Pushing down with his foot, the ten-year old pulled with all his strength on the blade his father had buried in the beast's chest in his last desperate act to save his beautiful brown boy. The result was the same: Nycolos Arcadia flew backward with great force and landed hard. He was angry with himself. This was his father's knife. No killer bear was going to keep that, not even a were-bear.

It would be more than a decade before Nycolos would understand the full ramifications of what happened next. But he knew immediately was that his life would never be the same again. The third time the little boy climbed onto the monstrous chest the knife came free, but Nyc still flew into the air and fell hard to the ground. His jaw snapped shut with a loud click when he collided with the earth and stars exploded in his eyes, obscuring his vision to such a degree that he almost missed what happened next. The bear grunted deep and hard, black blood shot from the open wound in its chest, splattering Nyc's shirt. The bear's arm twitched twice and Nyc realized that there was another sound: the rustle of meadow flowers coming to life, twining themselves around the bear's arm and legs. Whipping through the air, as though there was a stiff wind, the movement of the stems was audible. Black and red, bloodied stems became cordage, binding the massive monster, leaving only its head exposed. When Nyc turned his head, he saw that his father too was already bound, eyes closed, and being pulled downward into the Earth Mother's dark bosom.

Nycolos tried in vain to rescue his father, pulling at flowers that had become as strong as steel. He scratched until his fingers bled, the knife lying forgotten in the dirt. The earth around him moved, flowing down into the earth like sand through an hourglass. Nycolos Arcadia, ten-year old son of Rosa Arcadia, a black woman from Brazil, and Lyndon Arcadia, a white man from upstate New York, curly hair full of leaves and dirt; watched in horror as his father disappeared into the earth.

The meadow swallowed his father, wrapped in a shroud of white asters, buried beneath the open sky. The bear had been pulled halfway into the earth when it sat up. Nycolos nearly fainted, so tenuous was his grip on consciousness. The beast was alive, or come back from the dead, and struggling against the its bindings, large paws scraping the earth, sending sand in all directions, filling the air with a thick dust. The bear would not escape, Nycolos was sure. Nyc bowed his head and prayed to the heavens and earth to help his father. The bear was no longer struggling, but it managed to swing one great paw as he entered the earth, and dust and spores exploded around Nycolos. Waist deep in white asters, Nycolos Arcadia swore he could hear the dust and spores tinkling like little chimes, and see them twinkling in the sunlight as they fell. It was through this haze he saw the giant grizzly's head blur, like an image out of focus, and when it came back into focus, it was no longer the head of a bear, but the head of a man. A man with thick black hair and a thick black beard, dark eyes and a strong jaw. He looked like a mountain man who had never come down from the mountain, and never intended to. Then the image blurred again and he was looking at the grizzly. Nycols Arcadia screamed but no sound escaped his throat. The hawk cried, long and mournful, and Nyc thought he heard something in the cry about death and life's lessons.

Nycolos stared at the two bare spots, all that remained of his father and the beast. His mind devoid of all thought, even the questions he knew he should ask, the Earth tilted sideways and he fell to the ground. He knew he was losing consciousness, even as radiant white light filled his mind.

Chapter 3

Fly Agaric

Casting aside animal form,
Freely they walk among men.
Howling hordes stream forth,
From forest, hummock and hollow
Children of Gaia, hewn of earth, rock and stone.
Rain righteous retribution on mortal man.

Nycolos Arcadia floated in space not knowing who or what he was. High above, golden orb blazed to life, piercing the darkness. His eyes adjusted and he could finally see he was moving through a forest. Running, Nycolos tore through woods as fast as his feet would carry him. Sinkholes opened on all sides, threatening to suck him into the depths of the earth. His father's voice crying to him from the depths within. Branches bent low on trees, swiping at his head, seeking to shatter his skull on trunk or bough.

His foot caught on a rolling stone, and he fell to the earth. Vines shot out from the trunk of a nearby tree, wrapping around his neck, arms and legs. Even struggling for all he was worth he couldn't match the strength of the vines. They pulled him screaming into the blackness, a void of nothingness, where light and dark met in secret. He found himself sitting at his dining room table eating dinner with his parents. The table was set for dinner. His parents sat across from each other, mouths moving in mute conversation. The lights of the crystal chandelier flickered wildly, but his parents didn't notice.

Lightning flashed outside, silhouetting the dark form pressing against the large picture window that flanked the dining room. Massive bear, a monster, scraping long black nails down the windowpane, making the first sound that he could hear, curdled his blood and sent a shiver down his spine. Nycolos leapt to his feet screaming, but his voice would not come. Panic filled his chest, clutched his throat he inadvertently, bumped the table hard enough to spill wineglasses and knock plates to the floor. Shattered soundlessly without a sound.

His parents noticed nothing, their discussion growing more animated, their arms waving and faces grown intent with contained emotion. They rose, gathered plates and eating utensils from the floor, and moved their mute conversation into the kitchen. Tearing after them, Nycolos pulled on their shirts and pant legs, calling to them breathlessly. oblivious to his attempts to distract them, they moved through the motions, beginning to argue by the looks on their faces.

The bear paralleled their movements, moving from the dining room window, to the kitchen. Black ton of muscle and death tapped more persistently, saliva coating the glass where panting maw and broad black nose threatened. The glass cracked, and broke with a popping sound, showering glass into the kitchen sink. Lights flickered for the last time and faded before the arrival of death. Nycolos could see the dark forms of his parents, unaware of the danger they were in, verbally sparring in their soundless melee, feinting and parrying in the middle of the kitchen. Lightning flashed, anger painted their faces, but death cared not. An enormous paw through the void where window belonged, death's escort. Nycolos reacted, hurdled onto center island ceramic tile cutting board, jumped nimbly through the darkness from island to counter top, more tile. Pushed off of father's shoulder and jumped through the broken kitchen window into the dark, furry chest of the beast. He passed through the creature as through shadow, more like plunging into a dark, cold pool, reflexively inhaled breath , more darkness.

He landed with a thud, not outside the kitchen, but in the meadow where his father had been killed. He felt small and exposed, asters towered over like trees with thick stems like trunks. A hawk screams, somewhere high above she circled, crying out her delight, there is prey. Nycolos was afraid, scrambled to escape, claws tearing at the earth, pushing himself to dodge left and right around massive stems. Whiskers vibrated wildly, aiding to make sharp turns, vision was limited beneath blades and stems of the massive asters. The hawk drew nearer, imagined wings cutting through the air.

Fear drove him onward, hawk's cries whip and carrot. Cut left, cut right, footing lost, careening into a large stem, crashing through plantain leaves. Landed on a rose thorn, which tore a large gash in his brown fur.

Nycolos Arcadia looked down in shock at his white chest covered in fur; he was a mouse. The hawk's talon ripped him from the earth, the vice-grip threatening to sever his small body in half. The hawk held her head high, choosing a landing site to devour her prey. He felt his tiny ribs cracking and popping in his chest. She alighted on a nearby limb and brought her beak down to rip off his head.

****

Nycolos woke kicking and screaming, his left hand hit something soft, and promptly both of his arms were restrained. His eyes adjusted, and soon he could see again.

"It's all right little one, I'm here now, you're ok." The woman from the campfire the night before was cradling his head to her bosom. Her dark eyes were beautiful, almond-shaped and full of compassion and unshed tears.

"Daddy...," Tears sprang free and Nycolos was blinded once again, this time by grief. The woman in red moved his head to her lap and cradled it there, shushing him gently. She wore the same shades of browns and reds she had been wearing at the campfire the night before. She sang a few notes in his ear, a strange sad song he had never heard before. It made his body feel light, and strength infused him. The pain in his chest was obscured, somehow distant, as if pain could be moved behind a cloud. He still ached everywhere, but less intensely. She helped him to his feet taking care to be sure he was steady before letting go.

"My name is Lora." She whispered.

"My dad, we have to find him." Nyc's desperation was bubbling free, effervescing to the surface.

She sang again, and it was as if she shut off his brain, or thrown him into some sort of trance. The world became faded and dull, colors removed from everything, leaving the world in shades of gray. Nyc could do nothing else, not even think. Lora led him to the campsite, though Nyc did not feel like he walked there so much as arrived there. The ground jumped and blurred with their steps, and in three short steps they were there. At the campsite she left the four-season tent where Lyndon pitched it. Lyndon had planned for them to hike the mountain trails and return for dinner. She took his pack from the tent and fitted it to his back. She sat him on a log and told him to wait, which, for some reason he was completely contented to do.

Most of what happened next was lost to Nycolos Arcadia for the next decade. Upon the discovery of his memories however, he would remember Lora stopped next to a large cherry tree on the edge of their campsite. She placed her palms together and muttered an incantation, most of which Nyc missed except for one word, "Agaricus." A mushroom sprouted next to the cherry tree, popping out of the earth in an instant. The cap flipped open like lid, and a small, white ball of light flew up and out of the basidiomycete's stem. Immediately following the will-o'-the-wisp, a slim fairy flew out of the stem. She wore beautiful garments that were the color of budding tealeaves. The blouse she wore looked like overlapping leaves, covering her tiny chest, leaving her stomach and shoulders exposed. The fabric was sheer and shone like a silver lining.

The fairy alighted on the cherry tree and spoke at length with Lora. The mysterious woman looked chastised, as the fairy wagged her finger and spoke down to her. The white ball of light flitted around, bouncing up and down in time with the conversation, turning red when the two women started yelling at each other. The fairy made herself clear with a firm gaze, a pointed finger and hand on her hip. The will-o'-the-wisp was bright red, flying in and out the cherry tree frantically. A large root of the cherry tree unrolled from the earth and wrapped around Lora's foot. The tall woman with ivory skin, and lustrous brown hair, was not pleased at all. Finally the fairy with green wings to match her clothes kicked open the toadstool cap and flew down the stem like a diver entering the water. The red will-o'-the-wisp disappeared into the bole of the tree. Lora leaned on the tree, supporting herself with both hands and shook her head.

After several minutes she took Nycolos by the hand, and for a moment synapses fired in his ten-year old brain, memory blossoming to life. He remembered being a mouse, ribs broken, head twisted awkwardly, about to be eaten by a hawk. Lora's eyes shone with a ravenous glint, and he wondered if she was going to kill him. She considered him for a long time, then took out a small purple bag. She poured some white dust into her hand and blew the powder into Nyc's face. She shook her head and led him down the path, humming her nameless tune. After she blew the powder in his face, Nyc had jumbled and confused memories of being led down the mountainside. What should have been hours of hiking blurred into a slide show of streams, boulders, and gray mist. Everything was suffused with the gray mist and the sensation of moving, down and down and down.

What may have been hours or mere minutes later she whispered a song in his ear again, and the washed-out world surged anew, becoming bright and vibrant. Nycolos could hear birds in the trees, and feel the breeze on his face. He could control his movements again, and turned to face the mysterious woman. He was not at all upset, but instead overwhelmed with a sense of gratitude and thanks. He grabbed her hand of his own volition, pulling her towards the foot of the mountain and the dale that opened up beyond it. She stopped after a few steps forcing Nycolos to stop as well.

"I can go no further little one." She spoke with finality and remorse, her eyes glittering dangerously. "There are people at the bottom of the hill that will help you get to your mother, just tell them what happened." Sadness settled in her eyes, like she knew the consequences of some action he had yet to take.

She tapped a nearby tree with two nails and a white orb emerged from the bole of the Ash tree, settling in front of Nycolos. The orb bobbed in mid air as if waiting for him.

"Follow the will-o'-the-wisp child. Have no fear, this one is mine."

"Yes, I will. Well, goodbye then." He waved goodbye and was ready to begin his descent but she leaned close and whispered one last song in his ear, a new one unlike the other two. A gray mist settled around Nycolos Arcadia, and he walked down the foot of the slope and out into the afternoon sun. He never looked back, it didn't matter anyway, even if he did there was nothing to see save trees, bushes, and birds. The most beautiful of which was a red-tail hawk circling high above the woods. The will-o-the-wisp bobbed along, guiding Nycolos through the impenetrable fog. After several minutes of descent Nyc's boots crunched onto a gravel trail, at which point the glowing ball dove into the ground and was gone. The gray mist stuck with him and only disappeared as he entered a wooden building that looked like a big log cabin. The mist took several moments to disappear completely, but once gone he could see people wearing green uniforms running around screaming at each other. One pretty blond lady with short hair and first aid kit ran over and practically slid across the wooden floor to Nyc and started checking him for wounds. She ripped off his blood stained clothes and fired questions at him. Nycolos didn't have to fake the tears once they started rolling down his cheeks as he told her what he remembered. A bear had killed his father on Hawk Mountain.

****

Rosa's heart hammered in her chest, each beat thundering in her ears. She rocketed through the darkness, pushing the station wagon for everything it had. Tires squealed as she navigated through twists and turns at dangerous speeds unbecoming an immigrant housewife. The road snaked through a mountainous pass sloping downward sharply at the far end. She stomped down on the accelerator, sending the car shooting off the top of the incline. The engine revved loudly, roaring as the tires left the ground, the car slammed onto the highway, orange sparks shooting out behind the family wagon. Rosa's face was covered in tears, which she rubbed from her cheeks violently.

Thoughts collided in her mind like caged birds trying to fly to freedom beyond the bars that confined them. Lyndon was missing, and Nycolos was alone at the ranger station. She couldn't fathom how something so horrible could have happened. She felt like the universe was determined to destroy her little family, one way or another. Their favorite camping location was only fifty miles away, but it had already been dark when she got the call from the ranger station.

She had been sitting in a hot bath, up to her ears in suds, bubbles tickling her ear lobes and nose. Rosa had ruminated all evening, before that she had been walking around sighing all day, and was quite sick of herself. Her logic was that a long hot soak would help ease her mind, and as it turned out she was right, if just barely. Her mind finally quieted while she imagined the boys sitting around a campfire, maybe talking about the divorce, or Lyn's new girlfriend. She didn't hear the phone ring right away, and it took several rings before she snapped to and recognized the sound. Even then she didn't move when the answering machine clicked on in the next room, she hadn't expected any calls and the only people she really wanted to hear from were on the side of a Hawk Mountain, fifty miles away. The voice sounded garbled and muffled, echoing down the hallway from the bedroom; the only word she understood was "forest ranger".

Sitting in the driver's seat her wet hair had finally stopped dripping, but her sweat suit was wet down the back, as she put it on before toweling off. Lost in thought, she blew by the state trooper parked on the right shoulder. The woop-woop of the siren made her heart jump, but brought her back to the present of blue and red lights in her rear view mirror, cutting the night and stinging her eyes. She pulled over cursing in Portuguese,

"Filho de puta! Puta que pario!"

The officer stepped from his cruiser once her vehicle stopped completely. Strangely enough, he jogged to her car, and stuck his head in her open window.

"Hey, Rosa, figured it might be you. Dispatch called with a message from Chief Ranger Thompson, he said you'd be high tailin' it through here." John Duda was a local guy they knew that liked to hang with Lyndon once in a while. Hunting with Lyn in the woods or fishing for hours. He was a nice guy in his early 20's, with dirty blond hair, a very unassuming nature, and a belly just starting to stretch his uniform.

"Figure I'll give you an escort since you're driving so damn fast. Follow me." A pitying expression played across his face at the mention of her speed.

He recovered, ducking his head and pulling the brim of his hat low. He jogged back to his cruiser, pulled out in front of her, turned on his lights, and gunned it. Already more than halfway to the ranger station, they covered the remaining twenty-odd miles in an eye blink, pulling into the parking lot of the ranger station, squealing tires announcing their arrival. A figure stood in the doorway of the park office. Rosa couldn't make out any features of the person, backlit as they were, face obscured in shadow.

A mist filled the mountain valley, obscuring sight beyond 30 meters. The park office was lit from the inside, and a few tall streetlights illuminated the parking lot. The streetlights shone as eerie ephemeral globes suspended in the mist. Rosa ran up the wooden steps and through the door held open by a red-headed man wearing a park ranger uniform. A young man as well. He was not surprised when she dispensed with the courtesies—asking where her son was. He nodded to Rosa and gestured with his arm, pointing down a hallway. She ran.

John Duda already forgotten, had not entered the station, instead pulled out of the parking lot, heading back to his speed trap.

Rosa Arcadia pushed open glass doors leading into a large back office. Behind a large oak desk, Nycolos sat in a comfortable looking leather chair, drawing on paper with crayons. Chocolate curls fell over his ears and mocha forehead, he looked up with puffy red eyes when he heard the door open and they lit with joy.

"Mom!" He was around the desk in a heartbeat. The little boy crashed into his mother's arms and the two of them sobbed together on the floor in the middle of the Chief Ranger's office. Rosa hadn't been told everything in her brief conversation on the phone, but she knew Nycolos had come down the trail alone and covered in blood.

Rosa disengaged from her son and stood, noticing the park ranger sitting on the corner of the desk mumbling to himself.

"Ma'am, the boy has had quite a day, I have a few questions, but brief ones, so you can get Nycolos here home to bed."

"What happened?" She barely let the Chief Ranger finish before speaking over him; she stared deep into Nyc's eyes, holding onto his shoulders when she spoke, making it was obvious to whom she was talking.

"It was him, Mom, the bear from the ravine; only mean this time." The boy blubbered unashamed, dammed up desperation and fear spilling forth in the safety of his mother's presence.

Rosa froze; her heart hammered in her chest harder than ever in her life. Nycolos, her beautiful boy shook like a leaf, his face buried in her bosom. The ranger sitting on the edge of the oak desk pursed his lips and glanced at them from the corner of his eye. He coughed once and stood; garbed in green his eyes seemed soft as he regarded the two of them. His hair was dark and curly, covering his head and arms like a thick coat of fur.

" I sent a couple of my men up the trail once we figured out what your son was saying. They haven't come back yet, and I don't expect to hear from them before morning. They're camping where your son and husband camped last night." He motioned toward a brown leather chair on one side of the room, and Rosa mechanically obeyed holding her beautiful little boy to her breast.

The park ranger extended a callused, thick-fingered hand.

"My mother always said I had lousy manners." He grimaced and shook her hand. " I'm the Chief Park Ranger Daniel Thompson." Stepping back he settled on the corner of the large oak desk once again and took a deep breath.

"Mrs. Arcadia, your husband was mauled and probably killed by a bear today. Probably sometime this morning, given Nycolos had time to hike down to our station by this afternoon. Your son showed up in our office today in a most particular fashion." He paused, his eyes shifted to Nycolos who had stopped crying and was nodding off on his mother's chest.

"Honestly Mrs. Arcadia, If I hadn't seen it myself I don't think I'd believe it. Nycolos appeared in the foyer there like a shadow come down the mountain, covered in blood, dirt and pine needles, but unhurt." He added the last quickly, seeing her eyes widen in horror.

"Another ranger has a boy his age and his wife brought some clothes over once we got Nycolos calmed down."

"And Lyndon?" Rosa couldn't get the rest out.

"Your boy says the bear killed him." He stopped abruptly as if biting something off. He looked at Nycolos again, considering something.

"My ranger's radioed in, they found no signs of a struggle, just some pieces of clothing, and Lyndon's knife, but no body." He looked at her, pity playing across his face. Rosa didn't feel the tears streaming down her cheeks until he passed her some tissues. She wiped her eyes and looked into his round face.

The ranger was well built given his age, he looked to be in his late fifties, with salt and pepper wavy hair, and a barrel chest that had just started to settle into his gut.

"Do bears usually come so far down the mountain?" She knew they did, but he was a professional.

"Well, yes, sometimes. That's the thing, ma'am, your husband and son weren't close to town. They were at least twenty miles in. It is incredible that your son walked so far in his condition." Rosa's eyes stung, shining with unshed tears that pooled in the corners of her green eyes.

"I can't believe..." Words failed her.

"Well, your son in quite amazing, but there's more."

"More?" Rosa thought she might cry out in anguish, only just managing to bite back on her despair. A weight pressed on her chest and shoulders, it felt as if it would crush her where she sat. If Nycolos hadn't been sitting in her lap she was quite sure she would have thrown herself on the floor wailing.

"I'm sorry, ma'am." He handed her the entire box of tissues. "Would you like to put this off for a while?"

"No, No, I want to hear it." She put her head on Nycolos's, pushed her lips through his curly locks, and squeezed him tight.

"Well, not only did he hike twenty miles back to the Ranger Station, be he appeared in here like a ghost." He raised his hands and continued before she had time to ask any questions. "Believe me ma'am, like a ghost, as in not there one second then standing in the middle of the room the next. None of us saw him walk through the door, and as you can see, this is not a large office. He brought this fog you see outside down the mountain like it was tied to his ankle. I know this sounds nuts, but it is the god's honest truth. Even the office fogged up for an hour or so. About the strangest thing we've ever seen in this neck of the woods."

Rosa said nothing, only hugged Nycolos tighter, he had finally stopped shaking and his deep even breaths told her he was sleeping. Seeing she was not going to comment the Ranger continued.

"Then there's the lady..." He stood and walked to the opposite side of the office, gazing out of the large window towards the foot of the Hawk Mountain Trail, the peak of which was visible during the day. Rosa was thankful that he had his back to her, she could taste blood in her mouth from her bleeding tongue. She knew exactly which woman he was talking about, a beautiful and graceful woman with almond eyes and a slightly hooked nose. A woman that had taken the moment of Lyndon's death from her like a thief in the night, making off with Rosa's crown jewel, her golden-hearted giant.

Rosa was sure the Ranger couldn't see her tightened jaw, so spoke into the silence.

"There was a woman with him?" Her voice was shaking.

"A woman wearing a red dress with brown and white according to Nycolos, he says she stopped by the campsite the previous night, and walked him down today, though he doesn't remember how or when. Nobody saw her by the way, or your son, and the lower trail was definitely busy today, this being the last weekend before school starts. I myself asked at least a dozen hikers who should've seen him, and none did." Park Ranger Thompson turned from the window, his arms crossed over the badge on his chest, and regarded her for a mere second. Abruptly he crossed the worn wooden floor and knelt in front of her.

"Again, Mrs. Arcadia, I'm sorry for your loss. If we find anything more I'll call you personally, I just thought you should know everything we do, you can go home now and get some rest. We can try to make sense of this craziness when you two are ready."

Rosa did not hesitate, she picked up her sleeping son and walked out of the station. Once in her car, she sat in the driver's seat staring blankly through the windshield, her keys forgotten in her lap, when the Chief came to the windshield.

"Mrs. Arcadia, I want you to know we're going to do our best to find your husband, and I want you to let Nyc know I'll bring his father's knife to him as soon as I can. He seemed most distressed about having left it on the mountain."

Rosa nodded numbly. The Chief nodded to her once, put a hand on her shoulder and squeezed. With a gentle smile and sad eyes he walked off into the mist.

Chapter 4

Ravens and Crows

Nycolos and Rosa spoke little for the next several days. The fog filling the valley below Hawk Mountain followed the pair home, attracted like a magnet to their heartache, at least that's what Rosa thought. The mist settled around their house and forest slipping through cracks in brick and mortar until Rosa would've sworn the house was full of fog as well. Mother and son stayed hidden in bed, staring out windows and blankly at walls. She tried to exercise, but had nothing to give, her heart hurt too much. They ended up watching old cartoons they had both seen a thousand times; not really watching, but holding each other tight, trying not to drown on their tiny island of grief, battered by waves in an ocean of foggy misery.

Rosa trudged out to the orchards one morning a week after the accident to check on the chickens, turkeys, ducks, pheasants and other poultry she had left to fend for themselves. The animals got most of their forage from the orchards, in which they dwelt the entire year, and as such were probably fine, she guessed, but her duty was to check none-the-less. The fog refused to dissipate the entire week; instead it grew denser, if that was possible, obscuring one of the many gates that lead into the orchard. The animals were usually fat and happy this time of year. Apple, pear, and plum trees overflowed with fruit, hedgerows were laden with blackberries, raspberries, hazelnuts, and currants just to name a few. Today was no different, though she couldn't see beyond the first row of trees, she knew their limbs hung heavy with fruit. In the distance she could hear the chickens clucking, they sounded excited.

After twenty minutes of searching for birds but seeing none, she was ready to head inside to her down comforter and fuzzy slippers. Since the accident if she got out of bed, it was a good day. She could barely pull herself together most days, and if it hadn't been for Nyc she wouldn't have bothered. Her chore had been as much about getting out of the house as it had been about checking on the birds. Something big moved through the fog beyond the trees, causing the fog to undulate and contort in the breeze. Chickens clucked off to her left and a rooster cock-a-doodled. A horse whinnied far away, Rosa heard galloping hoof-beats and Mirage rocketed through the mist. Dappled white and brown, the mare galloped nearly to the gate before pulling up short, nostrils flaring. The horse stepped close and rubbed her muzzle on Rosa's outstretched hand.

"Mom?"

Rosa screamed and nearly jumped out of her skin, she hadn't heard Nycolos approaching.

"Yes, sweetheart," She managed not to bite his head off, but just barely, "Sorry I left you—I thought you were sleeping, honey, so I just came to check on the animals." Neither of them had grown comfortable with solitude yet, and she felt a pang of guilt in her chest.

"It's O.K. Sorry I scared you." She saw a glint of humor in Nyc's soft brown eyes, but it was lost beneath the raised hood of his sweatshirt.

"You saw something, didn't you?" Though phrased as a question, Nyc's tone was a statement. He stood at her shoulder, stepped up onto the lowest crossbar of the gate and caressed the affectionate mare, absentmindedly peering into the fog.

"Yes," she replied, "I saw something moving around, stirring up the chickens. Turns out it was Mirage up to her usual tricks."

Nycolos peered into the orchard as if his determination alone could burn off the fog. Mirage snorted and stomped her hoof several times and Nyc would've sworn he heard tinkling laughter deep in the orchard.

Mirage was beautiful. "Her usual tricks" earned her the name Lyndon gave her when she was still a filly, and Nycolos just beginning kindergarten. The mare played tricks, hiding in the orchard, her dappled browns hidden deep in shadow. Other times she stood motionless in full sun, surrounded by wheat or barley, maize. The mare was skilled at eluding them in any of the orchards, dappled mare flitting through dappled sunlight.

"She misses Dad." Nycolos never stopped stroking the horse. Mirage stood with her head practically on his shoulder, and Rosa knew Nyc was right. Lyndon was Mirage's favorite; she loved him with abandon and would follow him all over the farm when she was able.

"Yes she does, we all do." Rosa rubbed the mare on one cheek and wrapped an arm around her son.

"Let's go inside and get some food." She didn't need to suggest twice. Nyc hopped down from the fence, waved goodbye to Mirage and walked inside with his mother.

***

Their loss went unnoticed to the outside world save their close friends and neighbors the Millers. Lyndon's parents were dead and he had no brothers or sisters. Rosa's family was in Brazil and not much better. Her brother lived in Queens, NY, but they had fallen out of touch for some reason, separated by age and circumstance. One of the reasons Rosa and Lyndon had fallen together so hard had been because neither of them had anyone until they had each other. She taught him capoiera, he had taught her English, and they taught each other how to love.

Some of the regulars noticed Lyndon's absence when she opened the organic grocery three weeks after the accident. Their little store sat across the street. A small and simple affair, the genius of Lyndon's idea was bearing fruit in so many ways. She decided to open the store again to give them something to do, and because neighbors started calling asking for squash and onions. Nyc wasn't ready for school, the camping trip had been the last weekend before school started, it was still too soon. The principal was understanding and told Rosa that Nycolos could take all the time he needed. So he stayed home and was a great help to her, harvesting and preparing products for the market.

The store was small, consisting of only two rooms. The front room had wooden crates around the perimeter, filled with whatever was fresh from the farm. She and Nycolos filled the large center bins with apples and pears. The side bins she filled with tomatoes, zucchini, squash, some pumpkins, radishes, greens, etc. A long counter topped with white ceramic tiles divided the front room from the back of the store. The back was open with a long wooden table, along one wall, that they used to clean veggies. Opposite the wooden table stood a metal sink and grooved stainless steel counter, topped with a wooden cutting board at one end. Lyndon used to clean and prepare the birds and livestock they sold on the cutting board. The job fell to Rosa now. In the back corner of the store were two freezers they used to keep already butchered meat and whole hanging carcasses.

Wrought iron potholders hung from the ceiling beams, the iron shaped to look like leaves of rambling Boston ivy. Bundles of herbs hung from every other beam, flower ends hanging down with brightly colored string binding the base of the stems.

The walls were lined with wooden shelves and glass casements filled with small glass bottles full of liquids herbs. Other sections were soaps, teas, lotions and salves. All made by Lyndon and Rosa in the lazy days of summer, before mention of divorce or death.

Rosa moved behind the counter, checked the register, opened the shutters and windows. The fog had finally lifted from the flanks of the Mount, and the sun shone weakly, like her resolve. The organic grocer had been Lyn's idea, and had started really slow. After a couple years though, business was booming, and with food contamination in the media, people in town were becoming more conscious about where their food came from. As a result their business was growing by leaps and bounds. Nycolos was moving in and out of the back door, bringing in what vegetables remained in the truck. He had been quiet for the three weeks since the attack, but last night that had all changed.

****

The phone rang while they sat having a quiet lunch of chicken soup with fresh carrots, tomatoes, and greens from the garden, finished off with a salad of sliced tomatoes, cucumbers and cilantro. Rosa answered and the voice of Chief Ranger Daniel Thompson reached her ear.

"Mrs. Arcadia, we've finished our search for your husband. I'm sorry but we were unable to find his body." She could hear papers rustling in the background as if he were going through a file.

"I have your tent and equipment from the campsite, if you'd like I can send someone to bring them by."

"That will be fine, thank you."

"Yes ma'am." He hung up.

Rosa returned to the table and told Nycolos what the ranger said. She and Lyndon had always been straight with Nycolos. They told him long ago who Santa, the Easter Bunny, and the tooth fairy were. The funny thing was, he hadn't really been surprised.

"They aren't going to find him." Nycolos spoke nudging some peas floating in his soup.

"Why not?" She was afraid to push the subject; he hadn't opened up about what had happened on Hawk Mountain. All she had been able to learn had been because of his nightmares. She held him tight when he woke screaming, crying out in fear of being swallowed by the earth. Other nights he didn't wake but spoke loudly, screaming nonsense about the bear-man or the hawk-lady.

"The bear-man and Dad were swallowed into the ground." Tears gleamed in his eyes, but he refused to let them fall. "But I don't think he's gone." He met her eyes and held them, starlight star bright, first star I see tonight.

Rosa sat with her mouth open, unsure how to respond to Nycolos. Was he just a frightened boy grasping at an impossible hope? One she herself was desperate to believe? She needed to know what had happened. Could it be possible that Lyndon had abandoned Nyc? She couldn't bring herself to believe it, Lyndon may have thought their marriage was over, but he would never put Nycolos in danger.

"What do you mean, honey?" Tremulous and tentative, her voice was nearly a whisper.

Nycolos stared out the large picture window, his mind far away, beyond the distant horizon and the realm of the living. "I don't know." His voice sounded as if it was coming from some far-away place.

They finished lunch in silence, each lost in their own thoughts. Afterwards she suggested they move to the orchards to harvest some fruit and vegetables so they could open the store. Nycolos thought it was a good idea so they headed out. The fog that had settled on the farm finally burned off that morning, to the delight of both mother and son, allowing the weakening autumn sun to warm the orchards on a perfect September afternoon.

Mirage stomped and snorted when they came out into the noonday sun, and the mare nudged them both a little too hard. They had been neglecting her since the accident, not in the sense of food or water, but in time. Their absence was tough on Mirage, she was accustomed to constant companionship. Nycolos watched his mother work for some time, unsure of what he should do. She had been treating him like he was made of glass for the last three weeks, but he knew she was desperate to know what had really happened. At lunch it had almost been too much for him to bear, she looked ready to beg him to tell her.

They picked apples from the lowest branches whilst he pondered how much she could handle. He knew Mirage hadn't been up to her usual tricks a few days ago. He felt something in his chest, that morning, a presence that reminded him of his father, and yet totally foreign as well. He wanted to tell her but there was simply too much, so he started at the beginning, or what he thought was the beginning. He told her everything he could remember. The mysterious lady that visited the campfire, the following morning, hiking to the clearing and their meeting with the bear. He told her he thought Lyndon's accidental offering somehow enraged the beast. He told her of the battle, knife vs. tooth and claw, to the death.

Tears salted his words of Lyndon's greatest sacrifice and his final words of love.

Rosa broke down during his story, dropping the basket she had filled with apples and pears. She fell with her fruits, sending firm, green and red fruit, bouncing around the roots of the apple tree they stood beneath. She grabbed him, pulled him close, and buried her head in her hands weeping.

Nycolos swore he heard someone else weeping, another female voice, but he couldn't investigate without leaving his mother, and that was not going to happen. He told her what happened when he pulled the knife from the bear's chest, how the bear came back to life when he did; the way the ground opened, swallowing bear and his father, and he saw the bear shape shift. The rest was a blur and he told her so, all he could remember was the lady in red singing, sparkling sunlight and the fog of a dream.

Mirage whinnied loudly behind him, as if she was listening to his tale and was incredulous at what she heard. Rosa stared at Nycolos for a long time saying nothing. The ten-year-old did not recall his experience flying as the hawk, the glowing orb that the lady in red had argued with, or the fairy that flew in and out of the mushroom that ascended and descended like an elevator into earth. He did not mention he thought it had been his father in the orchard the other night. He couldn't explain it to her anyway, and she was already upset enough. As it was, she didn't speak to him for almost the rest of the afternoon. They worked long and hard, picking fruit, collecting eggs from the chicken coops in the corners of the orchards. They picked squash, and zucchini, greens and broccoli, combing through the seasonal vegetables that were replete throughout the orchard, grown unruly and rotten, lost and forgotten since the accident.

Nycolos was pushing a wheelbarrow full of acorn squash down a hedgerow when she put an arm around his shoulder and turned him around. She squeezed him tight, kissed him and walked into the field of golden rods holding pruners for the harvest. By the time they finished the sun had painted the sky gold and pink.

When they finally came back into the house Rosa sent Nycolos upstairs to take a shower, telling him she would call him when dinner was ready. For the first time since the accident he felt almost O.K. being in a different room than his mother. Apparently she felt the same, telling him she'd be fine after patting him on the cheek. He climbed the stairs, his mind quiet and still, another first in a long time. He pulled some of his favorite p.j.'s from his dresser, a blue and green one piece with padded feet and a zipper that ran from his ankles to his neck, that he called footsies. He threw them on the bed and glanced out the window.

Mirage stood shoulder-deep in the goldenrods field, grazing on something. The mare raised her head looking toward the tree-line and the forest beyond. Nycolos realized with chagrin he left the orchard gate open, and would have to get Mirage in before dinner. His reflection looked back at him from the bedroom window; apple leaves and hay decorated his afro, but there was something was different about his eyes. Without any more thought he dashed downstairs.

Rosa wore a green handkerchief to hold back her tight curls, her muscled brown shoulders flexed as she pierced an acorn squash cutting it in half cleanly. She heard Nyc jumping down the stairs as he took five at a time, and turned, mouth opening to say something.

He cut her off, "Mirage is in the meadow, I left the gate open, I'll put her back." He didn't give her time to protest and bolted out the door. He knew she could catch him if she tried, but at least he had a head start.

Nycolos flew from the kitchen before Rosa could get a word in edgewise. She couldn't help but smile. That was more like it, at least a little more like the boy she knew. Normally she would've scolded him severely for leaving the room while she was still talking, but not today. She went through the motions, making her miso soup and zucchini stir-fry. Nycolos had always been an honest boy, never prone to tall tales or lying. Sure, like any kid he used to lie when he spilled something, or broke a glass, but she and Lyndon had been quick to teach Nycolos the lie he invented was a much greater infraction than any broken window or spilled drink.

Which meant he believed his outrageous tale, and perhaps she should too. Ranger Thompson had been cryptic describing how Nyc arrived at the Ranger station. It was just a really hard pill to swallow. One bear attack was a freak accident, but another in the span of a few weeks, by the same bear, fifty plus miles away was testing the limits of credulity. Who was this lady that had been with the boys at the campfire? Was she Lyndon's lover like Rosa had surmised? Had Lyndon been trying to introduce Nycolos to his lover so soon? Not likely. Lyndon was handsome, but never smooth enough to be a player. Rosa was convinced Nycolos must have invented the story about the earth swallowing his father, an attempt by his ten-year-old mind to protect him from the violence of what he witnessed. Maybe he had seen the bear eating Lyndon and his ten-year-old mind couldn't handle it. *Maybe.*

Rosa tried to sort it all out in her head. She visualized for perhaps 100th time what Nycolos told her. Lyndon did lock up sometimes, and she had seen him do so several times when she surprised him during sparring sessions. He was strong enough and brave enough to tackle a bear, but the size of the bear Nycolos described seemed preposterous. She had arrived at the conclusion that she needed to talk to somebody about Nycolos; the doorbell rang.

She wiped her hands on her jeans, went to the front door and peeked through a side window. Standing on the doorstep, Ranger Daniel Thompson tipped his wide brimmed, green hat when he saw her at the window. She opened the door allowing purple twilight and Ranger alike to enter.

"Good evening Mrs. Arcadia, I live out this way so I figured I'd drop off the tent and equipment." He gestured to the landing behind him where a pile of familiar camping equipment lay.

"Oh, thank you Mr. Thompson, I'd forgotten, would you mind?" She stepped onto the landing with him and the two of them managed to get all the equipment piled in the foyer in one trip.

"Thank you again, Mr. Thompson, I appreciate your help."

"No problem Mrs. Arcadia, you all having a problem with the crows eating your crops?"

Rosa hesitated before slowly answering, scanning the Ranger's face for hidden meaning. "No, why do you ask?"

"I just saw a whole bunch landing in your back yard."

She turned and peered through the dining room and into the kitchen but couldn't see what was going on in the back yard. Nycolos had been out back with Mirage for some time, it would soon be completely dark.

"Well, let's walk around back and see what's up shall we?" She couldn't help but ponder what compelled her to invite him; perhaps she was grateful how he looked after Nycolos that sangrient day three weeks prior.

She pulled the front door closed and they walked around the house towards the meadow. She didn't see it at first until she heard Daniel Thompson swear under his breath and point to the sky.

Hundreds and hundreds of crows and ravens descended on the meadow, obscuring Nycolos and Mirage but for flashes of white and brown. Rosa knew Nycolos was in the center of the undulating mass and her breath caught in her throat. The mass circled boy and horse, black-winged forms whipping around and around the boy in an ever-expanding sphere of black feathers. Black beaks made a terrible din.

She screamed to Nycolos, good luck that. The mass of avian flesh settled and the ranger swore again. The crows and ravens alighted in innumerable concentric rings. The birds stood as if frozen, heads craned towards the sky. In the center of the circle stood Mirage, Nycolos perched atop looking for all the world like a prince of something. *The undisputed King of Hide and Seek,* echoed in her skull. Regal and beautiful Nycolos also looked to the sky unaware of her arrival. Somewhere high above and lit by golden rays of the sun was a red-tail hawk, crying loud for all to hear. Somehow, above all the din, Nycolos spoke, in a deep melodious voice that carried all the way to her ears as if he were standing at her shoulder.

> Earth Mother mourns, for the world gone mad
> Scars of strife, mar her flesh.
> Prodigal people, the fruit of her loins,
> Rape, ravage, and tear her asunder.
> Black blood of her bosom, stains the hands of man
>
> Tears trail through slate gray skies.
> Whipping winds and waves rise to her call,
> Calamity crests o'er levy and sea wall.
> Chosen children, flora and fauna,
> Answer her beck and call
>
> Casting aside animal form
> Freely they walk among man.
> Howling hordes stream forth,
> From forest, hummock and hollow
> Children of Gaia, hewn of earth, rock and stone.
> Rain righteous retribution on mortal man.

He spoke those words and tumbled from the horse's back, the ravens and crows exploding upward as he hit the ground.

"MOM!" Nycolos yelled.

She snapped to, she was behind the counter of the shop daydreaming; he must have been talking to her for some time.

"Mrs. Rodriguez would like to speak to you." He looked exasperated, moved past her and out the back door.

"Hello Rosa...," the elderly lady barely needed an instant to get her chatterbox running at full steam, it seemed she had heard. Rosa thought at least she looked the grieving wife, distracted, distraught, and barely listening to the woman. Rosa's eyes followed Nyc as he moved out back; he stopped just beyond the threshold and gazed upwards into the apple tree behind the store. Rosa saw his lips moving in conversation and heard the distinct caw of a crow. Rosa turned to face Mrs. Rodriguez; it was only polite to receive her condolences. She didn't hear a word. She had the feeling the King of Hide and Seek wasn't going to be hiding any more.

Chapter 5

Hymenoptera

Times of trial,
bear man down.
Woes, war and waste,
secreted like steam.
Hardworking hes and shes
Lay low,
animal and tree,
Earth and sea
burn and boil,
Wither and writhe,
Children of Gaia,
answer their cries.

The next morning Nycolos felt the fog had moved into his head. The sun shone clear and bright, blinding eyes and waking him unwanted. He hadn't risen so early in a while, and it was painful to say the least. The aroma of bacon hit his olfactory as soon as he woke, pursued closely by the sound of his mother's voice, light tapping on his bedroom door. Bleary eyes, warm bed he stared at the wall opposite, waiting for the fog to clear out of his room.

She returned in five minutes, opened the door and curtains, allowing the sun full access into the recess of his room. The light was so bright he had to shield his eyes, pupils contracted, he could see again. Going back to sleep was no longer an option. Rise and shine, good morning sunshine, he rose to his feet and migrated to the bathroom. Music danced up the stairs, a pleasant bossa nova his mother loved so much, of soft melodies and caressing voices. He loved the lilting, longing the familiar standards evoked.

Eggs, bacon and a couple pancakes waited for him, kitchen table, served with sliced pears and apple cider. The butter he spread on his pancakes was freshly made, goodness knows when she found the time; and the maple syrup was from their trees as well.

Nyc knew his mother was trying to soothe his nerves with his favorite breakfast. Most days breakfast consisted of oatmeal, waffles, and 'huevos rancheros' on Sunday. Rosa wasn't a morning person, and it had been Lyndon who had usually assumed morning duties such as preparing breakfast and packing lunches.

She tousled his hair, grabbed the coffee carafe, poured herself a cup. She wore his father's bathrobe and her pink slippers, she tapped the clock on the microwave.

"Twenty minutes; I'm going upstairs to get dressed, make sure you have your stuff together." One eyebrow arched over green eyes, checking his face for agreement. Around a mouthful of pancakes he mumbled compliance. Nycolos watched her walk up the stairs, unconsciously sniffing Lyndon's bathrobe. They had both been drinking in what pieces they could find of Lyndon. Yesterday, Nyc found her sitting in the closet, not crying or moaning, just sitting on the floor with Lyndon's clothes like she was in some meditative state. He was going to leave her to it, but she beckoned to him. He sat in her lap and they stayed there, breathing in memories of father and husband.

She hadn't mentioned Nyc's insistence that his father was alive. Which he was glad for, he didn't think he was ready to explain what had happened on Hawk Mountain again anyway. His mother was generally a practical, no nonsense type of person, but she did acknowledge the importance of spirituality and the sacred. First he had been afraid she would laugh at him, tell him he was just a kid looking for something to believe in. Once he finally mustered up the courage to tell her she hadn't laughed at all, instead she had stopped talking to him for half of the day. He had given her space, which seemed to work; and they toiled the day away harvesting fruits and vegetables. An esoteric activity so ingrained in them it was a cathartic and meditative exercise, clearing the mind by keeping it too busy to think.

She did not bring up the conversation again, though she was acting in a most peculiar manner ever since he told her his story. He was sure his mother did not believe his story concerning the curious circumstances of Lyndon's death, but the way blood drained from her face when he mentioned it wasn't a good sign either. He knew she would broach the subject eventually; she wouldn't be able to leave it alone. As per her character she was waiting to catch him off guard, like when they were sparring. He didn't mind, he would tell her as many times as she could stand to hear it, just not today.

The crows were something else altogether. Mirage had been waiting for him when he bolted from the back door. He mounted her in one smooth motion; jumping off the picnic table onto her dappled back. They trotted into the back meadow following the hedgerow of currants, filberts, serviceberry and wild rose that served to divide the meadow form the orchards. They visited the teahouse, whitewash and pink, looked up at the tree house nestled in a spruce grove. Both built by the three of them as a family, marking the passage of summers past. The sky soft purple, golden brilliance of autumn sunset receding from the heavens, he saw the hawk. He knew she was there though he could not have explained how to anyone, not even himself. The crows were there before he knew it, flying around him until flapping black obscured everything. No fear chilled his blood, in fact he had been intrigued. The crows were deafening, their cries sounding to his ears like they were saying "Look, look."

When the black birds settled to the earth he was unsure if the goldenrods had been blown over, trampled, or had lain down themselves. He sensed the hawk like a hum in the back of his head, but there was another presence he felt. A familiar sensation that reminded him of what he had lost and where. It was a sensation that he recognized, like the earthy and fresh mountain stream smell of his father's shirts.

Lyndon Arcadia was out there somewhere, hidden, but nearby to be sure. Nyc's head felt full, like it had been stuffed with thoughts and feelings that were not his alone. He was aware of many creatures, crows, ravens, field mice, and Mirage, so much awareness it threatened to overwhelm him. Crows screeched, Mirage whinnied, stomped her front hooves and reared up onto hind legs, kicking the air like a dappled steed from a cowboy movie. Nycolos wished he could fly too, the hawk could probably see his father from up there, he knew how strong those eyes were.

The hawk cried out, and the crows settled in circles, commanding each other to "look, look," in a deafening cacophony. Nycolos considered his mother standing with Ranger Thompson a hundred meters distant, beyond what must've been the outermost ring of crows. Their mouths were agape, and his mother was as pale as he had ever seen her. His eyes were stronger than they should've been, saw the fear in her face even at that distance. Darkness.

***

Rosa appeared, gliding down the steps, pulling him from his morning daydream and assessing his progress.

"You seem to be done, why don't you go brush your teeth and we can get out of here."

The routine was the same regardless of how different they felt. Pack a bag, pack a lunch, hi ho, hi ho, off to work we go. They went through the motions as they had so many times before. Rolling up to the elementary school she stopped beneath a sugar maple whose changing leaves were so red it appeared to be ablaze.

"You and I are going to practice tonight, right?" Her tone left no room for doubt. Capoeira it was

"Yes." He kissed her on the cheek and jumped out of the car.

Sidling up the walk he joined the groups of kids waiting by white double doors. The morning air was crisp, autumn crept from green toned to red and yellow. Children's voices carried easily as they spoke eagerly about this and that. A skinny white kid with unkempt blond hair made a beeline for Nyc. He wore a wrinkled, plaid, button-up shirt that was red and black like a lumberjack's, and jeans a little too short. Benjamin Miller was Nyc's best friend. They were weekend adventurers, getting lost in the woods around their homes for hours at a time. Abigail Miller called a few days after the accident and spoke to Rosa for hours. Rosa broke down, crying during the conversation, and took the phone upstairs to her room. She came down later with puffy eyes and told him Ben missed him and loved him.

"Hey." Ben looked at his face, then lowered his eyes and shuffled his feet.

"Hey." Nyc knew there was a lot to say, but decided they'd get to it later. Ben opened his mouth to say something just as the bell rang. Nycolos heard the "Sorry", and acknowledged the comment by resting a hand on his friend's shoulder as they walked inside, biting back tears he dared not shed, lest the floodgates open: not here, not now.

The day unfolded as usual inside the brick and mortar confines of locker covered hallways and linoleum floors that never shook the scuff marks. Nycolos was two weeks behind in class work, but that wasn't such a big deal, at least it kept him busy. His teachers were worse, as were all the adults around the school that treated him as if he were something delicate and broken. They coddled him like a wounded bird or lost dog, each one making a point to come see him at some point or another, offering soothing words and pearls of wisdom. Even Mr. Pritchard the Gym teacher; one of Nyc's favorites because of his no nonsense attitude, told Nyc he could "take it easy" if he didn't feel like taking the physical fitness test. Nyc didn't mind the physical fitness test, pull-ups, sit-ups, the mile run, were fun and made his body feel strong. All good considering his mother had capoeira practice slated for him that night. In fact "taking it easy" was far more painful than any push-ups or 100-meter dash.

Most painful were the kids that treated him like the adults. They spoke to him cautiously, as if afraid they would hurt his feelings, or catch his sadness. None of his teachers called on him that day, or even for the rest of the week. He was summoned to his guidance counselor's office several times that week, "Let's talk about feelings," so he obliged. It was much easier to talk about how he felt than what had happened. Mr. Wright was an decent guy who dressed in old suit pants that he had probably bought in the early 1980's. All shades of brown and blue; why did ugly pants have vertical stripes running from leather belt down to his brown loafers? His dress shirts were pastel and nearly every color of the rainbow. "One for every day of the week," he liked to joke. The conversations were uninspiring, but seemed to do the trick for Mr. Wright, who like to muss Nyc's afro after their sessions.

His catch-up work was easy, so by default he spent most of the time looking out the window across the soccer and football fields. He stared at little yards, little houses flanking the school, ticky-tack, good hood. Little houses similarly sized, similarly shaped, similar cars and similar dogs, on similar streets running down into town and onto the valley floor of New Hamlet.

At long last Nycolos reached the end of his first week back. Friday dismissal bell released them beneath a slate gray sky, freed of their confines to begin their several mile walk home. He and Ben could have taken the bus if they chose, but Friday's had certain magic about them, and they preferred to walk home. They had been friends since infancy, living on different sides of the same hill. The 'Mount' they called it. When toddling troublemakers, they roamed onto each other's property at will, only recently beginning to mark trails and routes on the Mount. They had great plans for the Mount, which included forts, fishing holes, no-girl areas, and spots to stash their treasure. Plans that were on hold, but they could both feel the urge to head up the Mount again.

Unknown to the two boys, roots of friendship between them had long ago grown firm, sprouting the seedling of a mighty tree that would grow strong like ironwood and bind them together through their lives. A friendship that would weather the storms of many years, bending in the blowing tempest, but one that would never break.

Ben's parents were divorced, and had been since Nyc could remember. Ben's father was nice, he lived a few towns away. He visited every other weekend, and Ben went to his father's house for a couple weeks in the summer. Ben told Nyc it wasn't that bad, he got to have two Christmases, birthdays, all that good stuff, but they both knew he preferred to stay at his mom's house.

"Got a new bow." Ben's eyes shone with excitement as he cocked and loosed an imaginary arrow. "My dad..." his voice trailed off. He looked guilty and ashamed at having touched the taboo subject. "...brought it over." Nyc could barely hear the last couple words. Irritation flared in his bosom, born of suppressed rage and a week's worth of coddling.

"C'mon Ben. What?! You can't mention your dad now that mine is dead?" He hadn't told Ben anything about what happened the day he lost his father, or in the days since.

Ben grimaced and said "Sorry," then grimaced again and looking even guiltier. He seemed stuck a repeating loop of guilt and grimace, so Nyc tripped him, nearly sending the blond boy to the ground. Ben stumbled a few steps, righted himself and threw a handful of fallen leaves and soil at Nycolos. They resumed walking and Ben continued where he left off.

"Yeah, I told my dad how many turkeys were cruising the mount. So he showed up last Sunday with the bow and told me he thought I should catch a turkey or two for Thanksgiving this year.

"Cool." Nyc was an O.K. shot, but Ben, who practiced religiously, was excellent.

"Yeah, I know," Ben was grinning from ear to ear, blue eyes practically shooting sparks, "so you wanna come hunt with me this weekend?"

"Sure," Nycolos answered before thinking. "Actually, let me see if my mom wants me around, but I'll ask."

"Good." And with that they moved through the woods in silence.

Halfway home the trail forked. At the fork, a charred circle glittered as sunlight reflected off of hundreds of shards of broken glass littering the area in and around the fire pit. Two kids stood near a log that sat near the charred circle. They were smoking cigarettes and tossing firecrackers at chipmunks, squirrels, and any birds foolish enough to show their faces. Nycolos recognized Damian Fontane and Jacob Watts immediately. Local problem children, it was no town secret the 13-year-olds had grown up in troubled homes. New Hamlet was a small town, but like all human endeavors, it had a dark side. Damian and Jacob had grown up in the shadow of that dark side, on the wrong side of the tracks, in a run-down trailer park called Evergreen Heights. A name that was painfully inappropriate, some developers twisted humor, considering the trailer park was in the lowest spot of the valley, next door to the materials recovery center. The only height was the overhanging cliff that was ready to fall on the trailer park, the evergreens cut down long ago.

The water table in the trailer park was so high the residents were constantly calling plumbers on account of septic systems that never drained correctly. Furnace Creek snaked through the valley, diverted years ago in an effort to stop the seepage of wastewater into its relatively clean waters, to no avail. As a result the residents of Evergreen Heights were accosted by the foul odor of their own waste, coupled with the stench of the materials recovery center next door.

The odor seeped into their pores and the psyche of residents until they themselves could no longer discern the rankness they carried with them. Damian Fontane and Jacob Watts were two residents of Evergreen Heights that were never able to get the smell off completely. It sank into their bones and flesh; Nyc wondered if that was the cause of their unpleasant disposition.

"Well, hey shit-stain." Jacob Watts greeted Nycolos, lit the wick of a firecracker, and flicked it at Nycolos and Ben. It exploded in the air behind them, making them jump. Damian Fontane laughed a little too hard.

"Yeah, it's pond-water and Paul Bunyan." Damian added. The two bullies laughed malevolently, snickering and pleased with their witty put-downs. Damian Fontane dressed like his older brothers. Black hair slicked back above a large forehead and Romanesque nose. Italian heritage long forgotten by family members, but not by genes. The leather coat he wore was a throw back from the 1950's, black leather with a high collar, with silver zippers here and there. His pant legs were rolled up, evidently too large hand-me-downs, displaying leather boots that laced up past his ankle.

"No, No I got it, chocolate milk and 2%." Jacob Watts was chubby with sandy brown hair that cascaded down over his forehead and into beady black eyes. The flight jacket he wore was black on the outside and bright orange on the inside, Nyc saw fireworks hanging from one pocket. Black jeans that were several sizes too large hung halfway down his butt, his boots were unlaced, the tongues hanging forward to the tips of his shoes. His chubby face was starting to sprout hair in some places, his acne grew much more proficiently. Their last put-down pleased them mightily, such that the bullies bent over double, slapping their knees and laughing.

This sort of encounter wasn't a first for Nycolos, much of this treatment was standard fare when you were the only black kid in town. Nycolos and Ben kept walking, feet moving toward the right fork that meandered along the valley wall for another half mile, then turned sharply climbing up and out of the valley on an old forgotten road, past broken down foundations and rusted-out car hulls. Ultimately leading to an old farm field across the street from the Mount. Damian Fontane side stepped a few feet, blocking the trail, and their escape.

"So, your daddy's dead isn't he, shit stain?" The taunt glittered in Damian's eyes. He exhaled smoke in Nyc's face causing the ten-year old to break into a coughing fit. Watering eyes stung, throbbing wound pulsed, Nyc felt something bubbling in his chest like molten lava.

"Look, he's gonna cry." Damian shoved Nyc backwards into Ben.

"I heard they didn't find no body neither," Jacob Watts was pleased to share his knowledge with anyone that was willing to listen to his drivel. "Maybe your daddy ran away, I'd run away from a couple of niggers like you and your immigrant mama too."

Benjamin Miller put a hand on Nyc's shoulder and spoke up. "Bug off, guys, we didn't do anything to you."

As if waiting for protest, the bullies pounced. Jacob stepped through the charred fire pit grabbing Ben, looping arms in front of Ben's shoulders and locking his hands behind the blond boy's neck, immobilizing Ben in a full nelson. Jacob's cigarette burned forgotten on the ground, crushed beneath Damian's boot as he grabbed for Nycolos, malice ablaze in his eyes. Damian Fontane had never seen the Arcadia's capoiera barn, inside a studio used for capoeira training, classes, and even seminars. If the bully had known of the training space he may have thought twice about his actions.

Damian Fontane shifted his weight forward to strike. At the same instant Nycolos stepped in to meet him, and simply jumped straight up, slamming his forehead into the taller boy's chin. He heard the loud click of teeth a grunt of pain and Damian Fontane fell backwards holding his mouth, his hand muffling a scream trapped behind tightened fingers. Nycolos turned to the stunned 's Jacob Watts, mind churning to help Ben. Jacob's eyes were as wide as saucers, slow wit unable to comprehend what was happening. Benjamin Miller, no stranger to capoeira classes, or older brothers with a grudge, stomped down with all his might on Jacob Watts's boot. The bully howled and released the full-nelson, Ben spun, elbows raised and caught Jacob squarely across an acne-covered cheek. Bully #2 went down, eyes dazed, and the ten-year olds fled. They hauled ass out of there and didn't stop running until they could see their houses and the Mount sitting between them.

The boys collapsed in the old field under a half dead apple tree. They laughed and held their bellies until tears streamed down their cheeks. They took turns imitating the two bullies. When their laughter faded they settled on a large branch of the apple tree fallen to the earth years before. Ben chomped on a red apple, sending juice running down his chin. He had grass in his hair, his cheeks were flushed with laughter.

"My parents were getting divorced." Nycolos spoke suddenly, gauging his friend's reaction.

"What?" Ben asked around a mouthful of apple, brown eyebrows furrowed, he wiped the juice from his chin.

"My dad took me camping so he could tell me that they were going to get a divorce. Only, the first night he was going to tell me," he shrugged and looked at his friend, " this lady showed up, so he never said boo." He buffered his sentences with long silences, which Ben endured patiently. "The next morning I'm pretty sure he was going to say something when we got up to Hawk Mountain, but well, you know." He left it at that.

"Then I guess you're just like me." Ben said after several quiet minutes.

"I guess so."

"So, uh, you wanna go shoot my new bow?" Excitement peppered Ben's voice again. The boys crossed the field banking north towards Ben's house. They didn't discuss the divorce again.

***

Rosa Arcadia didn't mind that Nycolos wanted to camp on the Mount with Ben Saturday night, in fact she was pleased he wanted to do something...normal. She hashed it out with Ben's mother, quick phone call, with the one condition that Nyc help out at the store Saturday morning.

The rooster started crowing at 4:30, and there she was at his door a few minutes later.

"Rise and Shine." She said.

The rooster didn't stop until Nycolos, standing on the back patio, whipped a rock at the bird. Nycolos breathed deep in the pre-dawn light, holding a buttered piece of toast in his other hand. Rosa whistled and waved him over to the shed where she had a wheelbarrow loaded with empty baskets for collecting fruits and vegetables from the orchard. She gave him his marching orders and sent him into the orchards. They worked while the sun rose, chase the mist before it burns off. Nycolos started collecting eggs from the chicken coops, moving from orchard to orchard visiting each coop in turn. The chickens roosted in the orchards most nights, perching in the numerous fruit trees that made up the orchards. The females would roost in the coops when they were laying eggs, facilitating egg collection.

The greater orchard as a whole was on the order of ten hectares—or twenty–five acres, and was divided into seventy small orchards. Each one a tenth or two tenths of a hectare in size, divided by hedgerows of serviceberry, currants, filberts, elderberries, blueberries, hawthorns, too many to name that served as forage for the resident livestock. Years earlier Lyndon constructed coops in the corner of each of small orchards. These the birds used during the winter months and for egg laying. Nycolos filled the baskets easily, moving from one section of the orchard to another. The orchards were planted with a poly-culture of fruit trees. Planted in long, undulating swales that ran north to south or east to west, depending on which orchard one was in. Inter-plantings of corn, tomatoes, eggplants, peppers, wheat, barley, you name it, undulated down the length of the orchards companions of the large fruit producing trees. The large orchards were used for animals like Mirage, the cows, goats, sheep, partridges, geese, ducks, turkeys, and even a bunch of pheasants lived in the cornrows. The large orchards were planted to corn and gourds this year, and he could hear the beating wings of anxious pheasants when he cut through one.

The hedgerows were traversed via wooden gates. Each one unique and like some doorway out of a fairy tale. Lyndon's artistic touch was evident in the curving lines of the sunburst on one gate, moonbeams, fairy's wings on another and one with mosaic tile-work that looked like violets was one of Rosa's favorites. The gates to the large orchards were adorned with the animal busts of a horses, goats, cows, sheep, a raven an owl, a bear. Rosa had instructed Nycolos to collect eggs then meet her in the barn. When he got there she was in the northwestern corner working over steaming pots and piles of dried herbs.

"Mrs. O'Connell will be coming in this morning for her hawthorn and ginkgo tinctures," she gestured with her head in the direction of the counter. A dozen brown and blue bottles sat in a wooden basket with ribbons attached to each of the necks, indicating the type of tincture and dosage.

"Carry those to the truck for me, would you, sweetheart?"

The rafters in the corner of the barn were lined with hanging bundles of goldenrod, lavender, sage, mint, hawthorn berries, ginkgo, Linden flowers, and St. John's wort, and those were only the plants he recognized, there were dozens more he didn't know.

Double boilers puffed away beneath hanging plants while Rosa made infusions, oils, tinctures, ointments and salves. Bundles for tea, sachets for drawers and any number of herbal creations lined shelves and counter tops in every direction. Their store had a stock supply, and filled requests as ordered, though no orders had been filled for the last couple of weeks due to familial crisis. New Hamlet was small enough that most everybody knew what had happened to Lyndon by now. Rosa and Lyndon started the business 13 years before—goodbye meager savings—when they first moved to the area, straight from Brazil. Lyndon made a mess in their kitchen for a year before Rosa made him build the workspace in the barn. Since then more than a few locals had come to appreciate Lyndon's herbal remedies. Rosa and Lyndon caught the fever, and now enjoyed making the remedies as much as espousing them.

They gained a following locally, every week new orders needed to be filled. Rosa hadn't fallen behind yet, but Nyc felt a pang of guilt as he lugged a box out to the truck and stood there huffing and puffing. His mother would be making different remedies all day and into the next. There were orders for goat cheese too, he should probably do that for her now.

Rosa called him, he jumped down from the truck and hurried inside.

"All-right kiddo, I'm almost done, go get me a couple wheelbarrows of pumpkins and acorn squash while I finish up here. Then we'll head down to the store.

Mirage was waiting at the gate when he returned to the orchard. She was amazingly resourceful and moved in and out of the orchards at will. Mirage was his constant companion of late, she followed him like she used to follow his father. He hadn't sensed anything strange since the day with the crows., but that didn't mean anything. Corn grew between apple and pear trees running in rows with squash, pumpkins, green beans, and peas in the orchard his mother sent him to.

Ducks quacked in a corner, splashing in their pond, unappreciative of the arrival of horse and boy. Acorn and butternut squash shaded the feet of the corn plants, keeping the soil moist and relatively weed-free, while the corn stalks provided poles for the twining tendrils of green bean and pea vines to climb in pursuit of the sun. Nyc left the wheelbarrow at the end of the row and moved up and down the length picking, pumpkins, acorn and butternut squash alike. Mirage moved in and out of sight through the shadows of the orchard. She whinnied loudly, frisky with morning energy, glad to be alive. Nycolos stopped to enjoy her beauty.

Mirage jumped over a compost pile of pruned branches. She landed cleanly, clearing the pile easily, but her flank brushed stacked white boxes, beehives and honey, down it went. The hive exploded into the morning air. Black buzzing cloud enveloped the dappled mare, eye blink to a gallop at the first sting. Nyc dropped his gourds and ran to intercept Mirage. She pulled up in front of him, rearing up kicking the air just above his head. He put his arms out a tingling, flicker like horse hair moving up his skin.

"No!" He yelled to no one in particular. "Leave her alone!"

The most peculiar thing happened. The hive swarmed them, did not land on either boy or horse, buzzing madness flew around the two of them. Such numbers the orchard was blocked from sight. An unyielding mass of hymenoptera surrounded them in a perfect sphere, from the ground beneath them to the sky above their heads. The buzzing was so loud Nycolos was sure Mirage couldn't hear his calming words. The horse whinnied and screamed, ears flat, teeth bared. Nyc touched her side in a vain attempt to control her. He feared she would try to bolt through the insect mass. The ten-year-old boy acted on instinct again, guided by an unconscious he didn't understand. He knelt on one knee, bowed his head and placed a closed fist to the earth. Words came from his throat, in a voice much too deep to be his own.

"May the Earth Mother bless us and guide us through harm into the arms of the creator." At the utterance of the last word, the sphere exploded outward with a loud bang. And just like that, the bees were gone. As quickly as he could, Nyc righted the hives, grabbed his wheel burrow and high tailed it out of there.

When they reached the store Rosa and Nyc pulled all the produce off the truck and loaded them into the bins in the store. She carried the tinctures herself, placing them in a wooden cabinet behind the main counter. Once Nyc was done she pretended to look for a chore for him. He bounced from foot to foot and she could tell he was going to explode sooner than later. When she finally opened her mouth to tell him he could go, he barely waited to hear the words before he shot out the door into sunlight.

"Hey!" Rosa opened her arms wide, and he ran back to embrace her with a crushing hug, he was getting stronger, she decided. She kissed him on the head, "All right get out of here," but she added gravely, " be very careful and don't shoot Ben or get shot." She patted him on the bum and watched him tear out the door.

****

The Saturday crowd was full of her regulars, and the day whizzed by. Unexpectedly, she received six requests for her chickens and collard greens. A breakout of salmonella out west had her older clients panicking. Rosa realized with chagrin the number of orders she was agreeing to fill would have her chasing chickens and ducks all of next week. *Lyndon would've been pleased,* she thought with a smile. He always hoped their neighbors would start growing their own food or buying it from their neighbors. He had hated manicured lawns, pesticides, fertilizers and everything they represented. Lyndon was hard to stop once he got going, but that was one of the reasons she fell for him in the first place.

Morning rolled into afternoon, Rosa sold out of acorn squash, pumpkins, corn and eggs. Late afternoon orders of goat cheese were added to the list of things to do. She hadn't quite mastered the soap making yet, she told a couple named Trish and Don. An older couple, she was a retired school teacher, and he a retired firefighter. They smiled and laughed a lot, and were generally pleasant to have as customers. Disappointed at not finding their favorite soap the couple was mortified when Rosa explained why she couldn't say when their order would be ready. Trish always had a crush on Lyndon, and practically broke down leaning on the counter.

Her gray and white ponytail feigned acquiescence while errant strands rebelled openly, falling into her sun bronzed face. She was still beautiful, thought Rosa; white jeans clung snugly to curved calves above canvass shoes. A healthy glow spoke of laughter and happiness. Don was around the counter before Rosa could say spit, he gave her a hug so genuine she almost broke down.

Fifty-something and muscular, Don looked like well-hewn mahogany with a glint in his eyes. He cupped her chin and murmured sweet confidences of her profound beauty and indomitable strength, and laughed out loud when she blushed through her cacao complexion. Trish called him a scoundrel, grabbed Rosa's hand from the other side of the counter.

"We'll stop by this week if that's O.K.," her tone told Rosa they would be by regardless.

"Yes, that's fine."

The couple bought entirely too much after that. Once Don saw the hawthorn tinctures he bought almost all of them, pointing out to Trish in a loud voice that his family had a history of heart problems. Trish suggested he would use any excuse to buy a new type of liquor. Departing as loudly as they had entered, the couple left Rosa with a distinct sense of longing for her native Brazil.

Those two would love it there, she decided to recommend it to them when they stopped by. Infectious allegria (which means happiness) marked those two and it showed. *They made it,* she thought, *a mixed couple out here in West Nowhere.* Maybe she and Lyndon could've too, didn't matter anyway. She hadn't noticed the man in the corner selecting some collard greens and carrots until he came to the counter to pay. Chief Ranger Thompson gave her a sly smile.

"Mrs. Arcadia."

"Hello, Mr. Thompson." She hadn't seen him since the day Nycolos had fallen off the horse. They hadn't spoken much last time either, after carrying the boy inside she had dismissed him rather briskly.

"Driving kinda far to pick up some veggies aren't you?" She cocked an eyebrow at him.

"Not as far as you'd think," long pause, "and I wanted to check up on you and your son after the other day." She was grateful he didn't mention the details, even though they were alone.

"That's kind of you, we're fine thank you."

He eyed her for an eternity before pulling out some money and paying for the veggies.

"I also wanted to ask you why you didn't mention to me you were on the mountain near the boys' camp?" He had been palming a small piece of fabric that he let fall to the counter top.

Rosa realized with terror it was a patch from her pants. The patchwork pants she wore hiking because they were thick enough that thorns and thickets proved little obstacle, the pants she had worn when she followed Nyc and Lyn up Hawk mountain to their campsite. The pants she had worn when she saw the other woman for the first time, huddled in a thicket of Witch-hobble thirty yards on the other side of the trail from the campsite. She had seen the beautiful woman with long brown hair stride into the firelight like she owned it.

The same pants she had been wearing when the Ranger stopped by to drop off the camping equipment. Rosa's blood froze, eyes on the blue corduroy patch with a kitten playing in the center of it. She told the truth, most painful, least suspicious.

"I hiked up there to beg Lyndon to rethink the divorce, that was why he took Nycolos up there in the first place." She sighed pushing through raw emotion and humiliation.

"I got to their site around dusk, they didn't see me and I was going to say something, but I saw a woman with them. I thought she might be Lyndon's..." swallow the bile in her throat, "lover. So I hid in the underbrush for a while and then hiked out, which took all night. Then I went home and cried." She was ashamed to say these words out loud.

"I know it was silly, but at the time I wasn't thinking straight."

"So that's why you believed Nyc," he didn't blink. "You saw the lady."

"Yes, I saw her, and she was just as Nyc described her. Tall beautiful, dark hair, red skirts."

He nodded as if half listening to her. "You should know some of the other Rangers and Troopers think your husband abandoned your boy up there. Not often we don't find any remains, or the animal that did the killing. We haven't found anything." He winked so quickly she almost missed it.

"Don't worry, I'm the only old timer with enough patience to find that little clue," he motioned to the patch, " and after what I saw the other day up at your farm, I'm ready to believe. But none of my people have seen what I saw, except the fog."

Rosa didn't know what to say, so said nothing. She had already said too much.

"I'm sure we'll be seeing more of each other Mrs. Arcadia." He winked again and left the store.

Could Lyndon really be alive?

Rosa Arcadia didn't believe it, she didn't' want to believe it, because to believe it she would have to acknowledge the mountain of hope she had ignored. Somewhere in the back of her mind she had piled hope atop hope, until she had built a mountain that teetered precariously on Nyc's strange story, and the mystery surrounding Nyc. Maybe Lyn was still around somewhere, a mountain of hope was threatening to crush her beneath its awesome weight.

CHAPTER 6

Boulder Dash

Smiting with seasons
Flood and fire
Hurricane and hail
Tsunami and typhoon,
Works of wise men
Burn like brimstone
Melting mountains
Glow golden beneath
Snow capped waves.

Nycolos ran across the street and up the long driveway to his house. He dashed inside. grabbed his backpack—packed the night before—and was outside again, tearing through tall goldenrods. He cut through old fields and windbreaks until he reached Ben's backyard. Ben was in his backyard airing out his tent. Abigail Miller stood a few feet away hanging a sleeping bag over the clothesline. She saw Nycolos first and waved to him as he drew near. She was pretty and tall like Ben would be, her hair a pale blond with hints of strawberry when the sun hit it right. She had it tied up in a bun with a pencil pushed through to hold it in place. She wore blue jeans, a white button up shirt and was peering at her work through rimless glasses. Freckles dotted her nose, which she wrinkled often when scrutinizing one of her numerous books. Abby said something over her shoulder and Ben backed out of his tent. Nyc always had a small crush on Ben's mother, and he loved the small bookstore she ran downtown, and tried to stop in as much as possible. She always seemed to have a smudge on her cheek and a book in her hand. Even in the garden, or hanging clothes she looked like she belonged between bookshelves.

"My mom already knows about your crush, and no I didn't say anything."

Nyc blushed and dropped his gaze, kicking the grass. He had been staring at her.

Abigail Miller strolled over and gave Nyc a big hug from behind. "Don't mind him, handsome, I already told your mom if you were only twenty years older you'd be all mine."

Nycolos was so uncomfortable he genuinely considered leaving. Before he could both mother and son laughed together, snapping Nycolos out of his stupor.

"We're just giving you a hard time, Nyc," Abby hugged him tight and kissed him on the head. "Let's all go inside and have some lunch before you guys head up the Mount."

Relieved, Nyc walked inside behind Abby and Ben. The house was an old timber frame farmhouse originally home to a larger family than the Millers. Everything in the house was wood and one could easily hear the murmur of voices slipping through the cracks in un-insulated walls. The wood stoves and the large fireplace in the living room were perpetually lit from fall till mid-spring. Adjacent to the kitchen, the large coal-stove was the most utilitarian, thought the family used wood instead of coal. The living room was spacious, with large sliding doors along the southern wall, and the hearth was large, with thick rugs lining the wooden floor three feet from the fireplace. Several racks of antlers lined the walls, though lacking the heads they had been attached to. Abigail had hung small figurines of fairies with gossamer wings in various stages of flight from the antlers, making the room feel occupied even when it was empty. Every other wall in the room, and every other room for that matter had been fitted with shelves. The shelves were lined with books, organized such that room corresponded to a topic.

Another reason Nyc enjoyed Ben's house so much were the books. He could get lost for hours in Ben's room, reading selections from the book-laden walls. Abby selected graphic novels, and adventure novels for the walls of Ben's room, full of superheroes, super villains, mutated turtles, and teenage ninjas. Novels of every sort lured him to Ben's room on those nights when the sun bedded down early and darkness filled woods and fields.

***

They lunched on sandwiches and some fresh tomato slices. Afterwards they opened their packs and made sure they had everything they needed. Repacking the tent a half-hour later, Nyc watched Ben bring out his bow. Abby had more sandwiches she packed inside a paper bag, which she instructed them to eat for dinner. Lastly, some trail-mix and apples she indicated were for breakfast the next morning. Nycolos and Ben had their backs to the house as soon as they could manage, waving goodbye to Abby below, who waved back, jumping up and down melodramatically, blowing kisses to the departing boys.

Nycolos and Ben hit the tree line, their pace slowed as they cut straight up the slope, wading through Hobblebush and raspberries. Shortly they were on the trail that circled the midriff of the Mount, connecting both families' properties. The foot of the Mount sprawled with orchards and plantings of the homesteads at its skirts. The summit was a community of beech, maple, oak, and hickory, nearly a century old after clear-cutting during colonization. The entire area was logged then, to meet the demand for woodstoves and home building alike. They walked several minutes to the southern slope of the Mount. They forged upwards again, through the forest to a wooded glen that perched atop a ridge, settled in a hollow a few hundred feet from the summit.

A lean-to in one corner was backed by a stand of spruce, several grills hung from the sides, a few blackened from use. The lean-to was a little more than ten years old. Lyndon built it with Ben's older brother Jackson Miller, who had been 14 at the time, and deeply troubled. His parents Abigail and Keith, together since high school, had given their ailing marriage one more try. Coincidentally, Benjamin was conceived, the only good thing that had happened for the little family that year. Emotionally damaged, Abigail and Keith were often angry and selfish that year. Jackson suffered, acting out repeatedly, in and out of school. When a school aide called and suggested counseling for the divorcing couple, Lyndon took Jackson up the Mount and they built the lean-to.

Rosa had been pregnant with Nycolos at the time, staying with Abby Miller as Keith packed his belongings into a pickup truck with a trailer hitch The women sat on the front porch and watched him make the trips necessary to move to his new place. Lyndon and Jackson came down from the Mount on a beautiful Sunday morning at the end of that weekend, and the teenager seemed stronger and more sure of himself. Jackson tearfully joined his father and they took the last load to his father's new house together. From that time on he had been a different boy. He developed a distinct interest in capoeira and martial arts in general, an obvious result of his weekend with Lyndon. Jackson Miller soon became one of Rosa's best students at her tri-weekly classes. Jackson would retreat to the refuge of the lean-to when he was having trouble "dealing", as he so eloquently described his melancholy, during those awkward teenage years.

Jackson Miller straightened up after that, with the exception of a few parties he threw on the Mount during high school. Parties diffused by Lyndon and Rosa, who were barely 25 at the time.

They appeared at the bonfire and relaxed with the kids for while before sending them on their way. Jackson may have been upset, but never said anything to Lyn or Rosa.

Jackson and Benjamin Miller were textbook examples of hybrid vigor. Tall and fair like Abigail both boys were smart and nerdy too. Lacking their mother's poor eyesight, the boys were excellent physical specimens like their athletic father.

Graceful athletes, they excelled at sports, becoming principal players on any team's roster. Jackson had been a proficient baseball player during high school and had been recruited by several Universities though he chose to attend a local community college. Benjamin had fallen for soccer; he and Nycolos were both excellent, and each other's toughest competition.

Jackson attended the local community college for a couple of years, during which time he fell in love with carpentry. As a result he ran a business out of Abby's garage. He converted the upper attic into a loft apartment with his workspace below. Jackson had cut and installed the walnut and apple shelves that lined his mother's home and her bookstore in town. His business was booming, with local interest in community crafts steadily increasing.

"He's not over it yet." Ben spoke as they arranged their equipment, preparing to pitch the small two-man tent on the wooden platform of the lean-to.

"Who?" Nyc asked just to be sure Ben's thoughts had been drifting the same as his.

"Jackson."

Sure enough, Nyc thought,

"He's been working a lot and only comes over to eat or wash his clothes. He doesn't mess around with me or mom anymore, he just works in his shop. Sawing and cutting all day and night."

Nycolos sat quietly for a while. His own sadness still ached like a wound in his chest. The pain had dulled slightly, but still felt raw and exposed. He and Rosa had been very insular for nearly a month, perhaps all the weeping and holding each other had begun the healing. Nycolos realized he hadn't thought about the other lives his father had touched. The other people that must be aching and missing Lyndon too. Then there were the times he felt his father's presence nearby, like he was standing outside his window, or just around the next tree. The hawk called to him from the recesses of memory, pulling on the wounded heart in his chest. He could feel things were different somewhere deep inside him, though he had not addressed what since he had met the lady on the mountain the day his father died. This was all too new to him.

"You should tell him to come to class again, it really helps, and we can talk if he wants." Nyc didn't know what else to say and shrugged his shoulders.

"Yeah, that's a good idea."

A comfortable silence stretched between the minutes. The two boys pitched the tent, gathered firewood, unrolled their sleeping bags and moved through a routine that allowed their minds to wander fantastically through the adventures that would unfold. Half an hour later they were contented with the status of the campsite, passed around a water bottle and decided on their course of action. Both boys had the layout of the Mount memorized, and spoke without the need of maps or drawings. Ben thought they should hunt the western slope so they could better utilize the sun. They walked over to the western slope ten minutes later, moving stealthily between the trees. A fair-sized meadow halfway up the slope provided a good location with visibility, downwind of any game approaching the meadow.

Ben selected a spot in the northwest corner that was upslope from the dale. Five meters into the trees, he pointed to a windfall where a large spruce leaned precariously against its neighbor. The spruce was long dead as evidenced by the gray branches and lack of bark. Lyndon called them widow-makers. Such treacherous individuals had claimed the lives of, or caused serious injury to many loggers, hence the name. Beneath the widow-maker grew a large honeysuckle, leaves still bright in the autumn afternoon. They settled into the honeysuckle to wait.

Nycolos was patient, glad to be in the woods again with his friend. Ben was so excited to shoot his new bow, his normal patience was limited. He was quiet for the first thirty minutes admiring the re-curved Mongolian bow his father had given him for his birthday. After which he spoke for the next thirty minutes in a hushed whisper, espousing his fervent admiration for the detail and artistry of fine craftsmanship.

Ben lapsed into silence eventually, watching the glen intently for many minutes. Nycolos engaged him in some light banter, they debated a melee between their favorite giant robot mecha. The conversation ended eventually with the boys agreeing to disagree, which was fine. This was one of their old arguments that never seemed to end. After another hour, an apple and a half sandwich later, Nycolos told Ben he was going to hike around for a little while and would meet him back at the spot in an hour or so.

Ben was concentrating on the prey he expected to walk into view any moment and waved him off with a curt, "Sure, alright."

Nycolos set off, cutting through the underbrush for several minutes, making so much noise he knew he his friend was sitting in a honeysuckle feeling very irritated. Once through the underbrush he moved slowly, his mind wandering to his father. Nyc knew his father would've visited them if he were around. He wondered if it was possible for his father to step from behind a huge ash tree he knew stood around the next bend. *Probably not,* he kicked a rock and it flew into the underbrush of raspberries. He lollygagged his way around the shoulders of the Mount, meandering down the summit through stands of hickory, maple, apple and spruce, lost in thoughts of father and family. If his parents had divorced he would've stayed with his mother, but where would his father have moved? Nycolos wished he had come to the Mount with his father for their talk instead of Hawk Mountain. Some wild rose grabbed his pants. Rosa multiflora, in fact. Large rose hips hung heavy on the arcing branches, ready to be eaten or picked. The thorn pierced through the weave of his jeans and embedded in his skin. Nycolos Arcadia stopped and disengaged from the thorny autotroph. He pulled the large brown thorn loose, grateful it had not remained stuck in his leg. He watched the blood paint a dark circle on his jeans.

He reached a glen above his house. From that vantage the youth could see the rectangular outlines of the different orchards. He could make out his house, and a black mark where lightning struck the maple tree. He saw the meadow and forest that covered the foot of the Mount below him. The ridge dropped off nearly ninety degrees, a precipitous cliff, falling to the ravine below where all this madness started weeks ago. His father said glaciers had carved out the valleys and hills that dotted the landscape around New Hamlet. Nycolos tried to imagine giant mountains of ice moving through the landscape, ripping fissures in the earth, dropping boulders and scouring the earth down to bedrock.

Icy tendrils melting and gushing through cracks in rock, ripping loose stone with the weight of a mountain. He imagined the mega-fauna his father told him about, roaming the earth, monsters like wooly mammoths, saber-tooth tigers, giant beavers, giant deer and elk, and goodness knew what else. They used to guess how big the mega-fauna would be. Lyndon always urged Nycolos to imagine them moving through the forest in groups.

Nycolos pushed through an American cranberry bush, also known as Vibirnum tricuspidata, stepping into the clearing he knew Ben was on the other side of. He froze, checking for game that might cause Ben to loose an arrow. Seeing none he moved through more shrubbery of honeysuckle, calling to Ben. Cranberry, rose and raspberry, pulled at his feet. His foot caught on a root, and he stumbled forward in in the tall grass. He barely regained his balance, in the process stepping on a dry twig that snapped with a loud crack. Somewhere in the distance he heard a dull twang or rather he felt the vibration in his chest.

The sun was in his eyes, blazing a brilliant orange and gold. The far treeline was shrouded in shadow, sun blocked by thick spruce, low in the sky, retreating from the encroaching night. The sun's rays lit the tops of the maple trees, only just holding on to the remnants of red and gold leaves. Nyc saw the glint of a metal arrowhead arcing high through the air. Ben had angled high to cover the distance between himself and Nyc, whom he apparently thought was worth shooting.

It was already too late, Nycolos had seen the arrow at the apex of its flight, it had since traveled towards where he stood, rooted to the ground. The ten-year old pivoted, hoping the arrow wouldn't pierce his chest if he turned sideways. Ben screamed in horror from the far side of the clearing, just as something nearby grunted loudly. The sound emanated from the earth beneath his feet, and sounded eerily foreign, like a rasping cough pushed from a stone throat.

It caused the Mount to vibrate violently. Grouse burst from the wild rose bushes around him, frightened into flight by the shaking earth and scraping rock. Ben's arrow fell, piercing a large rooster as he rose in front of Nycolos Arcadia, wings beating furiously at the air. The grouse fell twitching to the herb covered ground, beating his wings for the last few times, red mohawk bright against the green earth.

"Nyc, Nyc!" Ben sounded desperate, and made a ruckus running headlong through brush and bramble. Nycolos was panting, and when his friend reached him they took a moment to catch their collective breath. Nycolos didn't say anything, but pointed to the ground and the grouse.

"Holy guacamole."

"I know." Nycolos leaned on Ben, aware that in the second before the arrow pierced his flesh, he had fired off a prayer in that instant to any higher power willing to listen. He begged for survival, not for himself, but for his mother. She needed him, and he was all she had left. Nycolos ran to the nearest stand of trees and relieved himself, glad that he hadn't messed his pants.

Ben found Nyc after he finished gathering up the bird and stowing his bow. Nycolos was leaning against a spruce tree when Ben patted him on the shoulder and gestured in the direction of the lean-to.

"Did you feel the earthquake?" Nyc managed finally, halfway back to the campsite.

"Earthquake?" Ben eyed him quizzically.

"Yeah, didn't you feel the earth shake so bad you almost fell down?"

"No, I smelled this awful odor and I think I dozed off, but I swear you were a fat turkey gobbling around the meadow." Ben stopped walking, listening to the absurdity of his statement.

"Well, what about the mountain coughing or roaring or whatever, are you going to tell me you didn't hear that either? It was like a giant stone lion or something was hacking up a lung. You didn't hear that?"

"No, Nyc I didn't, but as soon as I fired you were standing there instead of the turkey, that's when I screamed."

"Well..., nice shot." Nycolos Arcadia was at a loss for words.

"That's the other thing," Ben stepped off the trail holding a large branch out of the way for Nyc to pass. "I just hurried the shot, there's no way I should've been that close. I'd swear a breeze picked up and carried my arrow."

"Maybe you're just getting better."

"I am, but not that good." Ben was no nonsense when it came to shooting arrows.

"Hmmmm..."

They reached the campsite and quickly broke into their duties. Nycolos gathered up more firewood and got the fire going again. Twenty minutes later he was throwing a lit match onto the pyramid of kindling he had constructed. Ben hung their food in a bear bag from a nearby maple, and the grouse from a lower branch of a hickory, remarking to Nyc that they would have to drop that off at the house in the morning so that it would not go bad. The boys sat, mute and content, eating cold sandwiches before the fire. The night grew cool, chilling their backs and ears.

Nyc kept the fire big, managing to keep them warm without getting burnt. They picked up the threads of old conversations, half paying attention to each other. Eventually the lads lost each other amongst the stars, making a game out of pointing out shooting stars to each other. Before long they were stretched out on their backs flanking the fire and passing yawns back and forth, eye-lids like sandpaper. Nyc was dozing off when he heard a voice.

"Hey." Came the whispering from behind them. Nyc sat up, trying to keep up with his skin.

Jackson Miller stood beyond the firelight, barely visible in the darkness, with a flashlight in his hand. Nyc wondered if the older Miller had used it at all. He was also adept at hiking around the Mount in the dark. As a maladjusted youth Jackson had spent so much time up there he could walk the trails in his sleep. Stepping into the firelight, he was a larger version of Ben. Dirty blond hair was matted to his head by the grey knit hat he wore. His face was scruffy with a few days growth and he was wearing work clothes. Nyc guessed he had been sent.

"Mom sent me up here to check on you guys."

"See Nyc, I told you she'd send him." Ben remained stretched on the ground next to the fire, staring into space. He covered a yawn with the back of one hand.

"Looks to me like two little kids falling asleep next to a campfire." Jackson wasn't trying to goad them; he just called it like he saw it. Nyc remembered what he had wanted to say.

"Jackson. you should come to class again, I've gotten better, and Mom is still the best, but I bet you could give her a run for her money now." Nycolos rose and danced the jinga, stepping into a spinning back kick.

"Maybe I will Nyc, I'm so stiff these days I'm sure you'd give me a run for my money. Ben told me about your walk home the other day."

"Oh, yeah." Nyc sat down inside the lean-to, a few feet from the shadows.

"Sounds to me like it's a good thing the two of you never stopped playing." The Brazilian word for training and sparring translated to playing in English, another aspect of Rosa's home country, language, and martial art that Jackson had absorbed. Jackson moved closer but did not sit.

"I think I will come to class, Nyc, it will probably be good for both of us." Jackson smiled a deep infectious smile, a genetic trait Ben and Abby possessed as well. He punched Nyc on the arm, walked by to the hanging grouse and asked,

"What happened?" The question seemed strange, considering they were on the Mount; Ben raised a hand from his prone position next to the crackling fire.

"That would be me," Ben sat up, suddenly animated talking about his shot, "it was awesome, you should've..." he stopped. Nycolos was glad Ben was staring into the fire and not at him, "should've seen it Jack." Ben said and lay down again. "Nyc walked in front of me a pace or so and threshed a couple of bushes and POW!! They practically exploded in Nyc's face, he almost wet himself." Ben's laugh was genuine and Nyc supposed it was, since he wasn't dead. Though he wasn't sure he preferred Ben's version of the truth.

"Nice job, little brother," True pride and surprise tempered Jackson's voice. "Looks like you're both little more than you seem. I better watch out. Well, I'll tell mom you two are O.K., she was sure one of you would be hurt or maimed by now." Jackson looked at the boys, gauging something in them, then clapped his hands loudly.

"All right, fellas, looks to me like you two are already half asleep, why don't you turn in?" He ushered the boys into the lean-to with practiced mannerisms of a man used to dealing with children. They slipped into their sleeping bags, pulled out of the tent and placed outside on the raised wooden platform of the lean-to. Jackson hung a battery-powered lantern from one of the hooks on the wall, made sure the boys were snug in their sleeping bags, and kissed them both on the top of their heads.

"I'm going to put the grouse down in the freezer for you, Ben." Ben barely murmured a reply, already off to sleep.

"Goodnight, Nyc." Jackson waved goodbye.

"Goodnight, Jackson." Nyc watched the older Miller brother go, but he didn't leave right away. He spent several minutes putting out the fire and disappeared around the corner of the lean-to. Nyc heard him untying the bear bag and then, several minutes later, raising it again. Nyc never heard him move away into the night.

****

Nycolos Arcadia clung to semi-consciousness for some time, but ultimately let awareness slip from him. Giant boulders crashed into each other like marbles beyond the smoldering fire, tumbling down the Mount and back up again. Sticking to one another like magnets, the boulders were of all shapes and sizes. They were irregular, some perfectly round, others completely flat. The rocks fused together into a massive mound of bouncing granite and quartz. A mound of stone that unfolded, revealing arms and legs of stone, rising like the earth come to life. In the center of the mass, an assemblage of smaller rocks formed the chest and head of the Golem, swarming in a writhing unit around a massive round boulder. The Golem opened its mouth and the rasping sound of rock scraping over rock echoed through the night.

Jackson Miller stepped from behind the monster's legs and loosed an imaginary arrow at Nyc. Nycolos felt a tug in his gut and realized with horror an arrow was sticking through his chest. He touched the shaft, it was one of Ben's, homemade of arrow-wood, with lovely duck feathers. Jackson stood above him, the rock monster mute in the darkness behind.

"You never should've given up on him." A grouse sat on Jackson's shoulder and puffed out its chest at Nyc. "And you should've fallen to that arrow today. Lucky for you, huh?"

****

Nycolos Arcadia woke with a start in the cool darkness of the autumn night. He sat up, snug inside the warm sleeping bag and held his head. He didn't want to wake up Ben because he was scared; too much weird stuff had already happened that day. Which was why when he heard the clicking of rock on rock as if someone had caused a rockslide, he put on his shoes and jacket and moved into the darkness alone.

The spruce stand behind the lean-to was a pool of darkness that did not frighten Nycolos. But nervous apprehension banged around his chest, making him jumpy. He stopped for a long one-hundred count, straining all of his senses, searching for movement among the boughs. The clatter of rocks had ceased, though the memory rattled through his mind. Circling the wooden lean-to, Nyc checked the fire-pit. All but a few embers were extinguished, smoldering orange in the bright moonlight. Moonbeams illuminated the dale in front of the lean-to, save for a rock outcrop that jutted from the shadows beneath a cluster of huddled trees. Shrubs looked like crawling animals to Nyc's overactive imagination, and dry branches rubbed in the darkness, creaking in the passing breeze.

Nycolos Arcadia, a boy known for formidable mental attributes, considered the shadows a long time, as was his nature. The little brown boy considered what he heard, and concluded it was the call of nature. He moved into the darkness of the spruce stand and made his way to a darkened outcrop where the moon beams were barred entry. Under a particularly grand spruce Nycolos arranged himself to take care of business in the night air. Facing the spruce Nycolos heard the sound of rocks bouncing like marbles. It sounded like someone was kicking rocks. Nycolos froze, straining his ears for more sounds. Convinced he was still half asleep, Nyc leaned against the spruce, zipped his fly, and his nightmare came to life.

Giant boulders shifted impossibly, rising from the ground to tower above the dale. Easily as tall as the nearby spruces, the monolith of stone was illuminated by the moonlight. Rocks clung together in ordered chaos, the arms and legs of the monster looked like pillars of moving stone. Massive boulders covered with moss and ferns formed the darkened shoulders and broad chest of the monster. Cobbles undulated across the thing, filling voids between the larger boulders. Nycolos watched the monster in profile from his vantage, as it scanned the dale. The creature stood still, except for the massive head, which continued to turn from side to side in a scanning motion, Nyc saw glowing gold orbs filling otherwise empty eye sockets. The constant sound of dropping rocks prompted Nycolos to look closer. He moved to the edge of the shadows, and the little boy watched and listened as a monster, unable to hold itself together, fell to pieces. Showering the earth with cobbles and gravel, filling the air with dust and clatter. The giant's arms and legs undulated as if a swarming mass of creatures moved there. Rocks jockeyed and crunched against one another, cobbles fell from the creature's shoulder, sparking and shattering loudly, sending more dust into the air. Broken pieces tumbled of their own volition, attaching to the monster's pillar-like leg, pushing into what would've been a calf. The larger boulders comprising the skeleton of the monster were the only stable pieces, while the rest of the rock armor shifted upwards to fill in gaps falling pieces left.

"Nyc?" Ben's call sounded faint. Nycolos looked toward the lean-to, just as Ben stepped from behind a boulder into the moon-lit, boulder-strewn dale.

The monster froze, literally, undulating rock faces of pillar-like arms and legs ceased, and with them the continuous shower of falling earth. Nycolos hoped Ben would stop and go back to the lean-to, he hoped with all his might. Ben stopped in the clearing, scratched his behind, and searched the shadows with his eyes. Nycolos saw Ben's tousled hair clearly in the white light of the half-moon, and could almost imagine the puzzled look on his friend's face. Ben guessed correctly, unfortunately for him, and Nyc watched his friend walk up the slope, towards the dark outcrop where Nycolos crouched, with growing trepidation. The rock monster stood, a giant rock statue towering at the top of the incline, rocks shining in the moonlight, seeming to glow against the shadow filled spruce forest. Ben neared the shadows and the tree-line, ghosting through the dale and a pool of white light. A mere twenty meters from the shadows Ben called out.

"Nyc?"

Nycolos didn't have time to answer, the monster crumbled into a crushing rain of limestone and granite. Ben let out a cry as he stumbled backwards throwing his arms above his head. Thick dust rose from shattering cobbles and impacted earth.

The rock monster lost form completely, with giant arms raised to its head, gravel armor fell in a continuous shower of stone. Finally, the largest boulders stood bare and silent, silhouetted by the moon, within a cloud of dust. The left arm tumbled to the earth, two huge elongated boulders embedded in the ground with a loud thud, a third rolled down the incline, missing a shocked Benjamin Miller by a meter. The stone face contorted and a massive black maw opened, emitting the same rasping cough Nycolos heard earlier that day, the golden orbs glowing in dark, cave sized sockets extinguished. The grating sound of rock on rock chilled his blood and the stone monster crumbled to the earth. Boulders large enough to crush houses bounded toward Ben, who would surely die crushed beneath boulders that hadn't moved since the last ice-age.

Nycolos burst from the shadows, exploding into a full run. He jumped between two rocks sticking up from the earth, and pushed off with his arms and legs, begging his body for more speed. Heat welled up from the earth, passing through his arms and legs, and he felt lighter than he ever had before. Time slowed, and Nycolos blasted across the space separating him from Ben without taking another step, parting the roiling dust cloud like a strong breeze. He slammed into Ben with a grunt, carrying him beyond the boulder's path and certain death.

"Nyc?"

Nycolos didn't answer his friend; instead he ran toward the lean-to, pulling his friend behind. Each step pushed him with the force of canon blasts. The dale passed as a blur of boulders and grasses bathed in white light. A blast of wind tousled their hair as Nyc turned sharply, tearing toward the safety of shadowy darkness next to the lean-to. When Nyc tried to stop they were moving so fast they slid five meters over the gravelly earth on booted soles.

The two boys turned to see the last few of the boulders rolling out of the dale, crashing into the forested darkness , felling trees and splintering wood. It took several minutes for all the rumbling and rock slides to cease. Nyc could still see one large boulder well into the forest, glowing bright white in the moonlight, surrounded by the darkness of spruce and shadow.

"What was that?" Ben doubled over, gasping for breath. "What the hell is going on Nyc?"

"I don't know, I went to take a piss, then it showed up!" Ben was already breaking camp, and Nyc pitched in immediately. They didn't make any efforts to be tidy that night, and simply threw everything inside the lean-to and took off running. The two ten-year olds ran all the way home, through the darkness of forest paths black as pitch, navigating more by memory than by sight. They crashed through Ben's back door, collapsing onto the couch in the living room.

Abby came down, but didn't ask any questions, if she assumed they had been too frightened to stay on the Mount all night, she would've been right.

She gave them milk and cookies, and ushered them up to Ben's room. Nyc drifted off to sleep for the second time that night, feeling Ben's stare on the back of this head. Nyc fell asleep thinking about golden glowing eyes, golden orbs that greeted him in his dreams. Dreams in which he dodged rolling boulders with wings for arms.

CHAPTER 7

A Shrinking Feeling

Nycolos Arcadia stole from the Miller's house in the pre-dawn light. He slept fitfully for a couple hours. Wading through dreams of golden orbs waking him over and over. Walk home was brief , quiet, save for the birds chirped, geese flying south in formation. The back door of his house was open, he slipped upstairs to his room, flopped down atop the bedspread and lost consciousness.

Rosa woke to the phone ringing. Third ring she rolled over and picked up the black cordless receiver, eyes still closed.

"Diga." She spoke in Portuguese half-awake.

"Rosa, It's Abby, is Nyc there? He left here early this morning, I didn't see him go." One breath, worried mother.

Rosa flipped back the covers and padded down the wooden floored hallway to Nyc's door. Naked flesh goose-pimpled, tightening in the cool morning air that filled the house. Peeking through his door she saw Nyc asleep on his bed, booted feet hanging off the side.

"Yeah, he's here Abby, did something happen?"

"I don't know, the boys came down from the Mount around two in the morning, I sent Jackson up there around ten, he came down around twelve and told me the boys were sleeping." Long pause. "But you should've seen them when they came down from the Mount, they were covered in dirt; it was in their hair, and clothes, pockets, everything. I think maybe they had a fight."

"Is Ben up yet?" Rosa thought maybe Abby was right, the boys were usually inseparable on weekends. She slipped back under the fluffy down comforter on her bed.

"Not yet, but when he does I'll talk to him."

"I'll do the same and then we'll talk."

"Alright, bye, Rosa."

"Chou, Abby." She hung up the phone.

Rosa looked at the clock on the bed stand it read 7:30. She decided to sleep for a couple of hours then get up and make some breakfast. She lay there for the rest of the morning thinking of ravens and crows

****

Nycolos woke to Rosa pulling off his boots, socks and pants. He crawled under the covers, thankful to be home.

"You O.K. sweetheart?" He wasn't completely awake so murmured an affirmative.

"Did you and Ben have a fight? You've got some pretty good scratches and apparently so does he."

Nycolos sat up, awake. "What did Ben say?"

"He's still sleeping."

Nycolos relaxed and let his head fall back on the pillow.

"No, we didn't fight, we just felt like going back." He rolled over onto his side, so she couldn't see his face.

"Are you sure?"

"Yes."

"Alright." She didn't sound like she believed him.

****

Nycolos and Ben didn't talk for the rest of the weekend though their mothers did all day Sunday. Rosa didn't open the store either, she liked to lounge around the house and property on Sundays, though she had so much work already postponed. She suspected some thorn between the boys, as did Abby. Nycolos was content to let them think so, it meant Ben hadn't talked. Rosa tried prodding him with questions once he got out of bed. After that failed, she bribed him with food, typical. She spent the entire Sunday trying to get the truth out of him, between trips to the barn that is, but Nycolos refused to cooperate. By dinner she conceded, but Nyc knew that his mother was waiting to strike when he wasn't looking.

That week at school Nyc kept his head down and focused on schoolwork. He and Ben ate lunch together, mute camaraderie, shield and spear, deflecting bully Damian Fontane and Jacob Watts. They had not forgotten their humiliation, Ash and Beech witness. Nycolos wondered if Ben would have talked to him if not for the threat of the bullies. Ben didn't look at him the same anymore, Nyc caught Ben staring at him several times over the course of the week. Ben would blink when Nyc looked back at him,evil eye, take that, but wouldn't look away. Instead he would look at Nyc more intently, like he was studying an insect.

Between the two of them, their mothers picked them up the week after their encounter with the bullies. The clattering stones of the Mount overshadowed the bullies, but had not eclipsed grade school circumstance. The grade-school bullies seemed like a trivial threat, but Ben intelligently took the initiative and circumvented any unpleasantness by arranging for Abby to pick them up Monday and Tuesday.

Nyc had Rosa the rest of the week, using lame excuses like his sore back or bum knee. She knew he was full of it but didn't call him on it since the boys were at odds. The mothers would've been much more concerned if they had known the boys really did have sore backs and legs; thank you, adventure.

Their arrangement worked for the first week, and after an uneventful weekend Rosa showed up early the following Monday. Once the boys were loaded in the car she took Ben down to his mother's shop.

"Your mom wanted me to drop you here today, Ben."

"Thanks, Mrs. Arcadia." He jumped out and shut the door.

* * *

"You and I are going to see a counselor today."

Nyc could tell by her voice that she wasn't thrilled.

"If you don't want to go then why are we?" He countered.

"I think you and I have some issues we need to work out about Daddy."

Nycolos didn't reply, he had nothing to say. They drove for about half-an-hour before turning into the drive of a two-story Victorian, all white with navy-blue shutters. His mother pulled around back down the gravel driveway, crunch beneath the tires. They stepped from the vehicle, entered the rear of the house through a large door painted to match the shutters. A sign to one side read 'Dr. Rosen' , in gold letters on an oak plaque.

The foyer was all shiny hardwood floors and wooden paneling on the walls. Recessed lights in the ceiling lit the entryway with a muted white light. Wooden pegs lined the walls providing spaces for jackets and coats. Beyond the foyer the office opened to a larger waiting room. Two leather couches sat kitty-cornered, fronted by a wooden coffee table covered with magazines. Nycolos sat on the cool hide, it creaked with the sound of fitted leather. Rosa stepped to the reception desk, behind which sat a grandmotherly woman with very curly white hair. Her spectacles were thick and gave her a comical appearance of large over-sized eyes. She nodded as Rosa spoke and pushed a button on her phone, speaking softly into the speaker.

A door opened behind the desk and a man stepped out. He was wearing brown corduroy pants with a soft-looking red v-neck sweater. He had curly hair like the woman sitting at the desk except his was dark brown with larger curls. His smile softened his eyes as he took in mother and child.

"Mrs. Arcadia, thank you for coming." He moved forward and shook her hand.

"Dr. Rosen, Thank you."

He took Rosa aside and spoke with her quietly just inside his office. Rosa nodded slightly and they came over to Nyc together.

"Sweetheart, Dr. Rosen would like to talk to you." Rosa looked over her shoulder at the doctor.

"What about you, Mom?" Nyc didn't like the idea of talking to the doctor alone, but was not alarmed or surprised. After his talk with the school counselor he had imagined someone would suggest this to his mother sooner or later.

"I've seen him several times, sweetheart; he wants to get to know you, since he already knows me." She looked at him and saw the question in his eyes. "We'll go in together next time, I promise."

Dr. Rosen stepped into the opening. "Hello Nycolos, I'm James Rosen, would you mind talking with me for a while?" His smile was deep and his gesture genuine, Nyc couldn't help but smile a little to himself.

"Sure." Nyc hopped up, walked over to Rosa and hugged her around the waist. He turned to the office and followed Dr. Rosen in. The office was big with more of the same recessed lights and wood paneled walls and ceiling. Both walls were bookshelves of dark wood that were lined with books of all sizes. The wall opposite the door was a large map of North and South America. A third rather large sofa was placed in front of a dark and deep leather chair. Both chair and sofa were positioned in front of a desk, tidy with a notebook, files and computer.

Statues and busts were interspersed among the books. A globe here, a marble head there, served as bookends as well as decorative art. Nyc slid onto the leather sofa and settled in for the duration. The first half hour wasn't bad, Dr. Rosen really just wanted to figure out who Nyc was and how he had grown up and so on and so forth. They played some word association games, some board games and even some video games. It was during the second half hour that the doctor felt ready to start feinting and dodging.

"I'd like to talk about your father and what happened to you two, is that O.K., Nyc?"

"O.K." *Here we go,* thought Nycolos. He hadn't given this type of conversation too much thought, though he and Rosa had agreed he wouldn't tell any of the strange parts, which of course was going to be difficult for Nycolos, considering the whole encounter had been the strange part. Rosa had assured him the shrink would want to talk about his feelings more than the details. Nycolos knew he wasn't going to say anything he shouldn't, but it was necessary for him to play along so as not to look stand offish, which would inevitably lead to more scrutiny.

"Why don't you tell me what happened, Nycolos." The shrink like to say his whole name.

"Didn't my mother tell you what happened?"

"Well, yes, of course, Nycolos, but I want to hear it in your own words."

Nycolos had been well trained by his parents so he knew very well the snarky comments brewing in his brain would be the wrong things to say.

"We got up early, Dad made breakfast of ham and eggs, we ate, then left for a day hike. We hiked up to a meadow, we surprised a bear, they fought, Dad to protect me, the bear to protect his food, I guess."

Nycolos could see that moment in his mind's eye. He had been thrown to the ground, pushed by his father's fumbling hands, prostrate before the monstrous bear like an offering to the gods. His father bent double with horror frozen in his eyes and mouth, the bear roaring in outrage at Lyndon's apparent sacrifice of his son.

"Yes."

"They died." Nycolos was pissed he had to say the words for some reason but he said them anyway.

"Both of them?"

"Yes," Nycolos replied gravely, "they killed each other."

James Rosen looked honestly surprised by the answer and he blinked several times before scribbling in his little pad. He continued his questioning after a brief pause.

"And then what, Nycolos?"

"This lady showed up, and she walked me down to the Ranger station."

"What about your father? How did you feel about leaving him?"

"Sad, I cried a lot, for a long time before the lady showed up. I pulled his knife out of the bear's chest..." He tried not to remember the grief that had gripped him, or the terror of the bear coming to life again. The doctor didn't say anything, but was scribbling intently.

"So I walked with this lady down to the Ranger station."

"And who was this lady?"

"I don't know, she showed up at our campsite the night before, she wanted to talk to Dad mostly, so I went to bed after a little, she seemed nice enough." Nyc shrugged, it seemed like the right thing to do.

"Do you know why your father took you up there, Nycolos?" Dr. Rosen was looking at his pad when asked Nyc the question.

Nycolos took his time answering. This wasn't something he had gone over too closely with his mother. Nycolos decided honesty was the best policy, this time.

"Yeah, my parents were going to get a divorce and he wanted to tell me that weekend."

"Really?" While previous leading questions may have irritated Nyc, after the last one he wanted to pluck the arched eyebrows right off the forehead of the pretentious psychologist.

"Yes, Doctor, really."

"How did this make you feel, Nycolos?"

"Bad."

"As in not good, sick, or sad?"

"I guess sad."

"So what would that have been like?"

"Oh it never would've happened."

"How do you mean Nycolos?"

"Well after the attack my father was alive long enough to tell me that he loved us and the divorce was all a foolish mistake." Nyc hadn't told Rosa that part of the story yet and immediately felt a pang of guilt gathering; if she found out she would see his fault in confidence as a betrayal of trust. Family was his first team, everything else was supposed to come after; Rosa and Lyndon had never let him forget that.

"He did…, when was this?"

"When he was dying."

"Right before?" The shifting gears of the Dr.'s questioning seemed to have become jammed as he stuck to one line of questions.

"Yeah, he was all torn up, his arm was completely ripped off, but he killed the bear, he told me he loved us, then he died." There was so much more to say but Nycolos knew better, he had already come too close to the unbelievable truth.

"And that's when you broke down."

"I cried, then she showed up and walked me down."

"So why did you take the knife, Nyc?" The doctor peered at his notes again.

"It was Dad's, I wasn't going to let that bear keep it. Maybe one of us would need it in the future."

"One of whom Nycolos?"

"My mother, me,…?" Nyc just barely bit down on his father's name.

"Just the two of you?"

"Yes."

"Have you seen your father, Nycolos?"

"What?" Rosa had mentioned something like this might happen.

"Have you seen him?"

"No, he's dead." Nycolos could feel his face heating.

"I know he's dead, Nyc, but no one found his body; maybe he's still around."

"He's dead I told you, he's dead!"

"Are you sure?"

"Yes,…I don't know, stop it, leave me alone!!!" Nycolos stood, kicking the board games strewn across the floor as he moved to the door.

The doctor met him halfway, went down on one knee, hugged Nycolos and apologized. Over the doctor's shoulder through an old-fashioned window with imperfect glass panes, Nycolos could see a large horned owl sitting on the sill, with its head cocked sideways. The owl's face appeared warped and distorted even, one large yellow eye like a monocle; the other appeared squinted, giving the animal the appearance of having a black hole for a left eye. The bottomless darkness of that dark hole swallowed light and life. Nycolos froze in the psychologist's embrace not sure what to do. Sensing the alarm in the boy, the doctor backed away a few steps.

A strange force came over Nycolos, a voice emanated from his throat that was definitely not his.

> Times of trial,
> bear man down.
> Woes of war and waste,
> secreted like steam.
> Hardworking he's and she's
> Lay low,
> animal and tree,
> Earth and sea
> burn and boil,
> Wither and writhe,
> Children of Gaia,
> answer our cries.
>
> Smiting with seasons
> Flood and fire
> Hurricane and hail
> Tsunami and typhoon,
> Works of wise men
> Burn like brimstone
> Melting mountains
> Glow golden beneath
> Snow capped waves.

"Alright Nycolos, we're done for this time." His face relaxed into a sort of goofy grin while he crossed his eyes and moved his glasses around his head.

"Sorry for the questions buddy, we just want to help you get through this tough time." He smiled again, genuine and sincere. By "we" Nyc assumed he meant his mother.

"O.K." Nyc walked from the stagnant air of his interrogation parlor. Nycolos chanced a glance whilst retreating towards his mother's waiting arms, but the owl was gone, replaced by the purple hue of the sunset.

****

Mother and son rode home in silence, the metal skeleton cutting through the crisp air. Wool socks and wool caps to match combated the chill, they wore matching boots, matching eyes and matching frowns.

Nycolos tried in vain to hold on to his anger, he wanted to be angry with his mother but his gentle nature would not allow for any such resentment, and as the car pulled into the driveway Nycolos loosed the one remaining seed of anger that remained him with a cathartic outburst.

"Why did you do it, mommy? Why did you yell and scream at him so much, that's why he wanted a divorce." He was crying in the passenger seat.

Rosa felt as if her son had just stabbed her in the heart, the first snow flurry of the season drifted weakly from the sky.

****

Rosa and Nycolos Arcadia trudged through the next week just trying to get by. Ben and Abby nearly forced themselves upon mother and son but were repelled by work-related excuses. They were close enough to get the picture. Nycolos was fine and wandered the property freely, Rosa didn't even mention boundaries anymore as the cold winds gripped the countryside setting blades of grass erect and white in the frosted nights. Jackson showed up one night when Capoiera classes were scheduled, the look of regret and sorrow on his face when Rosa informed him she had temporarily canceled the classes so severe she felt guilty.

"We'll start them up again soon." She patted the tall young man on the shoulder. Rosa Arcadia couldn't bear her guilt for more than five minutes once Jackson stayed for a cup of coffee, and they all ended up in the exercise barn playing capoiera and the birim bau. Jackson was strong and lithe with amazing creativity and an infectious laugh. All had fun as they jumped, flipped, rolled and kicked to the sounds of the Brazilian rhythms.

What seemed an age later, though in truth only two hours, the trio emerged from the barn. Jackson's body steamed in the night air before he pulled his sweatshirt over his milky white skin. The three stood, heads steaming in the night air, talking over the good and bad of their sparring session. Cool and crisp, the air was easy to breathe and felt good in their lungs, tasting of fallen leaves and coming snow. Rosa scolded the boys gently about catching colds and they promptly covered their steaming heads with the hoods of their sweatshirts she gave students at the school. The Brazilian flag stitched on the left breast of each sweatshirt above the name of their farm, Arcadia.

Company waited back at the house in the form of a black and white Sheriff's cruiser and a green jeep of the Forest Service. With ice in their stomachs, Nycolos and Rosa realized there were three figures standing in the shadows by the front porch.

"Good evening Mrs. Arcadia." A sheriff's deputy addressed her with a condescending tone, perhaps less than pleased at having been left waiting. Though the Brazilian beauty with cacao skin noted that they couldn't have been waiting long or they would've heard the noise in the barn and come up to investigate. The deputy stood next to an older gentleman with graying hair that she recognized as the sheriff. The sheriff had a leathery face that had seen many sunny days with high cheekbones and a pointed nose. He seemed complacent and had contented himself leaning on the hood of his black and white Ford cruiser scanning the darkness for something none but he could see. He sucked on his yellow teeth before spitting through the air a long arcing shot that sank into the frosted grass.

"Mrs. Arcadia, if you don't mind, we would like to go inside and talk to you for a few minutes."

Rosa Arcadia did not hesitate to answer, nor in fact did she even blink before answering in the negative. No, they would not be continuing anything inside, it was not that she mistrusted all uniformed officers, she had met a few decent stand up cops that had been nice to her; but she had too many sour memories that burned acidic in her stomach, memories that all started with something benign like asking an officer for directions. Invariably those encounters had gone wrong as something implanted in an officer's brain required that they stick their noses as far as possible into Rosa's business. She could just see this gentlemanly sheriff sitting on her couch talking to her while his flunky of a deputy with a sneer on his face wandered through her house.

Her tone as well as manner effectively conveyed Rosa's thoughts to the sheriff, his deputy and Chief Ranger Thompson, who had been leaning on his jeep behind the Sheriff's car, and had not yet engaged in the conversation.

"Very well," the Sheriff turned his head and spit again. Raising his eyes he took in Rosa Arcadia, weighing her in his mind.

Rosa caught Jackson's eye, the responsible fair-haired young man wore an open scowl directed at the deputy. In an effort to simplify the encounter she asked the young man to take Nycolos inside. The boys moved up the walk and onto the porch, she didn't hear them move inside as she returned her attention to the uniformed men. The sheriff exhaled a deep breath; he seemed to have made up his mind about something.

"Mrs. Arcadia, we need to talk about Lyndon. Some loggers were mauled yesterday ma'am, apparently they disturbed the wrong pair of bears." He reflexively spit again, which made Rosa sick. Anger flared in her chest, that they should bring such ludicrous slander to her doorstep. She caught herself wishing she had made sure the boys were inside before beginning this nonsense.

"My husband is dead, gentlemen."

"Ma'am, we've been informed by Ranger Thompson about what happened to your son and husband. The problem is, ma'am, the lack of remains leaves many questions unanswered, and you and your husband have a history of environmental activism."

"Yeah, we know tree-hugging, granola-crunching hippies when we see 'em." The younger deputy's face was flushed and a vein bulged in his neck.

"Deputy Fontane, if you can't refrain from interrupting me, you can remove yourself."

The deputy swallowed hard at the reprimand from his superior, choking down his emotions with evident distaste.

Though inappropriate the deputy had a point. Lyndon and Rosa had been involved in a number of local protests against lumber companies, and had been responsible for organizing hundreds of protesters, using the farm as one of the regional bases of operations. They had gladly provided room and board for several days, filling their barns and haylofts with sleeping activists, many of which ended up chained to trees, laying under tractor treads, or perched high in trees refusing to move.

The local logging companies were incensed, and their employees, until an anonymous informer phoned the appropriate authorities and the local press; the town of New Hamlet had been appalled to discover the company had been logging illegally in an old growth stand far from their "legitimate" operations.

Lyndon had most recently been advocating aggressive measures to protect the Lollygag River, which majestically meandered through their green valley. The trailer park that sat along its banks had grown quickly with little regard for environmental ethics, and the brilliant planners of New Hamlet had deemed the material recovery center belonged next door, out of site and mind of the more affluent members of the community. The septic system and refuse produced by the trailer park had become increasingly evident on the banks of the river in the form of condom wrappers, soda cans, beer bottles, plastic baggies, toilet paper, etc. The Sheriff knew the deputy was right as well, though he was able to convey as much with more tact.

"Given your history, and the lack of the body, if you'll excuse my saying so, ma'am, but this is my job, given those factors it becomes necessary for me to ask some of these tough questions." He stopped there, leaving the rest unsaid, but she knew that wouldn't last.

"So, let me get this straight..." she held up her hand while shaking her head. Though she didn't realize it she projected strength, steam still rising from her head, wisps of power backlit by the porch light, illuminating the vapors of a ghostly aura flickering from her head and shoulders. "You gentlemen are suggesting my husband faked his own mauling, traumatized his son, leaving him abandoned on top of Hawk Mountain hours from safety, me a widow at 32 so he could work clandestinely to thwart illegal logging?!? Are you kidding??"

"We're not ruling it out, let's just say that." He looked her straight in her green eyes.

"Why don't you just get the hell out of here?"

"Well, ma'am, I understand it sounds preposterous, but we found this." He held out a plaid flannel shirt, criss-crossing red and black lines formed a checkerboard pattern, it was Lyndon's favorite flannel, and the one Lyndon had been wearing the day he died. One sleeve was missing and she remembered Nyc telling her Lyn's arm had been ripped off. Tears she hadn't felt coming tickled her chin and cheeks. The sheriff handed her the shirt, it was horribly dirty but she could see the initials stitched inside the collar, L.A., she had sewn the stitches herself.

"That is his shirt, isn't it, Mrs. Arcadia?"

"Yes."

"We found that just outside the logging camp yesterday."

Rosa's stomach dropped out and she thought her knees might buckle.

Ranger Thompson stepped forward making his presence felt at last. "As I explained to you gentlemen earlier, this proves nothing. Sad to say, but families like Arcadia's are not the only people that like to hike and camp in the forest for days on end. Unfortunately, unsavory individuals will hike into the forest and camp for weeks between their "activities". It is entirely plausible one of those loggers, or some other person found the item."

The sheriff looked at the ranger, "Thank you, Mr. Thompson. I know this is a tough time, Ma'am, but I needed to let you know what we found. We also have some testimony that certain acquaintances of yours have animal training experience, your husband included."

"So now we trained a bear to attack my husband, and the loggers? First of all, we had a professional animal handler here last fall to give all of us a lesson about wildlife biology, it was open to the public, and second of all those loggers are cutting old-growth stands again and deserve what they get, and third of all you're full of shit." Rosa was out of patience and this charade had gone on long enough. "If you gentlemen will excuse me, I have to make dinner."

"Yes ma'am, we understand, let us know if you hear anything and tell your son to stay out of trouble." The sheriff and his deputy stepped into the black and white cruiser and pulled off leaving Rosa alone with the ranger.

"I'm sorry about that, I told them it was crazy and down right cruel to do this to you. They also asked me about Nyc's story and what I thought about it."

"And?" Rosa could feel her pulse slowing finally, she hadn't realized how fast her heart had been hammering in her chest.

"I told them I thought it was true even if we haven't found Lyndon or this mystery lady, I've never seen someone come down from the mountain covered in as much blood as Nycolos was."

"Thank you, Mr. Thompson," Rosa put her head in her hands. "If you don't mind, I really need to make dinner."

"No problem, Rosa, I'll let you get some rest."

Rosa nodded before letting herself inside the house. Her head was spinning like a top. Could Lyndon really be alive? Given the nature of the last few weeks and the emerging nature of her son, the hope she kept locked deep inside her chest fluttered madly like a butterfly trapped in a jar.

Chapter 8

It's All Happening At The Zoo

Before the beginning of man or beast
Goddess Gaia chose her guardians.
Her celestial hands catching cosmic
Souls and stardust molded with magic and might.
None bear witness saver her sister, night.

Nycolos hated the Zoo. The school trip had slipped his mind until the Monday morning his mother brought it up at breakfast. She had been distant since the sheriff visited the other night. She started staring out windows and going for walks at night. Nycolos knew she walked the property line looking for Lyndon. Neither of them wanted to say it out loud but they were both waiting for something to happen.

"I hate the Zoo." Nycolos could feel a sulk coming on.

"Oh come on, honey, don't be negative." Rosa saw the sulk too and was amused. The rest of the morning passed as routine, mother and son lost in the ether of memory. That was until they got into the car to go to school. Once she had him cornered and unable to escape she lit into him with the sharp side of her tongue. She wasn't as upset about the fight as she was about the fact that the sheriff brought it to her attention. She was even more upset she had to pry the truth from Nyc and Jackson the minute the sherrif's car pulled down the driveway. If it was self-defense fine, but she didn't want to be the last one to find out.

She dropped him at school with a kiss on the forehead, tongue lashing already forgotten.

Benjamin Miller was already there, jumping around under a Redbud tree whose leaves had turned and fallen already, leaving slim seed pods clinging to skeletal branches.

"What's up?" Ben waved to Rosa as she pulled away.

"She just chewed me out for what happened with Damian and Jacob."

"Yeah, Abby tore me a new one too." Ben shrugged, rubbing his behind, trying to be funny, but his mind was already moving beyond their groundings. "You need to watch out for those two, they're on the rampage.

I think you knocked out one of Damian's teeth or something. They're looking to do some damage to us, and their class is coming on the trip too."

On cue Jacob Watts and Damian Fontane stepped from the brush on the other side of the street. The trail where Nycolos had put his head into Damian's jaw ended where the bullies stepped into the road. The pair of miscreants flicked cigarettes back into the woods then crossed the street with their pants sagging below their butts. Nycolos smiled to himself, those fools would never learn. With their pants like that they would never catch him if he ran, or stop him if he decided to stand and fight. Nycolos elbowed Ben in the ribs who nodded without taking his eyes off the bullies.

More than ever before, Nyc realized he and Ben were more than capable of handling Damian Fontane and Jacob Watts, especially when they worked together. The bullies of flesh and bone had nothing on a giant monster of limestone and granite, trying to crush his skull in with flying boulders.

The two 13-year-olds were less than impressed that the two sixth graders were not shaking in their boots. Damian Fontane made a beeline for Ben and Nyc, pulling Jacob in his wake. Nycolos mentally visualized two ways in which he would deal with the approaching problem. He had no need to use the defensive forms however as Mrs. Richardson the school Vice-Principal strode out the front doors in time to greet the two troublemakers. It seemed she had been informed about the altercation between the boys. She wrapped her generous arms around the shoulders of the troublemakers and escorted them inside, her plum-colored skirt suit wafting sickeningly sweet perfume in her wake. Damian managed to direct a threatening sneer at Nycolos. Nyc stuck his tongue out at the bullies retreating back.

"Told you," Ben pointed at the trio moving through the front doors of the school. "Watch out today; they'll try to stomp us for sure if they get the chance."

****

Their classes emptied out after roll call in homeroom. Raucous children were shepherded by teachers and aides equally happy to be free of the confines of brick and mortar, textbook and syllabi. The air was crisp with fall, though overcast and warmer than it should've been, still a welcome relief from the stale air that tasted of chalk. The wind blew in gusts, sending ball caps, loose papers and leaves whipping through the air. Once the children were wrangled onto the yellow buses, the wagon train headed southeast. The trip was a two-hour jaunt full of screams, shouts, giggles of laughter and the occasional interruption by teachers walking down the aisle shushing the children and asking them to pick up their garbage. In truth the teacher's effort was half-hearted, the few teachers on the bus had grown accustomed to the constant hum and buzz of the beehive of activity. The children obeyed perfunctionally, conversations cascading over the imposed silence as soon as the teachers turned their backs and headed back up the aisle. Notes were passed, laughter chimed like sweet notes, crushes were invented and smothered in transit.

Ben and Nycolos spent most of their time discussing possibilities of the trip, running through hypothetical encounters that might unfold if they were cornered by the bullies. They were no longer concerned that they would get beat up, but they did want to stay out of trouble.

Shock dulled and missing Nycolos, Ben was eager to talk about the madness on The Mount. Ben tossed about somewhat playful ideas, more jokingly than anything serious, though he watched Nyc intently.

Nycolos hadn't told anyone other than Rosa Arcadia about the bizarre, mind-bending experiences that had transpired that day and intermittently since. Nycolos allowed the preposterous absurdities flowing from his best friend's mouth to wash over him, thankful that he had someone he could trust. The Millers were practically family, much more than just neighbors. Abby and Rosa shared a friendship he recognized was deep and as profound as his own with Ben. The two little families clung to each other in good times and bad, weathering storms of divorce, death, teenage angst and now nature come to life. It seemed absurd, though if he were nuts at least it would be his family laughing at him.

Ben had run out of gas and was staring out the bus window lost in thought while waiting for Nyc's input.

"O.K." Nyc said. Ben licked his lips a little and sat very still. An avid reader with an imagination to boot, Ben's eyes already sparkled in anticipation. The truth was they both knew everything that was happening had something to do with Nyc.

So during the hour and a half remaining of the bus ride to the nearest city with a respectable zoo, the two boys, Princes of The Mount, spoke in hushed whispers. Casting furtive glances at those who approached too near, completely unaware of spitballs, gum, candy, crushes, or their arrival at the Zoo. It wasn't enough time. Nycolos Arcadia started from the beginning, from the night of the storm, the night he first saw the bear.

He wasn't through all of the madness that had occurred since but was close when the bus arrived at the zoo. Nycolos was just able to tell his friend that Rosa knew about the day Lyndon died but nothing since. Squeal of breaks, exhale of pressurized air, squeaky opening of bus door. Old timer bus driver's smile and huge sunglasses. Too few teeth. Their conversation cut short, the duo disembarked, Ben's mouth agape, gray matter struggling with it all.

The air was chilly as they stepped onto the asphalt, a breeze snuck down Nyc's jacket giving him a chill and goose bumps. His mother would say, "Someone walked over your grave." A morbid thought, but he was fond of her sayings. She had one for almost anything. Since Lyndon Arcadia died she was sure to explain to him that they were "taking it one day at time until they felt ready to climb the hill again." While the hill in her saying was a metaphor he thought it an appropriate choice of words. One day they would climb that hill again and see what they could see.

Their bus was the first in a long line; it was clear several schools had organized trips to the zoo that day. Nycolos Arcadia could feel his frustration massing into a tight ball in the middle of his chest, and he was still outside the gated community, don't forget to check in at the security booth. Wild animals forced into cages for the betterment of mankind.

Ben shoved him from behind, students were extracted from the buses in an orderly fashion and kids were lead bleating through the turnstiles. Nyc spotted Damian Fontane and Jacob Watts several times during the morning, but always from behind. The 8th grade group was several exhibits removed from Nyc's and under heavy observation.

Nycolos and Ben were being watched as well, teachers sneaking furtive glances, made lousy spies and informants. Ben remained silent through the first several exhibits. The darkness of the bat-house, the reptile-house, but became fidgety when they reached the monkey house. Nyc managed to keep him quiet if only by promising they would talk it all out, just not huddled in a group of students during a tour of the monkey house. The thing of it was, Nycolos Arcadia couldn't have been more sincere.

He wanted to talk it out, he wanted to tell his best friend everything. Ben had shared the danger and risked his life with Nycolos, and came through, still full of trust in Nyc, he deserved the same in return.

Damian and Jacob at the snack bar, eating cheese balls and throwing them at anyone unwise enough to pass. Nyc saw them later throwing rocks at the bears. They stood 20 meters distant, chucking rocks they pulled from their packs, bearing evident the premeditated nature of their malicious act. The bears didn't care at first but grew aggravated after several well-placed rocks. The bullies took off running and hid in the souvenir shop when a zoo keeper started chasing after them.

Nyc and Ben narrowly avoided them behind a bathroom on the other side of the zoo. They were smoking cigarettes and swearing about something. Nyc and Ben remained out of sight, let sleeping dogs lie and all that. The bullies almost nicked them by the elephant pen.

Ben was down in front leaning on the railing, staring at the family of elephants, flicking tails and floppy ears kept distant from the wall by a ha-ha fence. A gap 10 meters deep and 10 meters wide separated the elephant area from the crowds. Ben was pressed shoulder to shoulder with the mass of other sixth-graders, momentarily acting his age.

The wind shifted, from behind Nyc caught the smell of stale cigarette smoke mingled with the mildly sour smell of dirty laundry and sewage. Nyc jumped forward a few steps and saw a small rock bounce off the trunk of the tree next to him. He didn't turn around until he reached the iron rail, pressing into the throng of excited children.

Damian and Jacob stood behind a landscaped planter— oh, if looks could kill. A few sparrows flitted from one burning bush to another, the bright red bushes provided perfect perches for winged flitting jaunts.

One such sparrow burst from the bushes as Jacob beat the innocent shrubbery with his hand in frustration, arced above the bullies like a feathered torpedo, loosed a depth charge of white and green onto the startled face of Jacob Watts

Nycolos turned to the elephants, suppressing his laughter at the bullies' ineptitude. The animals were gorgeous as well as massive. Grey skin flecked with pink patches on the inside of legs and underbellies. The little boy's mood sobered; despite his small victory over inept aggressors, the elephants were stuck in that little space every day. In the opinion of one pre-teen boy, the holding area was too small. The elephants stood on a concrete pad several hundred feet across with a small shallow pool for water.

He could see a wooded area attached to this holding pen, he couldn't see how big it was, but he knew it wasn't enough. It never was. At least the elephants mostly just stood there flicking their tales from side to side. Watching the lions, or other big cats just about drove him crazy, all that pacing was more than he could handle. The herd was on the move again, as a teacher gesticulated and spoke in a loud voice ushering her children towards the avian building.

Ben nudged him and pointed out the older class moving off toward the other side of the Zoo. Still standing behind the Burning Bush, Damian and Jacob were being upbraided by an irate zookeeper. They hadn't taken their eyes off of Ben and Nyc, looking more determined than ever to do harm to the two younger boys.

The day was turning out not too bad, Nyc thought. The avian dome was a conservatory, a large greenhouse with full-grown trees, small shrubs, and colorful birds flying from one domed spire to the next. The tall palm trees and tropical foliage smelled rich and earthy, sultry bird songs called from all sides. The window panes were white-washed, muting the already weak autumn sun.

The children dispersed throughout the open space, screaming voices and hammering footsteps bouncing off the brick walkway up to the domed glass ceiling and back again. Perches of wooden branches and nests were numerous on the sides of the glass house. Some sections were netted off, containing predatory raptors, condors, vultures, and the like. Others had local birds, pheasants, grouse, and another with some endangered species like tanagers, finches, and toucans.

Moss grew in the cracks of the brick walkway in the moist areas of the winding path. Lichens hung from the rock façade built around the large support beams that were the bones of the birdhouse. The footlights running parallel to the footpath were dim but appeared to be lighting up slowly. Like streetlights coming on in the dusk the light was faint, growing stronger as he walked down the footpath.

The sky outside spoke of afternoon shadows; the short days of winter bring night to cloak them in darkness a little earlier every day. Mrs. Hughes bellowed from the other side of the atrium, the classes were done for the day, form in a line and move out towards the zoo entrance and the buses.

The conservatory was the building that upset Nycolos Arcadia the least, the wide-open space was only a little depressing, and the best of the day. The humidity was high and the air was sweet with floral scents of tropical lushness. Nyc decided this was the best enclosure to be trapped in—if he were an animal that is—but it was still a cage like all the rest at the zoo, just prettier. They were all just cages. Nyc spotted Ben already by the exit, he was waving to Nycolos to hurry up. The space seemed grander somehow and more eloquent lacking the hubbub of human activity. The calls of lush tropical birds sounded melodic and inspired tranquility and peace.

"Let's go!" Ben's voice echoed off the glass walls reaching Nyc's ears twice.

Nycolos Arcadia spotted the red-tail hawk in the corner just above the entrance. It was her, he knew it was, the very same hawk he had seen the day his father died. She had something to do with all the madness. Her eyes were piercing and he could feel their strength in his stomach when he moved to stand below her. Beautiful to behold, her tail feathers were splayed, striped with red, flecks of white at the tips. Nycolos wanted to ask her so many questions.

"Who are you?" He just barely managed to get the words out.

"I think it's a red-tail hawk." Ben's voice was loud in Nyc's ear and he jumped a little in fright.

"Sorry Nyc...," Benjamin Miller lost his voice when Damian Fontane and Jacob Watts stepped through the glass entrance, barely containing their delight at catching the younger boys alone.

"Talkin' to birdies," Damian Fontane might as well have danced a jig in delight, "If it isn't the porch monkey and the nigger lover." The bully picked up where he left off during their last encounter. Jacob Watts snickered as usual; his baby fat face belied the innocence left behind years ago.

Broken and abandoned by his father's beatings. Jacob was twitchy but could take a beating and orders, not so smart though, thus perfect lackey material. The hawk screeched breaking the spell of the encounter causing the bullies to look skyward. Nyc watched the hawk stoop; though only 30 meters above, her speed was incredible. In a surprising turn she plummeted for his face, talons outstretched. Something smashed into his side pushing him sideways, an explosion of feathers an instant later threw both he and Ben into the nets flanking the walkway.

The boys hit with such force a support cable snapped somewhere in the rafters. They rebounded from the net, catapulted into the rock façade on the other side of the walkway before crashing to the ground. Ben on his knees was holding the right side of his face, sandy hair stained red with blood, trickled in sickly scarlet tendrils through clenched fingers. Ben was moaning slightly rocking back and forth. Damian Fontane walked close, shock and awe plain on his face.

"What the hell, you two are a couple of freaks! Look what your acrobatics get you now; you're both all fucked up."

Nycolos was fine, he'd checked as Rosa taught him; more importantly he knew the bleeding on Ben's face had nothing to do with their fall. Watts wasted no time, stepping into a roundhouse he kicked the side of Ben's head with a sickening thud, and sent the ten-year old to the ground unconscious. Nyc stared in horror.

The birds in the conservatory went beserk, flying into netting, crashing into windows, screams deafening the humans standing in the refracted light. Nycolos rolled onto his back just in time for Damian to step on his chest, a glint of triumph dancing in his eyes. Destined to failure, self-imposed mediocrity and ignorance Damian Fontane and Jacob Watts once again suffered a defeat they didn't see coming, at the hands of magic.

****

The woman from Hawk Mountain stepped from behind a bush that was much too small to have hidden her body. She wore the same red skirt she had worn that fateful day, with vertical bands that ended in little inverted arrows at the hem. The menace in her gaze struck the bullies dumb. Her face was tight, gone was the soft air she had coddled him with after his father's death. She stepped with evil intent, no hint of anger marred her sculpted features, instead her visage was steely with a determination that spoke of death.

Regarding the four boys she placed her right hand on her generous bosom, red cotton pulled tight, she stroked down her solar-plexus toward the ground speaking quietly to herself. Nycolos felt a distinct thrum in his chest, like something huge had just fallen somewhere, a tree in the woods. A vibration that came from nowhere and everywhere. A strange and horrible smell flushed outward from the woman, a particulate storm full of spores and seeds, moving bushes and the net nearby.

The birds in the conservatory went berserk yet again. Flying into each other, windows and the netting. Chaos erupted like an uncorked champagne bottle. Calls and squawks echoed through the space, a deafening din so profound Nycolos couldn't hear a thing.

His head felt light, dizziness gripped him, and he fought to stay conscious for all he was worth, if he lost consciousness all was lost. Damian Fontane and Jacob Watts were impacted by the stench, swaying in place, eyes glazing over; they seemed to have become befuddled in some manner. Damian looked around, concern marking his face, alarm replaced stupor and the bully walked right into Jacob Watts who had remained in one spot scratching his head.

"Watch out, you fool," Damian shoved Jacob. "What's going on? I feel like we were doing something."

"I know... that lady." Jacob was scratching his head harder.

"Whatever. Let's go find those two freaks and beat them before the buses leave." He grabbed Jacob by the sleeve, Nyc watched the bullies leave the way they entered.

The woman turned her attention to Nycolos; he was scared for Ben more than himself. Stepping over the bushes that separated her from the walkway, her dark hair was lustrous and swayed forward to cover her eyes, which he realized were glowing amber.

"It's time, little one." No rage, she was merely matter of fact about it.

Backpedaling, Nyc tried not cry. "Time for what?"

"To go visit your father."

Nycolos froze, could she, or was this her sick way of messing with him.

"Where is he?" Anger began bubbling in his chest.

"He is not as far away as you think, little one, but very difficult to reach." She flexed a long-fingered hand, admiring her sharpened fingernails.

"I don't want to die." He didn't know why he said it but the words just popped out.

"It is going to happen sooner or later; I think sooner will be better." She opened the same hand, flexing again this time, she gestured toward the ground like she was opening a fan and her hand burst with plumage of white feathers topped with red streaks, they were red-tail hawk talons.

"I can sing for you like last time, that way it won't hurt." Pain exploded in Nyc's head, sending him to his knees.

Ben stirred, he rose to his feet and stood struggling to focus with his one good eye, squinting at the woman that had been a hawk a moment before. The lady in red, bringer of death, with a hand of razor-sharp talons ready to rip out their throats. Ben was still clearing the cobwebs from his brain after the viscous kick. The hawk-woman turned slightly and raised her transformed hand above her head, amber eyes hard with the already made decision.

Nycolos Arcadia felt fear melt away, replaced by resolve and anger to keep this woman or whatever she was away from Ben. He felt a thrum again, deep in his chest, this time he felt the vibration emanating from the ground beneath his feet.

Something snapped in his gut, similar to butterflies in his stomach before a soccer game; he felt like an entire bird was trapped there. He screamed, for his life, his friend's life, and he screamed for all the madness bottled up inside. He screamed for his father's betrayal, his mother's anger, the woman that wanted him dead. The woman looked over her shoulder in horror, mouth agape a threat dead on her lips.

The scream rooted in Nyc's entrails, reaching downward through his legs, awareness traveling downwards from his chest, gut, and down his legs to the earth. His awareness touched the earth, the scream was no longer his.

His mouth was a conduit, something deep emanated from his vocal chords increasing in active and decibel strength, a final thrum vibrated under the soles of his shoes traveling up from the earth, through his mouth and exploded into the conservatory. A shock-wave slammed into the woman in the red-dress, knocking her from her feet. She flew through the air into the mesh net which broke free completely from the roof supports with more loud twanging and popping sounds. The netting fell atop the prone woman.

The windows of the conservatory vibrated and shattered. Not one at a time, not a crack here a crack there, every window of the conservatory exploded outwards simultaneously as Nyc's earthy scream crescendoed into frequencies beyond human hearing. The invisible hand gripping his gut disappeared, like an octopus tendril retreating back into the earth. Nycolos staggered as it left him, fell to his knees for a moment before rushing to Ben. His friend was on the ground laying on his belly, holding his ears. Nyc rolled him over and saw the gash down Ben's face left by the hawk's talon. The wound was deep, running from his cheek up to his eyebrow. Nyc shook him a little till he opened his good eye.

"We need to go now." The space was quiet, many birds had fled through open windows or fallen dazed to the ground from the awful sonic blast. The only sound was the tinkling of falling glass, accented by the occasional large pane crashing to the ground. He dragged Ben dumbfounded to the atrium entrance and beyond. Outside the autumn sky had grown overcast, full of slate gray swirling clouds. The entire Zoo was complete pandemonium.

Glass windows were blown out of the buildings closest to the conservatory, exotic birds or otherwise moved through the food court appearing and disappearing behind wrought-iron tables and chairs, bright colors drawing the eye as they flitted amidst the tables. The animals in every building were going berserk. Some starlings native to the region, swirled en masse performing an aerial ballet as graceful as mesmerizing. Two different clouds of the black birds collided, crashing into each other, starlings fell to the courtyard's cobbled ground and manicured landscaped planters, most still flapping.

Nyc walked a half-blind Ben toward the Zoo entrance, clear on the far side of the zoo grounds, the conservatory was the exhibit situated farthest from the entrance, how convenient Nyc mused. They still had a two-hour bus ride back to New Hamlet, a grave situation indeed. At least Ben wasn't leaking blood from his ruined face. The bleeding had stopped for the most part, Ben's eye was swollen shut and had only just removed his hands from his ears.

"Are you O.K?" The question was stupid, Nyc knew it was, but he didn't know what else to say and he needed to hear Ben's voice. Ben gestured to his ears and shook his head no, so he couldn't hear. Nyc's heart sank, he had defended and perhaps blinded his best friend in a matter of seconds.

They used hunting signals worked out ages ago to slowly make their way from the war zone. Nycolos walked in front, Ben just behind, within arm's reach. The mayhem was all encompassing, glass shards crunched under the mad footfalls of panicked zoo-goers, panicked zoo-keepers; the latter trying to keep patrons from hurting themselves or animals in their mass exodus from the zoo.

Most of the smaller monkeys had escaped their glass walled enclosures; they showed up in the courtyard together with hyenas. A pack of hyenas strolled across the plaza grinning, brown and black hackles raised, strings of saliva stretched long from the corners of feral mouths. The screaming grew louder when some fleeing ladies saw the hyenas start to circle up around a zoo-keeper that had been shooing them away. The other hyenas occupied themselves snapping up starlings and tropical birds that were too slow or shocked to vacate the premises.

Feathers and fur, flying in all directions. More birds than he could count or possibly hope to recognize flitted to and fro. Serpents slithered across grass and cobble. Writhing walkways prompted more screams from the last of the escaping guests. Clickity-clack, crunch and crack, insect swarms ejected from some display somewhere buzzed through the air. Swooping birds, foreign and domestic were suddenly dive-bombing through gray clouds of buzzing insectidae.

Nycolos was sure most of the people had been evacuated from the Zoo. The only screams he heard were in the distance, and fading toward the main entrance. The only person left near them was dead. The Zoo keeper taken down by the mayhem lie prone on the cobbles. Nyc could barely make out the body, a slightly plump woman, apparently in her fifties was face up on the cobbles.

A large group of hyenas yelping and jostling over her abdomen. Nycolos was grateful he was too far away to see or hear anything clearly. Small monkeys jumped through the trees, scampered across rooftops and chased squirrels from trashcans. A few squirrels chattered angrily but lost ground, gobbled as morsels by hungry hyenas, or tossed out of trees by monkeys already occupying the heights.

Elephants trumpeting in the distance, the ground shook as some commotion disturbed the earth. An uprooted tree came soaring over the top of the elephant enclosure some 100 meters distant, and Nyc saw a zoo-keeper go down under the massive tree trunk with a scream. The ground shook mightily, quaking underfoot. The little old lady the keeper had been helping was thrown to the ground by the force of the impact, but was up and running again in seconds; Nyc could hear her screaming even from that distance. The zoo keeper didn't rise again. Now they were surely alone.

The hyenas and monkeys in the square stopped in place, destructive activities momentarily suspended. Ears twitched, hackles rose, hyenas laughed, monkeys screamed. Nycolos realized he and Ben had remained stationary behind a planter for too long, the animals focused their yellow and brown eyes on the boys, beginning to stalk. The hyenas spread out, looking to surround the boys, the monkeys approached through trees and atop parasols that shaded wrought-iron tables of the food-court. The monkeys threw sticks, feces and whatever else was on hand. The boys were cornered, bat house behind them, dark as a cave, a lone red light flickering somewhere inside. The hyenas and monkeys were between the boys and the exit, sharp teeth, and blood lust an effective roadblock to their escape.

Nycolos backed them up to the bat house. The entrance was a well-done fiberglass replica of a cave. All grays and blacks the seams and creases had been sculpted to perfection. Stalactites, dropping water and cool moist air most convincing. Maybe they could move from exhibit to exhibit, hiding inside each in turn. The futility of this idea was apparent as they scurried backwards toward the entrance of the bat-house.

The glass windows were blown out on both sides of the atrium entrance, the building would provide no shelter, just a dark cave with a flickering red light in the back and the squeaking of bats swooping through the darkness. The bat-house would only serve as a nightmarish dead end where hyenas would corner them and rip out their throats.

Nyc skirted the entrance, keeping the half-blind Ben behind him, ignoring the shivers that crawled up his spine and the companion thought that someone was walking on over his grave. Today of all days the saying rang a little too true. The boys hugged the side of the building, inching toward the end of the wall where they would be forced to run next to a chain link fence for 30 meters to the next exhibit, North American Canids and rodents. A hyena jumped atop a planter off to their right.

The animal was frothing, drool dripping from the corners of its mouth. The animal gnashed teeth, yelping that sounded distinctly like a laugh, a course smokers laugh, a cough as much as chuckle.

Monkey faces appeared through the juniper bushes, a rock exploded on the wall just behind Ben. Ben couldn't see out of his right eye, Nyc's friend was barely hanging on. Nyc needed to get Ben out ASAP. An orange lunch tray whipped through the air barely missing Nyc. Sticks followed and Nyc accelerated to a run, pulling a stumbling Ben behind. Moving into an open space his stomach dropped , three hyenas lifted their heads from a feast of Zoo-keeper.

The woman's stomach was gone already, left only the stained cobbles, crimson with leavings of liver, lungs, stomach, and entrails. Nyc was sure it was the zoo keeper the hyenas took down.

Leaving the feast of entrails, the hyenas approached menacingly, blood soaked muzzles shooting spittle with each yelp. Benjamin Miller and Nycolos Arcadia ran half the length of the chain-link fence but found themselves unable to proceed or retreat. The hyenas and monkeys hemmed them in yelping with excitement, the sangrient moment of truth imminent. The doors of the bat-house vibrated, setting the large bat shaped totem pole rocking to and fro, the doors opened and closed, banging fitfully.

Bats began pouring from the entrance, a few bats at first erupting as black leathery missiles from the cave opening, became a giant circling bait-ball of fur and leather darkening the sky with undulating chaos. The bats hit the hyenas and monkeys like a wave crashing against the rocks. Monkeys flipped into the air, jumping and grabbing at the cloud of squeaking rodents. Rabid hyenas nipped and yipped, likewise jumping into the air grabbing bats and swallowing them whole. A few monkeys were quick enough to grab a bat or two, but the bats were so numerous it made little difference. In the resulting melee monkeys fell from trees flailing, ran into each other, trees, and brick walls. The hyenas spun in circles, some fled immediately. One large male snapped at a passing bat but missed and careened into another male. The two males began fighting while a third ran into the courtyard frantic and frenzied biting at empty air.

Nycolos seized the moment and sprinted the rest of the rest of the distance to the next exhibit, pulling the still stupefied Benjamin in his wake. The North American Canids and rodent exhibit entrance was also decorated with two large totem poles. The two large poles were the corner support beams of the atrium entrance. The windows were blown out of this exhibit as well, the doors on one side of the atrium laying on the ground.

The loudspeakers atop the building blared to life sounding garbled but intelligible enough to decipher a voice asking all patrons to please exit the zoo in an orderly fashion. Nycolos paid no heed to the errant white noise, anyone with enough sense to still be alive in the madness would know getting out was the only way to stay that way.

Nyc took stock. He and Bend stood in front of the North American exhibit The courtyard was chaos of escaped birds, bats and hyenas still snapping at the air ineffectively. The monkeys had fled, the deepening gloom of the approaching night made it that much more difficult to see the mass of bats whirling through the air, or monkeys moving to the trees. Cutting through the courtyard was unwise to say the least, too many sharp teeth and raining twigs that could hurt them more than they already were. Continuing along the perimeter they would have to pass the penguins, bears and lions. The penguin exhibit had miraculously remained unbroken; finished a few years earlier the exhibit was plagued by leaks and problems.

The most recent work introduced plexi-glass, strong enough to withstand the banshee howl.

Nyc's head whipped around at the sound of a rasping laugh. The largest male hyena moved onto the footpath from the courtyard closest to the boys. The animal was covered in blood, open wounds dripping blood onto the cobbles that lined the courtyard. The victor of the engagement the hyena limped forward a few steps to claim his spoils. The boys backed into the atrium of the canine exhibit, crunching glass underfoot, trampling over the blown out door.

Nycolos desperately wished he could summon the strange abilities at will. Benjamin still in his stupor stopped at the building wall and put his back against it.

Nyc's resolve coalesced into action, his mind grown accustomed to the jogo of the roda, playing capoiera with his family, he could see the hyena's rear leg was severely damaged. If he and Ben could take out that leg they should be able to outrun the beast. He put his back against the stucco wall of the exhibit. The grainy surface felt rough under his fingers, he could feel Ben shaking on his right.

"You always get us into such crap." The first coherent thing his friend had said in the last twenty minutes, maybe his wits were no longer addled, at least his hearing seemed to be returning.

"You can hear again!" Nyc tried not to get too excited.

"Yeah, but it sounds like you're really far away."

Backs against the wall Nyc explained the plan in a staccato whisper, that became a yell out of necessity for his deaf friend, he only hoped these hyenas didn't understand English. What a strange thought. Speckled black and brown hackles stood on end, the hyena was a mere 3 meters from them it stank of death and putrescence.

The plan was simple enough and involved throwing rocks and some running, the boys did not have a chance to act however. A white streak shot from the North American exhibit and Nycolos watched razor sharp fangs tear through the wounded hyena's neck. The beast fell to the cobble, throat turned to dyke, running red with the blood of the slain menace. A white wolf stood just beyond the flailing carcass, as synapses fired for the last time, muscles spasming with random contractions.

The wolf sat on her haunches, uninterested in the death throes at her feet. High above Nycolos heard the cry of a red-tail hawk. She was alive; he imagined that she sounded furious. He wondered if she sent the hyenas on him when she failed in the conservatory. Then what of the bats? Had they been a stroke of luck or something more? Nycolos addressed the wolf with his eyes, gauging her intent. Was this she-wolf one of them or was she just a wolf? She sat with her long pink tongue lolling out the side of her mouth, panting with golden eyes regarding the boys with evident disinterest.

Nyc pulled on Ben's sleeve, if they were going to get out now was the time. They hadn't taken more than a step before a voice spoke.

"You have done well to survive this long, little one, but you will make it no further."

Nycolos stopped scanning the still green Privet hedge for approaching threats. The white wolf sat still, looking at the boys as yet uninterested. Ben walked into his back and grunted.

"If we're gonna go, let's go!" Ben's anxiety was recovering as well.

"You didn't hear that" Nyc yelled.

"Hear what, in case you haven't noticed, I'm half deaf and blind over here Nyc, I've been hearing ringing in my ears for the last hour but did I say anything? Noooo." Ben looked at the wolf with his one good eye, towards the courtyard where deranged bats harrowed monkeys to no end.

"So now the wolf is talking to you?" Ben was recovering nicely Nyc decided, except maybe for the fact twenty minutes had passed and not the hour Ben seemed to think.

"C'mon, Nyc, which one of us got kicked in the head after all?" A red fox trotted from the Canine exhibit. Red fur was thick and bright like the changing leaves of autumn. Brown socks matched the brown tips of pointed ears and bushy tail.

The fox walked lightly on padded feet like he was tiptoeing, pointed nose flanked by bushy whiskers sniffing the air.

"No Ben, I think it's the fox."

"Great." The lack of skepticism was startling to Nyc.

The red fox sat right in front of the two boys, white wolf joining her orange-red companion. A blue haze surrounded the fox and extended outward toward Ben, eventually enveloping him.

"Your friend has a concussion and a serious laceration on his face," the fox voice a melody in Nyc's head, reminding him of wind chimes tinkling on his porch, "I will heal the concussion and laceration, but he will have a scar." The hazy smoke coalesced, becoming a dark blue that was opaque, glowing from within. The color lightened little by little until the haze was gone.

Ben sighed, exhaling a deep breath and rubbed his head.

"That feels better. Man, did my head hurt," he turned to Nyc. "The Fox?"

Nycolos Arcadia nodded in the affirmative.

Benjamin Miller was down on his knees in a second, face to face with the magical creature. "Thank you, Mr. Fox." There was nothing but sincerity in his words.

"We must be on our way, though the entrance is not far, I suspect we will encounter considerable opposition to your exiting this hellish place alive." A very distinct tone of disgust entered the voice. "You will not survive without my assistance." The finality of the statement was unquestionable.

"O.K., let's do this!" Ben's confidence sounded forced, but it seemed he could hear the fox too.

The fox trotted around the boys, taking up the lead. The white wolf took up the rear. The quartet moved from the entrance of the North American exhibit, following the slow curve of the cobbled walk. Nycolos and Ben walked shoulder to shoulder bumping into each other in an effort to stay close.

The sun had nearly set and the sky grew darker as blue spilled from the eastern horizon. A cold breeze blew, ruffling the boy's hair and cutting through clothes. A trumpeting sounded from their left. Red brick walkway mixed with cobble as the group reached an intersection.

The red brick pathway wound away to the east toward the performance amphitheater where the zookeepers, dressed in shades of brown and green wowed audiences with animal tricks. That day, at the particular moment when all hell broke loose the elephants had been giving their last show before the zoo closed. Two adult females and one of their young charged down the red brick walkway toward the two canids and two boys, trumpeting loudly and obviously enraged. The elephant's heads bobbed up and down with each step, ivory tusks leading the charge, aimed low to the ground. The smaller elephant, unable to keep up with the larger females trumpeted his mother's triumph as she bore down on the minute humans.

The older elephants must've been left in the pen, Nyc thought, while the more manageable females and young were taken to the show pavilion. Tons of elephant flesh shook the earth, knocking statues into bushes. Down went Dionysus, down went the Three Sisters, a stone bust of Diana crashed to the cobbles, arms holding her bow survived the fall, but her quiver chipped and broke off. The fox flicked his bushy tail and the white wolf flashed past the boys, blazing white fire like the heart of a star. The wolf bounded through the air, jumping atop the largest elephant on her way to the baby.

With an explosive leap the wolf head butted the right side of the small elephant. In the blink of an eye the beast was blown off the red brick path, crushing a wooden park bench before leveling the bamboo fence that paralleled the brick walkway.

The two larger elephants stopped abruptly, massive gray hides twitching furiously. Nycolos could see eyes illuminated by a red light from within. Freckled trunks extended toward the boys, giant ears twitched furiously and the elephants were panting, contaminating the air with their foul exhalations. The monstrous wall of flesh towering over the two boys and the fox wavered, the mother turned her baby, just picking itself up from the remains of the crushed fence. The wolf stood facing the mother elephant. Snarling with raised hackles the flame blazed around the wolf like a comet.

Red light flickered in the obsidian depths of ancient elephant eyes, something happened inside the angry animal, rage battled with instinct. She turned to the boys again, bearing down, head ready to crush them, one foot raised to crush the fox and be on her way. The fox flicked his tail, sending the mother and her companion into convulsions of trumpeting and stomping. Nyc was sure he and Ben would die, squashed pre-teens, flattened like pancakes beneath the weight of the awesome juggernauts.

The red light flared bright in the elephant eyes, just for a second, then went out completely. The elephants turned to the wolf and charged.

"She will handle them for now, we must keep moving." The fox spoke in his head again, and Nyc didn't argue. He assumed "she" meant the wolf. His brain was beyond comprehending the impossibility of what was happening in this animal prison.

But the animals were pissed, and with him specifically. He knew he shouldn't have come on this trip. He hadn't realized he was speaking aloud until Ben answered him.

"A little late for that now. Let's just see if we can get out of here."

The group of two humans following one red fox moved away from the wolf and her battle, they continued along the perimeter of the large central plaza. The penguin exhibit was sculpted to look like crashing waves, with a tiled mosaic mural running just under the roof along the length of the building, artfully rendering scenes of brain coral, fire coral and reef life in vibrant hues of blues, oranges, greens and reds. Beneath this mosaic a long Plexiglas window ran the length of the structure and penguins were swimming in rapid curving arcs. The window was cracked in several places but no leaks were apparent. The fox glanced over his shoulder gauging something about the two boys.

They trotted past an entrance which was flanked by two sculpted emperor penguins easily 2 meters high. The fox paused, looking back towards the enraged elephants. The battle sounded ferocious. The glow of the white light was apparent even around the corner as they were. The gathering dusk, the witching hour if you will, was pierced by white light, casting wildly flickering shadows as the wolf moved somewhere out of sight. Nycolos could hear stone shattering and wood splintering.

An uprooted pear tree flew tumbling end over end, down the trail, branches cracking, bole snapping as leaves abandoned limbs in a shower of green, yellow and red leaves.

The white wolf appeared at the edge of the bamboo fence, balanced atop the narrow bamboo poles. She exchanged a long glance with the fox before disappearing again, the sounds of battle never resuming to the sound of trumpeting elephants.

"She tells me there is another elephant coming, a large male that escaped his bonds at the amphitheater. We must hurry lest..." a loud bang interrupted his relation and the three of them turned to see a bloody cloud in the blue water behind the plexiglass window. A small penguin body floated toward the surface, seemingly lifeless, immediately followed by another loud bang, like someone bouncing a ball off of glass. Another bloody cloud and another lifeless penguin. The fox growled deep in his throat.

"She has help apparently and they have gone too far." Nycolos was about to ask if the she he was referring to could be the same red-tail hawk that was circling high in the darkening sky above, but he never had the chance. A third thunk of penguin skull against the glass and water exploded around them. Ben, closest to the wall lost his footing and was swept into Nyc, who was in turn blasted off the path and underwater in an instant.

As quickly as it happened the water surrounding the two boys stopped moving and became thick like gelatin, slowly expanding to encase them in a pocket of air. Once the two boys were completely enveloped by the air pocket it zipped sideways and enveloped the fox.

The trio waited a few moments as millions of gallons drained from the fractured penguin tank, leaving suddenly awkward penguins slip sliding down flooded walkways. As the water subsided the fox lead the boys toward the center of the plaza where a few penguins flapped in the courtyard, riding the wave as far as they could.

From their vantage they saw the white wolf way down the red brick path that ran toward the performance amphitheater. The wolf was engaging three large elephants. The tables had turned and the white wolf was a blurred streak, it was all she could do to not get trampled. Bouncing off the large male she started jumping from elephant to elephant, smashing into the flank of each animal with that same explosive blast.

The white wolf was a blur of movement, inciting the ire of the larger male who trumpeted threateningly, stumbling a few steps when the she wolf smashed into his side. She stopped atop one of the females, just long enough for the male to charge. She was gone from the elephants and running toward the boys by the time the male crashed into the female with a sick thud of flesh on flesh. Her white flames extinguished as she drew close, where she sat on her haunches next to Ben, panting. The blond boy petted the wolf absently, and Nyc was surprised to see the wolf incline her head in pleasure.

"We have one more obstacle, children, and I think we may be free of this hell." The expressive tail flicked again, sending the white wolf trotting towards the entrance. As she approached the entrance walkway she passed between the cat and bear exhibits. Nycolos expected anything at that point, Bears swinging over the top of the barrier wall, or cats descending on them with claws of fire. But nothing happened, the wolf walked out of the zoo without incident.

"It would appear we may have been given a hand as well." The fox spoke as if to himself and Nyc wondered if he meant for Nyc to overhear these thoughts. The trio walked from the chaos of the zoo to the chaos of the parking lot. Dozens of zoo keepers ran among the groups of children and adults. They administered first aid where necessary, and yelled to each other in loud voices that carried on the autumn wind. The fox and wolf hung back, away from the mass of humanity, wounds, trauma and all. The vice-principal of their school found them almost immediately. She, like all the other people that saw them emerge from the zoo stared in obvious surprise. By the time the boys looked back the fox and wolf were gone.

Chapter 9

Malicia

Clutched close to her chest
Clothed and couched in fur and fern.
Pachamama planted on provenance of Pangea
Providencial progeny to pastor her flocks.
Stewards and shepherds both.

School was canceled the following day, no surprise for students or faculty, though not the next. All that had been on the trip were greatly subdued. Kids scurried to class, eyes wide like saucers and once seated whispered through classes. Teachers organized papers on their desks failing to respond with teacher-like authority, thoughts cast back to the previous day's chaos of screaming students, bloody carcasses, animal savagery. The classrooms fell quiet eventually, painfully so. Teachers and students alike tried make extra noise. Their art teacher put on Christmas carols and handed out chocolates while they made clay tiles as Christmas presents for their families.

Thanksgiving recess was only a few days distant and the entire school seemed to be on autopilot, students went through the motions, the teachers more so. The teacher's lounge was almost as loud as the cafeteria that week, boys and girls, young and old retold ferocious moments when it seemed animals would kill them all. Wearing humor as armor students feigned bravery, masking fear with shields of bravado. The same fear that would wake some for years, hearing again and again the banshee scream that deafened nearly everyone in the zoo, and broken every glass on the buses, and even the glasses on people's faces. The madness made all the local broadcasts and even the national news. Reporters droned of crazed animals running loose, deaths of animal and man, a mysterious noise breaking everything, deafening many people, great fodder for nightly news.

Oil shortages, global war, the immigration problem were secondary to the madness of the zoo, according to the press. The local authorities were looking into the occurrence as a suspicious incident. The school made an announcement in the form of a message on the local public radio station and in the paper. A parent/teacher general meeting was to be held in an effort to assuage concerned parents, horrified to think something like this could happen.

When the yellow bus pulled into the school parking lot that night, looking like it had driven through the worst neighborhood of crowbar-wielding hoodlums, everyone on the bus was cold to the bone. Once the bus started rolling the chill got worse. The wind whipped through the windows the entire ride back, sucking the warmth and any remaining fight right out of them.

Rosa took the boys to Abby's. The mothers were so concerned they nearly stripped the boys naked right in the living room. Once they ascertained the boys were indeed whole, the interrogation began. That is, after Abby cried over Ben's face.

The scar was red and ugly, looking newly healed.

Far better than what it had looked like, Nyc thought. *Abby would've been inconsolable had she seen the blood.*

The boys answered honestly as often as they could, but edited with great liberty, out of necessity obviously. The racist kids and attacking hawk were in, best to explain Ben's face; talking animals and new friend, out. Ultimately both mothers returned to Ben's face. The cut ran up his right cheek in a single deep slice, three small lacerations radiating outward from his eyebrow like rays of the sun drawn on his face. The mothers cried together, redressing the bandage the paramedics had put in place while the boys sat in an ambulance, getting their wounds checked, staring in vain at the zoo entrance, hoping their new friends would appear again. Nycolos had known they would not, they never showed themselves to "normal" people, although it seemed mistakes were made, the nightmare at the zoo being one.

As a consequence Nycolos Arcadia and Benjamin Miller were the most animated students in school that day, the most animated people period. An odd fact should anyone have been observing the boy's behavior. They were not jumpy like everyone else.

They spoke excitedly with shining eyes and flailing arms. The only other children that seemed unaffected by the madness were Jacob Watts and Damian Fontane. The exposed underbellies of peers and teachers alike emboldened the two bullies and they spent the day poking fun at the weak. They thrived in an environment of fear, and it permeated the hallways of New Hamlet Elementary that week. Like all predators once they smelled fear and weakness they were out for blood.

It was just after lunch when they caught scrawny Sean Colby in the bathroom. A fellow trailer-park resident. they recognized each other on sight. The scrawny white kid was spindly with sharp elbows and bony knees. He walked through life with a look of perpetual surprise, even more fixed since the zoo. Sean was one of the few kids that was able to get the smell of the trailer park off his clothes on account of the fact that his mother worked at a dry cleaners in town and was diligent about dry cleaning all of their clothing. Evelyn Colby wore a startled expression similar to that of her son, perpetually surprised she ended up in a hole in the ground trailer park and employed at a dry-cleaners.

Sean Colby had felt the knuckles of Damian Fontane and Jacob Watts before. The other kids in the trailer park didn't like him very much. He wasn't into stickball, baseball, or catching bugs down by the creek. Instead he liked to read his comic books and draw. His wide-open-all-the-time eyes captured beauty adeptly, skeletal fingers brought a blank page alive with sublime dexterity. Down deep. Sean thought maybe they all hated him because he smelled different.

Damian Fontane and Jacob Watts beat on him sometimes, although Jacob had admitted to Damian several times it wasn't fun, saying, "He always looks scared anyway, and he doesn't cry or fight back, he just lets us beat him, then gets up and walks away."

That lunch hour as Sean Colby moved through the bathroom door, greasy-haired Damian Fontane and dirty-nailed Jacob Watts stepped in behind him and shut the door. They decided during lunch Sean would be good pickings, he was more distracted than usual, spilling his first lunch tray as soon as he left the lunch line, walking into one of the dozen trashcans that were situated around the cafeteria. He was so distracted he sat at a table with some other trailer parkers, and didn't notice Damian and Jacob making plans at the other end.

The bullies cornered the twitchy kid in the bathroom. They made little noise and with no preamble they beat Sean Colby half unconscious. Minutes later the janitor walked in on the two boys torturing a spluttering Sean Colby. Damian shoved his head repeatedly into one of the toilets screaming, "You still smell better than us? Huh? Who smells like shit now?" Jacob Watts the lumbering oaf was cheering on Damian whose face was contorted in rage, a large vein bulbous on his neck. The two bullies were suspended immediately for an undetermined period of time. Nycolos and Benjamin happened on the scene a few moments after the Vice-Principal had escorted the bullies from the bathroom. Damian Fontane smiled at Nycolos and mouthed, "You're next," as he was led away.

Neither Ben nor Nycolos took the threat seriously, a mistake that would ultimately prove costly. Their minds were otherwise occupied with the dangers they had escaped and the magic they had seen. Since sharing the whole truth with Ben, Nycolos felt a profound relief that strengthened their friendship, if that was possible. They talked about what sort of powers they had seen, the falcon's stoop that had nearly cost

Ben his eye, but had endowed him with a badge of honor even the bullies had blanched at when they first saw it. The female teachers however doted on Ben incessantly.

Ben was eager for Nycolos to relive the moments between the kick in the head and the appearance of the fog. The fog was of course what he called the time he had lost in a fog of incoherent colors and sounds. At one point Ben admitted to him. "It's better you didn't tell me the whole story before that night on the Mount, if you had I probably wouldn't have believed you, I would've blamed your stories on your dad's disappearance."

****

Their classes blended into snippets of stolen conversation and hypotheticals. The real day existing between classes and tardy bells. When at last the bell rang for dismissal the two friends continued to wax poetic about all the strange events that were occurring. They stood under a big red maple, mostly bare limbs coated with a thin layer of damp snow. The first snowfall had come to the previous night, covering limbs with fresh snow. They talked for a few minutes before the realization dawned on them that Abby was down at the bookstore, and Rosa was harvesting ducks, chickens, turkeys, gourds and goodness knew how many other goodies from the orchards. Thanksgiving was a few days away and the store was usually sold out weeks in advance. Nycolos had helped that morning before school, riding Mirage through the orchard picking any fruits he could reach from the saddle.

He wasn't big on killing the poultry though he did enjoy chasing and catching them. Rosa didn't like killing the fowl either, that had been Lyndon's job, but she had assumed the duty stoically, just as she had so many others. Nycolos hadn't told her what he had seen that morning in the last orchard, furthest from the house, planted with corn between the trees, left to feed the pheasant that inhabited that orchard.

The pheasants weren't easy to catch though they recognized horse and rider slipping through a hole in the hedgerow of currants and privet that closed behind them. His father used a shotgun sometimes, but Nyc usually used his bow like Ben. Rosa asked him to get five, as she had two orders to fill. He spent the better part of an hour trying to get a few roosters and hens, they waited patiently bursting from the hedgerow only when he was nearly atop them. He thought about his sling-shot but it was all the way back at the house and if he went back Rosa would tell him to forget it and take him to school. Nycolos stopped and thought a few moments, leaning on a Serviceberry tree with smooth gray bark and naked limbs, wishing he had practiced shooting arrows with his Dad as much as they had practiced capoiera.

He picked up a good rounded rock and whipped it at a rooster that blasted out of a corn row when he stepped near. The stone shot from his hand like out of a gun, a gust of wind pushing from his hand, flattening a section of the corn row. The stone flew true and the rooster fell, beautiful plumage of green, browns, purples and reds. Nycolos stood above the unconscious bird and looked at his small brown hands. What was happening to him? He placed the speckled beast in his basket on Mirages's rear flank, and tried in vain for another twenty minutes but was unsuccessful.

Rosa's whistle sounded faint when it cut through the morning air. If he could hear it all the way back here, that whistle would've hurt his ears if he was standing next to her. She must've realized it was time for school and wanted him back. Giving up he turned to gather Mirage and saw the dappled mare standing at the back gate. Being the last orchard the back gate opened into the back of the large meadow of goldenrods, barely fifteen meters from the woodline and the ravine that snaked through the forest. She flicked her tail and whipped her head. Her whinny sounded pleased. Nycolos reached her after cutting through three rows of corn and jumping over some mushroom logs.

Just on the inside of the fence lay four pheasants. Still alive but apparently complacent, one rooster and three hens lay still, crooning softly and when he bent to pick them up they didn't even move. Placing them in the baskets Nycolos leaned against the horse's neck. A shape stepped from behind a spruce tree in the shadows of the forest. It was Lyndon, he recognized his father's figure anywhere, even at this distance. He had two arms, the severed right arm was whole and lifted momentarily as if he were going to wave but thought better of it. The silhouette faded as his father moved further into the woods, stepped behind a large oak and was gone.

Nycolos wasted no time, he jumped to the second rung of the fence and leapt to Mirage's back without hesitating. He wrapped his left hand around the leather pommel and kicked the latch of the gate open with his right foot. He and Mirage shot through the morning as fast as thought, reaching the tree line before his father should've moved fifteen steps. But no one was there. The soil was bare of footprints, the man was gone.

****

"Well I guess we should walk home, otherwise we'll be here for hours waiting for the Moms." Ben said, referring to their mothers by his newest moniker, coined since incessant doting post-zoo incident. Nyc nodded absently, he and Ben had divulged the truth to their mothers. They had gotten away with the half-truth for a while, but ended up cracking under the penetrating two-pronged attack of both mothers. Abby's eyes grew wide like saucers, the blood draining from her face, causing her freckles to stand out in sharp contrast on her milky smooth high-boned cheeks. They had to get her to sit down for the rest of the story. Nycolos knew from the beginning Rosa wasn't buying their half truth, and of course he told her whatever they had left out when they finally went home at nearly midnight. She kept him up till 1 am when he let slip something happened on the Mount. She finally sent him to bed when he nodded off on the couch. Not before she extracted his promise that he would tell her everything when he got home from school.

The boys crossed the deserted street. Buses were gone and most parents had picked up their kids. The elderly lady crossing guard that was sweet as candy to the kids, but would cut parents to pieces with a razor sharp tongue, was gone too. Into the wooded trail they last walked what seemed an age ago. Only honeysuckle and buckthorn hung tenaciously to their leaves. Numerous golden leaves covered the earth, forest floor like a golden field topped with a dusting of snow. The boys shuffled booted feet through piles of leaves, rustling at their passing. The fire pit where they encountered Jacob and Damian stood empty, un-melted snow shone white and fresh atop the blackened and charred earth.

"Let's walk to the bookstore, your mom is probably really busy, we can get some pizza from Jr.'s next door. I want to look at some of the books about magic and stuff, the ones I have at home didn't seem to touch on what I was looking for." Ben looked to Nyc for confirmation, which he received as a nod.

Decision made, Nycolos Arcadia and Benjamin Miller took the low trail, the one that lead further down the valley towards the center of New Hamlet. Most days they took the high trail which lead up the slope to the top of the western ridge of the valley, there cutting through farmers fields and a few thickets they reached the foot of the Mount and their homes. The lower trail sloped downward gradually consisting mostly of scrub, buckthorn, honeysuckle, and leafless brambles of raspberry. The trail was narrow like a bike trail, thin blades of errant grass peeking through the dusting of snow. The path ran between the two-lane road and the ever higher slope as the moved toward the valley floor. The woods thinned to their left, allowing them to see the cars zipping by.The road curved away to the east designed by the first settlers years ago when wagon wheels were more common, the switch back across the width of the valley where the gradient was steepest.

Loggers cut the switch-back years ago, through the virgin forest of Maple, Beech and Oak centuries ago when the trees were so tall one could hardly see the leaves. The trail continued south down a craggy outcrop that dropped off quickly and required the boys to step carefully using hands on large limestone rocks, loose gravel slipping under their feet causing them to slide several feet at a time. The slope leveled out and the path widened into a section that got more use. Shagbark hickory flourished with thick straight boles. Bark in long plates peeling from the bole of the tree gave them the appearance of whittled sticks left discarded by the hands of a giant hobbyist. While they walked Ben expanded on the theories that he had developed so far. The underbrush was thin between the tall straight hickory boles, and they separated a little picking up and absentmindedly tossing what few hickory nuts the squirrels had not taken, at each other.

Ben's mind was running on overdrive, his mouth barely able to keep up. Usually he asserted, powers came out at the beginning of puberty around thirteen, or sometimes this could happen at the end of puberty around 18 to 25. Ben though it was extremely rare to have powers manifesting at ten, an in between age according to his theories. The scar around his right eye wrinkled and stretched with Ben's waxing and waning intensity. The scar tissue was still light pink on his freckled Caucasian complexion. Nycolos Arcadia had to admit his friend had a battle scar other kids would be envious of, but Nyc knew if it hadn't been for the red fox his friend would probably only have one eye.

The trail narrowed again as it skirted the edge of a small cemetery with faded tombstones of marble and Granite. Grass had grown tall around the stones, a large solitary willow clinging to leaves, long branches hanging like long green locks falling to the brown shoulders of the earth.

Ben connected the threads of his theories moving from nascent abilities to those appearing in times of extreme strain. The path flattened out grading into underbrush and thickets before ending in the curving cobble substrate of the Castle Creek. The creek was narrow where they broke through the rose thorns, booted soles stepping through pockets of water.

Leap frogging over white cobbles and boulders rounded by the water's touch over the course of millennia, the boys crossed to the other side. The creek curved away to the east, small riffles a result of the dry fall, widening into a flat shallow pool that arced away out of view as it jogged south toward the far side of New Hamlet.

They scrambled up the far slope entering an industrial area, comprised of storage spaces, a huge warehouse for some shipping company and an old junkyard decorated with barbed wire, chain-link fence and threatening signs. They walked down the driveway that ran between the warehouse and the storage place. Stepping over the railroad tracks that ran East-West, perpendicular to the driveway they cut left moving east once they reached the end of the driveway. Shadow pooled under the overpass that carried the cars descending into town. The industrial park smelled fetid and sour after the pleasantness of the wooded trail. Cars zoomed over the bridge momentarily drowning out conversation.

They didn't see the people under the bridge until they were almost on top of them. The people Nyc saw step away from the cement wall of the overpass were silhouettes until they stepped into the light. Nycolos barely suppressed a groan, Ben failed and groaned loudly, cursing at the end. Nyc noted his friend had become more liberal with his cursing of late. They did have many good reasons to swear lately, Damian Fontane and Jacob Watts stepped into the sunlight, cigarettes held in their childlike fingers.

"Well if it isn't the porch monkey and his trainer." Damian Fontane hadn't stopped walking, and drew closer with each step. Nycolos could see three other figures moving from the shadows, stepping into the light, illuminating their greasy hair and soiled jeans. Damian Fontane's two older brothers, ages 16 and 17, had decided to bring back the greaser look of the 50's, somehow the grease stuck to them a little too much. Johnny and Bobby Fontane were born a mere 13 months apart. Johnny the older of the two wore an old leather jacket like Damian's with zippers in more places than actual pockets.

Like Damian he was muscular and looked fit but carried an angry chip on his shoulder that repeatedly and incessantly enraged Johnny to the point of violence. Bobby Fontane was probably the least malicious of the Fontane boys, but did love a good fight. Shorter and stockier than the older Johnny, Bobby followed orders to the T and he was excellent muscle.

Nycolos turned his back to the approaching threat, " Let's try attack plan R." He spoke in a harsh whisper though it was unnecessary. The second he saw realization in Ben's eyes and his head nod yes, Nycolos took off running the way they had come as fast as his legs would carry him. The bullies exploded in shouts, hoots of joy, the chase had begun. He knew they had enough of a lead to pull off "plan R". Plan R was a bit of Brazilian capoiera malicia, or trickery, the essence of the game. Nycolos in the lead zoomed around the corner of the warehouse, only to feel Ben gaining on his right side, odd since he had always been a little faster than his friend.

"Drop your pack." Ben barked while running, Nyc realized the logic of the statement. Letting the straps slip from his arms, he left his friend in the dust. They reached the end of the driveway and split up. Nycolos dove left, hugging the warehouse wall stopping just out of sight of the driveway, Ben doing the same on the opposite side. The beauty of plan R was that R stood for run, the essential feint of plan R. Once the enemy was committed to the pursuit the prey turned the tables and attacked, by then it was often too late for the attackers.

They could hear the footsteps and Damian and Jacob hammering down the driveway, the echo of their footsteps bouncing back and forth off the metallic aluminum siding covering the buildings. Their footsteps slowed a little as they reached the halfway mark, passing the dumpster Nyc had thought about hiding in but had passed up as too vulnerable. He hoped they could make it to the end of the driveway so his plan could work, and it did, perfectly. The bullies plodded by Nycolos, visibly winded and slowing with each step. Nyc and Ben sprang their trap. Ben had discovered an aluminum garbage can lid somewhere, he slammed it into Damian Watt's shins as the older boy rumbled past the corner, sending Damian Watts face down on the asphalt screaming and clutching his shins. Nycolos took out Jacob's legs with a leg sweep that tripped the chubby boy similarly, sending his mass slamming into the asphalt like his co-conspirator. Both Nyc and Ben kicked their prey in the stomach, Ben's righteous retribution fueling his fire, kicked Damian in the head just as Damian had kicked him a few days previous.

"Let's go."

Both bullies lay on the ground, Damian was dazed and holding his head, Jacob wheezing, trying to find the air Nycolos had expelled from his stomach with the second kick.

"Hey,...what the...Bobby, Johnny, get over here!!!" Jacob Watt's older brother Joseph Watts had jogged over to partake in the beating or maybe just watch and was obviously surprised. A genuinely handsome boy, the twenty-year-old had his pick of the plot in the trailer park, but had long tired of the slim pickings there. His beauty was such that the more lonely women of town were perpetually saving him. From young twenty-something high-school teacher trying to save him with her young idealism and passionate lovemaking, to an elegant forty-something who sighed like a schoolgirl when he turned his gaze her way.

A little over six feet he appeared the dirtiest of all of them, dirt-darkened jeans, red and black plaid lumber-jack jacket. His long hair fell past his shoulders and into his face. The long silky hair framed a gorgeous face with a strong Italian nose, though his skin and hair spoke of Irish roots. His blue eyes were hidden by the tumbling mane, but the hair could not conceal the menace and anger they could sense in his voice.

"You little freaks, you're dead!!" The 20-year old was fast, even in boots, Nyc and Ben had little time to make a decision as the larger menace bore down on them. Lightning fast Nycolos pulled Ben towards the stream, ducking right to parallel the rear fence of the public storage buildings. They stumbled, feet catching in brambles, slipping off rocks, clumsy with panic and a fear that was justified. A large metal post marked the boundary between the public storage and junkyard fences. Nyc stopped and pointed upwards at the fence line.

"If we climb this fence here we can cross over into the junkyard." Ben nodded again and the boys scaled the fence in unison. Nycolos, closer to the tall corner post stood atop the fence balancing with the post, before stepping carefully between the razor wire that ran like a stretched spring atop the fence. He dropped lightly to the ground , Ben joining him seconds later. Ordinarily they would've complemented each other on navigating such an imposing obstacle as the razor wire with such elegant thinking, but time was short.

They split up without a word, looking for places to hide. Nycolos saw Ben Miller disappear behind a mound of metallic refuse. An old Cadillac stood on its front end curiously, apparently leaning on something out of sight. The blue hood and body was faded with time and rust, the canvass top peeling, no longer white but an ugly shade of gray. The front windshield a dirty brown was no longer transparent.

Old washers flanked one side of the Cadillac, stacked atop one another like a pyramid. The opposite side was not visible to Nyc, confident his friend had found a hiding place Nycolos bent his efforts to finding one of his own.

It took little time. Beyond a box-spring lacking fabric, another cluster of junk lay across the earth like it had been dropped from a great height and exploded in all directions on impact. A commercial size drier lay upside down among the toilet bowls, a VW bug, family caravans, old tractors, air conditioners, and such waste. The door to the drier was intact but the locking mechanism was busted, inside the space was large enough that he could hide out of sight, but see out the window.

"I saw them duck in here." A voice trailed though the air and Nycolos ducked behind a mound of rubble and scrambled into the drier. Backing into a shadow Nyc was unnerved. He knew the flaw of this hiding place was that it had only one exit, a no-no according to what he had been taught.

He scarcely made out the sound of the chain-link fence clanging as bodies pushed against it. He heard a loud thud and a storm of swearing, followed by laughter of two individuals and two more thuds, three people moved into the junkyard.

"You two fools stay there, we'll be back in a minute." Nycolos Arcadia wasn't sure whose voice he was hearing but the authority of the command made him think it was probably Joseph Watts. The cursing continued unabated, one of the two Fontane boys had severe diarrhea of the mouth. From his hiding spot Nyc could see Bobby Fontane limping a few steps, then stop and crouch down on one knee, holding his outstretched leg. A large rip in his right pant leg oozed blood, turning the top of an exposed sock red. Standing, he yelled at the other two boys who were still out of sight shifting through rubble by the sound of it. Their laughter erupted yet again, put-downs like dumb-ass, and idiot floating through the air, falling metallically to the piles of rubble.

Johnny exploded, running out of sight fist raised, face red, Nycolos feared for an instant they had discovered Ben. He was dissuaded of this notion when Johnny and Bobby came into view throwing punches, faces contorted in rage. Johnny the older brother was quicker and faster than Bobby. Bobby punched his older brother without effect, Johnny punched his little brother in the gut, doubling him over, then put a foot on his rear and kicked him, sending the stocky younger boy flying. Bobby stumbled forward and crashed face first onto the box spring. Through pure dumb-luck the sixteen-year old trailer park resident looked into the industrial sized drier as he picked himself up. The anger dissolved into a grin of triumph. In an instant he had the door open and dragged Nycolos Arcadia out by his pant legs. Nycolos fought against the rising panic that threatened to sap his strength and dull his wits, goodness knew he needed all he had at that moment.

Nycolos turned once he was clear of the drier. Bobby Fontane was screaming at his two partners in crime for help.

Nycolos crab walked with his hands until he was close enough to tangle his feet in Johnny's. He hooked his feet behind Johnny's heels and the boy fell backward hard, head bouncing off of the compacted soil. Nycolos stood quickly and stomped down on the gash in Bobby's leg before tearing off toward the fence on the opposite side of the junkyard. He hoped he could lure the bastards from the junkyard and give Ben Miller a chance to escape. Bobby screamed, clutching his leg, cries becoming sobs, the bully wept unabashedly, overwhelmed by pain.

Nycolos took half-dozen steps before a hand closed on his curly locks and pulled him backwards so hard his feet left the ground momentarily. His back slammed into the ground as Bobby's had a moment earlier.

"Looks like I caught me a nigger!" Joseph Watts' stale cigarette breath was nauseating, he grinned his perfect smile over his prey.

"Where's your nigger-loving friend?" When Nycolos didn't answer, Joseph Watts mimicked Nyc's attack and stomped down on his calf. Nycolos screamed, tears forming in the corners of his eyes, Ben was gone he said. Their plan was for Nyc to hide while the bullies searched for them and Ben went to get help. Not satisfied with the answer but limited in manpower Joseph quickly made a decision regarding the ass-beating at hand.

"Bobby, Johnny get over here, ...Damnit, Bobby, stop that sniveling and get over here." Joe kept his booted foot on Nyc's chest, pressing down with his considerable mass. Nycolos had not recovered his wind yet, and was unable to see the other two from his prone position. Bobby limped over, eyes hot with anger, spittle mingling with tears at the edge of his mouth.

"You little coon fucker, you're dead." Bobby stomped down on Nyc's leg again, sending pain shooting up his extremity, calf muscle was being crushed like a grape beneath boots. Johnny Fontane stood next to Joe and when Nyc rolled onto his side clutching the wounded calf, Johnny kicked him in the gut like he was kicking a fifty yard goal kick.

Lights exploded in Nyc's brain , speckles of light and dark migrating into his field of vision, the day seemed darker, he hadn't realized how late it was getting. Ben was still safe, and Nycolos Arcadia clung to that thought like a drowning sailor, the early winter afternoon growing colder by the second. Nyc's mind kicked into gear, he grasped at another desperate thought. Ben thought he might be developing some powers, evidenced by what Nyc like what he had done with the bees, on the Mount and at the zoo. Groping for clarity he sat up enough to clap his hands together with all his might. Nothing. Clawing through the dimness of his vision, he sat up and screamed, clapping his hands again with as much strength as he could muster. Nothing happened, no explosions of sound, no gusts of wind, no attacking trees. The three assailants looked at him for a few seconds, Joseph Watts stepped on his chest again, forcing Nyc back to the ground.

Breathing was hard, he felt like he was slipping down a greased pole into a bottomless pit of pain. Nyc looked up to see Johnny raising a metal pipe high above his head. Nyc raised his arms up to cover his face just in time. He felt something break in his arm and the dull thud of the metal pipe rebounding from bone. Pain was everywhere, his body was made of pain, all that was left was to embrace it, he did. The darkness crashed over him like a cresting wave, crushing him into the earth.

Benjamin Miller watched in horror, emotions a jumble in his chest and heart as the bullies beat his best friend. He sobbed in silence, he could see everything from his hiding place inside the hood of the upended Cadillac. The engine block had been removed and he had managed to crawl into the open space from behind. After rounding the pyrimid of washers he had moved under the caddy and found the entire undercarriage removed. He stacked some old appliances around himself, lay down peeking out of a crack that ran along the length of the hood.

He thought for an instant Nycolos might get away, but his stomach bottomed out when he saw how fast Joe Watts was.

Joe snatched Nyc so easily and threw him to the ground with such force Ben though his friend lost consciousness as soon as he hit the ground. The bullies were hooting and hollering over Nyc's unconscious form. The sound of Nyc's arm breaking had been like the snapping of a dry branch. His right forearm was bent unnaturally, Johnny Fontane and Joe Watts were laughing, slapping Bobby on the back, stomping on Nyc's chest between hollers.

Ben nearly gave himself away when Johnny Fontane pulled out the metal pole. He bit his lip until he tasted blood, but still blubbered and sniffled, loudly. Nyc was getting pummeled to save his hide and he knew it. If he were to go out there, even if he caught them by surprise the bullies were too big and strong for him to defeat them all. If the trailer trash hadn't been hooting and hollering about knocking Nyc out and breaking his arm they would've heard him for sure.

Joseph Watts patted both younger boys on the back and doled out orders to his lackeys.

"Go get those dumb asses and get them home. They both look pretty beat-up, but it's Damian that got his marbles rattled."

"And what are you gonna do?" Johnny Fontane didn't like taking orders from anyone but he seemed to have cooled a little after loosing his bile on the ten-year old brown boy.

"It's my turn to punish this here nigger, get the fuck out of here and keep your eyes peeled for that nigger-loving white kid. He's next, so check his mommy's store on the way home."

The Fontane brothers followed orders with alacrity, eyes widening momentarily before they scrambled to hop the fence. Only Bobby hesitated a little unsure in his decision, but was soon on the other side of the fence, footfalls pounding away from the junkyard. Their footsteps receded then disappeared. Joe Watts stood over the small boy's body. He rubbed his hands together excitedly looking over his shoulder and checking in all directions. His eyes became furtive and his perfect features deformed. Juxtaposed within this perfect specimen and prime example of poor white trash, darkness festered, pushing against the near perfect exterior and bubbling over as often as not.

Licking his lips Joseph Watts reached down and grabbed Nycolos by the belt and flipped the boy over. Pulling out a boot knife he cut through Nyc's belt, pulled it out and threw it in a pile of rubble. Ben froze in horror. What became evident was that Joe Watts had something perverse in mind for the unconscious brown boy face down in the dirt. A frog the size of a rock caught in Ben's throat and his heart hammered in his ears, this could not be happening, not to them. Muscles frozen, he lay on the ground trying to will himself to action. His brain was screaming at his body to do something.

Joe Watts yanked down Nyc's trousers and exposed his smooth brown prepubescent bottom to the cold afternoon air. The pedophile grabbed the little boy's bottom, flinty eyes shining with excitement, lips twitching unconsciously, he lusted for the ten-year old. Something snapped inside Benjamin Miller, and he vacated the mound of appliances and bolted from his hiding place beneath the Cadillac's undercarriage. Benjamin Miller picked up the same pipe Johnny Fontane used to break Nyc's arm and hurried toward his friend. He ran toward the pedophile bastard wielding the smooth metal like a baseball bat, ready to swing for the fences. He never got the chance, the rear window of the Junkyard office blew out, the biggest German Shepard Ben had ever seen jumped out of the window, enraged. Glass shards exploded outward glinting red in the rays of the dying sunlight.

Joe Watts still unhooking his own belt rolled off of Nyc's unconscious body. He ran towards the corner of the junkyard they had scaled to enter. The shepherd's fur was mostly black, brown only on the shoulders that bunched with each stride, muscles rippling as the enormous dog sped at them. Joe Watts ran past before Ben could set himself to swing and the opportunity was lost. The bounding dog bore down on Ben, but bounded past the boy without a second glance.

The beast closed the space in two strides, catching the pedophile at the fence. The dog was so big when it leaped its maw closed on the thigh of Joseph Watts as he tried to pull himself over the top of the fence. Watts screamed and beat the dog's face with his fist, slicing his arm deeply on the razor wire. The dog only released his lock jaw when Joe Watts thumbed it in the eye. Ben watched Joe topple from the top of the fence, and hit the ground hard, belt buckle still unfastened. The German Shepherd barked madly at the retreating villain.

Ben pulled up his friend's pants and rolled Nyc onto his back. Nyc's face showed little bruising beneath his complexion, his right arm was a sickly shade of purple below the elbow. Ben looked up when he heard a man's voice swearing.

"Damn dog, goin' crazy in the car like that, then bustin' out my window like that." A large white man with rosy cheeks, greasy coveralls, and a greasier cap reading Al's junkyard ambled into view. His white hair tumbled to his shoulders, and his jowels tembled with his expletives, ceasing momentarily as he stopped to check the window sill.

"What the...?" While inspecting the sill the large man had seen the bloody Nycolos Arcadia and his friend. The obese junkyard owner named Al hurried outside, ruddy cheeks gone pale. The tough as nails middle aged widower had a hard outer shell, but a soft gushy center, and the sight of the two children in such a bad way broke his heart into pieces.

Benjamin Miller watched numbly as the big man rushed to them, murmuring soft nothings to sooth and comfort the two children. The massive German Shepherd had given up her barking since Joe Watts fled. She trotted over to where Al sat crouched over Nyc, checking his pulse while he spoke to the 911 operator on his cell phone. The German Shepherd licked Ben, as if noticing the boy for the first time, then moved to Nyc and sat next to him whining softly. Snow began to fall, fat flakes drifted lazily out of the slate gray sky. Settling on Nyc's brown curls and brown nose, Ben wept for his friend, for himself, and for all the hurt that ached in his chest.

Chapter 10

Guess Who's Coming to Dinner

Ages, ancients, rise and fall
civilizations, castles, crumble all.
Earth beneath, sky above
mankind stumbles, without mother's love.

Rosa Arcadia sat at the kitchen table drumming her fingers incessantly on the wooden top, muddy booted feet tapping accompaniment on the tile floor. She was in a foul mood, due mostly in part to the three uniformed men positioned around her modest kitchen. Sheriff Ward sat in a chair to her right while Chief Ranger Thompson sat to her left. She had a rule about letting police in her house, but the warrant the sheriff shook in her face told her she had no choice. The sheriff agreed not to rip up her house, or take her downtown if she told the truth.

Rosa knew she was in for trouble when they came around the back of the house and into the barn where they found her plucking the feathers from one of the pheasants Nycolos brought in for her that morning. She was up to her elbows in plumage, guts and boiling water when she saw them coming down the path from the house. Quickly deciding it would be better to go out and meet them. She walked out of the barn holding six pheasants that had been rubbed down with herbs and spices. Rosa knew her white butchering apron was red with the blood of butchered poultry and her curly hair full of feathers.

"Gentlemen, is there a reason you're all on my property this fine morning?" Which was when Sheriff Ward informed her that they had an urgent need to talk to her.

"It has come to my attention Mrs. Arcadia that you were in the woods the night before your husband's disappearance. I believe we have some more questions for you."

She led them inside, but only after hanging her birds in the smokehouse. The smokehouse was a little timber-frame gem Lyndon and Jackson Miller put up to help with the farm stand. She left the mess of feathers and guts on the wooden chopping board in the barn, but made the intruders wait while she brought the two-dozen birds she had prepared that morning and hung them in the smokehouse. The hickory smoke folded our of the doorway and streamed into the sky every time she opened the door. She left the bloody apron on.

Now she found herself sitting at her own kitchen table feeling like a caged animal. The men surrounding her were asking her to confront the possibility that Lyndon might still be alive. The bigot, Deputy Eric Fontane arrived with the Sheriff and stood away from the table, leaning on the kitchen counter, barely managing to conceal his look of contempt.

"Why were you in the forest that night. Rosa?" The sheriff, was true to his word so far and hadn't trashed the house. He had walked through every room though, checking every closet, under every bed, the basement and the attic.

"I was spying on Lyn, I wanted to see if he was going to tell Nyc about our divorce, and then I was going to beg Lyndon for us to try to make it work one more time..." It still hurt when she said the words out loud, stirring up pain in her chest that ached like a ton of stone on her chest. "And then I saw him with another woman and I assumed she was the reason he wanted a divorce. As soon as I saw her I left."

"So let me get this straight. As angry as you were, you didn't confront him with his new lady?" The sheriff's raised eyebrows were nearly as grayed as the hair on his head.

"Humiliated is a more appropriate word I think, Sheriff. By that point I was distraught, afraid that I had pushed my husband away and was not going to humiliate myself further by begging for him in front of his lover." She practically snarled the last word.

"And the woman—did you recognize her?"

"No, I've never seen her before, or since." The hair stood up on the back of her neck. She tried not to think of Nyc's version of the story, and how much he could have told Park Ranger Thompson. On cue the Ranger spoke up.

"Mrs. Arcadia's description of the woman matched that of the boy's, it was definitely the same woman, both days."

"Thank you Mr. Thompson." The sheriff didn't seem to appreciate the information. His gaze settled on Rosa's tapping fingers.

"Then you wouldn't know anything about Lyndon running around wrecking illegal logging operations, Mrs. Arcadia?"

"No, I'm afraid not." Hope fluttered in her chest, banging around her insides like a mad insect. "And unless you have more proof than an old shirt that Lyndon has been the one attacking these logging operations, this is a very cruel tactic, officer."

"We have evidence..." Deputy Fontane sounded like he wanted to add a few words to the end of his sentence, but was cut short by a gesture by the sheriff.

"Yes, Mrs. Arcadia, we have evidence, hence the warrant. We found several fingerprints that matched your husband's on some of the wrecked equipment. Mrs. Arcadia, the attack happened the same day as the incident at the zoo. I'm beginning to believe your husband faked his own death and joined some eco-terrorism group."

"Quite a theory." Rosa mentally stomped on the hope that was no longer fluttering in her chest but banging around like a caged monster, maybe it was her heart. It was all she could do not to jump out of her chair and scream.

"Homegrown terrorists that rise from the dead." She prayed that her shock was not evident.

"I know it sounds a little far-fetched, Mrs. Arcadia, but the fingerprints are Lyndon's and the incident happened yesterday." The sheriff hadn't stopped watching her since the conversation began, apparently he saw something that made him want to believe her.

"Now, Mrs. Arcadia, from the look on your face, I'd say this is news to you, or maybe not," a very long pause, eyes probing her face. "But if Lyndon shows up you need to let us know. He and whomever he's working with haven't killed anyone yet, though I don't know how. The damage they caused and the equipment they destroyed costs hundreds of thousands of dollars."

"That equipment belongs to thieves and crooks, raping the forest in an uncontrolled destructive manner. Even if some eco-guerillas did wreck it," she made a smart-ass face at the Sheriff, happy with her small victory, making this word her own. "They should lose their rights and their equipment as soon as they start cutting illegally."

"Something like that, ma'am, though I don't like anyone getting away with this in my county."

"You're right about the logging though." Ranger Thompson spoke up. " It was in an old-growth stand, some really big old trees." The ranger didn't look at the sheriff, he looked deep into Rosa's eyes.

The conversation wound on, the threat towards Rosa not imminent but recessed in the undertones of their talk. Thinking to better her situation Rosa offered a tour of the grounds, which of course was accepted with professional ease by the sheriff. She escorted the trio through the repaired back door, over the brick patio, where the stump of the giant maple reminded Rosa of Lyndon all over again. She took them back to the barn, showing them the smokehouse on the way. Moving then to the barn, the men examined the butchering area. Tables, sink, and stove still covered with feathers, cast-iron pots full of water blackened from use. Rosa used to opportunity to take off her bloody apron before leading them around the barn. She showed them the timber framing and joinery Lyndon had worked with Jackson to construct.

They poked round the cooking area where herbs hung drying from nearly every rafter and crossbeam. The loft was the same, bundles of herbs tied and hung from the southern yellow pine cross beams. They checked a trap door in the floor and Eric Fontane even went down a little ways before realizing it was a root cellar with wooden shelves lined with roots, mason jars, and bottles of homemade wine. After that he told the sheriff he'd be in the cruiser, apparently the threat to Rosa having dissipated too much to interest him further.

Once the underling was gone the sheriff was slightly more pleasant towards Rosa, almost polite. She walked them out to the orchards, exiting out the back of the barn, large doors open wide allowing the animals freedom to move in and out at their discretion. She showed them the pheasants, ducks, chickens, geese, and turkeys. Moving from orchard to orchard, the Park Ranger was intrigued by the variety of species planted. He engaged her in a long discussion about ecosystems and animal husbandry.

The sheriff didn't say much, so she decided to make the tour an interpretive nature-walk. She finished the orchard tour leading them from the last and largest orchard, the same she sent Nycolos that morning to fetch the pheasants. The gate was simple, horizontal boards in a frame, Lyndon's touch apparent in the braided arches that bowed their braided limbs up and over the gate.

She led them to the forest edge pointing out the teahouse Lyndon had nestled against the spruce trunks and the tree-house perched in a large oak a little farther down the tree-line. Rosa Arcadia stayed outside while the two men checked the tea-house. The tree-house sat astride the crotch of an old red oak with a massive trunk. Brown leaves clung tenaciously to black and gray branches. The Sheriff wasn't interested in climbing up to the trap door entrance, but Chief Ranger Thompson obliged, moving up the twenty-some-odd meters of ladder quickly and disappearing inside. He reappeared shortly and made his way down with the same alacrity he ascended.

"All clear, Sheriff, no one up there." His words sounded sincere, though his eyes sparkled with mirth. Rosa lead them through the brown field of goldenrods and beyond. Down the wooded trail by the ravine giving the officers running commentary on species diversity of their little farm and the Mount that loomed beyond. She estimated the age of trees and enlightened them to the history of the farm before their arrival and the migratory patterns of some of their local fauna. She saw Mirage creeping around in the orchard and woods, staying just beyond the edge of sight.

Rosa Arcadia wished North American police officers were as openly corrupt as those on her native continent, where in most cases a handful of cash would get her out of scrapes. Not that she was guilty of anything, but she wanted these men to leave her wounded family alone. She and Nycolos had only just begun to talk about Lyndon again. Just that morning Nycolos returned from the orchard with the birds she had asked for, brimming with questions about his father. What were Lyndon's favorite foods, colors, sports, etc. The boy was particularly animated, his brown corduroy pants wet on the knees and bum from snow and mud.

They ended up talking about Lyn so long she forgot to send him inside to change his muddy pants, and he ran off down the driveway when they heard Abby honking. She thought she had seen Lyndon that morning, walking through the orchards in pre-dawn light checking on the animals. Both she and Nyc were sharing fantastic phenomena, swirling around Nycolos since Lyndon died, but she didn't want to mention seeing Lyndon, for several reasons. Three of which showed up at her house with a warrant several hours after her son ran down the driveway.

****

Rosa had called the psychologists few days earlier to cancel any future appointments. In light of strange occurances centering around Nycolos she thought it unwise to continue the charade. Dr. Rosen was not particularly pleased and had not been reticent to share his opinion.

"Mrs. Arcadia, the school counselor recommended at least three visits. I have only seen each of you once. I think both of you would benefit from several more sessions."

"I understand, Doctor," she tried to be tactful. "We just need to take a break for now. I'm sure you heard about what happened at the zoo."

"Yes, Mrs. Arcadia, I have; all the more reason you and especially Nycolos need further counseling. I think you both have un-accessed grief which has led both of you to disassociate from your emotions."

"Doctor, thank you for your concern and we will resume the counseling eventually, we need some time right now." Her hand itched to hang up on the doctor.

"Your disassociation is not healthy, Rosa, and given the strange circumstances of your husband's death both you and Nycolos are evidencing signs that you think Lyndon is still alive. Next, one of you—or both—will say you saw him somewhere, and I wouldn't be surprised if Nycolos becomes angry, and acts out."

That was all Rosa needed to hear. He had come a little too close to the mark and she couldn't help but think about Nycolos and Ben fighting with bullies from school. The image she had seen that morning of Lyndon's shadow moving through the orchard like a specter had her nervous. She would've sworn what she saw was her eyes playing tricks on her if Mirage hadn't been so happy, whinnying like she did when she saw Lyndon Arcadia.

"Listen, Mr. Shrink, you don't know anything about unaccessed grief, you got that? That little boy and I cried ourselves to sleep, we cried ourselves awake, and cried ourselves through every minute of every day for the better part of three months.

"We made it through, but only just, now we have the holidays coming and all we have is each other. We had so much accessed emotion we've been doing all we can, not to drown in it. So please, Doctor, respect my decision and trust that we will return to counseling." With that said she slammed down the receiver.

****

At long last she finished the tour, looping the two officers back around the front of the yellow house. Deputy Fontane stood next to their squad card talking on the radio, responding to the squawking coming from inside the car. Forest Ranger Thompson took off his hat and scrubbed his forehead. Large knuckles on his hand and calluses spoke of years of hard work. He turned his soft eyes to Rosa as the sheriff strolled to the car to speak to his deputy.

"I'm sorry, Mrs. Arcadia, but in light of the evidence, when the sheriff called I had to tell him what I knew. I tell you, this uniform never chafed so much." He spoke genuinely, something she appreciated.

"I understand, Mr. Thompson," she patted his gnarled hand. "It's quite alright."

"Good, well, I hate to leave you with these two but I have to get back to Hawk Mountain."

"Drive safely, Chief." She waved goodbye as he strode down the driveway to his green park jeep.

The sheriff was speaking on the radio, while Deputy Fontane strolled to Rosa, gravel crunching beneath his big black boots. His pale face was drawn and his cheeks looked hollow. The dark circles under his eyes belied too few hours of sleep. His black hair was shaved close to his head giving him a martial look. He checked the sheriff before speaking to Rosa, "Listen, Rosa Arcadia, here's what I think. I think you and that tree-hugging husband of yours are behind this and if you don't want to get into trouble you need to take your immigrant ass back to the jungles where you came from, and your little half-breed boy with you. Nobody wants you here—even those commie punks you let have meetings here talk bad about you, they just use your space."

"Hurry while there's still time, get out of here, go back to the jungle where you belong." He bared his teeth at her, pulled his sunglasses over his eyes and walked back to the squad car.

"Mrs. Arcadia," the sheriff beckoned from the driver's side of the black car. When she moved close he lowered the cb and spoke to her quietly. "Mrs. Arcadia, you should come with us immediately."

Her stomach dropped into her boots; Rosa though her voice sounded weak when she spoke. "Sheriff, I am not hiding my husband, in fact I have been grieving for him for three months; if you see him I have some choice words for him as well."

"It's not you or your husband, ma'am; it's your son, he's been hurt, we'll take you to the hospital."

Rosa Arcadia flinched as if he had taken a swing at her, but for once didn't argue. "Let me just run inside and get my jacket."

She did. Stepping inside the foyer to examine herself in the oval mirror with a polished brass frame of tangled vines and blossoming flowers. No tears, her face was dry and she intended to keep it that way. She would not allow herself to cry in front of these bigots; green eyes flared in her reflection and she grabbed her key off the rooster-shaped hook next to the door.

****

One of the worst decisions previous city planners of New Hamlet made was to put Evergreen Heights trailer park next to Castle creek. Septic systems only worked for so long before they needed to be dug up. As a result the creek adjacent to the park had become turbid and littered with refuse, surely as offerings, left by the downtrodden inhabitants that lived there. The stink of pooled human waste was less severe this time of year, the almost frozen ground didn't allow the vapors to rise and assault the senses.

Sanctioned by the DEC the owners dug up the offending septic tanks the previous year, the progress was slow compounded by the fact that nearly all of the systems failed within a few months of one another. Installed nearly thirty years prior, three decades of human excrement pushed through the guts of blue-collar men and women took a toll.

Born of burger joints, processed meats, snack foods, cheap booze, high fructose corn syrup, and the sorrows drowned in such vices, the waste festered for years, until the one-hundred year storm, flooded the park, raised the watertable, freeing the noxious toxic waste to contaminate the beautiful creek and shock the whole town.

The stench sank into anything and everything in the park, people included. The municipality came in, re-routed the stream away from the park, leaving a small ephemeral stream to remind the park residents where the water used to flow. Clogged with debris, children's toys and trash the ephemeral stream was washed clean every spring with the snowmelt. The re-routed stream would swell sending tendrils of water down to its old ox-bow. The smell was intermittent now, but it lingered in the minds of every resident. A memory, an idea so putrid, and so fetid they could smell it every day of their lives as if the rottenness had sunk into their souls.

The aluminum-clad containers of human squalidness were festive that time of year, colored lights adorned small windows and smaller Christmas trees. Stilted and several feet off the ground voices drifted through too small windows into the purple light of evening. Names like Bounder and Eagle painted on the aluminum hides displaying which manufacturer assembled said boxes. The trailers were scattered in a nonsensical fashion, appearing dropped accidentally into the chosen locations. Group mailboxes stood on wooden posts like checkpoints for travelers passing through purgatory with dozens of pigeonholes marked with numbers following no sequential order. Dirt roads were rutted, and uneven, sediment ran off the dirt roads in tons, rilling and sheeting into the now dry streambed.

Aluminum siding hid crawl spaces where pipes ran under the temporarily gay footsteps of residents several bottles into Thanksgiving merriment. As abhorrent as the trailer park was, full of aluminum containers, thirty meters long by 10 meters wide the ticky-tack boxes were home to several hundred residents that knew more than they would've liked about neighborly dysfunction.

Rusted propane tanks of all sizes were clustered against northern walls, jerry-rigged by the mother of necessity to power water and stoves. In one corner of the park, down a barely visible dirt road, sandwiched between an abandoned truck containers waiting for trucks that would never come, so badly rusted light shone through the swiss-cheesed corners, sat a group of mobile homes that looked like all the rest. Just past the containers, old lengths of chain link fence leaned against the mustard yellow chassy of an ancient bulldozer, likewise oxidizing toward infinity, treads and front end hopelessly seized. On the northern side of the dirt road, an old wooden building sat behind the containers with walls painted gray except for the large letters in a faded yellow reading Sigfreid's Poultry.

****

One trailer stood clean among the rest. The white of the trailer sides crisp like cake frosting, with a small greenhouse sweating on the side, shovels and plants evident pressing against the corrugated plastic. Navy blue shutters flanked the normal sized windows that looked new. Vibrant red wind chimes like twisted candy canes spun in the wind. A wicked looking inflated Santa was whipping his deer inside a large plastic globe which sat next to the only functioning jungle gym in the whole trailer park. All plastic and no wood, the blues, reds and greens were sharp against the whites and grays of the aluminum boxes.

Hemmed in on four sides like a castle of decency surrounded by a dirt moat, the nice trailer lay under siege by the malignant forces of vice, rage and ignorance. Four trailers with aluminum patches slapped haphazardly on their hulls, surrounded the nice moat. The patches looked like a quilt of aluminum with rivets for stitches and off color aluminum salvaged from who knows where as fabric. So numerous were the patches in fact they made up most of the siding on all four trailers. A dilapidated deck with faded wood and peeling red paint hung from the north side of one trailer. An abandoned weight bench discarded in the corner, weights rusting on the earth beneath the deck. The remaining space on the small deck was occupied by a pink toilet and sink. Distorted sounds emerged from the innards of the beached white whale.

The Watts household was active and lively from the sound of things. Alcohol and motion worked to keep the inhabitants warm, as the temp inside the trailer was not much warmer than outside, due in part to the rusted patches next to the leaning deck waiting to be replaced. The second and third patchwork trailers stood dark, seemingly uninhabited, except for the occasional twitch of a curtain or opened mini-blind. One was originally gray, now patched with lime green pieces over the years.

****

The other white with a long yellow line circling the equator of the vehicle, patches of yellow, white, silver and green, was just as dark as the other. Lacking any signs of life, what little snow that had accumulated since the afternoon remained un-shoveled and unsalted.

The residents of said trailers had given up caring, if they ever had. The green trim of the smaller domicile blending into the browns of rust that abutted the window frames. The larger trailer with the yellow stripe housed the forgotten elderly Mr. Smith. A pedophile that prayed on children before it occurred to anyone to keep track of sex offenders, the old man was the oldest living inhabitant of Evergreen Heights trailer park. The benignly mediocre man abused decades of boys and girls, many of whom had grown to raise their own dysfunctional families; a bare few addressing the rage that stemmed from Mr. Smith's violations. Through some twisted weaving of the tapestry of life the evil man had never been reported.

The same twisted weaving of the fates brought the Watts and Fontane families to that corner of the trailer park 20 some odd years earlier. Old Mr. Smith had grown weak and faded in those years, though no less perverse.

One afternoon in summer when Joseph Watts and Eric Fontane were 14 and 18 respectively, they noticed the seventy-year-old man eyeing them lustily as they sat in the sun. sweating and counting the money they had taken off some rich kids in town. Joe Watts and Eric Fontane gave into temptation that day and followed the old man inside when he offered them ten extra bucks and some cold beers.

Mr. Smith wished he could die at that point in his life, karmic seeds he had planted inadvertently fruited, bearing him long life and adolescent neighbors who embraced violence. Vengeance was delivered piecemeal for years as broken windows and empty threats. Joe Watts smashed the old man in the jaw and knocked out some of his teeth—once they got inside the old man's trailer—after he pulled a shotgun on the boys with trembling hands, demanding some money for his most recently broken windows. Eric and Joe dragged the semiconscious old man into the darkened back room of the trailer. There the teens visited upon the old man the hell on earth he deserved.

Without pause or hesitation, the boys shed their innocence with their clothes, demonstrating their dominance just like their fathers had shown them. In the dark, with the old man's face buried in a pillow so no one could hear his screams.

****

The fourth trailer, patched like the rest, had three old picnic tables strewn around the perimeter. The lights glowed yellow from behind dirty curtains that were thick with dust and appeared to be from the seventies. The loudest of the trailers in this corner of the park voices were laughing inside the trailer. Mostly yellow, the patched hull of the little aluminum box was as yellow inside as out, within faded fake wood paneling covered the walls, an old shag carpet lined the floor.

Damian Fontane and Jacob Watts sat at the picnic table closest to the trailer. Their heads were bowed in submission, shoulders slumped under the barrage of insults crushing their already malnourished self-esteem. Damian Fontane's new teeth felt loose in his head and a bandage was wrapped around his right shin, his bloody pant leg pulled up to his knee. He would've scuffed his feet but his legs hurt too much. Jacob Watts sat next to him, looking equally downtrodden, he wore no bandages but his pride was sorely injured. Their older brothers were clearly upset by the second beating they had suffered at the hands of young Ben Miller and Nycolos Arcadia.

"...always told you niggers were sneaky sons of bitches. You two should've known better than to get fucking blindsided like that." Johnny Fontane was running his mouth as he was prone to, his right hand stroking a 12-gauge shotgun.

He stood in front of the two younger boys trying to make himself seem older. Joe Watts sat on the table top, not looking at any of them, but with his face turned to the sky, white flakes melting on his white flesh, but remaining on eyelashes and dirty looking hair.

"I don't know, Johnny, those kids seem pretty tough. In fact, I can understand why these two had so much trouble." Joe Watts had a bandage wrapped tight around his thigh.

"Yeah, whatever Joe, I know you could've handled them both yourself." Johnny Fontane spoke with a bit of reverence, but sarcasm laced the undertones of the comment. They all shared skeletons, and their closets while not literally, were figuratively huge.

Abused mentally and physically from a very young age left all of the boys scarred. No rhyme or reason to the selection, why one child chosen and another left alone. Johnny escaped, but not Joseph or Bobby, not since they were little, but they never forgot. Charged with such, the children had grown close, safety in numbers, banding together to distract, stupefy, and escape from the drunken advances that finally ceased when they were big enough to fight back, and to punch with force.

Joseph Watts considered putting Johnny on the ground to remind them both who was boss. The snow felt too good on his hot face to interrupt his thought process. Gears shifted in Johnny's head and he jumped tracks to consider the beating they dished out to Nycolos.

"Lucky for you two we were there to stomp the shit out of that little nigger for you." A lopsided smile climbed the pimpled cheeks of his face, he bared uneven teeth.

"And boy did we stomp him good, hey Joe, you heard his arm break? Oh man!!" Johnny Fontane couldn't hold in his laughter and threw his head back and laughed hard. Bobby Fontane stood next to his older brother and ran a dirty hand through his greasy gelled hair. He eyed the laughing teen, curled lip betraying the disgust he felt for his brother and his maniacal laughter.

"You shit-head, that little fucker would've gotten away from you too; so stop laughing, you dumb fuck." Joe Watts spoke quietly but sounded louder than Johnny.

The sharp edge of his words shut Johnny down, he finally stopped talking and sat on the table top. Mimicking the silent Joe Watts, he raised his pimply complexion to the sky. Bobby measured Joe's disposition, he knew Joe could turn at the drop of a dime, like a rabid pit-bull, when he bit down he didn't let go. Bobby Fontane had known immediately what was on the 20-year-old's mind when he sent the Fontane boys to gather up Damian and Jacob at the junkyard. Bobby sent Johnny to gather up the boys and remained by the fence of the junkyard long enough to see what Joe Watts had in mind for the ten-year-old black kid. Boby had seen the white kid sneak out of a rubbish pile with a metal pipe ready to clear Joe's calendar for the rest of eternity.

If the massive German Shepherd hadn't shown up Bobby was ready to let the kid try to crush Joe's skull with the metal pipe. Joseph rubbed Bobby the wrong way, he was an admirable fighter and good looking enough to live off of his looks. Joseph Watts reminded Bobby of his own father, Carl Fontane. Bobby hated Carl Fontane. Carl was a son of a bitch that had raped him when he was still a child of thirteen, sneaking into his room at night stinking of booze and crack cocaine. A rough year for their family; Barbara Fontane had died of dirty heroin in February, foaming at the mouth and seizing up on the yellow shag carpet on the trailer floor. That had been four years earlier. Bobby still thought about her every day.

Bobby thought she was beautiful, her eyes spoke of sadness and misery that her mouth dared not utter. She aged badly during the twenty-some-odd years of alcoholism and vice to numb the pain. Only Bobby knew the truth, she would have run and never looked back if she could have, but she stayed to protect her children. Barbara Fontane stood up to Carl Fontane. Beatings and rapes her reward. Eric Fontane asserted that was how Damian had been conceived, which explained his rage.

Carl Fontane had gone through several women since his wife's death. Cast from the same mold, the women were desperate enough to put up with beatings and forced sex to get drugs or to get off the street. They all left sooner than later, most stealing as much as they could carry when they left off like ghosts in the night. Carl Fontane had inherited a mom and pop general store from his parents.

The store had been in downtown New Hamlet, a success until Carl got his hands on it. Carl squandered what he was given, falling hard and fast. He sold the property to a young couple hoping to open a bookstore. He had the wherewithal to purchase the trailer and lot in the trailer park before smoking and drinking the rest of the money away.

Carl met Barbara during the first months he tried to run the store himself after his parents' death. Barb had been a sweet little thing, barely 19, working for him at the general store. Long platinum blond hair shone silver in the sun, and her curvy legs and perky bottom had been more than Carl could bear those twenty odd years ago.

He wooed her and wed her as quickly as he could manage, promises of milk and honey for the rest of their days. He sold the shop against her wishes and moved her into the trailer before she realized all was not as it seemed. Carl took her by the hand and lead her into the abyss of vice and resentment. Her once-beautiful features became haggard and drawn, thanks to years of smoking and drug use. Wrinkles creased her eyes, neck and mouth, making her appear much older than the 45 years she carried.

Bobby Fontane was strangely relieved when she passed away; she hadn't deserved the life Carl Fontane had forced on her. The hatred for his father oozed like slime onto Eric Fontane and Joseph Watts, tainting their actions and everything they touched. Like the old shotgun that sat across Joseph's legs, Bobby knew where it came from. He knew what Joe was going to do to that little kid and he couldn't help think of his father's weight pressing down on him, his screams lost in repressed memory. So when he saw the little white kid, Ben Miller emerge from the junk pile and grab the metal pole, he didn't yell a warning. Instead he squeezed the chain link fence wishing he was the one swinging the pole. And when Ben Miller stepped close the Joe's back, arms raised ready to crush the skull of that bastard, Bobby wasn't going to say a thing.

****

Joseph Watts and Eric Fontane had never done anything so malicious to Bobby, but he knew what they done to old Mr. Smith, and sometimes still did. On cue, Joe began stroking the old gun, the stock shiny with Joe's constant affections. The metal was polished and brushed with care.

Sometimes Joe and Eric would drive a few towns over and pick up prostitutes. Sometimes men, and sometimes women, they would all come back and go into Mr. Smith's and they would all get loaded and hoot and holler. They promised Bobby a turn some day, but he wasn't looking forward to any such thing. They coveted the gun like some sort of trophy, even arguing over it when they were younger. Now Eric let Joe hold onto it as he had several of his own, shiny and new issued by the sheriff's office. Bobby Fontane left the crowded picnic table and walked away from the surrogate and blood brothers alike. The ground sloped downward onto a small dale, it used to flood before the stream was diverted. The grass was just visible, the tallest of the blades sticking above the newly fallen snow. Thanksgiving would be a white one this year. A lone willow stood tall next to a dry old creek bed, garbage littered the base of the trunk, snugly covered in rocks and leaves. Roots protruded from the walls of the creek-bed, green tendrils trailed down forming pools of shadow. The orange sulfur glow of street lamps pushed back at the darkness, buzzing as they turned on for the night. Bobby stepped into the creek, boots squelching in the mud and water not yet frozen, seeking the darkness of shadows to match the darkness of his soul.

He could hear the creek beyond the hedgerow, thankful for the gurgle as retching brought black bile to his mouth. Strange movement in the dark, upwelling of sulfur putrescence, he vomited and vomited until he could barely breathe. Lights flashed in the cul-de-sac and a cruiser from the sheriff's office pulled between the abandoned truck containers. Eric Fontane returned to their wretched little corner of the earth to dispense his rare wisdom. Snowflakes danced in the headlights, swirling around the porch light on the trailer behind them. Bobby Fontane trotted backward toward the dark shapes of his brothers, he could hear Eric Fontane speaking in quick, clipped, sentences, none of which was polite or endearing.

"...I guess it would be too much for you to realize, you bunch need to high tail it out of here. Here's Bobby, at least he had the sense to hide somewhere out of sight. The Sheriff's gonna have someone over here real soon, so you boys need to get inside, pack your bags. I'm calling someone to get you fools out of here."

"Eric, the water over there by the willow..."

"Later, Bobby, we don't have time for this now; go inside and get your stuff."

Bobby did as ordered, wondering why a mud-boil would be gurgling away in the dry creek bed. He had never seen that there before, but there it was gurgling and popping, shooting mud into the air, splattering when it hit the ground. Sounding obscene and smelling putrid, the mud-boil was not ashamed of its flatulence.

Once the younger boys scurried into their homes, intent on gathering their things. Eric Fontane drew close to Joe Watts who was still perched on the picnic table top, caressing the old shotgun. Eric Fontane stopped next to his childhood friend and eyed him for a long time in the darkness. Scruffy and chiseled, Joe was wrapped in a dreamy stupor that Eric recognized the beginnings of an obsession. Joe was like that when he tasted something he liked, and wanted more.

With an open hand Eric Fontane cuffed Joe on the back of his head. Joe's hair was greasy against his hand. Joe turned his head, violence dancing like flames in his eyes.

"You are the dumbest of the bunch. The first thing that little white kid did was start singing like a canary. He fingered you right away as some scumbag pedophile that was trying to rape his friend." The two men shared a close bond forged by the fires of the sins they had committed over time. Eric chose the Sheriff's office as his career path, and had helped Joe out of several scrapes over the years. Joe managed to live off of whatever woman was after him at the time, but grew bored quickly with posh elegance and down comforters. He would slip out of empty mansions with manicured lawns and more servants than inhabitants. He would then spend several weeks crawling through gutters and flop houses among low-lifes and miscreants whose company was more to his liking. Eric Fontane could tell Joe had spent the last week or two living the latter half of his cycle. He smelled like onions and garlic, but something more offensive had seeped into his dirty jeans and jacket.

"Good looking kid Eric, you should've seen him." His brown eyes were lost in thought when he spoke.

"I've seen him, you dumb-ass, I can't get you out of this one; you, Bobby and Johnny need to get out of here tonight." Eric checked Joe's face to be sure Joe was still with him.

"You're gonna take Mr. Smith's old truck and drive up to Uncle Gus's farm. I told him you guys are on the way, you're all going to stay there until this all blows over. It may be a year or two."

Joe Watts was hardly listening, he was sitting upright gripping the shotgun with white knuckles.

"Damn it, Joe, you don't wanna mess with that family of porch monkeys, half the town loves them." When Joe still didn't answer Eric moved to cuff him again, but Joe raised his hand.

"Look, what the hell is that?" A blast of sulfur stink, rank with rot and putrescence assaulted Eric's nose.

"Jeezus, Joe, you need to wash up, bud."

"Look."

Eric Fontane followed Joe's finger to the willow leaning over the dry creek bed. A cone of mud boiled violently in the creek bed, ejecting Styrofoam, beer cans, used toilet paper and all manner of refuse through the air. The mound teetered sideways onto the bank, like a slinky climbing stairs, it pulled itself up onto the bank. The plopping flatulent mound roiled and sank into the earth. A particularly large boil popped and the smell of sulfur rolled over the two men once again. Eric Fontane covered his nose when he felt the burning in his nasal passages. Joe Watts was un-fazed; he rose from the bench and moved toward the dale, where the mud boil inched toward them like living Jello.

Johnny, Bobby, and Damian Fontane clomped down the wooden steps of the deck that fronted their house. Bobby and Johnny wore backpacks stuffed to the gills with clothes and other items. A sock stuck in the zipper of Bobby's backpack evidence of rushed packing, the boys pulled up short next to the picnic bench taking in the scene before them. Jacob Watts came down from his trailer next door, but stopped well short of the red picnic bench, the stench of trailer park waste all too familiar in his nose.

The mass of bubbling waste expanded until the entire dale below them was covered with liquid refuse.

Surging upward mud geysered to twenty-five meters for ten seconds before the pressure was released and gravity carried feces, mud and trash to the earth in an explosion of refuse, staining Joe, Bobby and Johnny. Time stretched out like a seamstress measuring her threads for cutting. Eric Fontane heard the door of his family trailer squeak open behind him and a muffled curse.

"Smells worse than ever out there. Jeezus, Happy Thanksgiving." Eric recognized his father's voice, and was glad the foul odor scared him away. Hopefully he would keep his circus act inside with the Watts. The door slammed shut behind his cursing, the outside world forgotten in lieu of the bottom of a bottle and some cocaine.

The brown pool of refuse steamed in the cold autumn night. The surface calmed and became smooth like ice, a milk carton standing upright next to a Styrofoam beer cooler. Soundlessly the pool grew skyward like a plateau rising from the putrid soils saturated with the waste of indifferent trailer park residents. Oozing ever higher, sludge fell from the edges of the waste tower. Clumps hit the ground, solid as if frozen, thudding loudly and vibrating in the chests of the onlookers.

A head formed near the apex of the mountain of sludge. A light blossomed in those holes, glowing amber-yellow and alive. Sludge congealed and compacted to form a humanoid head, torso, arms and legs. Roots protruded from the head of the sludge figure like hair plugs, spikes in a Mohawk. The chest and torso criss-crossed by willow branches, a green vest bristling with a toilet seat, a plunger, an old propane tank, and uncountable beer cans that glinted faintly in what little light reached the dale. Human endeavor involves destruction; tearing asunder one thing creates another. Created things, cast off once usefulness is expired. The definition of usefulness established by human inhabitants of a given era. Useful and wasteful, ideas changed drastically over the 100,000 years of human evolution. A stick and stone will break your bone, more valuable to our prehistoric ancestors than cars today. Take your stick and stone and bash your enemy's head in. Hunt for your food, feast on the flesh, light the fire. One man's treasure is another man's stick and stone.

The explosion in waste production coinciding with the industrialization and commercialization of the consumer economy has not gone unnoticed. Coupled with mass exodus from rural environs to urban squalor, incipient epidemics waiting to burst. Swine and avian flus threaten you, supermarket dumpster overflowing with plastic wrapped everything. Can't breathe the air, can't drink the water. Drive your car down the highway forever, afford the gas if you can. Amnesia afflicted inhabitants blind to their waste assume this is the way it is, was, and always will be. Not true, but that's what they want you to think, keep you shopping.

The human brain, capable of a great many wonders. Humility, arrogance, hope, faith, despair. Humanity will wade through a quagmire of the entire spectrum of human emotion. A forced catharsis that looms precipitously over humanity, a wave cresting to crash. Destroy the norm, what then will rise in its place? Problems stop us or stretch us, or so they say. Which will it be for humanity. Stopped or stretched? Dark and light dwells in each outcome.

"You have been marked." A booming voice gurgled from an open maw some twenty meters above the ground. Strings of mud connected the top of the creature's mouth to the bottom like strings of saliva. Yellow smoke trailed from the maw as the monster spoke, settling over the boys, sending them into coughing fits and burning their eyes.

"You choke of the fetid stench of your own creation. Your disregard for the earth earns you punishments far harsher than you are now suffering, I have not come to even that score. I come for those that have transgressed against the Children of Gaia." The gurgling voice echoed around the cul-de-sac.

"What the fu..."Bobby Fontane's outburst was cut off by a loud scream from the trailer door. The rotund silhouette of Jacob Watts's mother filled the doorway. She slammed the door again and the screaming inside reached hysteria. Outside snowflakes whipped into a frenzy, ripping the cap off of Johnny's head. The wind whipped around the polished shotgun, snowflakes cycloning inside the barrel trained on the monster.

The sludge monster's legs and arms were wrapped in willow tendrils, less tightly woven than those on the chest, like a Muy-Thai fighter suited for battle. Ropes wrapped around the fists, forearms, ankles and shins. The snow didn't reach the monster but melted before reaching the steaming sludge.

"Repent your wrongdoings and I will be merciful. Cross me and your suffering will be great." The gurgling voice vibrated through the air pushing snow clear in front of it.

"Who is the child of Gaia?" Bobby Fontane sounded frightened, and rightly so.

"The nigger kid you idiot." Joe Watts spoke for the first time since the madness began. The monster opened its massive jaw and issued a mighty gurgling roar. A massive leg lifted from the earth making an obscene sucking sound, then stomped to the earth with such force that every car alarm in the trailer park went off. Eric Fontane and his brother Damian were thrown to the ground. Damian's nose was bandaged and his eye was puffy from the beating he took earlier that day. Snow gusted in the cul-de-sac of the Evergreen Estates. Jacob Watts was similarly thrown to the ground and watched in horror as Johnny, Bobby, and Joe stood before their executioner, the blizzard covering the boys with white. Hundred of car alarms blared, horns and lights flashing in warning. Shiny new mustangs, brand new trucks, an Audi and numerous motorcycles honked and wailed in the hurricane force winds.

Bobby Fontane fell to his knees, tears unseen in the darkness and begged for forgiveness. The frightened teen's voice was tight with fear, his tough guy persona gone, replaced by a kid scared to die.

"I'm sorry, I didn't mean for it to get so bad, I won't mess with him again."

"The child will die when the time is right and when we ordain." The monstrous voice changed, no longer that of an individual, the voice sounded as many, a chorus of monsters speaking through one mouth.

"Would you shut the fuck up, you pussy? Get off your knees, that little nigger got what he had coming!" Joe Watts sounded very matter of fact the last time he spoke, he kicked the whimpering Bobby Fontane.

A tendril of sludge and willow shot through the blizzard, hitting Joe Watts with a loud thump. Joseph Watts fired his shotgun with abandon. Mud and sludge flew from the tendril, but it did not break. Mud undulated up the length of the tendril, filling in the holes before he could fire the next shot. The tendril writhed, shaking Joe from side to side. The first tendril split in two, a second tendril shooting from a hole made by buckshot. Brown and green tendrils wrapped the twenty year old vagabond tight, and he dropped the shotgun with hardly a crunch in the snow.

The miscreant was thrown backwards, boots flying from his feet, crushing the picnic table. His real and extended family watched as he was enveloped by mud. Head lolled backward, arms and legs limp, he was unconscious. His right sock had a hole in the front and a few toes hung suspended in the air. Mud and tendril wrapped around his chest then recoiled smartly into the swamp monster's leg. Only Joe's hand remained visible, the rest of his body swallowed by the creature's mass.

Eric Fontane stood, firing his .9mm and screaming with no visible effect. They could all hear the bullets hitting the sludge, small sucking sounds as each round impacted the monster.

"His fate is decided." The resonant voice became that of one monster again, yellow eyes piercing the blizzard, waiting for something more. The ground vibrated under their feet as the monster stepped closer. The chest and torso melted, head sinking into the shoulders and into the waist of the beast.

A human head and torso exposed to the night, giant legs of the monster as big as tree trunks maintained their integrity, still mud and willow branches. The human torso steamed in the night air, eyes glowing yellow, gusting wind blowing sandy-brown hair.

"Holy Shit." Eric Fontane stopped firing.

Lyndon Arcadia was bare chested in the blizzard, an evil snarl playing across his face. Joe Watts remained unconscious, embedded in the mud and willow vines of Lyndon's massive legs.

"Johnny Fontane this is your last chance." Johnny shook visibly when Lyndon muttered his name. Lyndon sounded like he was speaking through sludge. Eric Fontane didn't need to hear any more, he fired again in rapid succession. The bullets hit Lyndon Arcadia in the chest.

They could see blood welling upward, black in the night, leaving black streaks running down his chest, only for seconds before the holes closed.

"What the...?" Eric Fontane stopped shooting, struggling to understand the bizarre reality unfolding in their cul-de-sac of Evergreen Estates.

"Your weapons cannot hurt me, your decisions have been made, retribution is at hand."

Eric Fontane, Sheriff's Deputy, ran to the trunk of his cruiser and grabbed two grenades. The young deputy was so disturbed by what was happening that he pulled the silver pin and threw the grenade at Lyndon Arcadia's chest without thinking of Joe at all. He should've thought of safety, the grenade exploded to one side of the monster, ripping a chunk from Lyndon's side. Lyndon's monster melted onto the earth, tree trunk legs, vines, toilets, cans, sinks, and Joe Watts among assorted trash, crashed to the earth. Lyndon also fell, but passed into the earth, absorbed into the giant sludge puddle. By some miracle Joe Watts, Bobby and Johnny had not been hurt by any shrapnel. The Fontane brothers sprinted to Joseph, leaving Damian and Jacob huddled together beneath the deck, where they hid when the madness began.

Eric grabbed Joe under the shoulders, Johnny and Bobby grabbed mud soaked legs. In a state of panic the trio slipped madly, disregarding the stench of feces so strong they retched as they helped their surrogate brother.

Grunted effort moved beyond the rim of the sludge puddle, up the small incline and out of the dale, backpedaling towards the trailers they tripped over the rubble of the shattered picnic table and crashed to the ground dropping their unconscious cargo.

Sludge bubbled to life, globes and domes of waste boiled spewing noxious fumes, growing larger and larger. With a tremendous roar the sludge monster burst fully formed from the earth. Exploding skyward the thing flipped though the air slammed to earth, impacting with such force earth and waste exploded in all directions, leaving a smoking crater. Mud and tendrils shot from arms and legs all at once.

Windows shattered on the deputy's cruiser, willow branches puncturing roof and sides. The monster hurled the cruiser in the air, headlights spinning wildly as the car flipped end over end one hundred feet into the night sky. Another steaming tendril ripped through the night, catching Johnny Fontane and Bobby alike. Bobby was hurled thirty meters across the dale, he felt something crack in his ribs, while Johnny flew in a wide arc before crashing into the willow tree with a loud snap, and the sound of his blood curdling scream splitting the night.

Eric Fontane was rendered unconscious by a tendril strike so quick he didn't get to see his cruiser flying through the air like a child's toy. Joe Watts was hoisted by his neck. a tendril dripping steaming sludge to the earth and down his clothes like noxious acid. The sludge moved, flowing up the length of the tendril and into the mouth of the twenty year old pedophile. Snapping to, Joe Watts struggled and gurgled against the noxious human waste and trash entering his mouth. He convulsed, hands bloodied and ripping at the tendril that was strong like steel and wrapped around him. His eyes flooded and black sludge pushed out of his nose, eyes, and ears. The vagabond twitched one last time, then twitched no more, cadaver covered in black sludge. Lyndon Arcadia, the sludge monstrous beast pulled the body into the sludge and sank into the earth. Once again dropping propane tanks, trash and human waste to the ground. Joe Watts was never seen again.

When Eric Fontane came to, the snow had stopped. Johnny and Bobby were strewn across the dale like scattered laundry. Johnny Fontane's arm was badly broken. Bobby limped over while Eric was checking on Johnny and reported he only had a few broken ribs. Eric ordered him to call an ambulance on his car radio. He was shocked when Bobby told him the cruiser was somewhere in the woods on the other side of the creek. Damian Fontane and Jacob Watts emerged from their hiding place, pale faces matching freshly fallen snow, and ran inside the trailer where they found the adults huddled in the back room, waiting for the world to end. Fifteen minutes later the cul-de-sac was full of trailer park residents and the flashing red and blue lights of emergency vehicles.

****

White faces stood crowded together behind yellow tape Eric Fontane had run around their trailer and the picnic table. Now was not the time for his family to come under scrutiny of ill-bred, ill-mannered neighbors. The residents of Evergreen Heights were convinced the good-for-nothing Fontane and Watts boys had finally blown themselves up. Enormous crater in the dale reinforcing that belief, Eric Fontane was not about to disabuse his neighbors of that idea.

Mrs. Watts in all her obese glory wore red spandex, stretched to the point of exploding, dimpled with craters of cellulite; ran from cluster to cluster of onlookers speaking of the swamp thing made of shit and garbage that had killed her boy. Her blond wispy hair blew about in the chill early winter breeze. She moved alone down the length of the onlookers breathing her whiskey breath on all of them. Mr. Watts and Mr. Fontane were sufficiently frightened, their inebriation left on the trailer floor in piles of sour vomit. They had hidden in the back room when the ground started shaking, leaving Mrs. Watts to her own devices, peering out the window at the earth come to life. They left her to her own devices now, not daring to support her claims that a massive sludge-monster attacked the cul-de-sac.

Eric Fontane watched the ambulance pull away, flashing lights piercing his cornea. Johnny and Bobby Fontane tucked into the back were headed to the hospital and surely the detention center after that. His mind was quiet for the first time that night, thoughts dissipating as soon as they formed, blown away like snowflakes in the blizzard. He could see the headlights of his cruiser shining skyward like white pillars reaching toward the heavens.

Sheriff Ward arrived with the ambulances and spoke only briefly to his deputy. If Eric had been less distracted he would've noticed how carefully the sheriff eyed him with those sleepy eyes. The young deputy did not notice however, he stood staring at the sludge covered dale, mud-boils gone quiet, steaming sulfurous putrescence so strong even the local residents were wrinkling their noses and wiping stinging eyes. Shivers ran up the deputy's spine. Someone was stepping on his grave, and he knew who it was. Lyndon Arcadia was risen from the dead.

Chapter 11

The Move

Mankind reaps, a gift supposed
Mankind takes, ownership imposed.
Righteous god, mythological might,
Man's misdeeds ordained as right.

Nycolos Arcadia liked his nurse. She was pretty, straight long brunette hair framed her full cheeks and pouty lips. She teased him thoroughly about his broken arm, she also said she remembered him from his visit there months ago with his father.

"You have a crush on me, don't you?" She winked coquettishly at him. "That's why you keep coming back." She stepped next to his bed, crossed her arms under her ample bosom and tapped her foot.

"Maybe a little." He liked playing along with Angelica's games. His mother arrived, and the two of them together managed to get several smiles out of him.

"Well, next time just visit me, handsome." She winked again and squeezed his cheek.

Angelica the nurse treated Nyc like a friend and was familiar with the visitors that came to see him. As a matter of fact she brushed off the Sheriff and Deputy Fontane just that morning, making quite a scene, flailing her white arms in the hallway and shaking her finger under their noses.

"I don't care if the boys who did this to him got attacked last night, he can't answer any questions now, he needs his rest, those little bastards nearly beat him to death." The tears running down her face were not forced. "Now he needs his rest, so please, gentlemen, you need to leave now. You can try again the day after tomorrow." The command was clear.

Sheriff Ward and Deputy Fontane looked through the window at Nyc before accepting the rebuttal. Eric Fontane's red blood-shot eyes had a harrowed look about them. Nycolos ignored their stares though he could feel their eyes boring holes in the side of his head. He didn't know which of his attackers had been put in the hospital, but he had an idea who put them there.

Rosa Arcadia snorted loudly at the nurse's attentions, stood and wrapped her in a hug.

"Thank you so much for taking care of him."

"The pleasure was mine, Mrs. Arcadia; he's beautiful."

"I know."

"O.K. Well, the doctors' are switching shifts now, and the sheriff won't be back for two days, I hope. I'm not happy you guys want take him out of here, but I can't blame you, so the time is now. Careful with his arm and keep the ribs wrapped tight, no hard work for at least six weeks." Her no-nonsense efficiency pleased Rosa so much that the dark-skinned Brazilian woman hugged the nurse again.

"Thank you, Angelica." Rosa pronounced the g in her name like an h. "You truly are an angel." It was Angelica's turn to blush, fair complexion turned crimson under Rosa's praise.

"No, Nyc is the real angel here." The young nurse turned and left the room, keeping watch in the hall like they agreed.

Rosa had Nyc bundled up lickity-split. She draped his coat over his shoulders, his cast and sling on his right arm wouldn't fit through the jacket. The rest of his clothes had been cut off when he arrived, so he left wearing a blue, yellow and green sweat-suit. Rosa had wrapped him in the colors of the Brazilian flag.

****

Abigail Miller sat in her tan Volvo station wagon looking all the world like a getaway driver. Oversized cop sunglasses with silver rims hid her blue eyes, a gray scarf wrapped around her neck and mouth like some bank robber. Rosa laughed when she saw Abby and ushered Nyc into the backseat next to a worried-looking Benjamin Miller.

"Thanks, Abby, let's go." The wheels screeched as Abby pulled away from the hospital leaving the smell of stale sickness and death behind.

Nycolos Arcadia, still a little groggy from the drugs for the pain, leaned against his friend and let the ride wash over him. The tan station wagon was pulling up his long driveway of their house before he knew it.

"So when are you leaving?" Abby sounded concerned.

"Tonight, I don't want to wait around for those bigots to figure out what's going on."

"Do you believe it was Lyndon?" By now the tall tale of Lyndon the swamp-thing at the trailer park had spread through the town like wildfire.

"I don't know, but we're not hanging around for the sheriff to tell us it was."

The four of them entered the little yellow farm house through the back door. Ben helped Nyc upstairs and onto his bed before going downstairs for marching orders.

****

The mothers were a whirlwind of activity, preparing the farm for their absence. Rosa and Abby agreed Rosa should pack light. Ben was put in charge of packing Nyc's stuff. Nyc was noncommittal when Ben asked him if he had any preferences, his only request was that his father's knife be included. Ben placed the military-style Ka-bar blade atop the clothes in Nyc's camping pack before zipping it closed. Minutes later he carried the pack downstairs.

Jackson Miller already arrived. He was carrying Rosa's bags and some shopping bags full of food out to their station wagon.

Rosa asked Jackson to move into their house for a couple of months, and he was more than happy to oblige. It had all been arranged, Jackson would move into the yellow farmhouse and run the store across the street. No rent of course, he was doing Rosa the favor, but he forced Rosa to agree that once she and Nyc were settled she would let him bring fruits, veggies and goodies down once a month.

The two families spent the rest of the day in a prolonged tearful embrace of sorts. Abigail and Jackson sat in the kitchen talking with Rosa about rumors bubbling up from trailer park septic tanks. After the Zoo incident, the adults were less skeptical than most residents of New Hamlet. They spoke in hushed voices about Ben and Nycolos, and their repeated confrontations with the bullies. Jackson flexed muscled forearms unconsciously while they talked, hands opening and closing like he was grabbing an axe handle. Rosa couldn't help but wonder if he was thinking about the metal pole Ben swung at Joe Watts's head.

Around noon Ben helped an obviously stiff Nycolos down dark wooden steps to the first floor. He spoke for Nycolos, communicating his friend's request.

"Nyc would like to say goodbye to Mirage."

The adults looked at each other, Rosa and Abigail exchanging motherly glances that spoke volumes. Nycolos could almost hear worried thoughts tumbling all over each other.

"We won't go far, just to the first or second set of orchards, so she'll hear us calling." Ben spoke up quickly, hearing the unspoken concerns in the drawn out silence.

"Alright Nyc, but don't over-do it." Rosa spoke to both of them but locked her green eyes on Nyc at the end. Ben Miller had the back door open and ushered Nyc out, his half-crooked smile igniting worry in the adults.

"I'll go check on them in a couple minutes." Jackson Miller reassured the mothers once the door closed.

****

Benjamin noticed Nyc stopped leaning on him once they were out of sight of the house. Nycolos opened the gate with a horse-head engraved on it and led Ben into the first orchard.

The sun was bright, the bare branches of fruit trees carried a light dusting of snow on gray branches. Nycolos whistled sharply, sticking his tongue between his lips.

"Whe-wheew," sounded Nycolos's whistle. He used Lyndon's whistle to call the horse. They stood quietly for a couple of minutes listening, hearing nothing. Nyc shrugged after a few moments turning to his friend.

"She'll be here in a couple of minutes; let's just walk around a little bit—I feel suffocated in the house."

"Alright. Hey, Nyc, I'm sorry." About what was clear.

"Don't be. We didn't do so bad, at least Damian and Jacob know who not to mess with. The rest was just bad luck, and don't apologize again." The brown boy looked suddenly larger to his friend, his eyes glowed with strength. "I just wish these powers I have would work when I need them to."

"Yeah, well…" Ben didn't say more, he didn't have anything to say.

They opened the next gate with a sheep carved on the door and walked into the next orchard. Mirage was waiting for them, she stepped from behind a beautiful plum tree, skeletal branches so dark they looked black. Her dappled coat was brilliant in the sunlight. She stopped short of the boys, which was when Nycolos Arcadia and Benjamin Miller realized they were not alone.

A wise-looking red fox with a brilliant coat sat on his haunches next to Mirage, pointed ears with brown tips sticking straight up. A brown owl perched in the lowest branch of the plum tree head swiveling from side to side. Nycolos recognized the owl and the fox. Ben did too, and Nyc heard his breath catch in his throat.

"Hello, little ones." Nycolos heard the familiar intonations of the fox in his head, and by the wide eyed expression on Ben's face, this time he did too.

"Hello."

"We came to say goodbye, Mirage told us you were leaving." Mirage flicked her ear at the mention of her name.

"Yes, we're moving to the city for a little while."

"Also as she informed us."

The Great Horned owl hooted twice.

"You two have been marked." The fox's thoughts echoed in his head like a gong.

"Oh great, so now we get killed?" Ben's voice cracked with emotion.

"Marked for protection, you will no longer be menaced by Children of Gaia, either human or otherwise, but you will not see us again."

"Forever?" Nyc couldn't help himself, he didn't know how, but these animals were somehow connected to his father.

"Forever is a very long time Nycolos."

"So not forever then." He was grasping at straws.

"Not forever then." The fox left it at that, and turned his eyes to Ben, sensing the coming question.

"Who ARE you anyway?" Ben's voice grew stronger when the fox didn't respond.

"What does that mean?' Nycolos spoke almost on top of Ben.

"Your questions will be answered in due time." The fox regarded both boys with equal intensity, moving his gaze between them. Amber eyes shone with intensity, shining like gold in the light.

"In due time? You just said we wouldn't see you for a long time." Ben laced his hands together atop his head, hair sticking between fingers.

"Come here, Nycolos."

Nycolos stepped forward immediately as he was beckoned. Standing before the fox Nycolos admired silky brown socks, tufted brown ears.

A blue glow enveloped the fox expanding outward like a growing bubble. The light enveloped Nycolos bathing him in warmth that burned hot in his chest. Seconds later the bubble was gone, red fox remained.

"A gift from us." Feeling dismissed, Nycolos touched Mirage with his broken arm without any pain. She nuzzled his hand happily.

"We are your family. We are your father's family, we are the Earth Mother's family, her children in fact," the answer was clear in both of their minds, though the fox's amber orbs were trained on Ben. "You two will not see us again for several months, lest untoward happenstance should occur. We will visit you again when the appropriate time has arrived."

"The time?" Ben squeaked again.

"The Earth Mother will tell us when, and if you two listen closely, she'll tell you, too." The owl hooted and this time Nyc and Ben heard the hoot in their heads.

"Jackson Miller approaches, we take our leave now. Goodbye, little ones."

"Goodbye." Nycolos and Ben spoke in stereo.

The owl flapped its wings, soared out of sight; the fox turned and stepped forward and disappeared in a red and orange blur of speed.

"Who are you guys talking to?" Jackson Miller—as was his custom—snuck up on the two boys to see what they were up to, finding them staring at the orchard gate.

"Each other." Nyc stepped into the question smoothly, feeling wonderful and excited at the same time. Without waiting for Jackson to reply the ten-year-old scampered up the plum tree and onto Mirage's back. Holding out his casted hand, Nycolos gestured to Ben to step close, and helped his friend onto the horse behind him.

"We'll meet you back at the house, Jackson; Mirage is going to take us back."

Jackson didn't chastise them like he should have, nor did he chase after them. He was struck dumb by Nycolos Arcadia using his broken arm to point and gesture as he rode away with Ben. Not a wince or sign of the pain he should've been feeling. Jackson Miller watched the horse step through an unseen gap in the hedgerow and disappear.

The adults were waiting for Nycolos and Benjamin when they emerged from the orchards some twenty minutes later. They hurried the boys toward the house, leaving Mirage on the back patio looking through the window.

Nycolos Arcadia felt strong and invigorated, confidence welled up in his chest , he acted before anyone could react. Spinning through the open door he cart-wheeled on his left arm and spun a back heel kick. His mother and the Millers pushed through the door way. Jackson wore faded work overalls and Rosa her Brazilian sweat-suit, she nearly knocked him over trying to get their hands on him.

"What are you doing?! Rosa screamed.

"I knew you were up to something!!" Jackson sounded triumphant.

Nycolos pushed them off and windmilled his broken arm like a batter warming up his arm. He would've demonstrated his miraculous recovery further had it not been for Abigail Miller who all but fainted in the doorway. She had seen him in the emergency room, crying then too. Rosa consoled her, telling her how tough Nyc was and that he would be just fine. Abby stumbled, catching her foot on the sill of the doorway. Her oversized glasses tumbling to the red stone tiles, bouncing across the room to Nyc's feet. He ceased his shenanigans and picked up the glasses with his casted arm.

"I'm O.K. Mrs. Miller, really." He looked up into her freckled face, glad he could make her smile. Which she did, lighting up her face with her perfect smile and puffy red eyes. Nycolos understood why Ben and Jackson were so protective of her.

"Be a little more obvious, why don't you." Ben's words dripped with sarcasm.

"About the arm or your mother?" Rosa's voice was similarly glazed.

"Nyc, be a dear and put your arm back in the sling," Abby saw a protest ready to spill from Nyc's eager lips but she cut him off. "Please, for me; at least until you two explain to us what is going on."

Seeing no reason to argue Nycolos did as he was told, returning his arm to the sling and had out with it. He was excited the animals mentioned his father, though what was said was as much a riddle as confirmation that he was alive. He and Ben spoke on top of each other, leap-frogging through sentences until the tale lay bare on the kitchen table. By the time they were done, all sat drinking tea and eating bread. Once he and Ben reached the end, Rosa told Nyc who put the Fontane boys in the hospital.

"They say it was your father, honey."

"Yeah, the fox seemed like he had something he was biting down on." Ben said, his chin glistening with glazed sugar.

"We've been marked for protection, maybe Dad was our protector." Nyc spoke quietly.

"Better late than never I guess," Rosa's tone was dry. "Then why haven't we seen him?"

"He's got a new family, they said we wouldn't be seeing any of them for a while. Besides I don't think he's the same person." Nyc's voice was even quieter.

"That's probably the best for now. Let everyone think the Fontane boys and the Watts woman are out of their minds.

"The last thing we want is anymore attention focused on you two boys. That is why Nycolos, you are going to keep that arm in a sling and walk like your ribs are still cracked for at least a month after you get out of here."

"But, Mom,..."

"But nothing, sweetheart. Right now they think the trailer trash are drunks and drug addicts imagining things in a drunken stupor. If Eric Fontane knows something, he's keeping quiet about it for now. If you show up in town with your arm fixed, and ribs as good as new, people will start to wonder if maybe your father was behind this and all the other attacks."

"That would bring scrutiny here to the Mount we'd all rather avoid." Jackson spoke matter-of-factly. Abby Miller stirred her tea, but didn't drink; of all the members around the table she seemed the most despondent about the departure.

"Well, I have an idea. Since it's barely noon, why don't we have Thanksgiving dinner together tonight? Rosa, you and Nyc can leave afterwards; you said you wanted to leave after midnight."

"Yes, Abby, I do want to drive at night, less traffic and fewer police. Alright, let's do it. But, let's eat at your house just in case the sheriff swings by. Boys, go get one of the turkeys out of the smoke house, and I'll run to the store and get some apples and pumpkins.

"Oh, great!" Jackson's exclamation startled them all, "I just got some new pumpkin and apple pie recipes I wanted to try." He grinned at his family, smile perfectly contagious, just like his mother.

****

And so it was, the two little families vacated the southern slope of the Mount and drove around to the north side to feast, frolic and give thanks. Rosa, Jackson and Abby hung out in the kitchen talking recipes, new and old. Rosa and Abby took care of the potatoes, yams, cranberries and the like, while Jackson stepped out back with the smoked, seasoned turkey, and cooked it in the deep fryer in the backyard.

The boys settled in Ben's room and played video games for a while. They didn't talk about Nycolos leaving anymore. Both knew their lives were connected by unseen forces and the inexplicable mystery of new family. They heard Jackson turn on the TV downstairs and the sound of some sports game filled the living room.

Afternoon stretched into evening and around six the mothers called their boys to dinner. Still several days short of Thanksgiving, the party of five laughed, teased and conversed animatedly. Years later they would all remember that Thanksgiving as one of the best of all time despite the uncertainty hanging over them. The conversation turned to Lyndon for a long time, a happy turn; they relived past moments with shining eyes and heads thrown back in laughter. Inevitably the conversation arrived at the recent events of the Zoo, trailer park and the attack on Lyndon. The adults had suppositions but no more than theories. Abby and Rosa watched Ben and Nycolos during the conversation, painfully aware that the two young boys were experts on the subject, but the boys were through with the conversation. Content in the knowledge that they would meet the strange animals again, a destiny in common, somewhere in the future.

Abby and Rosa stayed in the kitchen to clean up after they all tried two portions of apple and pumpkin pie. Ben and Nyc tromped upstairs once again and were soon dozing on Ben's bottom bunk watching some Japanese Anime that Ben liked so much. The mothers stayed in the kitchen talking long after the boys nodded off and Jackson returned to the Arcadia's home to assume his charge, after hugs and kisses of course. Free to discuss their concerns they chose not to. Somehow the confidence Nycolos exuded infected them all, leaving hardly a worry in their pretty heads. Instead they spoke of Rosa's brother in NY City, and what Rosa had to look forward to in the city. Abby was worried about Ben and Nyc, and wanted to send Ben down with Jackson when he made trips. Rosa was more than pleased to agree.

The final point of business was the story. Ben, Jackson and Abby Miller were willing accomplices to the Arcadian disappearance and were glad they could help. Rosa insisted to her tall blond friend that any lie would do, the most preferable would be to tell the sheriff's office Rosa had taken Nycolos to Brazil to recover from the attack. The only exception being Ranger Thompson. Rosa had taken a liking to the wizened park ranger and his affection for Nycolos. Everyone else was to be fed the same story until their return.

****

Rosa woke Nycolos around 2 A.M. whispering softy until he was awake. Ben woke too, still fully clothed and walked groggily downstairs with Rosa and Nyc. Abby and Ben Miller embraced the Arcadias tearfully and stood at the end of the driveway waving goodbye, lit by the retreating break-lights. Nycolos tried to go back to sleep but couldn't.

He watched the stars whiz by through the foggy glass the blurred shadows of the forest whipping past. Rosa hummed softly, apparently in high spirits as they rocketed through the night. The little brown boy and his mocha-skinn mother left their home in New Hamlet, leaving behind towering spruces, dirt trails and their cozy little farm. They descended out of the mountains toward the concrete jungle, towering glass edifices and the press of humanity. If Rosa and Nycolos Arcadia thought they could escape racism, and the strange happenings in their lives by disappearing among the rushed populace of NYC, they were wrong.

Chapter 12

CITY LIFE

Metallic phallic spin and whir,
penetrate, push, dig into her.
Soil, sod, earth and ore
Gaia our home, so much more.

Nycolos Arcadia decided he liked the city. It felt like a living creature with a pulse and circadian rhythms, vices and ugly parts too. Rosa told him he'd miss the farm, her eyes told him she already did. Though Rosa had grown up in the favelas of Salvador de Bahia, Brazil, among the throngs of humanity, adorned with refuse and waste lining the avenues of her childhood, she was only really happy in the country.

Nyc didn't have as many trees to climb, or trails to hike, but in lieu of those he scouted alleys and dumpsters, fire escapes and rooftops.

The wind was the same—well, not really. The towering buildings like canyon walls funneled the wind, turning breezes into gusts and gusts into gales. He didn't mind so much when the wind blew hard and cold. It smelled somehow cleaner, than what he couldn't say, maybe cleaner than he had imagined. He watched people lean into the wind, a man in a gray trench coat with a gray hat to match lost his garment to the wind; it tumbled down 7th Avenue, disappearing under a taxi. The balding man ran madly after his hat, destination forgotten. The people minded the wind, he heard them on the subway, brushing themselves off and acting cold. Maybe some things about the city did get on his nerves.

Manhattan was fun. They went there with the extended family a few times the first week. Cousins Nycolos had heard of but never met in the flesh were suddenly very present. Central park was a good time, it was almost possible for Nycolos to admire the trees, open spaces, massive rock outcrops and dark brown soil. They stayed in Queens with his cousins, Nyc was good at reading maps, but had so far denied himself the pleasure of pouring over a map of his new neighborhood. Instead he contented himself with back alleys and shortcuts. Queens was greener than Manhattan at least.

He had trouble sleeping the first several nights. Their cousin's home was somewhere near Steinway. They lived in a beautiful three story brownstone. There were some Brazilian neighbors a few doors down, the rest of the neighborhood was a hodgepodge of families from South and Central America, Jamaicans and Hatians and even some Russians and Polish clustered on their own little blocks. He shared a room with his mother, his uncle had cleaned it out when he got the call from Rosa that they needed a place to stay for a while. Rosa's brother Mauro de Silva was older than Rosa by a few years, just as dark as she, and his body rippled with muscle. He had the same full lips as Rosa, same nose, hair in tight curls, gray flecks marking the passage of years. His wife Carolina de Silva was a few shades lighter than Rosa, her complexion closer in color to Nyc's. Her hair fell in undulating waves to the middle of her back over fit, muscled shoulders. Nyc realized immediately they were fun to be around. Mauro worked as a butcher at a Polish butcher shop. He was taller than Rosa, about six feet.

Nina de Silva and her brother Sidney were a different matter altogether. Sidney was in high school and had a life. Never in the house for longer than absolutely necessary Sidney de Silva was a ghost moving through the hallways in the pre-dawn light. Taller than both of his parents he was lithe and supple, moving with the grace Nycolos recognized in Rosa.

Courteous and conscientious he rarely made a sound when he left the house. Nina was a bit louder and much more present. Her 15-year-old body was that of a budding woman. She attracted suitors with her perky disposition and flesh. Missy and junior clothing that fit loosely the previous spring now stretched tight over her newly plump bottom and enlarged bust. She greeted Nycolos with a large smile and a big hug that left the ten-year-old breathless, and stunned with his mouth hanging open. To the delight and teasing laughter of his entire family. Nycolos Arcadia was not yet old enough to care, still found himself staring at his cousin's chest when they were introduced. Nina was a slip of a thing, taller than her mother she had her mother's complexion. She was coffee with extra cream to her father's espresso roast. Her curls were broad and wavy, down to the middle of her back. Rounded calves stretched into forever, strong from years of soccer and dance. During the winter she wore jeans so tight her mother asked if she could breathe before sending her on her way. Green eyes like Colombian emeralds had skipped Mauro de Silva, but not Rosa, or Nina. Nycolos recognized them the moment he saw them, standing out in contrast to her bronzed skin, pale in the winter months. Nina retained the rosebud lips of her mother, but the long eyelashes of her father and the rounded shoulders of the de Silva clan; her soft eyes and sculpted cheeks looked more like Rosa than Carolina.

Carolina and Mauro da Silva were cool parents as far as Nycolos was concerned. They were open with Sidney and Nina about sex, love, the birds and the bees, relationships and the customs and vices of such subjects. Nina and Sidney were routinely embarrassed by their parent's jokes about doing it whenever either offspring had friends of the opposite sex over. Nina's undeniable beauty had not gone unnoticed and gained the blossoming teen, a second generation Brazilian, attention she would have rather done without. Most recent were the varied and diverse attempts of two men on opposite ends of the male spectrum. The first, a young black boy sixteen years who meant well, though his pre-developed habits got him off on the wrong foot with Mauro da Silva. He showed up on the front stoop of their brownstone after dinner one evening. Mauro da Silva answered the door and the young man did well to introduce himself and convey his interest in the beautiful Nina. Mauro was not impressed, the youth wore his pants below his butt and an oversized t-shirt that hung nearly to his knees, but gave the boy with corn-rolls the benefit of the doubt, that is until he called Mauro son.

"You know what I'm sayin', son, your daughter is so beautiful she's like a work of art, you know what I'm sayin'?"

The truth of the matter was Mauro da Silva did know what the kid was talking about. His little girl was a work of art, her beauty profound, at times simple and at other times complex. Her beauty was clearly present to her father, even when she was a baby. Mauro bounced her on his knee for years, drinking in her sweet laughter that sounded like bells chiming. She had only just stopped sitting on his lap last year, around the time her body started to develop, she became self-conscious about her womanhood, and more succinctly, now had a life of her own.

By the time Nina came downstairs to greet the boy; prompted by her mother commenting that her father was going to kill her 'little friend', the boy had already been burned by the heat of Mauro's voice. Mauro informed the boy in a less than polite manner that he was not the boy's son, in fact he was old enough to be the boy's father, and if he was his father he would tell him to pull up his pants and buy some clothes that fit him. Mauro chased the fool boy down the block, kicking him all the way. The boy with corn rolls stumbled and fell over and over again, hampered by the pants he had pulled below his ass. The boy never spoke to Nina again, she in turn swore never to speak to Mauro again.

She did, of course, just as Carolina said she would. Carolina was full of pearls of wisdom, the problem being she hid them in hours of lectures so boring Nina often cried, just so they would end. During one such lecture, Carolina advised her daughter, "if the boy can't forgive you for your parents then you don't want anything to do with him anyway, because your parents are your parents forever." Carolina's nostrils flared when she doled out wisdom, as they had that day. Nina made peace with her father the following week when she asked him to pay her cell phone bill.

Mauro didn't mention the temper tantrum, but Carolina did it for him, lecturing Nina for a good hour about recognizing the error of her ways and speaking without thinking.

The second suitor to come calling was a fellow expatriated Brazilian. An older man in his early fifties, he owned a store near Mauro's, though he sold religious artifacts instead of meat. The older gentleman showed up wearing a white and tan Guayabera, it matched well with his tan suit pants. Gold shone on pinky fingers, wrist and around his neck. He affected a courteous visit to the casa of da Silva. He spoke with Mauro in the dining room for several minutes drinking caiparinha before he got to the real reason for his visit. The older gentleman had seen Mauro's daughter walking home from her father's butcher shop several times. He lived in the neighborhood and was under the impression if he should express his good nature and intentions to court Nina, her parents would be forthcoming with their blessings. The finely-dressed Brazilian with gold chains and slim long fingers was careful to reiterate his hands off courting, he would treat her like a queen and comply with her every wish.

"Surely you understand, Senor Silva, in our country, age is nothing compared to love."

Mauro explained with butcher's hands and muscled arms that he did indeed understand and thrashed the man soundly. (the rest of the family was out) Mauro was quick and careful to clean up the blood from the wood floors before his wife got home with the kids. Mauro da Silva kept the incident to himself, but made a conscious effort to take the whole family to the Religious artifacts shop where he feigned interest and bought several extra tall candles decorated with prayers and the face of the Virgin Mary. After leaving he explained to all of them why the man's right eye was swollen shut and he was walking with a limp. Mauro was careful to explain to his wife, son and daughter that under no circumstances was Nina to be talking to, escorted by, or anywhere near the man who ran the religious artifact shop and wore guayaberas.

Nycolos and Rosa were conscious to stay out of the way of their extended family. Caroline, Nina and the fellows stayed out of their business as well. On the fourth night in their new home after a churrasco (bar-b-q) of rack of ribs and fejoada, Rosa had out with it. She told them about Lyndon's death, the logging attack, and his disappearance. Nyc's several encounters with the bullies and their decision to leave New Hamlet after the death of Joseph Watts and the accusations of Lyndon's involvement.

After the heartfelt talk with Nyc, Mauro took Rosa into the sitting room through the French doors. They stood close to the hearth and Mauro hugged his little sister and they cried together until the fire had burned to embers. Rosa and her older brother had been separated by age and geography for so long she hadn't thought about their two families really being one until her hand was forced by the fates. That night after supper they wept, and her brother wept for her pain. Rosa always said home was where the heart was, and once she waded through the guilt, her heart was joyful.

Mauro and Sidney treated Nyc as one of their own, filling a masculine void Rosa hadn't thought to fill. Nina and Caroline took to the boy as well, Carolina smothering with hugs that left him breathless, and Nina coddled him like he was her favorite brother. They started their mornings with fried cosinha, rounded cone of tapioca flour around chicken or beef and cheesy goodness filling the center. Rosa spoke longingly of the cosinhas to Nyc, of warm nights with the sea breeze in her face on the beaches of Salvador. But she had never endeavored to make them on the farm. Nycolos fell for the cosinhas immediately and the neatly packaged ball of fried flower quickly became his favorite for breakfast, lunch or dinner. He ate them with such delight his Aunt Carolina started calling him 'cosinha', which translated to little thing. *Great,* Nycolos thought, he hoped it didn't stick.

After eight weeks of laying low Rosa arranged for Nycolos to start at the local public school. Fine as far as Nycolos was concerned. Two months of being housebound had him stir crazy and ready to do anything. New Year's, and Christmas already fading into memory, gray blustery February morning walks to school were a welcome change.

Nina attended the high school nearby. She volunteered to escort him to school for the time being until he felt more comfortable. That night after dinner Nycolos scaled the fire escape outside his third floor room, ascending to the snow-covered roof of the brownstone. The snow crunched under his feet as Nycolos moved to the low wall that separated the tar-coated roof of each brownstone, and delineated the perimeter of the brownstone's roof. He sat atop the brick wall and felt the breeze blow across his cheeks. As good a spot as any, he ran through the meditation exercises his mother and father taught him in capoeira class.

He conjured the mental image of his private place. A forested patch in his mind's eye, spruce and birch trees that huddled tightly around a small pond whose surface rippled, stirred by the errant caress of the wind. The trees did not sway in the breeze, nor creak at the wind's passing. Nycolos quieted his mind and let thought slip away into nothingness of time. The small pond stilled, the surface becoming like a perfect sheet of glass, quiet surface reflecting the images of spruce boughs above. City sounds fell away into the distance of space and Nycolos saw himself seated at the pond's edge. The pond rippled as thoughts skidded across the threshold of silence. School again, among strangers he hadn't grown up with, whether he liked them or not. There would be no friends this time, only strange faces and new places.

He opened his eyes, aware of his surroundings, sensing the stillness on the rooftop and hearing the echoing noises rising on the wind from the street below. The sky glowed orange, the electric burn of the city below reflected on the underside of slate gray clouds.

Clean water fell from the sky through polluted air thick with ozone and smog, bouncing off concrete gargoyles and iron scaffoldings. Flowing downward over asphalt, mingling with cigarette butts, urine, saliva and refuse, coursing into the subterranean veins and arteries, rumbling bowels as runoff churned toward the city's nether regions, to be excreted through outlet pipes into the surrounding bodies of water, the Hudson, the East River, the sound, the Atlantic.

Nycolos watched himself from above, sitting still, cross-legged with closed eyes, his afro puff one shadow among many. The sky above his mental forest was gray and glowing orange like the sky above queens. The pond was still, like a sheet of glass shining an orange glow back toward the heavens. Nycolos knew beneath still surface the pond was deep, with a few large boulders and some millweed or some other such water plant his mind conjured up, a few fish of no significance.

At the bottom of the pond, recessed in a cave, was a large oak door. Behind the door a hallway stretched 50 meters or so. The hallway changed every time he visited, sometimes the hallway was shining wood with dark wooden floors and wrought-iron lamps lining the walls. Other times the passageway seemed to burrow through an earthen mound, walls like stucco with brass lanterns hanging from wooden hooks along the length of the hallway. Most recently there had been no lights, instead the hallway had roots protruding from the roof, and forming patterns along the walls and floor. A phosphorescent glow emanated from everywhere and nowhere all at once.

The hallway was dry, it never flooded, even if he left the door open, the pond surface didn't pass the oak threshold. Doors lined each side of the passageway, standing opposite each other. The first door to his right was a room full of boxes. Every surface of every wall was covered with boxes, the floor, the ceiling, they stuck to their designated places and didn't move. Many of the boxes were empty, in fact most of the boxes were empty.

Those directly opposite the door were labeled across the bottom. The boxes were wooden with silver lettering, the inside consisting of piles of papers, or in some cases filed folders of information. One box said Capoiera, another Mathematics, another Animals, and another said Farm. His father taught him how to make this room, explaining how to arrange the boxes and how to visualize the things he learned, put them in the boxes, and more importantly how to retrieve them. Lyndon Arcadia told Nycolos that one-day he would be able to recall most anything, even everyday occurrences if he used the room enough. One day he would have a photographic memory if he wanted.

The other rooms were empty, though Lyndon assured him they would fill with important things like music, conscious and unconscious pantries of decision and indecision. As it was, no matter which door he entered, they were all the box room currently. Sitting on the bank of the pond Nycolos was startled by two large yellow eyes and a reptilian head breaking the surface of the pond, diving downwards with a splash. Nycolos stood in his mental forest, shocked by movement in a construct of his mind. He mentally probed himself, brain, body, the air surrounding him in Queens, the sound of footsteps clanging on the fire escape, nothing. Someone was coming up the fire escape but he didn't feel a presence in his mind, or body, he felt good. He kept his focus on the mental image, preparing to dive with his consciousness into the crystalline depths. His mental self scanned the forest stand for signs of movement. The dry rustle of leaves, and Nycolos saw a turtle lurch next to a birch tree.

****

"Nycolos?"

His eyes snapped open and he heard metal clang on the top of the fire escape, boots on metal, the mental image faded into the recesses of Nyc's mind to be conjured again when he summoned it. It had been too long since he meditated.

Turning at the waist, Nyc looked over his shoulder and saw Nina come up and over the wall, holding the metal banister built into the stairs, stepping into the snow that coated the roof with a crunch.

"What are you doing?" Her voice was soft but carried in the still night air, curiosity shading the edges of her words.

Nycolos stifled a sigh, inner peace shattered as much by his cousin as by the reptilian images invading his mind, swimming in his pond. How could there be an animal in there? The entire visualization was a construct of his mind, a tool his father called it, designed for meditation and memory recall. How a snake or a turtle could be there and not be products of his imagination or under his control was beyond him.

"I'm meditating." Nycolos uncrossed his legs and let them hang over the side of the brownstone, waiting for Nina.

"Aren't you cold up here?" Concern replaced curiosity and he saw a blanket wrapped around her shoulders. Her loose curls were snugly pressed against the side of her head by the black knit cap she wore pulled down over her ears. She idled up to his side and looked over the edge.

"Not really." She sat next to him, but didn't swing her legs over the low brick wall, instead left her feet on the snow covered roof.

"Thinking about school tomorrow?"

"I guess, maybe a little."

"Well don't worry too much, the school's not in the best shape but the teachers are pretty nice."

"That's good."

Nina eyed him quizzically, sensing the lack of interest in his voice. "Will you teach me how to meditate Nyc?"

"Now?"

"No, not now silly, but soon."

"Sure."

"Good, I'll leave you to it; don't stay up here too late, o.k? That's your mom talking not me."

"O.K.," he gave the Brazilian thumbs-up, "I'll be down soon."

She crunched back across the roof and clanged down the fire escape. Nycolos didn't try to resume his meditation exercise, instead ruminated on the secret world he had come to know. As if on cue, pigeons began to alight on the roof. Not one or two, but hundreds and hundreds of pigeons descended on the rooftop, alighting along the length of the low wall and on all the rooftops. Every rooftop except the one he was on. Like the crows and ravens that day at the farm house, the birds stood still and quiet staring at him. Mystery shrouded the details of the unknown world he had stumbled into the day his father died. A world of magic and metamorphosis with animals and earth holding the keys to unseen doors that lead to unimagined places. A fox, an owl, a hawk, had just left his life, and now some reptile and a turtle were lurking through the nether regions of his mind. He was unable to explain logically how the animals were somehow connected to those that had appeared in his life.

Nycolos sighed loudly, breath misting and ears stinging with cold. He missed Ben and Mirage, Abby and Jackson. He missed his meadow and the orchards he hid in. At least the Millers were coming down in another couple weeks. Rosa was going to start selling her organic poultry out of Mauro's butcher shop; maybe some goat. too. Mauro said there were a lot of people that liked goat in their neighborhood. So Jackson, Ben and Abby were bringing down turkey, duck, goat and an assorted variety of bird species Mauro was confident would sell among the Caribbeans, Latinos and eastern Europeans that dotted the neighborhoods.

Communities blending from one to another seamlessly until Nyc felt the whole world could be found somewhere in one neighborhood or another. Nycolos looked forward to the Miller's visit, but would have to muscle it out for a few more weeks.

His initial excitement of moving to the city fading, left in its place a determination to disappear, to do his time in concrete exile. The buzz and hum of the city that never slept became white noise, no longer did he sit at the window for hours, just watching people and traffic flow by. The gray concrete of buildings, black marble and red bricks, and too few trees made him feel closed in, even outside. He felt the lack of trees strongly and contented himself with the large tree of heaven that had taken root in the too small backyard. He leaned on its gray trunk or sat between roots that conformed nicely to his back. His only reprieve the knowledge that Rosa assured him the move was temporary, within a year they'd be back on the farm doing their own thing.

Rosa's demeanor had changed during the first two weeks in Queens. Initially ecstatic about renewing her relationship with her brother, full of familial pride, Rosa engineered family dinners, trips to the museum and ice-skating. Her enthusiasm since cooled, Rosa spent the last three weeks cooking up a storm with her sister in law. The kitchen fires went out at night, but only just, they fired up again at six when Rosa had taken to making bread that smelled fresh and sweet. Nyc couldn't manage to stay in bed most mornings and ended up in the kitchen drinking tea with the ladies and eating hot buttered bread.

The thought of morning and bread made his jaw crack with a powerful yawn. Breaking his reverie, the little brown boy crossed the roof and clanged down the fire escape to the window outside the room he and Rosa shared. He climbed through the window and put his jacket and boots in the closet before brushing his teeth and tucking himself into bed. He slept deeply regardless of the nerves he felt about a new school.

In his dreams he sat at a toadstool table with toadstool chairs and had tea and fresh buttered bread with a snake, a turtle, a frog, a pixie, and a fox. They laughed and hinted at secrets, joked about the conveniences and unseen dark places of city life, and acted for all the world like civilized adults. Nyc woke in the morning, unsure if the bread he smelled was real, or remnants from a dream.

****

Nycolos wiped melted butter from his chin with the back of his hand. The house was a flurry of activity as Nina and Sidney prepared themselves for school. Nycolos, long since awake, sat at the table finishing his tea and bread, eyeing his cosinha still on the blue and white plate. His mother and Aunt were drinking coffee and discussing Latin American politics in Portuguese, most of which he didn't understand except for words like Fidel, Chavez, and Morales.

Sidney was gone by 7:30. Nina offered to walk Nyc to his school before heading off to the high school herself. He suffered through kisses on the head from mother and aunt, a pat on the behind sending him out the door. The morning was sunny if not warm; they walked past sad green ash trees and Norway maples that shifted sidewalk slabs like they were miniature tectonic plates or some such thing.

The school was darker than Nycolos had imagined, dark stone and mortar three stories high like a Gothic sanatorium, barred windows to keep the patients from pouring into the outside world, afflicting the world with their madness. The school occupied a half block, the remaining half block was cement and asphalt with basketball hoops and handball courts, Nyc assumed he would be having recess there. Nina stopped at the foot of the stairs leading up to large double doors opening and closing as students moved inside in droves.

"I'll meet you right here when you get out. all right?" Nina bent over and put her hands on her knees to look into his eyes. She winked at him and he noticed the glitter around her eyes.

She wore snug broken-in jeans that had a faded look to them with some yellow running shoes. Her blue jacket sat high on her waist like a pilots jacket.

She turned and waved goodbye and was running down the sidewalk, backpack bouncing up and down on her back. Nycolos turned to the dark stone building and moved into the halls of knowledge. The interior was no more encouraging than the exterior. A security guard sat at the base of two large curving stairways that arced on the left and right sides of the room up to the first floor hallway. Nyc was jostled and bumped by the other students engaged in conversations or half awake, not expecting someone standing stationary just inside the doors. He was eventually pushed to the security guard's podium and opened his mouth to ask a few questions.

"You must be Nycolos." The security guard was a black man wearing all blue with a patch on his jacket shaped like a star.

"Yes." Rosa told Nyc to talk to the security guard and the rest would be explained to him.

"Alright, Nycolos, let's go." The man's hair was cut short, a large bald spot occupying the back of his head. The man stepped down from the podium and Nycolos saw he was of average height but his girth was quite ample. They joined the flow of children and the current parted around the wide security guard like water around a boulder in a stream. Nycolos followed him, distracted by new surroundings. Glass partitions that flanked doors were cracked and shattered, only wire mesh running through the glass keeping it from breaking completely. A couple holes looked suspiciously like bullet holes, scattered high in the corners of exterior windows. The glass in most of the school's doors were also broken, shattered, or completely missing.

The overweight security guard jingled and jangled all the way to a classroom with the glass pane of the door completely missing, a plywood board instead filled the void left by the absent pane.

Room 209 seemed benign enough from the outside, the numbers painted in black on the plywood plank. No artwork or other accomplishments hung above the lockers or around the door. The security guard gave him a smile and opened the door.

"Have fun."

Perturbed momentarily by the lack of decorations, Nycolos exhaled the breath he wasn't aware he was holding. The classroom was decorated with geometric shapes, angles, fractions and examples of long division crawling down the side of walls with remainders and decimals marching horizontally. The teacher had been wise enough to face the student's desks away from the door, leaving her chair and desk the only one facing the door. Nycolos counted off six columns of beaten wooden desks with uneven legs and scarred tops, by five rows for a total of thirty. He was grateful to see an empty desk situated at the back of the room and close to the window, barred or otherwise.

A lady rose upon hearing the door open, simultaneously 29 ten-year-olds turned to see who was entering their classroom. Mrs. Delisi had coppery skin, yet to pale with age and straight hair that must've been black like a raven's in her youth. Her eyes were strong enough that Nycolos felt them from across the room. She moved lightly across the floor coming to stand next to Nycolos. She smelled of baby powder and vanilla perfume. She wore a long green dress that nearly scraped the floor, white sneakers that reminded him of the nurse back in New Hamlet that had pinched his cheeks and winked at him.

Mrs. Delisi addressed the class and something occurred to Nycolos he hadn't thought of before, there were more brown and black faces in this one classroom than in his entire town of New Hamlet. 28 faces of varying shades of brown and black regarded him with unblinking eyes for a few very long moments. Nycolos couldn't help but be thankful yet again, for once he wouldn't be that one kid different than the rest.

The thought prompted guilt deep in his bowels, a little voice in the back of his head told him to be nice, he knew what it was like to be the one white kid at the front of the room.

"Children." Mrs. Delisi's voice was high pitched and slightly nasal, but not so much to be annoying. He could feel her long fingers resting lightly on his shoulder.

"This is Nycolos Arcadia. He will be joining us for the rest of the year. I expect each of you to treat him as you would like to be treated."

"Yes, Mrs. Delisi." The class replied as one.

And just like that the Undisputed King of Hide and Seek began school in Queens.

Mrs. Delisi wasted no time returning to her lesson plan and Nycolos was slightly chagrined when he realized the class was several units behind his class in New Hamlet, boredom evoking tears in his eyes. Mrs. Delisi wasn't as lenient as his teacher in New Hamlet and snapped Nycolos to attention several times when his mind wandered far beyond the iron bars and uneven desktops. She threw a few tough problems at him and even some conversions that he handled with aplomb not missing a beat.

After that Mrs. Delisi didn't try to surprise him again with any questions. She did pull him to the side once they were sent to recess and asked him in a very soft and kind voice that nearly made him blush.

"Mr. Arcadia , I would appreciate it if you could pay attention to my lessons. If you aren't feeling challenged we can find some extra-credit work for you, how does that sound?"

"That would be fine, Mrs. Delisi." His smile was polite, but grew deep and genuine when he saw surprise in her face. Surely she hadn't been expecting such a reply, but she rolled with it.

"Very well, Mr. Arcadia, I'll have something for you tomorrow."

"O.K."

She dismissed the matter with a nod of her head and offered to show him to the cafeteria.

Chapter 13

School Daze

*Send forth those siblings
long forgot.
Taught man his lessons,
though he remember not.*

He knew they had arrived by the rumble of voices and children speaking all over each other. The lunchroom was another of those gauntlets through which all children had to pass, and new kids often fell victim to. Mrs. Delisi left him at the door and he walked into the hubbub. The room was already busy enough that he detected no audible difference upon his entrance, though the tables closest to him did quiet to hushed whispers as other children saw him for the first time. A long line snaked from a doorway off to the right, winding across faded blue linoleum tiles the custodian could never get completely clean. Nycolos assumed the line stretched from the kitchen full of high-fructose corn syrup subsidized by the government both as corn and as the syrupy sugar, then asked why kids were overweight. Nycolos thought of Lyndon Arcadia for several moments as he scanned the lunchroom for open places and a safe table to sit at, his father had always gotten worked up over subsidies for big agribusiness, monoculture crops, and high fructose corn syrup the government bought from some agricultural producers and then put in all the government issue food. God forbid an inner city mother or trailer-park mom try to buy something healthy with her food stamps.

He spied a benign looking table off to the left with only two boys sitting at it. Nycolos traversed the gauntlet, thrusting past the prying eyes and open mouths full of half chewed food. He felt something bounce off his afro, which was puffy today, and ricochet to another table by the outcries he heard. As he drew close he saw one boy was definitely Latino with a rather large nose and dark greasy-looking hair. He looked tall and his cheeks were splotchy and flushed with red. When Nycolos asked if they minded, he stood immediately and extended his hand to Nyc. Nycolos shook the boy's overly sweaty hand and sat down opposite. The second boy's name was Kofi Everett, he was a nice kid about the same complexion as Nyc, Mocha with milk. He told Nyc his father was from Ghana, West Africa and his mother from Germany. She was living in Africa for many years where she met his father. Kofi was proportionate to Nycolos if a little thicker in the middle.

They were both in his class even though he hadn't noticed, but they both said hello to him when prompted by Mrs. Delisi. She wasn't a bad teacher according to Kofi and Gino Cabrera, but didn't tolerate nonsense. The two boys were nice, if somehow selected against by the absurd social Darwinism of popularity. Nycolos immediately realized they were 'misfits', cast out and treated so by their more accepted peers, if acknowledged at all.

It was obvious to Nyc why Gino was an outcast. His greasy hair and sweaty palms were easy targets for the ire of other students. The other Latino kids—and there were plenty—found him too shy and awkward to accept. His unkempt hair and gangly feet ensured that he became a bulls-eye for Latino and black girls, hiding their own insecurities behind insults and sharp tongues.

Kofi was another story. His mocha with milk complexion should've passed as acceptable for all. It wasn't until gym class later that afternoon that Nyc understood why Kofi was a misfit. The class played soccer in the gymnasium with uneven floor boards and a draft from a pair of emergency doors that didn't close quite right. The class was split in half, Nycolos ended up with Gino and Kofi on his team. Nycolos Arcadia watched from the goal for the two minutes it took him to realize no-one on his team had any clue what they were doing, except Gino. Greasy, gangly or otherwise, the Ecuadorian kid was like butter with the ball, he was rendered ineffective by teammates who failed to run or blatantly kicked the ball to the other team.

Kofi, who at least knew where to be, was no help. Though less awkward in appearance, Kofi had not grown into his body and had no sense of space around him. Nycolos watched with chagrin as he stumbled over his own feet in a rush of jumbled excitement. The next minute he ran full tilt into a kid from the other team, focused as he was on an incoming pass. Nyc was forced to defend against three shots before he had a chance to vacate the post, handing it off to a black girl with pigtails and a keen disinterest in the game.

He stepped onto the pitch, whistled high and loud cutting through the yelling and squeaking sneakers. The Ecuadorian kid looked over immediately, recognizing the whistle as a call for attention. Gino passed the ball to Nyc and it was on. Nyc and Gino moved together like a well-oiled machine, communicating with claps whistles, and nods of the head. Nycolos and Gino scored immediately, a little give and go, three times back and forth and the ball was in the back of the net. Gino and Nyc racked up five points in quick succession before the kids on the other team organized enough to cause a problem. Kofi did have some latent ability, he ran great interference . His awkward physical control and stumbling buffoonery was perfect for crushing opposing players and running screens, effectively preventing the other team from scoring.

All in all, the three of them made a good team; the final score was ten to six. Nycolos scored a goal as the bell rang with a beautiful side volley, crushing an arcing cross sent into the box by Gino. That was how Nyc found himself as the new kid sitting at the misfit table, word of which passed quickly through the grade, such that Mrs. Delisi looked at him differently the next morning when he walked through the door with no window a little early. She complied with his request and gave him the problem set she was only just explaining to the class, which kept him busy until they all moved onto reading and such.

Walking through the cafeteria the second day no one threw anything at him. The misfit table had two new faces. Kofi and Gino introduced him to the two kids though they came off a bit obsequious. Jason Fields was a black kid from Queens and had an aloof attitude that conveyed indifference. Which seemed to impress Kofi, Gino and the rest of the grade. Nyc didn't hear any alarm bells, though Jason's aloofness came across as a little arrogant, especially when he sat waiting for Nycolos to address him. Nycolos could see the kid's mouth tightening as he spoke with Kofi and Gino and continued to ignore the new comer. As far as Nyc was concerned his cool guy attitude wasn't going to cut it.

Raymond Somcio was the other kid, he was excited to meet Nycolos and though not in the same class as Nycolos, he had been on the other soccer team in Gym the previous day, as had Jason. Ray wanted to talk about martial arts. Nycolos took the opportunity to check out Jason and Ray. Jason was paying attention, even with his back to the table. His pants were dark blue denim and a little big, his boots looked new and unlaced, the tongue pulled way out. His blue sweatshirt was unzipped but he had the hood up around his narrow face with big brown eyes and long eyelashes. His hair was cut short so that he was almost bald. Ray was as skinny as a bushel of bamboo, lightning quick and excitable to boot. He wore non-descript khakis, white and blue running shoes and a striped sweater with a blue background with green stripes. Nyc remembered them from the day before, particularly Raymond and his speed.

Nycolos explained capoeira to the boys and what training with his mother was like. He didn't extend an invitation to any of them, but left the door open for any of them to express interest. Ray, who was not shy at all, jumped all over the opportunity and offered to trade Kung-Fu and Tai-chi for Capoeira and soccer. Nycolos agreed and it was decided. Jason finally swallowed his pride and also asked if he could join just as Kofi and Gino spoke up together. Nyc scheduled a meeting for that weekend, they would meet Saturday on the hard asphalt of the schoolyard, begin the knowledge exchange, and talk about other locations.

The rest of the week was a blur of new names and faces, once he found a niche, it seemed the rest of the kids would at least talk to him. By Friday Mrs. Delisi had the class up to speed and Nycolos was out of extra credit work. His new friends were excited about the Saturday meeting and honestly so was Nycolos. His excitement was further heightened that morning when Rosa announced Jackson, Abby and Benjamin Miller were coming down that weekend to bring meat for the butcher shop. School was over in the blink of an eye and Nyc was home, asking Rosa for pointers and permission for what he had planned the following morning. She agreed happily, overjoyed Nycolos had friends already, and took him up to the roof of the brownstone to run him through his paces.

Nina and Carolina came up to watch and eventually Mauro and Sidney did too when they heard the ruckus. The work out turned into a jogo and exactly what the mother and son needed. Nycolos began by scaring her, he ran past her spinning meia lua de frente, jumping up on the low brick wall that bordered the roof. He was moving so quickly he heard his entire family scream out in fear, afraid he was jumping to his death. He pushed off with his right foot, flipping his body back and up, tucking his knees to his chest; he saw his mother's terror-stricken face upside-down as he back-flipped over her head. His feet hit the rooftop and he picked his head up in time to see Rosa whip around. Fear melted from her face, instead laughter glinted in her green eyes and an unspoken menace suffused her sly grin.

The Silva's were hooting and hollering, giving the first exchange to the kid. After that it took all of Nyc's skill to keep his mother from catching him with her heels. Such deadly heels she had. He cart-wheeled with no hands over ductwork shining silver and gray, he hid behind vents and even over the brick wall once. Rosa had enough restraint to refrain from breaking said vents and ducts, but she did crack a few bricks when she brought her right heel down on the wall Nyc was hiding behind. Mauro ran downstairs and came back with his birimbau while Nina and Carolina clapped along, singing songs of the roda.

Nycolos was forced to crabwalk backwards, just barely dodging his mother's foot as it cut through the air inches from his nose. He rolled toward her, and he hooked his foot behind her planted right foot and pulled. Her foot shifted easily and Nycolos was sure he had finally caught her off balance, only to see her back-handspring out of danger, to the hoots and hollers of the family; that round went to Rosa.

They kept it up until they were both jacket-less and panting. Rosa finally called it, telling them it was getting dark and time to make dinner. Mauro and Sidney slapped Nyc on the back so hard it stung, play-fighting each other on the fire escape all the way down. The extended family descended to the kitchen. Nyc sat at the kitchen table while his mother gave him some pointers.

He needed to keep his eyes focused on his opponent more, he needed to have a second and third move ready should his first prove ineffective. His technique and form looked good but she thought he should work on his spins and handstands for a while. She wrote down a lesson plan for him to follow and some basic rules about teaching capoiera. She urged him to keep it simple, and the sparring light to nonexistent. Definitely no contact. Rosa assured him she would look for a place to show them the jinga, some basic kicks and punches.

"Don't bother trying to teach them about the game of it, or the malicia, they won't understand yet."

"O.K., Mom." He had to agree.

****

Mauro brought home some flank steaks and cooked them on an indoor grill he constructed. The kitchen was full of the noise of cooking and family. Mauro and Sidney continued to laud Nyc's skills in a fight, breaking the compliments only long enough to tell Rosa what a good job she and Lyndon had done. Dinner was delicious, bar-b-que steaks, dry rubbed with cumin, salt, pepper, vinegar and lime juice cooked medium rare. Fried yucca, plantains and ocra rounded out the greasy comforting meal. Mauro was in a good mood, glad to have his sister coming to work with him, he drank cold beer pulled from the fridge and cracked jokes in Portuguese that Nyc was sure were not for children's ears. The women laughed heartily, telling Mauro he was a scoundrel and had a dirty mouth to boot.

The ladies sipped red wine and talked, Rosa let Nycolos have some soda if he ran down to the corner store run by a pair of Lebanese brothers, and back with his caffeinated booty. Mauro let Sidney drink a beer and made a big deal about pretending to hide it from the women, Carolina made a big deal about pretending to be scandalized and Sidney drank his beer with a smile that just wouldn't quit. Nycolos dozed off at the table listening to Mauro play Bossa Nova on his guitar, and Rosa woke him around midnight and walked him upstairs to bed.

Nycolos had trouble sleeping at first, his mind spinning like a top once he finally got his pajamas on and tucked into bed. Rosa put on a movie that was awesome and always made him want to learn kickboxing. Rosa agreed if she could find a place for him to take classes around the neighborhood. He was asleep before half of the movie finished and somersaulted and flipped through the nightscape of his dreams.

****

He woke to Rosa's gentle prodding at 8 am, and rambled downstairs answering the call of nature, after which he stood in the kitchen scratching his head and trying to rub the sleep from his eyes. His brain was slow to process the new arrival sitting in the kitchen. Abby Miller sat at the kitchen table with Rosa, looking as beautiful as ever with her slim librarian glasses and sandy-blond hair tumbling into her face. Her golden locks blocked her face from Nycolos but he heard her speaking in a low voice to Rosa, holding Rosa's hand in one of her own and a steaming cup of coffee in the other.

Her eyes lit up when they landed on Nycolos, she cut her sentence short and stood, spreading her arms wide and beckoning to Nycolos she spoke loud enough for him to hear.

"There he is, my handsome boy."

Nyolos was too tired to be embarrassed and rubbed his eyes one more time before burying his face in her chest.

"I missed you, Abby."

"I missed you too, honey." She hugged him tight and kissed the top of his head. "Go say hi to Ben, he's in the living room."

And so he was. Ben was sitting in a recliner watching Saturday morning cartoons. The boys shared an awkward hug that was as sincere as Abby's had been.

"Still have a crush on my mom?"

"Not so much," Nyc lied, "but she's still really pretty."

"So's your cousin."

"You met Nina then?"

"Yeah." Ben's face flushed, capillaries dilating in his face, blood suffusing the tissue.

"She's a little too city for a country boy like you." Nyc had to say something to fill the silence.

"Whatever..."

****

Nycolos was finally awake and excused himself to brush his teeth and get dressed. By the time he was done, everyone was outside. Ben and Nina sat on the stoop watching Jackson, Mauro, and Rosa go through the inventory. Jackson brought down in the medium-sized yellow truck with freezer lined walls and shelves in the back. Jackson and Ben came down from the hills along scenic byways, trailed by Abby in her faded wagon. When Nyc crossed the threshold of the brownstone's front door Jackson Miller extracted his tall freckled frame from the inventory of pheasants, grouse, lamb, chicken, pork, goat, and duck, tinctures and oils from the shop and even some of his woodwork to boot. He hopped down from the yellow truck and gave Nyc a monstrous bear hug, grabbed him by the feet and hung him upside down for a couple of seconds until chastened by the powerfully exhaled breath of Abby Miller. Jackson promptly go back to work.

It was a brisk morning. Nyc briefed Ben on his plan for the day while the adults yelled commands and responses until the van was locked and on its way, puffed exhaust smelling of French fries. The days were warmer in the city, hours south as it was, such that even the crisp morning air felt warmer than what Ben was used to in New Hamlet. They chatted for a few minutes after the adults finished up, enjoying the sun on their young faces and the comforting camaraderie of family and friends.

They were inside having a bowl of oatmeal when Nina hugged Nyc from behind his chair.

"Hey cuz, I know you're busy with your friends today, but you said you'd teach me to meditate, remember?"

"Yes, how about Sunday, tomorrow?"

"Great; alright, boys, have fun."

"Can I come?" Ben's tone was mocking but his face had sincerity written all over it, his battle-scarred eye marking his honor. Nyc thought Ben might already be crushing on Nina.

Rosa, Mauro, and Jackson had all gone to the store. Abby Miller followed, wondering all the way if she could find a place to get some French fries.

Jackson brought more than Rosa had expected, and Mauro was very pleased. Carolina remained home with the boys and Nina, seeing them off with a kiss on the top of the head for each of the boys. She warned them to behave, and not to hurt themselves or anyone else, the latter directed to Nycolos specifically.

Ben Miller overflowed with excitement, spilling stories, one atop another, all over the sidewalk. Nycolos admitted to himself that it felt good to be walking and talking with his friend again. The school yard was empty, a black moat of asphalt surrounding the school, Ben caught him up on the news from home. Joe Watts was dead, and rumor had it Lyndon was the culprit. Mrs. Watts made a huge scene at the cemetery when they buried Joe. She screamed for Lyndon Arcadia to die.

"Funny," Nycolos didn't sound amused. "He already died."

Ben continued; word on the street said Lyndon was some kind of monster. Eric Fontane was still a deputy but was warming the vinyl of an office chair behind a desk until he recovered from his nervous breakdown. Bobby Fontane only cracked a couple of ribs, but Johnny Fontane had broken his arm exactly like Nyc's. Everybody in school thought Nyc and Rosa had escaped—not because they were not guilty, but because people thought Lyndon's ghost was haunting them.

That got a laugh out of Nyc and Ben joined him. If only people knew the truth. The sheriff stopped by Rosa's several times only to find Jackson working the fields and keeping the house in order. "All bark but no bite," Jackson said. "They had nothing. No proof other than eye witness testimony from frightened teens, a sheriff's deputy on the edge of sanity, three drunken residents of the trailer park and a cruiser 100-yards on the other side of the creek and standing upright with the trunk sunk three meters into the forested floor with not a road or wheel tracks anywhere to be seen."

Ben went over the evidence with Nyc as he loved to do and they both concluded the only real piece of evidence was the cruiser that had somehow been lofted into the forest like a plaything.

Lacking a driver or tire marks of any kind, the only sign of the auto's arrival were the broken canopy limbs where it crashed from the sky.

As strange as it all was, most people—the sheriff included—had a hard time believing something could have thrown the cruiser two-hundred plus yards. The plausibility of a monster terrorizing a trailer park was far-fetched to say the least, though Ben admitted several loggers caught wind of the story and insisted the bear that attacked their camp had been accompanied by a similar monster. The loggers' story caught the public's attention, it was old news that they were attacked by bears.

Eric Fontane had taken a keen interest in their story, interrogating the loggers at length, he was now even more convinced Lyndon was some sort of shape-shifting monster terrorizing New Hamlet.

Interestingly enough, Bobby Fontane started visiting Abby's bookstore, reading an assortment of comics, books, and magazines. Abby was cool about it and since he hadn't given her a reason, she refrained from squishing the pimply teen with her thumb and forefinger. Bobby Fontane asked questions about Nyc, Lyndon, and Rosa. Carefully at first, pretending to find more interest in his comic than in his question. But now he was confident and comfortable in Abby's bookstore and no longer feigned disinterest. Her answers were always the same, "I don't know, they haven't contacted me."

Ben seemed to think Bobby Fontane was now the odd man out, his brothers were treating him differently. The conversation was cut short by the arrival of Nyc's new friends. Raymond Somcio, Kofi Everett, Gino Cabrera and Michael Fields walked into the asphalt playground together. A flock of pigeons alighted on the fence surrounding the asphalt encrusted earth. Gray brown and white shades of pigeons wooed the boys loudly. Stray cats and dogs were beginning to appear along the fence-line, settling onto their haunches to watch.

Nycolos went through the motions and introduced everyone to Ben. Something about Michael's demeanor stank of dislike, a problem to be sure.

"Is there a problem, Mike?" Nycolos wanted to squash issues before they could fester.

"Who's this?" He gestured with a sneering lip, his city accent thicker with contempt.

"I told you who he is, Michael; he's my friend from upstate."

"Why'd you bring him?"

"Let's find out, Mike. Let's start today with you and Ben jogando, that translates to playing, but in Brazil it means sparring, or fighting. You game Mike?"

"I'll kill this white kid, man; you know what I'm sayin'?"

"Just give it a try, Michael, O.K.?" Nyc tried not to sigh and winked at Ben as they stood up.

Ben nodded. Standing slowly, he stood in one place in a fighting stance, looking timid and fearful of what was to come. Michael had his guard up immediately and bounced on the balls of his feet, shifting from foot to foot, Nyc could tell Michael had probably been in a few fights himself, or maybe boxing experience. Michael feinted a punch and Ben cowered, raised his arms in front of his face and murmured in a scared voice, "No."

Michael's cocky grin was beautiful and white, his perfect grin grew bigger, he drew back his right arm and unleashed a powerful punch at Ben's covered head. Which of course was just what Ben had been waiting for. Ben danced the jinga sideways, smoothly ducking under the punch. He pivoted on his right foot and spun full circle kicking his left foot in an arcing meia lua de frente (½ moon crescent kick) that caught Michael Fields on the brim of his Yankees ball cap. The hat flipped off to the side and the pigeons exploded from the fence, shaking with the sound of rattling metal and flapping wings. The birds flew low, swooping down and past the boys, Nyc felt the breeze of one pigeon that streaked past his face.

Michael, a little embarrassed charged Ben with quick jabs which Ben danced away from, simply moving around the other boy, dancing all the way. The next time he got behind Michael, Ben stepped deftly on the Michael's pants, the waist of which he wore pulled well below his buttocks, an obvious target for

Ben. The effect was Michael fell on his face to the oohs and aahs of the other kids.

"Well, there you go. Now you know why he's here."

Ben was careful to help Michael to his feet, hoping not to damage Michael's pride any more than it already was.

"And the importance of proper clothing." Nyc sounded like his mother.

Nycolos and Ben led the boys through stretches as the sun climbed from the horizon halfway to mid-day. They taught the four boys from Queens how to jinga, and evade. Nycolos made them practice walking on their hands, moving quickly, then slowly, then quickly again. He made them all practice, he and Ben included, the negativa and role, defensive moves both and integral foundations of the art. The negativa and role were ground movements, the first a controlled sit with one foot extended, the latter a kicking strike used to stand up again. Both moves took time for people to become comfortable with, he watched them falling and rising, kicking the air with alternating feet, wishing he had brought his cousin's boom box.

Raymond Somcio was highly flexible and stronger than he looked. The kid didn't seem to tire at all and Nyc could see playing capoiera with him would be fun and challenging. His martial arts training was evident in his high arcing kicks and easy muscle memory. Kofi Everett and Gino Cabrera were a different story. Kofi was strong, but heavy and plodding just like on the soccer pitch, slow and methodical. Kofi's creativity was evident and Nyc bookmarked a few pointers for later. If Kofi could get some speed behind his kicks and straighten up his technique he would be able to do some damage.

Gino was smooth and supple like a willow branch, also like when he played soccer, but his hair kept getting in his face and suddenly his feet were a little too big for his body. Nycolos paired Kofi and Gino together, Michael and Raymond together to dance through the ginga, negativa and role. Before anything Nyc clarified the no contact rule of the roda (pronounced hoda) which was not to be broken, and when rarely broken it was either an honest accident or someone got hurt, bad.

Raymond held his own with Michael and more importantly was not intimidated as Gino and Kofi were. In fact the Chinese-American, second generation Queens native was comfortable with Michael, given they were classmates and gym partners.

The morning went well once awkwardness and egos were dissolved by sweat. Nycolos made sure they all stretched for a good ten minutes as a cool down period, taking the time to speak to all of them again.

"Michael, I 'm sorry I tricked you in the beginning, but that was a good first lesson for all of you. Looks can be deceiving. My friend Ben is skinny, a little shorter than you and white. You—on the other hand—look intimidating with you baggy pants, baggy shirt, and that scowl you're always wearing. What you all saw Ben do at the beginning is another fundamental idea at the root of Capoiera called malicia. Maybe the most important fundamental root of the game. Similar to all is fair in love and war, so Ben pretended to be afraid of Michael, making Michael more cocky and less likely to defend himself, he was thinking he could easily stomp a little white kid.

"So what's up with the menagerie? Do they get involved too?" The most lively Nyc had seen Michael, his new friend gestured with his chin at the edge of the schoolyard. The chain-link fence was draped with pigeons, crows, starlings, and sparrows. Below the avian horde representative shaggy dogs were present. Many with shaggy coats looking dirty, though just as many looking shampooed and groomed, all sat with lolling tongues, haunches relaxed even in such close proximity to several dozen cats that paced up and down the length of the sidewalk. Tabbys, Siamese, toms, and dames, collars jingled and jangled, stopping occasionally to inspect Nycolos and his friends, before continuing their pacing. A flock of geese steered their V-formation over the school and a white swan broke off, leaving the formation and diving low to swoop over the boys, so low they could easily make out black feet folded to its belly.

"Wow," Nycolos spoke to no one in particular, and not surprised in the least for some reason. "That's quite a vocabulary word, Mike." He hoped something like this wouldn't happen, but tried not to make a big deal about it. The ten-year-old mulatto walked to the chain-link fence as casually as he could manage and spoke to the assorted menagerie of dogs, cats, starlings, pigeons, doves, crows, and he guessed a swan somewhere on the roof of the building.

"Alright, everyone," he kept his voice low, "thanks for coming out and keeping an eye on us, I'm trying to keep it low key these days, so tell our friends we're O.K., low key. I can't have you guys hanging out like this wherever I go, got it? I'll call if I need help; We're done so you can go, and thanks again."

As he spoke cats meowed, dogs barked, crows cawed, and doves cooed, but as he wound down they began to disperse almost immediately, the chain-link fence rattling as yellow and black scaled talons pushed off, sending hollow-boned bodies skyward.

"What the hell was that?!" Michal Fields sounded shocked and taken aback, but his smile was bigger than ever, and his eyes glittered with excitement.

"They are my friends." That was the best Nyc could come up with at the moment.

"Holy cow, does your menagerie fight with you too?" Nyc couldn't tell if Mike was being a smartass or being sincere, so he answered honestly.

"Only when my life is in danger." Nycolos Arcadia looked Michael in the eyes so hard Michael broke eye contact almost immediately. Mentally Nyc dared him to say something else. He didn't. Gino's whistle broke through the tense moment. "Whew-wheeew."

"Que loco, Nyc, remind me to stay on your good side." They all laughed a little too loudly in an effort to hide their discomfort. Ben Miller found one of those moments he always waited for, like stalking turkeys, it had to come to you he always said.

"You should get used to some strange…," Ben watched their faces ensuring he had their attention, but didn't pull the trigger, "if you're going to be Nyc's friend you better get used to it." Nyc wanted to step on Ben's foot but the damage was already done.

"Cool." Ray sounded optimistic.

"Nice." Michael too.

"Awesome." Kofi.

"Bueno." Matter of factly from Gino.

"Alright you guys, let's not worry about my friends, they're all gone now." And so they were, save for a few pigeons that moved from the fence to the power lines that crisscrossed through the morning sky.

"Why don't we all go get something to eat from the corner store?"

Heads nodded all around as the boys realized how thirsty and hungry they really were at half-past noon. Nycolos herded his group of friends from the tar-covered asphalt playground to the cracked and heaved sidewalk and city streets. They headed back towards his house and the deli on the corner run by the Lebanese brothers, who were very nice to his whole family, if a little overpriced. Not a bodega at all, the boss kept the shelves stocked and fresh food. Nyc bought a six-pack of some juice drink and handed them out to his friends when he returned outside. Six boys sat on the curb, feet tapping absently on the concrete street and metal storm grate. They talked loudly excited after their morning of jogando capoiera, and were flush with energy, having uncorked the wellspring of youthful exuberance. More comfortable with each other now, Nycolos could feel bonds forming and walls falling away, they talked that way for many minutes hardly allowing one another to get a word in edgewise.

Somewhere between having his pants pulled down and walking to the corner store Michael Fields became genuine. His bad attitude evaporated like sweat in the sun, leaving behind the salty residue of his real personality. Nycolos arranged for their Saturday meeting to become bi-weekly, and they would alternate between Capoiera, Kung-Fu, and soccer, dedicating an entire month to each sport. They were winding down, Nycolos heard stomachs grumbling and knew it was time to head home for lunch. He made a mental note to have his mother prepare a lunch for all of them next time.

Michael stood smiling down on the other boys, farewell dying on his lips. His eyes flicked over their heads and his face took on aloof indifference again and his eyes went flat just before he flipped his hood up.

"Great." He muttered under his breath.

"What?" Ben asked, standing next to Michael, who surprisingly enough didn't move away.

"What up, stick and bones?"

Nycolos Arcadia stood on the other side of Michael Fields and beheld a young black kid, taller than all of them, and definitely older. He took in their motley group with arrogance and disdain.

"Hey, Isaiah." Gone was Michael's true personality, as well as his confidence, replaced by the same docile attitude Nyc observed in Kofi and Gino when Michael first sat at their table.

"You got any money?" Isaiah's question didn't leave room for doubt, and didn't really sound like a question either. He sounded like he was used to taking money from Michael.

"Naw, man, my friend bought me this." Isaiah scanned the five boys standing with Michael, his lip curled horribly when he reached Ben Miller, and he actually spat on the ground near Ben's feet.

"What about it, nigga'?" Isaiah settled on Nycols as his target, and it was all Nyc could do not to sigh—another bully just in different clothes.

"No." Some of Nyc's own disgust must've crept into his voice because Isaiah stood up taller and stepped so close to Nyc he was breathing in Nyc's face.

"What if I don't believe you, son?"

- 227 -

"Well that sounds like your problem, not mine." Nyc stepped back off of the storm grate and onto the sidewalk. Isaiah's nostrils flared and Nycolos saw his pupils contract just a fraction. Isaiah feinted a punch at Nyc's face, stopping a few inches from Nyc's cheek. Nyc didn't flinch, or even blink.

"I'm gonna make it your problem, you little..." Commotion behind Nyc caught Isaiah's attention and he craned his neck to see the other boys for a moment before spitting at Ben again, who was visibly laughing now.

"What's so funny white boy? You're next."

"That's fine," Ben chuckled. "Could you tell your pets I don't want to play though?" He pointed at Isaiah's feet.

In his attempt to bully Nycolos, Isaiah stepped onto the storm grate. Nycolos Arcadia looked down at the bully's feet. They could hear tremendous rustling emerging from the depths below. The source of which was twofold. The cockroaches streamed up first, wings humming in flight, carapices rubbing together in brown chitin strengthened exoskeletons. Antennae and hairy legs explored the creases and seams of Isaiah's oversized pants, rustling all the louder as more and more emerged from the grate, crawling over each other to find purchase on the bully.

The second arrival were the large sewer rats that seemed content to gnaw on Isaiah's work boots, which looked well cared for and almost new, but industrious rats had several holes started.

The black bully screamed, high-pitched falsetto. Isaiah jumped up and down like a mad man, brushing at his coat and pant legs. Hairy legs and biting teeth drove the teenage bully to madness; he ran into the street, nearly getting run over by a taxi. He jumped on the hoods of a car and rolled around, fell off the hood and onto the street, still rolling. Finally, he stood and removed his jacket to beat at the bugs on his legs. He ran down the street stomping his feet like he was step dancing, flailing at his arms and legs, screaming all the way.

Nyc's new friends stared at him again, eyes like saucers, except Ben who shook his head still laughing and holding his sides.

"Alright, maybe not only when my life is in danger. Michael, who was that?" So complete was Michael's shock it took several attempts for him to get the words out.

"He's a bully that lives on my block, he's known me since we were both little but he's never been very nice; he used to beat me up and take my money." Michael didn't make eye contact with any of them.

"You got beat up?" Gino sounded as shocked as Kofi looked, and Nyc stepped in to help his new friend save face.

"Well, number one, Michael that won't happen again because we're going to make sure you learn how to play his game, and number two," he turned his attention to Gino, Kofi. "most people that become bullies were bullied by someone else themselves."

Michael was kicking pebbles and looking at the ground while Kofi and Gino regarded him critically, something clicking into place in their minds and they both reached up to pat Michael on the shoulder.

"That's right bro, si se puede." Gino was no longer intimidated by Michael.

"We got your back, man." Kofi laid it all out there.

"Thanks, guys." Michael scuffed the ground a few more times. When he looked up the huge grin and salty humor were back. "So cockroaches and rats too, that was pretty crazy, Nyc."

"I know, but if you guys don't mind can we talk about this later, Ben and I need to get home and eat some lunch."

"Sure," Ray stepped up, communicating his understanding with a squeeze of Nyc's shoulder. "Alright, guys, let's go home, we can quiz the new kid on Monday. It was nice to meet you, Ben." Ray's display of manners seemed to prompt the other boys as they politely extended their hands to Ben, repeating Ray's words.

"See you guys again; I'll be back down to visit next month."

"Cool," Michael's turn to surprise them. "We look forward to it; see you Monday, Nyc."

****

Though a mere half block from his aunt and uncle's house Nyc and Ben took twenty minutes to get there. They walked past it and circled the block talking for a while. Nycolos knew Ben had more and more questions. He told Ben the truth: no, he hadn't consciously summoned the animals at the playground; yes, he suspected that insects were fair game too; no, never cockroaches. But he told Ben about the bees in the orchard. No, he never summoned rats before and had not even thought about it. No, he didn't know how to call them. What was up at the school? He didn't know, things had been quiet until this weekend, maybe having Ben around did something, after all the fox and the owl had spoken to both of them months ago.

The two friends finally walked through the front door close to three in the afternoon. The house was quiet for the moment save the muffled sound of a T.V. audience laughing. Nina was the only one home, they could hear her talking on the phone upstairs. They called up to her and she waved from the second floor landing. The boys ate some sandwiches Nina made earlier, and left in the fridge with their names written in her neat hand on the paper lunch bags she had packed them in.

After eating, they ascended to the roof and sat in the camping chairs Mauro left up there. A hibachi sat in one corner of the rooftop, evidence of Muaro's cooking, past and future. The two friends sat in comfortable silence, gazing across the rooftops toward the distant Manhattan skyline.

Horn blasts and squealing tires were like white noise, as were the planes coming in to land at La Guardia, soaring over head they would've drown out any conversation, attempted or otherwise. Nyc regarded his best friend's scarred eye and torn visage for several minutes. Ben made being his friend sound like an adventure. Nyc wished he could fix his friend's face and give back all the adventures they had survived. The wind picked up and tossed the sandy-blond hair that was long enough to get in Ben's eyes. His blue eyes sparkled in the sun and he squinted against the sun as it drifted slowly westward. The hawk's talons left an impressive scar that puckered and wrinkled when Ben squinted, giving the ten-year-old a deceivingly menacing appearance. Ben must've felt Nyc's eyes, and ran his pointer finger up his cheek and over his closed eyelid and up to his brown eyebrow, where the single line became three just above the brow.

"Pretty awesome, huh?" Those familiar eyes sparkled anew

"I'm so sorry Ben, I never meant for any of this to happen to you."

"Are you kidding me? Not only is the scar bad-ass, but we've had more fun in the last couple months than in our entire lives, more than most people's entire lives!"

"I know but..." Ben didn't let him finish.

"Whatever, Nyc, I have a feeling we've only seen the tip of the iceberg. There's a lot more going on and you are neck deep in whatever it is. I bet you my best bow so is your father."

And that was that. They sat again in silence and watched the sun sink through the pollution filled skies, blushing shades of pink and orange, dipping behind Manhattan Island, silhouetting man made monoliths of steel, glass and plastic. They heard the truck pull up front of the house and the sounds of their families returning from the store. In a matter of minutes they were all in the kitchen talking, the adults were excited about how well the day went.

Rosa's fresh organic meat from upstate was such a hit they almost sold all of the pork and goat meat, something Jackson and Abby hadn't anticipated. Mauro explained the Caribbean, Latin and African communities were lovers of goat, and the more they bought the better.

Dinner was loud and lively. The Millers, the Arcadias and the Silvas laughed, teased and toasted as they broke bread together. Mauro had set aside some delicious rump-roast cuts of venison, left marinating in a chile-ancho sauce after dry rubbing with cumin, salt, pepper, garlic and ginger, and a dash of vinegar, and the juice of two entire limes. The venison marinated all day and was cooked so wonderfully it practically melted in their mouths. Jackson surprised them with a salad of dandelion greens and spinach he said just started growing in the greenhouse last week.

The food was fresh and local, grown and harvested from the earth that was Nyc's home. The conversation rambled on like the tides pushing up the shoreline, receding hours later. The talk was loud and jovial, that is until Ben asked Nyc a little too loudly when he and Rosa were moving back. In a matter of minutes and brewed coffee later the adults were excusing themselves and all save Nina, Sidney, Ben and Nyc moved into the sitting room. They took up the conversation Ben had prompted, coffee cups in hand.

"I guess we'll find out soon." Nyc watched the parents sitting on the couch while Jackson was futzing with the fireplace preparing to light a fire.

Nycolos Arcadia and Benjamin Miller never found out the answer to Ben's question. Not that night anyway, it wasn't until the following day as Ben sat in the truck with Jackson rocketing up the thruway that he was informed as to what the adults discussed. Nyc likewise didn't hear the answer until long after he stood on the stoop waving goodbye to his best friend and extended family. Unknown to them all was that their discussion meant nothing. They would all be leaving sooner than any of them imagined, and for reasons not magical, but mundane and heartbreaking to boot.

Chapter 14

The Lizard King

Twining tendril, padded paw
flowers bloom, crow's ca-caw.
Teach the women, teach the men
perhaps they will remember again.

Rosa and Nycolos were happy and invigorated to have new projects of their own, and all the better that it involved the Millers coming down every month. Weeks jumbled into months, winter into spring. The transplanted country pair made do in the hustling bustling, enjoying the fast-paced cosmopolitan nature of it all. One aspect of their new family routine were the Sunday BBQ's. Smoked meats, fresh fruits, the sound of Samba and Bossa Nova, smell of wood smoke, a little piece of Brazil there in Queens. Nycolos stuffed himself at dinner one Sunday night. Perhaps a bit too much, but it was all so good. He fell asleep with the smell of wood smoke permeating the entire house, his room included.

Nyc's dreams were troubled that night. He waded through sewer tunnels with wastewater up to his chest. The stench was horrible, rats and roaches accompanied him on either side. The sewer tunnel ended in a pipe that stuck out into space, where the brown water cascaded down a hundred feet to a dark lake with a pile of refuse like an island in the center. An alligator sat in the middle of the midden heap, and the monster looked to be 20 feet long if it was an inch.

"The Master summons you, you must obey." A large rat stood at the end of the pipe, whiskers twitching, speaking to Nyc. "El Rey Lagarto must be obeyed." The filthy brown messenger jumped into space and Nyc watched the rat hit the water below, small ring rippled outwards.

The alligator lifted its head and peered up at Nycolos, gigantic tail whipping back and forth. The giant maw opened, the walls began to shake, threatening to crumble around him. Nycolos woke with a start, covered with sweat.

The Lizard King is what the name translated to if Nyc's Spanish was correct. Great, more crazy animals that wanted to hurt him. That rat looked familiar believe it or not, and to where was he summoned? The little brown boy flipped his pillow over and lay his head down on the cool side and promptly fell into an untroubled dreamless sleep, positive the summons was the work of his imagination.

***

The next morning Nycolos Arcadia walked to school with Nina da Silva. He was distracted, thinking about the remaining months separating him from home. Rosa and family decided to remain in Queens until school was out before returning. Abby thought the plan prudent, considering the sheriff's Deputy was still nosing around. Nyc and Ben would be entering a new school year and would be able to fish and hunt in summer and fall. His thoughts wandered, as thoughts are prone, to the day his father died. It would be a year by then. He would ask Rosa if they could do something.

"Esta bon?" Nina asked if he was O.K. in Portuguese.

"Yeah, I'm fine. I guess I just miss my dad." Big mistake, giving voice to those words was nearly equivalent to opening the flood gates. The ten-year-old bit down hard on the frog that climbed up his throat. Nina hugged him and wiped a tear from his cheek.

"I love you, Nyc; maybe you want to play hooky today?"

He shook his head, unable to speak, kissed his cousin on the cheek, squeezed her tight and ran into the school before she could say more.

His new friends were excited to see him and their enthusiasm pushed his melancholy into a small corner of his brain. By lunch he was talking loudly; as excited as his fellow misfits. The day was routine, even a little boring. Mrs. Delisi's class went to the library after lunch, Nyc nodded off while trying to read a book about alligators. The Lizard King swam through the recesses of his brain all day.

He asked to go to the bathroom, and walked down the hallway with a bathroom pass, a large piece of wood shaped like a book that read pass of the front. Nyc reached a junction in the hallway where a large black man sat behind a desk, bottom lip out turned in a relaxed, unfocused look. Cecil the hall monitor knew Nyc and had no reason to give him trouble. The three kids standing around his desk were another matter altogether. Isaiah Rawlins was evidently the ring leader and the beneficiary of special treatment by the obese hall monitor, who was usually quick to hand out detentions and sharp words for students without a pass.

Isaiah's companions were similarly dressed, a bunch of look-alikes. Pants pulled well below their bottoms, baggy clothes all but hid their arm and legs. Isaiah's mouth curled into a horrible rictus of a smile when Nyc approached, preparing to turn left towards the boy's room.

"Yo," Isaiah's mouth curled horribly, a hitch in his walk so deep it almost looked like the kid had a limp.

"Yeah?" Nyc didn't want to stop walking but the older kid stepped in his path.

"What are you? Are you black?"

"Yes." Nyc was shocked, he hadn't seen that coming at all.

"You're not black, look at you, I see who you hang out with, I see the way you act." Triumph glittered in the bully's eyes, Nyc saw approval plain as day on the faces of the other two kids, even a smirk flit across Cecil's face before he hid it behind his newspaper. Like a sucker punch in the gut, the comment forced the air from Nyc's lungs and made his head spin. Isaiah sneered with malign satisfaction, and Nyc couldn't help but think he was going to stick out his tongue. Pleased with his saved face, Isaiah stepped out of Nyc's way. By the time Nycolos returned from the bathroom, the bullies were gone and Cecil the fat hall monitor napped behind his newspaper.

Nycolos was subdued that evening and even though a gorgeous spring day slid into a beautiful spring evening he stayed in his room or on the roof, but he didn't leave the house. A ten-year-old has little notion of his own psyche, or how experiences in one's life can influence it. Nyc knew the psychologist told Rosa they were both suffering from transitory hallucinations brought on by a mental break and distancing from their emotions in the trying time of familial loss. That was the last time his mother spoke to the doctor, hanging up loudly after calling him a quack that couldn't tell the difference between up and down. That night as Nycolos Arcadia waded through the depths of his own psyche, he found things that frightened him.

The dream started out benignly enough, though a little oddly. Nycolos Arcadia sat beside an oval pool in his meditation place. A small wigwam visible through the trees, belching smoke from a round hole in the center of the roof. All thatch and lashings, Nycolos didn't remember visualizing this medicine hut or evoking one. Well, his father told him dreams had different rules than meditative exercises. In dreams details and scenarios dragged from both the conscious and unconscious.

He was dressed in ragged clothes that were torn in many places. Welts and scars criss-crossed across his arms and legs, dried blood all over his raggedy clothes. Strangely enough his fingers were decorated with sparkling rings and ornate bracelets, heavy chains of gold hung from his neck. Distracted as he was Nyc didn't see what surfaced in the pond but instead heard the splash as it dove, slapping the surface with an unseen tail. Nyc jumped to his feet, walking the perimeter of the pool, scanning the crystal clear waters for any sign of movement. The ten-year-old was about to dive in when he heard it. What sounded like a swarm of bees several hundred yards distant grew in decibels until he could tell it was the screaming and hollering of humans out for blood.

The mob crested the top of a small ridge and the leaders in front held up a hand. With hawk-like hawk vision Nyc's eyes were powerful enough that he might as well have been two feet from the group. Eric Fontane wore his deputy uniform and shouted orders to everyone; Joe and Jacob Watts, Johnny Fontane charged forward when Eric's hand pointed at Nyc. The entire mob surged like a mudslide and Nycolos nearly fell into the pool in shock. He turned and ran, as quick as he could through the forest toward the only immediate shelter, the wigwam. He shot through the tall poplar forest, triangular leaves trembling in the cool morning breeze. He could hear the blood-thirsty mob coming closer, "nigger" floated in the wind, along with "monster", "fraud", and even "witch", attached to sayings like "stone him", "burn him", "string him up", "where do you think you're goin'?"

Nyc opened the wigwam door and looked back. Eric Fontane led the charge, his face deformed by rage, spittle foaming at the corners of his mouth, made him look rabid. Joe Watts ran next to him, face blue-gray in death, he looked like a zombie, screaming louder than the rest, "let me finish what I started, you little black bastard!"

Nyc slammed the door, as he turned the earthy darkness of the wigwam morphed into the fluorescent bright, white and brown disorder of a convenience store. He recognized it as one of many in his neighborhood, but wasn't sure he'd been there before.

The mob crashed into the convenience store windows, banging with hands, feet, sticks and stones. The window held, and would not break. The store clerk didn't seem to see a thing, nor the patrons that were giving him a hard time. One black kid was waving his arms and arguing with the Pakistani store owner over the price of a cigar, apparently he wanted more change back. The Pakistani was frazzled, his hair—brushed at one point—was now unruly. His eyes were wide like saucers and he made great effort to keep his eyes on all the kids in the store. The one in front of him yelled something and the owner yelled back and opened the register. Another kid took the opportunity to pocket at least ten cigars before the cashier turned around. The Pakistani man slammed the refunded money on the counter and told the boys to get out, which they did, laughing all the way at the frustrated owner.

Nyc watched as the rogues opened the door and walked through the lynch mob without noticing, and vice versa. Apparently they only wanted Nycolos Arcadia dead. The clerk didn't waste time, spotting Nyc immediately.

"Hey, black kid, what you want?"

"I just needed to rest for a minute." Nyc gestured at the mob, but the expression was lost on the Pakistani.

"No buy, no stay, get out." It was hard to believe the man couldn't see the mob outside the window, or hear the loud bangs of wooden posts, and boot tips, thrown at the window.

"Don't you see all those people out there that want to kill me?"

"No money, no stay, black, get out!" With the spryness of a young man the skinny Pakistani leapt over the counter and pushed him to the door. Nyc didn't resist, instead he braced himself for the wooden boards that would surely crack his skull and the flaming torches that would melt his flesh. The noise of the mob exploded in his ears when the clerk opened the glass door. He shoved Nycolos outside, delivering the ten-year old sacrifice to the altar.

Nyc opened his eyes and realized he was standing in front of Isaiah, who seemed larger than ever.

"What are you?" The older boy asked with a sneer. "You're not black, I see what you are." Isaiah shoved Nyc backwards and the ten-year-old realized he was surrounded by shades of Isaiah, he couldn't see any of their faces, but he knew he wasn't black enough for any of them.

"We see what you wear." One shade threw pants at him that replaced the rags he was wearing. Oversized and baggy he could feel the waistline snug beneath his butt and the extra length settled over his ankles.

"We see how you act," Another threw books at Nyc, hitting him in the head, "trying to be all smart and shit."

"We hear the music you listen to." Another shade threw old CD's at Nyc. Whipping them like throwing stars, sharp edges cutting Nyc's hands and arms. He threw up an arm to protect his face.

"You're not black." They chanted in unison.

"We see who you hang out with." With that the black boys broke gold chains from their necks which grew larger immediately. Isaiah whipped his chain over his head and brought it down next to Nycolos, shattering concrete and leaving a gaping hole in the ground. All the specters were striking out with their golden chains, cutting through the air, the clink of metal and the explosion of concrete all around made it hard for Nyc to move.

First one, then another of the chains wrapped around his arms, then legs. Their weight was incredible, so heavy Nycolos fell to the concrete ground just as his own necklace had swollen to such a size Nyc was having trouble breathing. Isaiah stood over him.

"You're not black, only these chains of bondage can truly make you black like us." The bully raised his foot to stomp on Nyc's face, cruel grin victorious and triumphant at the same time. Nyc screamed, chains exploded, bullies disintegrated and the world around him melted away. He was on his hands and knees next to a little oval pool in the middle of a poplar forest, a place very like his own. Lying on his back he breathed heavily for a few minutes, feeling the fear leak from his bones.

"You were summoned." Like the intonations of a giant gong, the deep resonant voice filled the entire forest.

"The Lizard King has no interest in the nightmares that haunt children, you will come now." Ruby-red eyes poked through the surface of the oval pool. Glinting with reflected light Nycolos would've sworn those eyes really were rubies. He had not the time for contemplation.

As quick as thought, two Jacare—small striped caimans, native to many places on the Earth—jumped onto the bank, grabbed him with sharp teeth by the ankles and pulled him into the pool. The water was cold, very cold. Odd, Nyc thought, the water in his meditation was never cold, it just was. This water was so cold he had to fight not to inhale a mouthful of water. The jacare pulled Nyc down into darkness. This was not his pool at all, there was no heavy wooden door, millweed, or large rocks, just unending blackness. They pulled him down and down, blackness filled his vision and his mind. His consciousness was full of blackness so absolute he couldn't hold on anymore.

Nycolos Arcadia fell with a start into the murky putrescence of a Queens sewer tunnel. Cold, vile waste of humanity coated his hair and contaminated his clothing. He pulled himself out of the main channel and lay with his back on the maintenance walkway that paralleled the main channel. The smell of it all caused him to vomit, repeatedly. The main channel ran brown and black, white wads of toilet paper, dime bags and kids toys floated by, forgotten forever by those above. Nyc had emerged from a rusty door standing ajar, looking unused for centuries. A mirror-like substance filled the doorway, like quicksilver or liquid mercury, save this silvery liquid was framed along the edges in runes that glowed orange, red, and yellow, flickering on and off in some pattern like Christmas lights.

"It seems the little one has survived after all; Master will be pleased."

Nycolos Arcadia spun around to confront the voice. The owner of the voice was a run-down looking vagrant of a man. Wearing clothes much like Nyc had been wearing in his dream, the shaggy-haired bum snickered in the shadows of the sewers.

By what little light there was Nycolos made out torn pants and shirt stained brown with dirt, grime and probably bodily fluids. The man had few teeth left and what few he had were yellowed.

"Who are you?" Nycolos found his voice at last.

"I am a familiar, the master's familiar." The bum bowed when speaking this time, as if introducing himself as a man of status.

"I thought familiars were animals." In fact Nycolos knew they were.

"I am but an animal to the master, but let us not dally any longer. You are quite as amazing as the master claimed, you must be to have survived the Door of Perception, few mortals have ever crossed through and survived, and you are the first to retain his sanity." He looked at Nyc with raised eyebrows, and Nyc felt a shiver run down his spine.

"The master has nearly infinite patience, but he knows you walk his halls, we must go to him." The vagrant turned and began walking along the service platform, heading down the long tunnel that ended in blackness.

Nyc followed the familiar, unsure if he was awake or if his dream had taken some frightening turn. The vagrant stank of refuse and rotting flesh. Nyc was shocked he could differentiate the man's stink from the rest of the human waste that flowed down the channel. It was several minutes before he realized the squeaking and skittering he heard were the rats and cockroaches trailing behind them.

The vagrant stopped next to a connecting tunnel and put his hand on a stone pillar. He whispered something Nyc couldn't hear and a rune lit up red on one side of the pillar. The rune looked like a greater than or less than symbol, Nyc wasn't sure which. A doorway cut itself from the brick wall of the sewer tunnel and he led Nycolos through. They crossed through a pipe-chase that was less odoriferous but stiflingly humid and hot with steam. On the opposite wall the vagabond repeated the process, another rune lighting up red, revealing a door that was not there seconds before.

They continued the journey through dark labyrinth of sewer tunnels, every once and a while cutting through secret doorways, activated by some magic rune and the bum's incantation. Nyc tried to keep track of where they were going in case he needed to make a getaway, but soon realized the futility of such an idea. They made so many twists and turns, cut through so many secret passages, there was no way he could have returned on his own. The rats, roaches, snakes and lizards were never far behind. Sometimes the creepy crawly mass was lost from sight when they cut through a secret passage, but the sound never escaped them, slithering, skittering, scurrying, multiplied a billion times. It was enough to scare Nyc to the core.

They moved deeper and deeper into the bowels of the city, criss-crossing through forgotten and abandoned subway terminals, only to return to the sewer again. The greatness of the civilization above apparent in the complex and convoluted system of waste water flowing through the subterranean strata. The knowledge of man compounded and condensed in pipes, stonework and excrement. Thousands of years of knowledge functioning beautifully to whisk the waste away from those it could harm. Cholera, Typhus, all the diversity of the most complex ecosystem. Bacteria by the trillions, trillions of trillions. Take the waste away, away, out of sight out of mind. So easy to forget away only means to nearby body of water, be it lake, stream, ocean or river. Another brick in the wall separating man from the natural environment on which he is so dependent, and to which he is so vulnerable. People are such fools, Nyc shook his head with a heavy heart.

Nycolos never had a weak stomach, but he was forced to stop and vomit several times along the way. After what seemed hours, but could have been minutes—it was hard to gauge time in the darkness—they reached something Nycolos recognized. A six foot diameter pipe dropped off into nothingness. Standing on the edge of the pipe, Nyc's eyes followed the arcing stream of dirty water that fell nearly 40 meters to a large retention basin below.

The water didn't look any cleaner down there. Just as in the dream, a large midden heap formed an island of waste rising from the chocolate-colored putrescence. In the middle of the island, the largest alligator Nyc had ever seen lay motionless, eyes lidded, mouth open.

Nycolos Arcadia felt bony hands shove him hard between the shoulder blades and he fell through space, windmilling his arms and legs hoping to land feet first. He hit the water with teeth jarring force, feet straight, hands at his sides. The force of the fall sent him deep into the murky waste-water, he forced himself to keep his eyes shut as he swam upward. He surfaced and treaded water until he reached the midden heap. Carefully wiping his eyes, Nyc checked his face and hands to be sure no refuse or excrement coated his skin. He couldn't hold his stomach any longer and vomited again.

Even after he emptied his stomach he continued to retch for a couple of minutes before his stomach stopped spasming. Human filth coated his hair, and dripped from his pajamas. He stank from head to toe.

Still on hands and knees Nycolos scanned the room. The vagrant familiar was nowhere to be seen. Nyc faced the biggest alligator he had ever seen. Nyc guessed the monster was nearly ten meters long and at least three meters wide. He could think of nothing more to do with than to follow this through to the end.

"You summoned me." Nyc shifted his weight back so he was sitting cross-legged on the waste pile facing the wide gaping maw. The alligator's jaw closed with a snap that made Nyc jump, the sound echoed around the entire chamber.

" I did." Like the fox, the alligator spoke in his mind, and his eyes opened to regard Nyc. The voice sounded like bubbling gravel.

"Then you are the Lizard King."

Chapter 15

Nagas and Nightmares

Time draws nigh, uncertainty grows,
mankind reaps, seeds he sows.
Darkness, pestilence, famine, fright,
hope, sustenance, community, light.

"I am." Nyc didn't know what to do next and let the silence stretch, taking the opportunity to examine the huge chamber. The room was cavernous, Nycolos found it hard to believe such a large space existed in the city's bowels, like a giant subterranean tower. A large arched doorway pierced the wall on the far side of the room. Directly behind the alligator, of course. The entryway was blocked by iron bars, but looked big enough to drive a dump truck through if necessary. The road that lead from the doorway was flooded with wastewater and piles of refuse blocked a clear view, but Nyc though he saw the road slant upwards in the distance, and his nose itched at the hint of fresh air.

The other three walls of the great chamber had similar tunnels leading away, all grated, none as big as the main gate. Cast iron sconces lined the walls, flickering flames protected by hurricane lamp design of the things. They circled the cavern with imperfect illumination, for the vast majority were unlit. Perhaps every third provided meager light in the cavernous chamber. The walls stretched upwards several hundred meters, numerous pipes pierced the brick, mortar and cement on each wall all the way up. Some, like the one Nyc had been pushed from streamed wastewater, oozing intestines of the city's bowels leaking excrement into this general settling tank or retention basin or Alligator nest or whatever. The effect was impressive, the constant sound of falling water lent an air of tranquility to the concentrated waste, the flickering light lulled the mind to quiet, or panic, circumstance dependent of course. The room was much warmer than Nycolos expected, perfect for a giant reptile. The faint candle light did not penetrate the shadows, and there a green phosphorescent glow coated the walls in uneven patches. A rune on the wall off to one side burned red and a secret doorway carved itself and opened.

The familiar stepped forward into the room and bowed deeply, touching his forehead to the stone walkway.

"I brought him as you requested, Master."

"Very well, wretch, leave us, I will send for you when we are finished."

"Yes, Master." The vagabond turned, and Nycolos watched the same rune light up, the door opened, closed and the familiar was gone.

"Tell me, boy, do you know why my familiar pushed you into the water?"

"Because he's a mean man with no teeth." The alligator opened its maw and coughed, what Nyc supposed may have been a laugh.

"He was once a very mean, very wealthy man that did whatever it took to survive. He is no longer that person, he is now my familiar and does my bidding. And yes, he has no teeth. He was a very wicked man, and did whatever it took to get ahead. Including horrible things to other humans. I couldn't care less, but he insulted the earth in so many ways he was mine for the taking. He did not push you in the water because he is a mean man. I commanded him to push you, can you think why?"

"So I would nearly drown in filth and waste." From his sitting position Nycolos could see all the way down the Lizard King's maw. Intimidating to say the least.

"Yes, I wanted you to taste the waste, the filth of your people. A small example of it but this is what your people do. You defecate in our waters, bury waste in our soils and commit egregious crimes against the Earth and the others you share this planet with."

"I know what you're saying." Nyc spoke only after the Alligator remained silent for several seconds, "I live on a farm, where we use organic farming and recycle our waste..." The Alligator barked or coughed, cutting him off.

"I know all about your human life little one, but the time of man comes to a close, and you are the herald of his downfall. If your friends and family knew what you were, they would run screaming into the night, even your brave comrade in arms." The last little bit knocked the wind from his lungs like a kick.

"I'm not sure I follow." Nycolos was sure the conversation was about to get much stranger.

The alligator struck without warning, Nycolos scolded himself mentally. The whole encounter had been trouble from the beginning, he should've known better and run for his life, regardless of roaches, rats or whatever other subterranean denizens lurked in dark corners. But no, he stayed to converse with this pangean monster that belonged in a Homeric epic; and as dictated by such epics would now devour him.

The monster didn't bite, instead it whipped a prehistoric tail catching Nyc full on his chest. Nycolos was thrown backward, he skipped across the surface of the water like a well thrown stone. Like those irregularly-shaped rocks, his body twisted and turned, arms and legs flailing outward, his screams cut short every time he hit the water. Head over heels he twisted like a stone ragdoll, hoping he wouldn't break his neck. Nyc skipped all the way across the murky pond, and crashed into the concrete wall on the other side of the chamber.

It took Nycolos several moments to recover his senses. Once he did, he was shocked to be alive, and for all intents and purposes, undamaged. His impact with the far wall was so violent he was embedded a meter into the concrete. He pulled himself from the boy-shaped hole and fell to the walkway that circled the perimeter of the giant room. *Enough groveling,* Nyc thought, he'd been on his hands and knees enough for one night.

He tried to stand but prepubescent muscles froze when he saw his hands and arms. Covered in gray-green leathery skin, plates like oversized scales ran from the back of his hand to his shoulder, growing progressively larger and thicker as they neared his torso. His wrist and the inside of his forearm was gray-green with little green dots like spots on a frog. Touching his head and back, Nycolos was cognizant that the plates and scales ran along his back, head and legs. That would explain why he hadn't been hurt, but what was going on?

The Lizard King bellowed, what sounded like a cough to his ears was wicked laughter in his head.

"Your resonance is astounding. That's my scale-mail I believe, for surely a human child never learned such things. Absolutely marvelous, I didn't believe until now. Let's continue; this promises to be interesting."

The trash island quivered as the thirty foot monster splashed into brown murky water; gracefully slipping below the surface. Nyc's heart hammered so loud all he could hear was blood in his ears, and his own panting. Maybe the Lizard King meant to kill him after all. He ran down the walkway, grateful to hear the slapping of bare feet on concrete. The scale-mail armor his skin had become felt ungainly and heavy, and apparently didn't cover his feet.

His skin felt tight at his joints, making it difficult to straighten his arms and legs. Scurrying as fast as his body would let him, he hunkered down next to a huge pipe with bars across the mouth. No sooner was he on his haunches than the alligator burst from the pool, smashing into the wall. The beast destroyed concrete like it was dust, smashing a hole as big as a subway tunnel in the chamber wall. The monstrous body was too wide to fit on the narrow human-sized walkway and the Lizard King slid back into the water. The monster resumed swimming, maniacal laughter echoing through Nyc's brain.

The monster head whipped sideways, crushing the pipe Nycolos hid behind. The ancient pipe crumbled, raining stone chunks down on Nycolos. Nyc was so close to the reptilian nightmare he saw the milky second eyelid; a membranous eyelid the alligator used to protect his eyes while swimming; blinking back the foul water the beast looked at Nycolos. Nyc hoped against all odds the alligator was done, or maybe couldn't see him through the concrete dust kicked into the air by destruction.

The Lizard King backed into the water, but did not submerge, his eyes remained above the surface, scanning. Nyc scurried further down the walkway while the monster searched for movement. Like playing red-light, green-light Nyc tried to stop as the monster turned in his direction. His foot caught on a loose rock and he fell on his face. He didn't make a noise, but was sure he was done for. The alligator was looking directly at him but didn't move.

Perplexed, Nycolos looked at his hands, expecting to see gray-green scale-mail. Instead he was shocked yet again, he was able to see through his flesh. Looking through himself, objects appeared slightly distorted, like looking into a clear pool. Nycolos Arcadia was invisible.

"Whoa." The words escaped before he thought better of it. The alligator head trained on him, the huge jaw opened, exposing row upon row of broad teeth, curving to life ending points. Nycolos watched a cloud form in front of the maw, and darted to the left, hoping to lose the monster with his mirror coat.

As well he moved when he did, a jet of super heated water shot from the beast's mouth, hosing the walkway where Nyc had been. Nyc pumped his legs, begging his body for speed. He was lucky enough to only get singed in a dozen places. Drops burned his exposed hands, feet and neck. It was all he could do not to cry out in pain as boiling water seared his skin.He stumbled into the next pipe, barred like the first, offering no escape.

"It is called mirror coat, you pink monkey, it is an advanced power. Again your resonance amazes me. It took me the better part of a century to perfect that skill."

Nycolos didn't answer, he knew the alligator couldn't see as well as he let on, the only reason Nycolos got burned was because he spoke. How he had known the name of the power was mystery however.

"I have many ways to find you little one, you cannot hide from me." The creature smashed the water with his tail, splashing down with such force, murky brown water surged outward, splashing up onto the walkway. The little boy heard a tremulous gurgling sound behind him, turned just in time to see brown water pouring down the three foot diameter pipe. Surging water crashed into Nycolos, catching him with his mouth open. He was pushed from the walkway and hit the murky water with a loud splash. In an instant the monster was after Nycolos. He would've been bait if he hadn't seen the giant head lunge in his direction as he hit the water. No longer caring if he got scum in his eyes, Nyc opened them, and saw through white membranous eyelids of his own. Murky, polluted liquid grew dark as an enormous shadow closed upon him.

Panic filled Nyc's mind. He kicked upward as the gator's jaw closed around him. He kicked, death and desperation threatening to crush him, swimming for all he was worth. Fingers suddenly webbed, the human boy stroked through the water like he was pushing off a rock. He exploded upward, bursting through the surface with all the force of a hunting shark. He soared into the air, nearly ten meters above the pool, it was barely enough.

The Alligator leapt after him, and would've caught the boy in his mouth had the beast been on the same trajectory. As it was, the arcing leap of the Lizard King left a scant meter between his maw and Nyc's feet. Time stretched and slowed the prehistoric reptile snapped at Nyc's feet as they hung, suspended for a nanosecond, high above the water. The arcing momentum of the Lizard King's jump carried tons of mass into the chamber wall, adjacent to the first hole. Tile and cement rained down on the creature's scaled back, the entire front end of the reptile lodged in the sewer wall.

Nycolos windmilled his arms as he fell, hoping he would have enough time to climb back on the walkway before the beast managed to extract scaly reptilian flesh from pulverized stone and sediment. Nycolos landed on solid ground with a tooth-jarring thud, more painful because he was expecting to hit water. He looked down, the water beneath his feet was frozen. Not everywhere, just directly beneath his feet. Nyc looked at the ice around his feet more closely, fractal patterns spiraled outward from his feet, he wished he had more time to appreciate the beauty of the expanding crystals. The Lizard King thrashed violently, reptilian tail swishing a few meters from Nycolos. The Lizard King struggled to extract his reptilian mass from concrete wall, showering debris in all directions. The boy hop-skipped out of the way, like he was standing on a frozen lake, sliding feet from side to side.

Breaking into a sprint, amazed the ice beneath his feet melted into nothing as he moved on, Nyc headed for the garbage island, mind racing to formulate a plan. The ramp looked promising. The bars blocking the ramp looked wide enough for him to squeeze through. The Lizard King finally freed himself with a mighty roar that would've paralyzed Nyc with fear if he hadn't already been running for his life. The maniacal laughter exploded in Nyc's head as the King resumed his hunt.

"Marvelous little rat you are! I haven't had this much fun in an age." Nycolos struggled to ride the three foot swells that rippled outwards from the Gator's splashing tail. "Let's try something different, shall we?" The laughter ceased, but was replaced by a whispering that sounded like it was right in Nyc's ear. He didn't turn around to see what the mad reptile planned, he kept running, not daring to imagine what was to come.

He reached the garbage island, squelched up the shore, and nearly broke his face when muddy refuse froze solid beneath his feet. He struggled on all fours until he was running again, still skating on frozen ice. He tried to stop, and slid, barely catching himself on an old coat rack protruding from the midden heap. The coat rack froze, but Nyc didn't care. The alligator was no longer visible, obscured by a mist that was expanding rapidly.

Nyc wasn't sure because of the distance, but he thought he could see water bubbling violently beneath the fog. The whispering continued unabated, and Nycolos entertained the idea he might actually escape. He turned and ran, jumping off the opposite end of the garbage island. He skated across the water. Twenty meters remained between him and the ramp that sloped upwards towards fresh air and freedom. The whispering in his brain stopped abruptly, an icy sense of dread crept up Nyc's spine like he could feel hundreds of blood thirsty eyes staring at his back.

A terrible din erupted behind, sounding like a mob of people after him. The voices were not in his head, real female voices echoed around the chamber calling him back to them. A golden voice sounded above the others, freezing his limbs and setting his heart a flutter. Joy swelled in his chest and he longed for nothing more than to see the owner of that golden voice. A fair-skinned woman, ageless and perfect, sat atop an enormous lily-pad, bare save for her hair. Lustrous blue-white locks, like ocean spray, tumbled over her shoulders and down her chest, concealing everything save her golden shoulders and arms.

Something in the back of his mind screamed, like a caged animal banging against prison bars, Nyc's awareness clawed and scraped for freedom. Struggling against the haunting melody for all he was worth, Nycolos Arcadia pitted his will against the Siren's song. He burned within, his skin felt as if it would burst into flame if he didn't dive into the water to join her. He reached out his hand, longing to hold her and caress her perfect face.

Moments from succumbing to the desire of lilting melody the last cell of his being reacted. His outstretched hand clenched like he was grabbing the Siren's neck, the lily-pad and the water immediately around it froze solid. The pad crunched, breaking into pieces, dumping the siren into icy waste that quickly climbed up her legs, torso and into her mouth and face. The frozen siren toppled sideways and her blue green fairness sank beneath the waves. Nyc put his hand to his head and shook it from side to side.

"Human kind has reached a precipice, Nycolos, a very precarious precipice. Humanity can begin to climb down, carefully, slowly, with great care. Or humanity can fall, Nycolos, and fall far. An apocalyptic fall that will bring death and destruction, war, famine and all the truly horrendous qualities of the human character into the here and now. It looks to me Nycolos, like humanity is going to fall, and fall hard. They will not be wiped out of course, you are like cockroaches after all, and the Earth Mother has a place in her heart for all her creatures, even the cockroach. But your numbers will be drastically reduced and the global landscape of cities and societies will be changed forever." The Lizard King was directly in front of Nycolos. Bobbing in the water like a small island on the move, truly immense. The massive jaws opened, dry voice like lizard skin resounded in Nyc's head:

> *Earth Mother mourns, for the world gone mad*
> *Scars of strife, mar her flesh.*
> *Prodigal people, the fruit of her loins,*
> *Rape, ravage, and tear her asunder.*
> *Black blood of her bosom, stains the hands of man*
>
> *Tears trail through slate gray skies.*
> *Whipping winds and waves rise to her call,*
> *Calamity crests o'er levy and sea wall.*
> *Chosen children, flora and fauna,*
> *Answer her beck and call*

Terrible Children

Casting aside animal form,
Freely they walk among men.
Howling hordes stream forth,
From forest, hummock and hollow
Children of Gaia, hewn of earth, rock and stone.
Rain righteous retribution on mortal man.

Times of trial, bear man down.
Woes of war and waste, secreted like steam.
Hardworking he's and she's, lay low animal and tree,
Earth and sea ,burn and boil,wither and writhe,
Children of Gaia, answer our cries.

Smiting with seasons, Flood and fire
Hurricane and hail, Tsunami and typhoon,
Works of wise men burn like brimstone
Melting mountains glow golden beneath
Snow-capped waves.

Before the beginning of man or beast
Goddess Gaia chose her guardians.
Her celestial hands catching cosmic
Souls and stardust molded with magic and might.
None bear witness saver her sister, night.

Clutched close to her chest
Clothed and couched in fur and fern.
Pachamama planted on provenance of pangea
Providential progeny to pastor her flocks.
Stewards and shepherds both.

Ages, ancients, rise and fall
civilizations, castles, crumble all.
Earth beneath, sky above
mankind stumbles, without mother's love.

Mankind reaps, a gift supposed

Mankind takes, ownership imposed.
Righteous god, mythological might,
Man's misdeeds ordained as right.

Metallic phallic spin and whir,
penetrate, push, dig into her.
Soil, sod, earth and ore
Gaia our home, so much more.

Send forth those siblings
long forgot.
Taught man his lessons,
though he remember not.

Twining tendril, padded paw
flowers bloom, crow's ca-caw.
Teach the women, teach the men
perhaps they will remember again.

Time draws nigh, uncertainty grows,
mankind reaps, seeds he sows.
Darkness, pestilence, famine, fright,
hope, sustenance, community, light.

Once we roamed
hand in hand
Stewards and brothers
loving the land.

Joy and sorrow
brothers twin
embrace humanity
in death spin.

Herald and prophet, flesh of the earth
Jaguar Princess, her magical birth.
Ancient blood call Children to warn

the Herald and Prophet of Gaia are born.

"And what does all this have to do with me?"

"You feign ignorance, Nycolos Arcadia. You know something is different inside you and has been since your father's death." The massive head moved from side to side, the Lizard King continued when Nycolos made no response.

"Your birth marks the arrival of the turndown, Nycolos. Mankind is falling and your lifetime marks the beginning of the contraction for mankind and the petroleum age as man knows it.

"Gaia, The Earth Mother seethes, ready to rise up and castigate the unrepentant. Already she flexes her muscles, sending many of us on tasks large and small, all aimed at one thing. We destroy the works of man, wielding earth and sky, so he might consider the impending danger, so far I don't think your people are getting the message."

"So I'm..."

"You were chosen." Loud gongs sounded in Nyc's brain, crumpling him to his knees, runes danced like Christmas lights in a circle around him. The lights faded as did the gongs and the ten-year-old pulled himself off the ground, suddenly very afraid.

"Are you going to kill me?" Nyc knew the answer before the monster spoke.

"So you are not completely ignorant after all? No, I am not going to kill you..." There was more there, something the beast left unsaid. Massive jaws smashed down, chomping sound echoing through the entire chamber and its churning waters.

"The time of your death is not at hand, little one. Gaia has strictly forbidden it."

"Gaia? The Earth Mother?" Nycolos hoped his tone sounded genuine and not incredulous as he felt.

"The very same."

"But why?"

Nycolos should've known better. Fool him once shame on you, fool him twice, he had it coming. That's what his mother always said anyway. Before Nycolos could blink, dense fog bubbled from the watery depths. Surrounding him in a sticky, hot mist, like the depths of swamp. The buzz of mosquitoes instantly loud in his ears, stinging and biting his face and ears. Mosquito madness of a mangrove swamp, swat and slap, panic and run. Nycolos nearly slid off the walkway in his panic. Mosquitoes flew into his mouth and eyes, stinging him everywhere. Madness crept through the panic, threatening everything.

Slithering rattle, hiss and flicker of tongue. Nyc's mind eye flashed with snake-like beauties climbing from the water on the far side of the chamber. Snake bodies followed the beautiful human torso of each woman, the Nagas slithered in his direction with death in their eyes. Just behind a beautiful armored warrior rose from the wastewater on a foaming green spray. The female warrior seemed human, though Nycolos knew she was not. Silver armor plates protected her arms and legs. Silver plates climbed from her silver winged boots to knee. Powerful thighs bare below pleated and plated skirt. Blue-green cloth rippled beneath silver plates with each step. Form fitting breastplate curved gracefully over bosom and shoulder, waves decorating the curving lines. She carried a silver trident decorated with waves and kelp vines, glittering beautiful death.

Nycolos screamed, curled in a ball arms protecting his head from the onslaught of mosquito blood sucking. He screamed and screamed, standing up angrily, swinging arms in capoiera movements. The mist and mosquitoes pushed clear, a perfect circle around him. Bright blue exploded from his chest, a perfect sphere rose from his chest. A drop of water from a leaf, slow and beautiful, crystal clear.

The blue ball flew from him and fell into the water, sinking out of view. The fog and mosquitoes began fading away ascending up and out of sight. The incessant buzz stayed though, setting his teeth on edge. As mist faded, glittering scales caught in the phosphorescent glow filling the chamber. Silver armor, reptilian scales, axe wielding Nagas, the armor clad warrior and her eviscerating trident caught his eye. They were coming.

A voice whispered in the back of his head.

"Give me form and fight we will." An image flickered in Nycolos' brain, and was gone. The water next to him bubbled violently again, bits of refuse rising to the surface, flying from the water, whizzing by his head. It rose from the surface of the water with an explosion. Nycolos couldn't see all of it clearly, but what he did see in the dim light of the subterranean cavern was a dragon on the loose. A long, lithe, snake blue body undulated like it was slithering through the air.

Impossibly fast it rippled through the darkness, visible by the blue orb glowing within its chest. It fired a green fire against the ceiling, there it stuck, like green napalm. The fire illuminated the room, scattering the darkness to shadowy corners. The fire dripped from the ceiling. Large molten drops, sizzling when they hit the water but continuing to burn. Sinking below the surface, molten green depth charges smoldering among the sunken waste. The dragon changed direction, undulating mass torpedoing for the alligator still floating on the other side of the cavern.

The slithering assassins were not halfway to Nycolos, a black snake twenty feet long and a foot thick lead the procession. That snake would crush him to pulp, the armored warrior and her trident would skewer him, and the Nagas would peel the flesh from his bones. The Nagas wore particularly nefarious grins, wielding their own razor-sharp teeth and spears. They meant terrible business, he felt it in his gut.

"Concentrate or all is lost," The whisper in his brain came through, "do not panic or flee." Nycolos stopped his shuffling feet, he had been inching away from the approaching threat. The dragon flickered, edges blurring, blue ball winking on and off. Nycolos concentrated, visualizing the indominable strength overflowing from the blue-green myth. Waste water solidified into flesh, overlapping scales, long sinewy whiskers, jaws and teeth solid enough to crush stone. The dragon descended suddenly in a tight corkscrew spiral, drilling downward quick as light. Icicle projectiles fired from the dragon, fired at the slithering horde coming to kill Nycolos. Icicles as big as sofas destroyed the concrete walkway in a shower of dust and ice, shaking the ground and deafening the ears. Nycolos stayed afoot, but only just.

The dragon collided with the alligator in an explosion of water and leathery hides. Serpentine length of dragon quickly wrapped around the alligator, constricting the Lizard King. The Lizard King wasted no time, spinning and diving in one fluid motion, the two disappeared beneath the surface. Visible only as shadows moving to and fro in the murky brown depths. The waste water glowed green with swamp fire smoldering below giving an eerie glow to the liquid and the blue ball swimming within. Nycolos concentrated, focusing on speed, power, strength. *Destroy the Lizard King.*

Never mind the twenty foot anaconda, slithering Nagas or armored warrior determined on dismembering him. The quartet surmounted the icicle obstacle and drew steadily closer. Clank of metal soles on stone. Nycolos had company. Closing his eyes he visualized safety and protection surrounding him. A fortification keeping death at bay. The approaching clank of armor stopped, sounding removed and muffled. Nycolos opened his eyes. He was seated in the center of what appeared to be an enormous nest of stone and mud. Expanding outward in ever expanding circles, jagged stalagmites jutted outward growing larger in size the further from him. The last circle consisting of stalagmites as big as oak trees. A mud dome capped each layer of protective stone, encasing Nycolos in a sturdy cocoon of stone and mud. A temporary deterrent at least. He heard weapons hacking on stone and mud.

The center of his nest was hot and humid, perfect for hatching eggs. He felt cool despite the heat and humidity, scale male armor covered him again, armor like an exoskeleton this time. Large spikes protruded from the shoulders, elbows, knees, thighs, feet. Nycolos stood, the armor was light, even buoyant, he felt lighter than normal. The joints of the suit were soft like connective tissue on a reptile. The suit breathed well, and may well have been air conditioned. He actually felt cool in the humid nest. Nyc stood at attention but refused to move. Focus, focus.

Blue orb rose to the surface, dragon and Lizard King blasted into sight, erupting from the surface of murky waters, mouths firing ice breath and hot steam respectively. Locked in a death embrace the dragon wrapped tightly around the Lizard's massive size. Enormous green wings flapped again and again. Wind whipped throughout the cavern, lifting garbage and foul brown water into the air. Thin tendril-like water spouts formed in the center of the pond. First one, spinning, spinning, then a second, a third. Nycolos stopped counting at ten.

Chop, hack, clang of metal on stone, thunk of metal into wood, hiss of black serpent. A black anaconda head pushed through a hole in the mud-packed dome, squeezing through little by little. The girth of the snake expanded as it moved through the hole, crumbling the roof around the snake, making the hole bigger and bigger. Silver axes hacked in the distance, turning the mud and stone to dust.

The trident-wielding warrior, flowing white locks fanning over her breastplate, shot high pressure water from the tip of her trident, dissolving mud and stone to nothing. The anaconda slithered through stone ramparts with ease, reaching Nycolos mere minutes after squeezing through the hole. It bit at his face, and his helmet dropped a face guard in place before pointed death fangs could find purchase. Pink inside of the serpent's maw, hooked white fangs, dislocated jaw stretched wide over his helm. The mass of the serpent wrapped Nycolos in a nightmare imitation of the dragon and Lizard King. Black scaled flesh coiled around Nycolos, coil, coil, coil, squeeze. Fangs disengaged and coiled muscled constricted. Nycolos was surprised it didn't hurt more. He imagined he would have been dead if not for the armor, which groaned and crunched but did not break.

The alligator and dragon writhed in battle, high in the cavern, just beneath the green fire that coated the roof. The green napalm continuously dripped from the roof like molten lava. Nyc wasn't sure whether the green fire burned but it sizzled and popped when it landed on the Lizard King. Immobilized by the constricting anaconda he was unable to dodge the trident staff when it came down across his helm. His head exploded in pain, helm shattering on the right side of his face, throwing him to the ground. The silver-plated warrior stood over him, eyes glowing a malevolent green. Nycolos screamed at her, defiant nonsense, bark and bluff all he had left.

The water dragon screamed with Nycolos, and the Lizard King struck. Giant prehistoric maw closed on the dragon's chest, piercing murky water made solid, closing around the blue orb, shattering it. Water dragon shrieked louder, rising to a crescendo, flapping giant wings one last time, and dissolved. Waterfall of waste fell from the ceiling, splashing loudly throughout the cavern. The wind in the chamber increased intensity, gale force winds thrashed everything, waterspouts spinning furiously.

The waterspout closest to Nycolos shot tendrils that smashed into the silver warrior and nagas, crushing them against the spikes of his nest before dragging them screaming into the water. Something gargantuan splashed down into the pool, Nyc saw the Lizard King plunging into the green water, no longer held aloft by the flying dragon.

The waterspout went mad. They propagated out of control, ten or more laying waste to the chamber, ripping pipes from walls, throwing waste like lethal projectiles, refrigerator here, toilet bowl there. The anaconda wrapped around him melted away, popping like a water balloon beneath the spikes of his armor. Nycolos knelt where he was, gripping the ground with his hands and feet. Trying as he was to stay in place he didn't see the Lizard King surface directly in front of him. Nor did he see the Lizard King whip his tail around, rocketing Nycolos through the air and into the murky water.

He hit the water so hard he nearly bit through his tongue. His armor exploded in the darkness, falling away from him. He sank like a stone, and the Lizard King was on him in an instant, dragging him down. Panic rose in his throat, inadvertent inhale, mouthful of murky brown waste. Foul, putrid, surely he would drown, lost, forgotten, a child corpse deep in the bowels of the city. But he didn't die, he kept breathing, the water tasted foul, like breathing the air of a cesspool, but breathe he did.

The Lizard King's maw closed around Nycolos and upward they sped, shooting from the water and crashing into the midden heap. The King unceremoniously dropped Nycolos in a pile of waste water and rags that remained of his pajamas. The Lizard King flopped onto the mud and wallowed with pleasure. Laughter echoed in Nyc's head, throughout the chamber as well. The laughter continued unabated, tears streaming down the Alligator face.

"My dear child, you truly are a marvel. I can understand why Lora and the ilk are so desperate to hasten your birth."

"You mean my death." Nycolos corrected the monster.

"Call it what you will, semantics really. Your resonance is unlike any I have ever seen, far exceeding your father's. I have never seen my own abilities used with such power and creativity. A water dragon! How entertaining, my boy!" Maniacal laughter replaced the cogent mind link.

The thirty-foot alligator raised his eight-foot head skyward as if scanning the ceiling far above them. His gaze returned to Nycolos, eyes glowing green, mouth smoking with steam. The monster bellowed the steam, firing the the hot vapor at Nycolos. Nyc, exhausted and weak, prepared for the burning of his flesh. Strangely enough he felt no heat. The vapor swirled around him, a miniature tornado. Runes flashed like strobe lights on the inside of the funnel. Each rune glowing a darker shade of red, searing his eyes and embedding in his brain.

"Very well, the task set for me is complete. Your resonance is now detectable by other Children of Gaia, not a problem if your father and Lucas Fox complete their responsibilities." Nycolos brain exploded with questions. What did his father have to do, and who was Lucas Fox? He had no chance to ask.

"I must go, my other lairs need attending and I have performed the task which she set me, I have no more time to waste with your human mind and sack of flesh. Remember the downfall of man is imminent, you are the harbinger of the end of an age. Make yourself ready and those you care for if you hope for your human family to survive the coming decades."

As if his mind wasn't spinning enough, the last comment raised new questions in the back of his head. The alligator spoke of decades like weeks, and centuries like months. The secret door outlined itself and appeared again, swinging open for the familiar who was chewing on a piece of meat on a skewer. He beckoned to Nycolos who was only too happy to leave the bowels of the city. He heard a tremendous splash and turned to see the gigantic tail slipping below the surface.

"The master must really like you, he despises humans, and almost never assumes his own human form anymore." Nycolos moved to the runic door with the vagabond, and realized with a start the man was eating a roasted rat. The wretched familiar spoke incessantly around his rat as he led Nycolos back to the portal. Nyc heard none of it. Why had Gaia forbidden his death, why would she need to? Well, he knew who wanted to kill him, just not why. What did all of this have to do with his family? After that he just thought about the human scourge raping the earth, fouling the seas and skies. Maybe the alligator had a point, the earth would be much better off without humans.

They reached the Door of Perception. Silvery blue rings and colors flashed across the mirrored surface that didn't reflect their images. The runes along the border of the door marched along the threshold, blinking on and off in a pattern that seemed more orderly to Nycolos the second time he saw them. The vagabond bid him farewell, greasy fingers and mouth glistening with rat fat.

Nycolos stepped through the door of perception into the darkness. He floated in a timeless void for what felt like an eternity, until his foot bumped something and again he was moving through water. He kicked his feet hard and stroked upwards toward a pinprick of light high above. After what seemed minutes his head broke the surface of the small pond in his meditation place.

Pulling himself up and out, he noticed smoke rising from the chimney of the little shack that stood a few hundred yards distant through the stand of poplars. Just considering if he could dry his clothes by the fire the grotto faded and he woke.

He was on the floor of the guest room between the bed and the closet. Disoriented and momentarily frightened Nycolos sat up considering the closet door. So confused was the boy that for a moment he entertained the notion that perhaps it had all been a really strange dream, he hadn't been anywhere. Until he noticed the pool of water under his bum, spreading across the hardwood floor, and the stench of his pajamas. There was no question after that. He threw away the clothes and hopped in the shower just as the sun peeked above the eastern horizon.

Somewhere in the east river an alligator the size of a subway car surfaced, leaving one lair and headed toward another. The rising sun was brilliant, splashing the heavens with rose-colored pastels, golden rays warming the back of a thousand year old giant. The creature rose again; slapping his powerful tail, he swam toward the bowels of the borough of Manhattan.

Chapter 16

The Fine Print

Once we roamed
hand in hand
Stewards and brothers
loving the land.

The next day was mundane, spring inched toward the lazy days of summer. Nyc's feet itched to run, jump, pedal and paddle while he was stuck in Mrs. Delisi's class. The wizened lithe teacher felt the infectious impatience bubbling in her students and set her own feet to tapping under her desk. She too longed for noontime strolls through botanical gardens, rolling meadows, and a slow dance in the moonlight on her patio. Summer vacation lurked behind a scant four weeks of class, and the respected teacher caught herself staring out the classroom window nearly as much as the students.

Nycolos forgot about his run-in with Isaiah concerning the measure of his blackness, too distracted by his crazy dreams until he heard the arrogant kid call Kofi a spear-chucker in the hallway. Anger balled in Nyc's chest, he considered doing something to the bully, but school was no place for righteous vengeance. Nycolos let it slide and moved through the rest of his day. He made plans with his new friends for more workouts the following Saturday and for every one thereafter until summer arrived and he left for home. His new friends promised they'd come visit him once he moved away. He wondered if the Lizard King was right, if these kids knew the truth about him and what he stood for, would they run away screaming?

Something was amiss when he got home from school that afternoon. The house was quiet and he didn't hear any loud music coming from Sidney or Nina's rooms.

The television was off, and the pots and pans in the kitchen were cold. Mauro stood before the cold fireplace in the sitting room, the entire family spread out before him on couches and recliners. Carolina was speaking in staccato Portuguese, her voice tight, just short of yelling at Mauro. She stopped when Nyc crossed the threshold. They all looked at him; whatever the problem, it was serious.

"What's going on?"

Rosa disengaged herself from the tension on the couch and walked Nycolos into the kitchen. She made him a snack of fried plantains and some miniature empanadas left over from lunch.

"Carolina, and Mauro are losing the house." She sounded sad, but more frightening to Nycolos, the tone of acceptance in her voice said the result was inevitable.

"Why?"

"Mauro signed some papers when he took out the mortgage on the house, he didn't fully understand the papers, and he didn't read the fine print. Now he can't make payments on the mortgage and the bank is going to seize the house, unless they sell it in the next few days."

"Is there anything we can do?" Nycolos, grown familiar with cousins, his aunt and uncle, found something happening to them frightening.

"Not right now, honey, unless you know someone who wants to buy a house."

"No, but they could always stay with us in New Hamlet right?" His mother's green eyes squinted, she regarded him, trying to peer into the mechanism of his brain.

"Yes, honey, I've already offered; they're still discussing it, and quite honestly, this is their family decision to make, so we better let them talk."

"O.K., Mom, I love you."

She moved to return to the sitting room, but Nyc had one more question for her. "Mom?"

"Yes, honey?"

"Am I black?"

"What? Of course you are, sweety; why are you asking me that?" Frozen in midstep.

"A kid told me at school the other day I wan't, he said he saw who I hung out with, that he saw the clothes that I wore, the way I acted and it wasn't black."

"Well, whomever this kid is he's ignorant and wrong. If he thinks being black is speaking with poor grammar, wearing his pants below his ass and behaving disrespectfully to everyone he sees and meets, he's got another thing coming to him in his life." Rosa was angry, he could see the fire in her eyes and knew better than to get in her way when her eyes burned like that.

"Our ancestors suffered through the middle passage, the same as millions of other blacks, shipped from Africa like sardines in a tin. Our ancestors felt the whip of the slave masters, escaped into the jungles with the quilombo of escaped slaves. Maybe we were in Brazil instead of the U.S., growing sugar cane instead of cotton and tobacco. But our family bled at the hands of oppressors, just the same. Your tell that kid if he asks you again, your family was whipped too, and playing the part of a stereotype doesn't make him more black than you, just more of an idiot."

She left him eating platanos fritos; returning to the living room to participate in the decision making, he assumed. By the time the adult women came out of the living room Carolina's eyes were red and puffy from crying and her voice was hoarse. Mauro kept trying to talk to her, apologizing from the sounds of things, but she wanted none of it. Sidnei and Nina looked crestfallen as well, the awful reality plain for Nyc to read in their downcast eyes and slumped shoulders.

The family reached a conclusion, they would sell the house ASAP, pay off the remainder of the mortgage and skyrocketing interest accumulated before moving to New Hamlet with Nycolos and Rosa. They would use whatever leftover capital remained them to invest in the farm and maybe add to the small house so they all fit. If not for the long faces and sniffling noses Nyc would've thought this good news. But his cousins so obviously in pain, broke his heart. To say, "You'll like it up there," seemed silly. He hoped time would heal their pain.

****

The store was fine, the previous owner left it to Mauro in his will. He had thought of Mauro as a son, and rightly so. Mauro loved that man like a father. So Rosa would run the store in New Hamlet, Mauro the one in Queens and the farm would provide the resources for both. A small apartment above the the shop used for storage would now be Mauro's home three days a week. Carolina didn't come to dinner that night, so Nina took a plate up to her around 8 o'clock, which came back half an hour later empty.

Nyc's family was subdued for the rest of the week, and Mauro slept on the couch, still there every morning when Nyc came down for breakfast. He stayed on the couch for nearly three weeks. Until the last week in June, the service berries plump shades of red and purple, and children counted the minutes until summer break. That Friday morning, the last day of school, Mauro whistled his way down the stairs and bright eyed Carolina kissed him smack on the lips when he entered the kitchen.

"You forgave him then?" Nyc spoke without thinking, too late to take the words back. No matter—cousins, aunt and uncle all exploded in laughter.

"Yes my little bon bonsinho. I forgave your uncle for being a hard-headed, ignorant fool and making such an important decision without consulting his wife."

"Good! You'll see, you guys will like the farm." He hoped they believed him.

"I know, honey, your mother was talking to me about it. It's because of her I forgave Mauro."

"That's what sisters are for, right, Sidnei?" Nina spoke to her brother who merely nodded in mute appreciation of his breakfast cosinha.

Nyc left for school before he realized Rosa hadn't been in the kitchen, today she opened the store and Mauro met her at 10:30.

School was an irritation to Nycolos that Friday. Mrs. Delisi nearly asked him to stand in front of the room and write on the board for her. So distracted was Nycolos, he walked right by Isaiah Johnson without a second glance. Gone were the insecurities of his heritage. His mother was right, as usual. Nyc's mind whirled through subterranean catacombs fouled with refuse and inhabitants who preferred the dark. Runes burned red and greens in the back of his mind. They might as well be branded on his forehead for all he could to to forget them.

The end of the age of man, he said. The ominous message delivered by the Lizard King was as frightening as the battle with the monster. Though now Nycolos Arcadia had more questions and even fewer answers. What was resonance, and why the Lizard King's amusement? Why didn't he always have awesome abilities? He looked up at lunch time, realizing the multicultural misfits were standing their ground. Defying logic and lunchroom hierarchy, they denied Isaiah Johnson access to Nycolos and sent him on his way; smoke trailing from the bully's ears. Isaiah Johnson was an insignificant speck, Nycolos had bigger problems than a teenage bully.

****

He saw her on his short walk home. There was no mistaking her white fur and pointed ears, or the way she cocked her head when she looked at him. Nycolos knew the white wolf, and she knew him. She only just let him see her. She darted around a corner as he drew close. He rounded the corner to see her tail disappearing down an alley. He raced over gray concrete, blackened with oil, dirty water and foul smelling refuse piles. At the end of the alley, a red door stood to his left, strangely out of place, freshly painted and clean. The rest was just as dirty as any city alley, but not the door. A fox's head served as a heavy brass knocker. No need to use it though. The door opened inward and Nycolos stepped across the threshold, heart hammering in his chest.

He stood in a dark hallway that ran toward the front of the building and bright sunshine. He could see the white wolf in silhouette, sitting in the doorway, he thought she was facing him but couldn't be sure. He inched closer, squinting and shielding his eyes from the glare. The white wolf nudged his leg and led him into the bright room. The door behind him closed soundlessly, he hadn't seen anyone close it.

He walked into a two-story room, gigantic display windows provided generous views of the city street. Tropical plants transpired from elephant-like leaves, palm fronds, and half a dozen leaf shapes, steaming the windows like in a greenhouse. Half-dressed mannequins scattered among the pots and planters positioned close to the window cared for the plants in still life, serving as an effective screen against prying eyes. Enormous red drapes were drawn back, surely used to cover the windows when more privacy was necessary, or the cold more insistent. The walls were lined with bookshelves, book cases, casements, chests of drawers and the like.

A wide array of books, bric-a-brac, and curiosities lined the shelves, all apparently older than dirt. A spiral staircase flanked the door, leading to the second floor walkway, similarly lined with bookshelves, book cases and the like. In the center of the room a huge desk sat on a dark red rug that looked very old and very beautiful. At the desk, back to Nycolos worked a man with bright red hair.

The man stood once Nycolos stopped behind his chair, and turned to face the boy. Sincere hazel eyes, almost amber, scanned Nyc mischievously. His hair a little curly and so red it appeared orange fell to his shoulders. Mutton-chop sideburns framed his face and wire-rimmed glasses perched on the edge of pointy nose. Thick eyebrows contrasted nicely with the brown suit he wore The jacket hung form a peg in a corner of the room. Standing in front of Nycolos, he peered over the top of his glasses, a roguish grin marking his face and extended his hand, gesturing to the chair in front of the desk.

"You made it! Good, I knew you would." The man patted the wolf on the head and rubbed her behind the ears.

"Excuse me sir, do I know you?" Nycolos knew the answer, but better safe than sorry.

"Oh come off it Nycolos. Fine, do you know her?" He pointed a finger at the wolf.

"Yes." There was no denying she was the very same wolf that saved his butt at the zoo.

"Good, well, the rest should be logic, my dear Watson." That settled it and he said no more about the matter. The wolf curled up on the red rug under the desk and promptly fell asleep.

"I've been keeping an eye on you, Nycolos, as is my responsibility. It has come to my attention that your family may be in need of some financial assistance. Am I right?"

"Yes, my uncle needs to sell his house." Nyc's head was still spinning from his encounter with the Lizard King, and now he was meeting the fox in his human form. He was even more surprised by the conversation's turn to esoteric financial matters.

"What was that?" The man's tone was suddenly very serious. Nyc wondered if he had spoken aloud involuntarily.

"I said, so you're the fox." It took some effort to say out loud.

"Before that."

"Oh, I said first the Lizard King and now this."

The fox looked at Nyc's face, then checked him like he was checking for broken bones or lacerations. The fox was not rough but he handled each of Nyc's limbs closely, smelling and peering intently at something unseen.

"What are you doing?"

"Checking you for runes and markings, the Lizard King likes to play games."

"Oh." Scanning the room while the fox checked him, Nycolos realized small animals moved here and there in the large shop. Squirrels moved to and fro with acorns and achenes, walnuts and peach pits. Butterflies and beetles flitted from tropical bush to mannequin arm, and back again. Nyc swore a humming-bird buzzed by him, moments before hovering in front of a bright red spike protruding from one of the dark green plants. It flew so close he felt the breeze on his cheek, spinning as much under the fox's examinations as of his own accord he watched it shoot up the spiral staircase, which continued up through the ceiling to what Nyc assumed were more floors.

"There are so many animals here." Nycolos couldn't help himself.

"Hmm.." The fox didn't say a word he only nodded and continued what he was about.

"I am a creature of the Earth Nycolos, even here in my urban dwelling I must make allowances for my work, cataloging plants and animals, providing help for those in need, etc." He replied eventually, sighing he stood and wiped his face.

"So you met the Lizard King, what happened? I see you have been marked, it makes your resonance detectable by other children. It is very faint, in fact it can't be detected unless you know what to look for, but it is there. I should have known." He stared fiercely at Nyc and drummed his fingers on his arms, crossed as they were.

"I thought you did know! Don't you all communicate with each other?" Nycolos was shocked to imagine anything but.

"Yes and no, it is very complicated and not worth the breathe it would take to lay it all out, see I am already fatigued even thinking of such nonsense. But recall Lora is one of us and she nearly finished with you." The man stared into his eyes, sincerity lending gravity to his words. The memories did that too.

Nycolos instead wasted his breath and related his encounter with the reptilian monster, the rune doors, the marking, the battle and his father. The man sat back down in his chair during the telling and Nyc resumed his seat. The fox whistled when he came to the end, peering at Nycolos even more intently.

"I am at a loss for words, Nycolos, I felt the power surging last night, a massive amount of power, to think that was you. Every child in the tri-state area felt that one, my child. Fortunate for you it was so brief none were able to approach or intervene."

Nyc didn't say a word, he didn't know what to say, he hoped he wasn't in trouble.

"No, silly boy, you are in no trouble, none of this is your fault, only your destiny." He waved dismissively at Nycolos. It was strange having the fox pick thoughts out of his head.

"Well, maybe you shouldn't think so loud, it is possible to keep your thoughts to yourself. One of the first skills we learn after our birth is listening to thoughts, and would you believe it requires no power, humanity is blind to it of course, but that is the truth." He stared at Nycolos for a while yet. Considering. "Would you like to see the rest of my home, and perhaps some refreshment?"

"Yes, I would." Nycolos trusted the man with his life, but one thing bothered him, he tried to think quietly as it were. The fox smiled broadly and threw his head back roaring with laughter.

"You are a sharp one aren't you?" He handed Nycolos two business cards. Plain white, the name Lucas Fox printed in a flowing red font, underneath the title Antique Dealer, and in the background a solid red fox silhouette trotted across the card. One card was unadorned, while the other had a rune scrawled on the back, one of the symbols Nycolos had etched in his mind. It was like an capital F but the horizontal lines slanted down at an angle.

"The first card is for your uncle, give it to him. The second card is for you. If you ever need me, place your hand on the rune and speak my name or just think about me really hard, and I'll be there as quickly as I can, or she will." He pointed to the snoring wolf.

"Thanks, may I call you Lucas then?"

"Yes, Nycolos, you may."

"Thank you for everything, Lucas."

Lucas stood and led him upstairs.

The next floor was the kitchen and living area, beautiful wood timber-frame gave the space a lodge-like feel with ample light pouring in through the large picture windows. The cooking area was sleek, an island clustered close by stools was equipped with four burners and room for eating on one end. The cabinets and wood work all rough worked pieces with knots and undulating grain chosen for imperfections as much as character. Imperfect or not the wood was all polished and smooth to the touch. Close to the window plants flourished, offering fruits of nearly any variety, Nyc was sure. Apples, peaches, oranges, bananas, avocados, tomatoes, basil, cucumbers, he could barely see out the window for all the variety. He spun to look at Lucas.

"What is all this?" He gestured to the plants.

"We all have our gifts, in our mortal toils and after the rebirth. This is one of mine, it brings me joy, and food." He smiled and offered Nycolos a soda in a glass bottle, popping the top as he handed it to Nyc. The plant area was flanked by a sunken seating area on one side, sun streamed in there too, plush cushions formed a half circle facing the window all in shades of burgundy and light-brown. On the other side a dining area Nycolos barely peeked, but he noted that too was sunken into the floor. Lucas led him up the stairs again. He did not stop on the final floor, shrouded in darkness, the curtains allowed barely a sliver of light to pierce the black. Nyc detected the scent of incense and sandalwood, surely Lucas's room. Thy exited onto the roof and Nyc was surprised yet again. A large greenhouse occupied nearly half the roof, the other half was covered with a thin layer of herbs, the occasional shrub, chickens, and a coop.

"Wow." Nyc didn't have to feign interest. They entered the greenhouse. It was a steaming A-framed affair with orchids, bromleiads, ferns, ficus, lichens galore.

Nyc caught his breath. Lucas threaded his way down one aisle and led him to a small office with wood furniture and glass walls. Lucas sat him in a comfortable wicker chair and let him get settled. Lucas kept quiet so Nyc spoke up. "I thought you wanted to talk about my family."

Lucas nodded and began. "For your uncle and family I would like to make an offer on the house. I will stop by your house for dinner tonight. It is my understanding that this is the only way to retain the property and eliminate the debt. I will hammer out the details with your uncle this evening; I do not want to bore you with such nonsense."

Nycolos was grateful, realizing that what Lucas referred to as nonsense was not necessarily so; only perhaps beyond the scope of one's understanding. Nyc thought he might appropriate the saying, he had use for it of late.

Lucas pulled out a small terrarium with a bed of fuzzy red-green plants that looked like miniature spoons covered with red hairs, he wasn't sure but he thought he heard them whispering. Lucas removed the lid and sat back in a chair opposite Nycolos, sipping his own soda. In moments a fly alighted on the edge of the terrarium. The little red plants stiffened, leaves opened wide to the sky. A humming sound floated out of the box, the fly teetered on the glass edge, and fell on the red carpet of plants, quickly immobilized by red sticky suckers that elongated from the leave edges. Nycolos looked up from the box, Lucas raised his eyebrows.

"Did I hear them singing?" He pointed at the plants.

"The Sundews? Yes, a little touch of magic to help keep the pests down, they do sound nice don't they"

"Yes, they do. They really do." Lucas was running to another terrarium full of white webbing. "Wait till you see this spider." Lucas sounded excited.

Several hours, many fascinating plants and animals later Lucas sent Nyc on his way with explicit instructions, give the card to his mother immediately. Before he left he had one last question, he asked it just before they left the greenhouse.

"Isn't it kinda obvious? The name I mean?" Lucas considered the sky then answered.

"Well Nycolos, sometimes the best place to hide is in plain sight." Twinkle in his eye and a spring and his step Lucas and his wolf led Nycolos downstairs and out into the alley. The she-wolf walked him home, Nyc wished Isaiah would show up. A stab of guilt, glance at the beautiful wolf, Nycolos had forgotten to ask her name. Strangely enough, no one seemed frightened by the large wolf walking next to the little brown boy on the streets of Queens.

****

The doorbell rang at 8 o'clock on the dot. Nina opened the door for the red-headed man. Hazel eyes sparkled in light spilling from the foyer. Nina beckoned him into the brownstone.

A grand bow and flourish, Lucas Fox flipped bowler hat from his hand to coat hanger in the corner. Nycolos, a well mannered young boy, introduced his new friend to the family. Mr. Fox greeted the men with courteous respect, the women however, he all but fawned over. Nycolos thought it might be possible for Nina's face to grow as red as the man's hair. The girl blushed furiously under his praises, mothers not far behind.

In no time Lucas Fox stood in the kitchen with the family trading tall tales and enjoying a beer. They were all in shock, save Nycolos, come to expect the amazing when dealing with his new friends. They averted homelessness by pulling together as a family, the extended family becomes nuclear. Arranging to share living spaces and living circumstances. First in the city and soon they would head to a new home up north. The neighbors were sad to hear the news. Mauro told Mr. Fox about the store, the immigrant and local families sharing similar misfortune. The Polish gentleman who owned the bakery, the Colombians that owned a small restaurant, all rubbing elbows in his shop. Buying goat, pheasant and the like, all the while sharing tales of woe. All over the city, and in fact the country, people were losing their homes.

Mothers and fathers displaced, carrying their charges like boulders on their backs, barely able to stand the awesome weight of responsibility and death of a dream. For many an immigrant family the foreclosure of homes was the death of the American dream. Blood, sweat and tears are not liquidity in the eyes of the banker. The bankers told them they'd be better off taking their immigrant families back where they came from. If the bankers could've squeezed blood from a stone, they would have. The same bankers felt no compassion for the insolent, ignorant masses that defaulted on loans, losing their homes and hearth. If the masses had read what they were signing they would've known better. The banker didn't care, the local government didn't care, and the federal government didn't care. God bless America. No one cared until the number of people losing their homes started to bring down the economy.

Then bankers cared because the government cared, not about Mauro's home, or his neighbors home, but about the bank that no longer be received money from Mauro. The bank that made so many predatory loans, the whole damn ship was fixing to sink below the waves of debt and depression. Mauro, Rosa and other heads of households spent time commiserating about the injustices and fallacies of the government, bailing out big business, but stepping on the downtrodden. The small time businessman or homeowner was a small fry, a nobody to the large cogs and sprockets of industrialized neoclassical economy. Guided by an invisible hand that would as soon put true value on resources and commodities as it would pay immigrant workers a fair wage. Brothers and sisters, men and women, who were the true foundations of the American economy, picked all the food the fat cats ate, sprayed pesticides, applied fertilizers, and exposed themselves to carcinogenic chemicals. The very same people that washed the dishes, cleaned the toilets, cooked the food, the downtrodden and unappreciated, the teeming refuse come to the golden shore.

Come years or decades earlier, dreaming of roads running with milk and honey, only to find they ran red instead, with the blood of the have-nots.

Mr. Lucas Fox was no nonsense once they got down to business. The women scooted the men into the sitting room and generated a whirlwind of activity into the kitchen. The results were rounds of empandas, cosinhas, fejoida (black beans and rice), sopa do fruta do mar (fruit of the sea soup), churrasco of ribs, and some venison steaks marinated in garlic, ginger and vinegar.

Mr. Fox remembered their names, ages, and knew a little more than he should have about each of them. Birthday's and mannerisms were within his realm of knowledge, which he smoothly pawned off on Nycolos, claiming the boy briefed him beforehand.

The dinner passed quickly enough, Mr. Fox kept banter light and exchanges superficial. Nycolos and Rosa refrained from plumbing the depths of the mysterious man, whatever his intentions. Besides he arrived as their savior, making the superfluous questions moot.

Dinner drew to a close and Mauro, Carolina and Mr. Fox moved into the sitting room. Mr. Fox sat in a high-backed leather chair smoking a pipe like the one Sherlock Holmes had, puffing contentedly on the stem, filling the air with whispy plumes. Nina and Sidnei delivered coffee and tea to the adults while Nyc and Rosa finished the dishes. The four of them fidgeted in a lengthy silence that slowed the minutes to a crawl. Thankfully Rosa pulled out cards and they whittled away the time drinking tea and coffee, and playing cards.

The French doors to the sitting room opened and a beaming Mauro and Carolina all but jumped for joy walking into the kitchen. Hugs all around and Mr. Fox was encircled by six sets of arms. They hugged him tight, cheering for him like he scored the winning goal at the World Cup. The girls, Nina included, kissed his hairy cheeks, Carolina whispered in his ear and it was Mr. Fox's turn to blush.

Prompted by some need their mysterious friend excused himself, asking Rosa if Nycolos could walk him to the door. At the door the Child of Gaia turned and addressed his young friend.

"Your questions are ready to be answered. When you return home the answers will seek you out. Mirage misses you, by the way." He didn't wait for Nycolos to reply, turned and walked down the street whistling some nameless tune.

Nyc couldn't help but think it was about time he got some answers. There was no question in his mind who the messenger would be this time.

Chapter 17

Home Again, Home Again

Joy and sorrow
brothers twin
embrace humanity
in death spin.

There is something strange about the human heart. For juxtaposed within its walls Joy collides with sorrow, love and hate make their homes. Hanging hats on ventricles and arteries, valves and capillaries. Nycolos Arcadia and family were intimately aware of the paradoxical functioning of said primal organ. The brownstone disgorged belongings by the roomful, first onto the city sidewalk and then into the big white moving van that showed up driven by Mr. Lucas Fox himself. He brought along a half dozen strapping men of various sizes and hues. All were obsequious and gentle with Carolina's belongings, following her orders to the T. For all intents and purposes, completely different than your average moving company.

Mr. Fox didn't offer any explanations, he just rolled up his sleeves and helped Mauro and Sidney with the first floor. Just shy of three hours and the house stood empty and ready to hit the road. Rosa and Nyc sat in their wagon waiting while Mauro, Sidney, Carolina and Nina walked through the empty house one last time. They descended after a long while, all eyes wet and the two parents hugging their children tight. They moved to the back of the caravan, hopped into their four-door sedan with a Brazilian flag hanging from the rear-view mirror.

Nycolos shared their sadness for the better part of an hour, but as thy crossed the Tappan Zee bridge, heading north, he couldn't ignore the upwelling of joy that blossomed in his chest. He stuck his head out the window, loving the breeze in his face. Nycolos shouted with triumph, and got a bug in the back of his throat for his troubles.

Rosa roared with laughter, he retched and coughed in the passenger seat, spitting and sputtering all over himself. She passed him some water once he suffered enough. That aside, both were in high spirits and laughed all the way up north. Sadness and Longing fetched cloaks and hats, leaving to make room for the new arrivals. Joy and Happiness.

They pulled into the driveway of the little farmhouse around six that evening. Waiting at the end of the drive the Millers stood grinning and waving excitedly. The convoy stopped in front of the house, the car barely stopping before Nyc was out hugging the Millers. The rest of the travelers, not as quick to disembark, were out in short order, stretching backs and arms, sighing mightily. Rosa declared unpacking postponed, and everyone obeyed, even Mr. Fox. All of the travelers, especially the drivers she stressed, should decompress, maybe drink a beer. Mauro, Lucas Fox, and the rest of the adults were only too happy to agree.

Jackson obliged, disappearing into the house and emerging with a cooler loaded with ice and beer for just an occasion such as homecoming. In fact the Millers had quite a feast planned for the returning residents and gifts for the new. Jackson served out the first round of beers and briefed Rosa, Mauro and Carolina on the living arrangements. The Capoiera barn was now a house for the da Silva family, Jackson had done it all and it was beautiful. There would be no need for anyone to sleep on the couch or the floor. Fight over rooms maybe. Nycolos Arcadia felt a warmth suffuse his family, at least, it felt that way to him. All gathered around the cooler, laughing at jokes, and enjoying good fortune provided them.

Clean air, homegrown food and people he would die for. Nycolos was sure of it, if he could, he would. His people, his family, his tribe. He saw bonds of energy binding his family tight, the flow woven like a basket of reeds or a straw hat. Mr. Fox caught his eye and nodded. Would wonders never cease?

Ben pulled on his sleeve, and like a gust of wind they blew across the field into the maze of orchards, happy to be together again. The adults did their thing, laughing and talking for a couple of rounds before Rosa and Jackson lead them all on the tour of the converted capoiera barn. After which, Rosa showed them the rest of the grounds, explaining to Mauro and Carolina the management practices she used, incorporating animal husbandry actively with produce production, the edible hedgerows and fertile orchards.

The adults bumped into Nyc and Ben leaning on some heavily laden Juneberry trees, Mirage wasn't far off, grazing on young oats. They gathered up the children and the whole lot of them unpacked the moving van. Once the last box was unloaded the festivities began. Jackson fired up the large grill in the back yard and he and Mauro went to work marinating, grilling and kabobing. Someone turned up the music and wine started flowing. Before long the adults were talking loud and laughing louder. Mr. Fox took turns dancing with Carolina, Rosa, and Abby, as did Mauro and Jackson. Nina and Sidney were content exploring the grounds at their leisure, settling in nicely. They talked with Ben and Nyc about life in New Hamlet. Though Sidney seemed more interested in what the town was like.

No one saw when, but at some point they realized Mr. Fox was missing, wolf and all. They checked the van and found a nice note attached to a large envelope, the van was theirs, to use in their new business ventures, and surely he would see them in the city.

The beautiful flowing script was impossible not to recognize. Mauro and Jackson hopped in the car and drove down the road looking for the mysterious fellow, but he was not to be found. Nyc thought he heard the yip-yip of a wolf somewhere far away.

It was an early night for all, the Silva family needed some time to adjust to the idea of country-life. Black nights, hundreds of stars, and strange sounds of country spaces. The Millers understood and left before the night grew late. Abby, Jackson and Ben walked home across the old fields that separated the two homes.

Nyc had trouble sleeping that night. He was waiting for the answers that were supposed to be coming, the answers to all his questions.

The family of the Jaguar Princess and the Undisputed King of Hide and Seek were transposed from county to city and back again. Tears of joy mingled with tears of sorrow that summer. Nyc spent half of the summer camping up on the mount with Ben. He re-lived the battle with the Lizard King at least a half dozen times. Ben couldn't get enough of it, and besides he said he wanted to catalog Nyc's powers. The concept of resonance was pretty easy for both of them to understand, but the reason why it might be necessary to mark Nycolos wasn't immediately evident.

Then the den of Lucas Fox was the next great mystery. Nycolos swore up and down he would take his friend if ever the opportunity arose, such was Ben's insistence. Nyc regaled Ben with accounts of fantastical plants and animals touched by Mr. Fox's magic, it was somewhat fun torturing Ben with tales of missed adventure. It was good to be home. Once everyone was settled Mauro started taking one of the trucks down to his shop Monday mornings, generally returning on Wednesday or Thursday. Carolina and Rosa threw themselves into the farming.

Carolina was a quick study and in no time she knew her way around well enough that Rosa could ask her to do anything. Jobs that reminded her of pleasant things Rosa saved for herself. She loved making the tinctures, oils, creams and salves. Mauro was amazed by the variety of animals she kept, and how healthy they all were, feeding on edible hedgerows and fruitful orchards.

****

The family settled, stretching through esoteric growing pains associated with such a transplant. Like a shocked plant, the family took time to send out new roots, probing the new home for sustenance and nutrition. Resilient as they were, it was only a matter of weeks before they had all found a niche. Evidenced by the pretty young girl that stopped by one evening to pick up Sidney. They went to the movies and got home late, but no one said anything.

Nina took a liking to Abby Miller and was lost as often as not between the shelves and bookcases of Abby's labyrinth of a bookstore. Abby hired her for the summer after the second day, to the delight of all, especially Ben. She would sit and read behind the counter, or chat with Abby about books and authors, happy as could be.

Nyc was not so contented as the rest of his family. The days were long and uneventful, the nights longer still, and he was plagued by bouts of insomnia. Night after night he watched shadows splay across his ceiling. By day he wandered the hills and dales of the Mount. His apprehension and anxiety were nearly maddening. He stalked squirrels, woodchucks, foxes and deer, waiting for something, anything to happen. Thankfully Ben was spending more time at the bookstore, affording Nyc ample alone time.Nyc was sure if he told Ben who was coming, Ben would have been with him everyday.

Nyc wasn't sure what was building inside of him, but got a clue one morning when he yelled at his mother after she reminded him of his chores. She didn't say anything, nor did his Aunt Carolina, they both just looked at him a little surprised. He apologized, left the kitchen and headed out the back door. His feet carried him, but he paid no attention where. His mind churned, he knew what was wrong. He was angry. He was angry at his father for wanting to divorce his mother.

He was angry they went on that stupid camping trip, angry his father had gotten himself killed trying to be a hero. Angry his life was turned upside down by a bunch of crazy animals and monsters. Who was the Earth Mother, and why did he have to be connected to some grand prophesy? If he was so important, why the hell did his father keep him waiting all summer? Was he merely a pawn in some greater game, would he still be in danger, or could he go back to his normal life? Feet stopped, and he realized where he was. Standing on the edge of the ravine, the limestone walls comforted him on some base level. Tittering female laughter teased his hearing. Dryads in the brush he supposed, he swiveled his head from side to side trying to catch a glimpse. Nothing, only laughter, they sounded so pretty. He almost called out to them.

The boy walked the length of the ravine until he found a particularly thick mat of tangled roots and mycelium. He climbed down like on a fisherman's net, save this net was living and was covered with detritus and boulders. Moss covered the ground, various outcrops and most surfaces along the length of the space. The air was distinctively fresh and it was as if a breeze was whistling through a crevice somewhere.

A particularly large boulder occupied one side of the ravine floor covered in moss and rock poly-pody fern. The huge piece of stone was almost perfectly round.

Nyc perched atop the surface, after scampering up the side closest the ravine wall using moss and ferns for hand holds. Surprisingly comfortable the mossy top was spongy to the touch. The ferns were arranged haphazardly but densely enough that when he lay down he was covered by them. Staring into the forest above, birds flitted to and fro like small black darts. The sky was clear, powdery blue and magnificent. A whistling sounded in the wood, loud and nearly in Nyc's ear. He sat up, pushing ferns aside. An eerie whistle sounded like a thousand whispers.

Scanning the walls of the ravine Nyc didn't see anyone on the rim above, nor down the length, scar in the earth's crust. A mat of roots parted, revealing a space in the limestone wall across from where he lay. There was no one holding the roots, they parted themselves. The whispering was louder inside the dark place and Nyc felt pulled toward the darkness. He jumped down from the boulder and walked into the cave entrance following the whispers. The roots closed behind him, plunging the tunnel into darkness. In moments his eyes adjusted, small mushrooms lined the walls lighting the passage with phosphorescent glow.

Heart pounding in his chest the child wandered on, sure he would fight or die at any minute. The tunnel spiraled downward into the depths of the earth. The whispering sounded as many voices. Not one, or two, to Nycolos Arcadia it sounded as if thousands of voices were engrossed in conversation. The last turn, downward, and out at last. Nycolos entered a large room ringed with the glowing mushrooms. In the center of the room a large slab of limestone sat like a raised dais, it was occupied by two figures. The larger one was an amorphous, unshapely thing that was more like a gelatinous mass than anything else.

The creature was slimy all over, coated with a fine sheen that reflected the blue-green glow. Nyc wasn't sure, but he thought the mass would've been yellow in the sunlight. The creature jiggled and shook as he drew near, the tumultuous voices growing excited, no longer a whisper. After distraction of the blob Nyc spied a second figure sitting behind the gelatinous mass, legs crossed and hands held together as in meditation. Lyndon Arcadia's eyes opened, Nycolos froze. Sitting on the limestone dais he was eye to eye with Nyc.

His eyes glowed blue-green, Nyc couldn't be sure if it was the reflection of the mushrooms.

"Nycolos."

"Dad?"

Lyndon uncrossed his legs and stepped down from the rock slab, he embraced Nycolos and they held each other for a long time.

"I'm sorry, Nyc, I'm so sorry. Please forgive me..."

"I do, Dad, I do." All the anger he felt was hard to find at that moment.

"Now, sit here next to me, we have to talk." He patted the limestone where he had been sitting. "I want to explain what has been going on, Nyc, and why. I know things have been really hard for you since my death, and I can't promise they'll get much easier, but at least you'll understand what is going on." He stroked Nyc's head and looked as if he would cry.

"O.K."

"The Children of the Earth are warriors for Gaia, Nyc, warriors for Mother Nature. She chooses us at birth, and calls us to her at the time of our mortal death. The bear you saw all those nights ago and the one that killed me was one. Nyc. You were right. The Earth Mother sent him to end my mortal life and to begin my immortal one." He let Nyc digest this, waiting for the boy to respond before going on..

"Immortal, you mean you can't die forever?" Nycolos sounded ready to jump out of his skin,

"I can die if my body suffers enough damage, but the Earth Mother heals and revives me should that be the case. You see, Nyc, my flesh, blood and bone are no longer like yours." Lyndon paused, perhaps he was overwhelming Nycolos.

"Suffice it to say I am no longer a human. I am now one of the warriors of the Earth Mother. I am a Child of Gaia. As are the Lizard King, Lucas Fox, and Lora, all of whom you've met"

"So you have an animal for you, too? Like them?" Nycolos was panting with excitement, he knew the moment was coming, but no amount of anticipation prepared him for the revelation.

Lyndon didn't answer.

In an instant the stone beneath his feet became liquid, flowing upward, his father blurred, becoming viscous and expanding. Grizzly Bear, 5 meters tall standing on hind legs. The animal's head scraped the ceiling of the cave. The panting animal dropped onto all fours, and looked into Nyc's eyes.

Lyndon's eyes glowed green, no doubt the light was coming from within. He heard his father's voice in his head, something he had grown accustomed to when dealing with the Children of Gaia.

"This form is mine now, just as my human one was, maybe even more so."

Nyc nodded, unsure of what else to do. The sound of squishing mud behind him, the blob pulsated wildly, jiggling up and down, thousand voices talking again. Talking on top of one another. Nyc faced the bear, his father human again. He nodded toward the blob.

"My familiar is a slime-mold, a rather extraordinary slime-mold, those voices you hear are from them."

"Them?"Nyc's mind raced, what was a slime mold?

"It is actually thousands of individuals joined together into one large mass, that is why you hear so many voices."

"Wow."

"Wow, indeed." Lyndon sat back down on the slab.

"You are of great importance to the Children of Gaia Nyc, and to Gaia herself."

"Is that what the Lizard King was talking about?"

"Yes, Nycolos, your birth marks the end of an age, the end of the Age of Man, and the beginning of something new. Mankind will be forced to descend into an age of decreasing energy. With the transition may come calamity or prosperity."

"The Lizard King thinks calamity." Nyc said dryly

"Yes, he does, as do many others. But calamity for man may mean prosperity for the other creatures of the planet. Therein lies the debate; can man and animal prosper, or has man proven too selfish to share? After your birth you will be tasked with this dilemma. For that reason various attempts have been made on your life."

"You mean the Zoo and the Mount?"

"Yes Nyc, on the Mount Lora tried to kill you with Ben's arrow, and would've tried something more had you not fled."

"What about the boulders?" It was hard to forget that.

"That was me. I was untrained and acting on emotion. I learned of the danger and tried to protect you with magic I was inexperienced with. I nearly killed you, and I am sorry."

"That was you?"

"With the immortality Gaia bestows us also comes great power, but these powers require decades of training and great discipline. Which is why your resonance is so astounding."

There was that word resonance. The Lizard King had used it over and over.

"What is resonance?"

"It is the reason you have power when you are near Children of Gaia. Like a mirror, you reflect each of their powers within you. Your own power is rising up to vibrate in harmony with those around you. This being so, you are able to use every power they have, and even amplify them in some instances, according to what I've heard. Lora and a few others tried again at the Zoo and failed thanks to Lucas Fox and his white wolf."

"That's for sure." Nycolos couldn't agree quickly enough.

"Lora has since been punished, as have her accomplices. They will accede to the will of Gaia ultimately, as do we all."

"You mean she's one of the good guys?" Nyc could hardly believe it, his father spoke as if he knew the woman well.

"We are neither good nor bad, Nycolos, we merely are. What is deemed good and bad are ideas constructed by man in his vain attempt to dominate nature, and other men. As I said earlier, what is good for the Earth Mother may not be seen as good for man."

"I see." Nyc knew he sounded confused, and he was.

"I hope so; the Lizard King was set a task, he was meant to mark you so we knew where you were, and to prepare you for your meeting with me. He did take liberties, as is his nature."

"He didn't mention you much."

"He marked you and started a process that will allow me to make your resonance dormant until the correct time. Until your birth. He doesn't like me much."

Nyc's jaw dropped. "You keep saying *until my birth*, I'm already born, shouldn't all the bad stuff you talk about be happening already?"

"Your birth as a Child of Gaia. Once your mortal life has ended, your immortal life will begin, and with it the time of contraction. Hence, Lora and the others hoped ending your mortal life would end this age that much sooner."

Nycolos Arcadia fell silent. He was to die and be born again, as something different. A warrior of the Earth, immortally a monster, just like his father.

"Will I be killed then?"

"Children of Gaia lead normal lives as mortals, but most do die in some way that is not old age, let's put it that way."

"Do you know when?" Nyc felt shivers and goosebumps climb up his spine.

"No Nycolos, I do not know when, Gaia alone knows that." His father looked down at the stone floor, when he looked up again his eyes were ablaze with blue light. Gone was any semblance of human eyes. He spoke with a voice that sounded like many speaking through him.

"Gaia has chosen this Child to harvest your mortal life when the time comes. As the one that sowed the seed of your first life, so shall he reap it and begin your second."

The light dimmed in Lyndon's eyes and he sat heavily on the limestone slab. When he looked up this time his eyes were almost normal, only the faintest glow visible in their depths.

"So you are going to be the one to kill me?" Nyc couldn't believe how steady his voice was.

"Yes Nycolos. I am." Lyndon looked sad. He took Nyc's hand and pulled him onto the slab. He directed the boy to the center of the stone, placing his large hands on Nyc's shoulders.

"Now, let's put that resonance of yours to sleep, that is the reason I was granted permission to see you after all." He stepped back, sat on the blob and it conformed to his body. Shaping itself around him and beginning to glowing with blue light.

Lyndon sat like a meditating Buddha, hands clasped, muttering incantations beneath his breath. A thousand voices took up the chant and the blue glow blazed bright within the slime-mold, blinding Nycolos and forcing him to turn his eyes downward. The top of the limestone slab had a blue line beginning on one of the outer edges. The line glowed with power like his father, spiraling inward around a central axis beneath Nyc's feet.

The spiraling blue line spun around Nyc, slowly at first, but gaining speed and intensity with the time of Lyndon's chanting. Soon the line spun around with such speed Nyc felt the whole slab vibrating. The line tightened and finally reached Nyc. His world exploded in blue light. He heard a thousand voices jumbled in his brain, his own among them, screaming at the top of his lungs. Blue light poured from his mouth and eyes, streaming to the roof of the cave like a fountain of water. The sensation grew and grew until Nycolos was sure he would burst. Abruptly the flow reversed, blue light sucked into Nycolos. He could feel the power flow down through his guts, legs, and into the earth. Down the power was sucked, shut tight beneath the stone, and then it was gone. The last thing he remembered was his father eyes all aglow, a blue aura surrounding him bright enough to blind the dead.

****

Nycolos woke on top of the round boulder covered with moss and ferns. He sat up, checked the matted roots covering the wall where the entrance to his father's cave had been. There was no cave, only limestone. He thought as much. He climbed up and out of the ravine, meandering absent mindedly toward the farmhouse. He could no longer hear the dryad's tittering laughter, though they called to him in earnest. A cause of great lament to the beloved earth spirits that loved the boy that frolicked in their woods.

He found his mother and cousins behind the house standing around the fire pit. A blazing fire glowed orange in the soft purple of dusk. Nina poked him with an accusatory finger when he reached them.

"'Bout time you showed up 'cuz, your mom was starting to worry." Rosa looked at Nyc from across the fire and shook her head.

"We're burning some of dad's things honey. I need some help letting him go, will you forgive me?" Her eyes were full of tears so Nyc squeezed her as hard as he could.

"I think that's a great idea mom, we need to learn how to let go." He stepped back and looked into her face. Her green eyes were as beautiful as ever and reminded him of the moss covered rocks in the woods. He leaned forward on his tip-toes and kissed her on the cheek.

"I love you, Mom."

"I love you too."

"Uh oh, Here comes trouble." Mauro spoke softly to all of them. Nyc and Rosa disengaged and looked in the direction of Mauro's gaze. Sheriff Ward and Deputy Eric Fontane rounded the corner of the yellow farmhouse and moved toward the family, looking grave.

"You're right, hermao," said Rosa " that's definitely trouble."

Nycolos Arcadia agreed with his mother, but was not alarmed. There was trouble on the road ahead, more than they imagined. Nyc was sure of only one thing: his death was coming sooner than later.

END

Meet our Author
Christopher Travis

Chris Travis is a plant scientist living in upstate, NY with his wife and children. He enjoys hiking, gardening and a multitude of outdoor activities. Currently he works a day job as a micro-biologist but aspires to run a farm like the Arcadia family when he grows up.